A DANGEROUS
SEASON

A Dangerous Season

A Sheriff Matt Callahan Mystery

RUSSELL FEE

Outer Island Press

Published by Outer Island Press, Oak Park, Illinois

ISBN: 978-1-949661-57-6 (ebook)

ISBN: 978-1-949661-56-9 (paperback)

Cover design and author photograph by Paul Stroili, Touchstone Graphic Design

Manuscript formatting and production by Fort Raphael Publishing Co.

For
Claire and Hazel

The Weendigo has no other object in life but to satisfy this lust and hunger, expending all its energy on this one purpose. As long as its lust and hunger are satisfied, nothing else matters—not compassion, sorrow, reason, or judgment.

—Basil Johnston, *The Manitous*

The Wendigo is simply the Call of the Wild personified, which some natures hear to their own destruction.

—Algernon Blackwood, *The Wendigo*

Prologue

She'd been warned, cautioned with tales of a creature with an appetite for human flesh; a creature who sought out the greedy and fed upon them; a creature possessed of an insatiable hunger. A monster so cold its touch burned, and its bite pierced like needles of ice. A monster with no heart.

Nights when she should have been asleep, she heard the pleas of her mother: What had her father done? What had he done to their family? He must atone for his sin. He must.

But her father hadn't listened, and now, it had come for them.

Her mother and father lay on the floor, the creature dancing in their blood, feeding on their flesh while she hunched, hiding; praying the creature wouldn't find her.

Chapter 1

The tourists and summer residents had abandoned the island to its keepers who had shuttered the restaurants and tourist shops, cleared the harbor of pleasure boats, and dry-docked the ferries. Tardy strings of ducks left the island in headlong flutters south, and the last lingering damselflies had died out. It was November when the lake roiled against the onslaught of winter, sending gales thrashing down its length and turning its waters lethal even to the largest freighters; when the mainland stayed hidden below a gray horizon during the day and appeared at night as a faint orange glow along a distant rim of black water; when the only way on or off the island until April was by plane, weather permitting. But the bars stayed open.

The early morning fog had folded itself until it thickened and lay like a heavy counterpane beneath which the island slumbered. But Sheriff Callahan was awake. While his partner, Julie, and her son, Max, slept, he'd filled a thermos with coffee, put on his boots, coat, gloves, and a wool watch cap. Before he sneaked out the door to the cruiser, he slipped on his mask, adjusting the restraint that held it tight to the left side of his face. He wore the mask more out of habit than necessity. The burns from the acid attack years ago in Chicago that ravaged his features and killed his fiancé had scarred over but would never fully heal. Though still repulsive to him, the islanders now barely noticed his disfigurement.

Callahan silently closed the front door to the house and walked through a grey morning fog to the cruiser. Despite the murky conditions, he had to drive the thirteen miles to the southern tip of the island to meet with Claude Demarest.

Demarest was an anomaly, someone not born on the island or of islanders but treated as if he had been. Which wasn't always a good thing. He wasn't Irish or of Irish descent, which should have been the first strike against him. He hadn't married an islander, which should have been the second. In fact, he had never married. The third strike, which should have sent him to the dugout, was that he consistently opposed funding any proposal to improve the infrastructure on the island. Among a permanent island population of just over five hundred, he often cast the deciding vote. Memories lived long, grudges survived lifetimes, and strong opinions resisted reason. He'd entered the island school at five years old when his parents arrived as teachers. After they left upon his finishing the twelfth grade, he stayed and never set foot off the island. His generosity and good nature endeared him to the islanders. These character traits lasted until just past middle age. Then they disappeared. A new generation of islanders knew him only as a curmudgeon or worse. Reclusive, bad tempered, and combative, he was conveniently blamed for contributing to many of the island's ills. Still, there remained those who remembered him for who he once was and who felt grateful to him.

Callahan only knew Demarest as a vexing old-timer so, at first, he was suspicious when Demarest called the station and demanded that the sheriff meet him early the next morning at his property. Demarest made his living selling eggs to the grocery store and markets, and he wanted Callahan to help nab the thieves who were stealing his prize chickens. The trap had been set, and all Callahan needed to do was arrest them. Demarest might be difficult, but he wasn't crazy. There had been reports of other disappearances of farm animals on the island, so Callahan decided to go. He also didn't want Demarest taking the law into his own hands.

When Callahan hadn't driven more than halfway, he had already chastised himself a dozen times for attempting to navigate the roads at dawn in a dense fog. At points, he could barely see more than a few yards ahead of the cruiser. He hoped that no one else would be reckless enough to drive this early and in these conditions. He'd turned on his flashing bar lights to make sure other drivers could see him.

*   *   *

As Callahan rounded the bend leading to Demarest's property, a red beam of light swung back and forth through the mist ahead of him. Callahan stopped the cruiser, and the beam steadily advanced until Demarest emerged from the fog holding a flashlight. Callahan lowered the driver's-side window when Demarest got to the cruiser.

"Thought you might be flashing like a cheap carnival ride when you got here. Was afraid you might scare the bastards away. Park here. The house is down the road about a quarter mile. We'll walk the rest of the way," said Demarest.

Callahan pulled the cruiser off the road and joined Demarest who turned off his flashlight and began walking toward his house.

"You sure this isn't an animal of some kind stealing your chickens, a fox or coyote maybe?" said Callahan.

"Positive. First, there's no blood or clumps of feathers like there would be if a chicken was dragged away by one of them. Second, the chickens didn't put up a ruckus like they do when a predator is around. Third, no screaming. Chickens scream when a fox gets 'em. Ever hear a chicken scream?" asked Demarest.

Callahan shook his head.

"They don't scream when a human grabs 'em. They fuss, maybe, or squawk but no screaming."

"What makes you think someone will try to snatch another chicken today?" asked Callahan.

"Cuz it's time. It's been happening regular. About every week or so. Been eight days now. I think they come in the early morning. That's when I'm usually gone. I take eggs to town very early in the morning and stay until about noon selling and delivering them."

Demarest stopped walking and pointed into the woods. "We go in there. There's a place further on to hide and wait," he said.

*   *   *

Callahan and Demarest knelt behind shrubs and a fallen tree, old and smelling of rot despite the heavy chilled air. Its bark had peeled off, and the grooves of wood-boring insects decorated its surface like wrinkles on the back of an old man's hand. Callahan wished they had found another place to hide. The ground was wet; and he could feel the moisture begin to seep into the legs of his jeans. But the spot did provide a good view of the fenced-in yard and the hen house in the middle of it. However, to call it a *house* was like calling the Getty Mansion a hut. The place was a veritable poultry palace. Callahan estimated it must contain at least a hundred chickens. He could hear a soft chorus of peeping and trilling coming from inside.

As if he knew what Callahan was thinking, Demarest said, "They're contented. They're also expecting to get fed soon." Then he nodded toward the far end of the yard. "There," he whispered.

A figure wearing a hooded sweatshirt and down vest darted from the shrubs and jumped the fence. In a few quick strides it was at the door to the house and inside. A smattering of cackles replaced the peeps and then exploded into a thunder roll when there was a loud squawk. The figure emerged from the door clutching a flailing and squawking hen and ran toward the fence. Callahan and Demarest vaulted the log and sprinted toward opposite sides of the yard. They each rounded the yard at the same time and tore into the woods after the thief. Demarest charged ahead of Callahan, launching a torrent of expletives at the escapee.

Callahan couldn't see the runner or Demarest but followed the screams of the chicken and the crunch of vegetation. Then he heard Demarest shout, "Got him. Over here."

Callahan turned toward the sound of Demarest's voice and plunged through branches and over bramble until he found him.

Demarest straddled the thief's squirming and kicking body, pinning it facedown to the ground as the chicken leaped and fluttered in circles beside him. "Help me hold him down. This bastard's not getting away," he yelled.

Callahan rushed to Demarest and wrenched the thief's arms behind his back and handcuffed his wrists. "Get him to his feet," said Callahan, and he and Demarest each grabbed an arm and yanked him up. As they did, the hood slipped off and they found themselves struggling to restrain a young girl who savagely sliced at their shins with her heels.

Chapter 2

As Callahan drove, Demarest sat in the front passenger seat of the cruiser, the chicken resting in his lap and clucking contently. The girl, separated from them by a steel mesh barrier, slumped in the back seat, sullen and mute. Callahan figured she was no more than ten or eleven. She hadn't spoken since Demarest had tackled her; she hadn't even cried out. The hood of her faded sweatshirt covered all but the tip of her nose and mouth, which she had screwed into a tight wrinkle of rage or fear. Callahan couldn't determine which. Despite the cold, she wore torn tennis shoes without socks, and thin cotton trousers at least three sizes too big for her that were cinched around her waist with a strand of clothesline. *Waif* came to mind when Callahan glanced at her in the rearview mirror.

"So, what you going to do with her?" asked Demarest who twisted to look back at the girl. The girl ducked her head even tighter to her chest.

Callahan shrugged. He didn't want to discuss her future in front of her; but, unless she could tell him where she lived and who looked after her, he would turn her over to the state's Department of Health and Human Services on the mainland. He looked up and into the rearview mirror. "You want to tell me your name and where you live?" he said.

The girl remained silent.

"Maybe she's a deaf mute," said Demarest.

"Maybe she's hungry," said Callahan, and when he glanced into the rearview mirror again, he saw her raise her head just for a second.

*　　*　　*

Julie was making the morning coffee when Callahan and Demarest arrived at the station.

"Oh, my. What's this?" said Julie as Callahan tugged the girl into the station and Demarest held the door open for them. He held her by the left elbow and forearm and had to lift her slightly to counter her pull against him and move her forward.

Julie rushed to the foyer counter and lifted its hatch to make way for them to enter the work area of the station.

"This here's a chicken thief," said Demarest. "We caught her red handed."

Callahan escorted the girl into the room containing the two detention cells, walked her into the nearest one, backed out, and shut the door. The girl rushed to the cot along the wall and fell into it face down, one leg hanging over the bare mattress; her hood still covering her head.

Julie came to Callahan's side, and they both stood outside the cell studying the girl through the bars. "I think she's hungry," said Callahan. "Would you mind going into town and getting her something to eat?"

"Honey, what would you like me to get for you?" said Julie.

The girl didn't answer.

"She's not talking," said Callahan, "but if I had to guess, I'd say she's partial to chicken."

*   *   *

In seconds, the girl had drained a chocolate milkshake, devoured four pieces of fried chicken, and inhaled a volcano of mashed potatoes and gravy.

"I don't think I've seen anyone eat so fast," said Julie, coming out of the cell room and shutting the door, "or fall asleep so quickly. She's in there dead to the world. She must have been exhausted."

"Did she say anything to you?" asked Callahan.

"Not a word," said Julie.

"Then we'll have to call the Department of Health and Human Services and report a case of neglect. An investigator can get here from the mainland within 24 hours. If we can't find her parents or someone who looks after her by then, Child Protective Services will put her in foster care. We can't take care of her here," said Callahan.

"Well, we certainly can't leave her in a detention cell overnight. She's coming home with us." Julie's tone of finality left no room for argument.

*   *   *

Callahan lifted the still-sleeping girl off the cot and carried her from the station out to the cruiser. Julie sat in the back, and he laid the girl on the seat with her head resting in Julie's lap. She didn't stir or wake all the way to their home.

Chapter 3

"She's gone. I've searched the house and she's not here." Julie stood in the bedroom doorway. She'd turned the ceiling light on, and Callahan covered his eyes with his hand as he sat up in bed.

"Did you check outside?" he said, his voice still heavy with sleep.

"I went around the house. No sign of her. The clothes I left folded by her bed in the guestroom are gone too," Julie added.

"Did she take anything else?" Callahan flung the covers off and swung his legs over the side of the bed.

"I don't know," Julie said and darted from the doorway.

Callahan shook his head in dismay as he listened to Julie's rush of footsteps down the hall.

*   *   *

The girl had taken two things from the house besides the clothes that Julie left for her: a jar of peanut butter and Max's blue down coat. Callahan typed and copied a detailed description of the girl to include the clothes she would be wearing, and he and his deputy, Amanda, posted it at the stores, pubs, restaurants, community center, school, gas station, and churches on the island. After three days, no one had called about her. In that time, Amanda had begun a check of the island's vacant vacation homes to see if the girl was squatting in one of them. So far, she had found no evidence of house break-ins. Callahan had also asked the school to see if any 4th, 5th, or 6th grade female students had been absent in the past two weeks and for how long—not a difficult administrative task as the school had only 51 students in its K-12 grades. No such girls had missed any days of school. Callahan wondered if a vagrant family now lived on the island. If so, it had to have arrived recently as it couldn't stay undiscovered for long on such a small piece of the earth.

"If that girl is alone, I'm getting worried," said Amanda. "We've already had our first freeze, and the temperature is beginning to plummet at night." She and Callahan were driving south to Millrace Road. Julie had radioed that a county pickup truck had hit a deer. The collision had immobilized the truck, and it was being towed back into town. The deer had also been immobilized—permanently—and lay in the middle of the road. Since animal control duties fell to the sheriff, dead deer removal had become Callahan and Amanda's specialty.

"If she is living in the woods somewhere, the weather may drive her to shelter in one of the vacant properties. So, keep up a random check. We may get lucky," said Callahan.

"There's the deer," said Amanda pointing ahead out the windshield. "It's not in the road though. It's off the shoulder by the edge of the woods. See it?"

Callahan pulled the cruiser onto the shoulder and slowed to a stop just short of where the deer lay. He and Amanda got out of the cruiser and walked to the animal. It rested on its side, forelegs curled as if caught mid-leap, its neck craned back and mouth open with protruding tongue as if gulping for air. Callahan stood over it and then crouched down for a closer look. "Damn," he said, standing back up and pointing to its bloody rump. "That damage isn't from the collision. The haunch has been cut away and the left leg removed."

Chapter 4

The deciduous trees of the island's forests had shed their leaves as if to make way for the faint light of a low sun to warm the ground. But such starkness, coming so soon after a carnival of colors blanketed the island, made those facing the sharp edge of a northern winter feel exposed and vulnerable. Nick, Amanda's boyfriend, was no exception. It would be his first winter on the island.

The family who owned the vacation home where he rented a converted attic had allowed him to stay for the winter. If he wanted, he could move out of the attic and into the house proper and the rent would remain the same, except that he would now have to pay for utilities. The added expense posed no problem. Callahan was keeping him on as a special deputy for technology until he passed the standard sheriff's deputy exam. When he did, he would become the second deputy sheriff of Nicolet County. The results of his test were due in days. Nick hoped he wouldn't have to retake the exam.

This hope was both irrational and ironic. In his wildest dreams, he never imagined becoming a deputy sheriff. The NSA had recruited him out of Stanford to become an analyst. After training, gaining experience, and proving a vital asset, the agency sent him to work at the University of Michigan's Center for the Study of Domestic Terrorism while studying for his PhD. His superiors predicted a meteoric rise within the agency. Then he met Amanda. At the behest of Callahan, she had visited the center looking for an expert in domestic terrorism; and Nick had been the only person on duty at the time. From that point on, it was as if he'd entered a portal to a parallel universe from which he never wanted to return. He'd come to the island for Amanda and was on the island to stay.

Nick had spent the last hour at the station searching the missing persons file in the National Crime Information Center's database and the NamUs Missing Persons' database. He hoped to locate potential matches for the missing girl based on geography, dates, and descriptors such as race, age, height, weight, hair color, and clothing. The number of missing Michigan children who possessed her descriptors shocked him. The information he had about the girl was simply too general for any viable matches. He was about to give up when "Green Light" by Lorde, the song's ringtone he'd picked for Amanda's calls, blared from his phone.

"Hi. How's it going with the research?" she asked when he answered her call.

"Not well. I haven't even come close to identifying that girl," he answered.

"Well, I've got something that might help. I went to see Mr. Demarest this morning to find out if I could learn anything else about the girl. I was hoping he might recall something he hadn't told us." Amanda paused.

"And?" said Nick.

"He told me that when he tackled her, her sweatshirt slid up her back and he noticed a red patch on the left side below her shoulder blade. He didn't mention it before because he thought it was just a scrape that she got running through the woods. I'm thinking it might be a birthmark."

"Maybe," said Nick. "I'll add it to the descriptors and see what pops up. Thanks."

*   *   *

Nick first added *birthmark* to the descriptors. He got several matches, but none described a red birthmark on the left shoulder blade. Next, he tried *burn,* which turned up an appalling number of matches, but, again, none on the left side of the back. Then he added *rash* and retrieved a single match for a girl who suffered from a skin condition which caused welts on her skin, especially on her back. She had disappeared from a foster home in Grand Haven, Michigan, two years ago. Not a conclusive match by any means, but certainly viable, he thought.

Chapter 5

No matter how high the octane level, the Dodge Charger did not leap into the fray at a muscled gallop. Instead, it hesitated before creeping up to cruising speed, all the while complaining in a grinding rattle as it bounced over the gravel roads. In its current condition, it was ill-suited to the island; but it came cheap as a hand-me-down from the Charlevoix Sheriff's Department. As Nicolet County's second law enforcement vehicle, it would have to do for Nick. The cruiser was reserved for the higher ranks.

Nick arrived early to pick up a package flown in from Charlevoix so decided to stop for coffee at the small diner next to the airport. He turned onto Donal Boyle Lane and drove to the Wing and Wheel Café. He parked next to the only vehicle in the lot, a dusty Ram 2500. Beside it, the Charger looked like a crushed beer can.

When Nick entered the diner, the only patrons were four large men seated shoulder to shoulder at the counter stools. All wore their bulky winter jackets and knit hats, and intently examined the menu. None of them looked up as Nick slid into a booth. Although it was almost two o'clock in the afternoon, all of them selected a breakfast of multiple eggs (scrambled or over easy), bacon, sausage, sides of pancakes with syrup, hash browns, Texas toast with butter, and coffee. The waitress wrote down their choices and then handed the order slip to the cook at the stove behind her who had already begun pouring oil over the griddle and cracking eggs into a bowl. She refilled their coffee then looked over at Nick, smiled, and held up the glass pot. Nick nodded, and she came from behind the counter and poured him a cup. Nick sipped his coffee while the men waited for their orders. None of them spoke as they watched the cook nimbly perform the acrobatics of short order cooking. He thought that if it weren't for the clatter the cook was making, the place would be as quiet as a mausoleum. Nick finished the last of his coffee and was about to pay and leave when one of the men got up and walked over to his booth.

"You the new deputy?" he asked, looking down at Nick.

"Yes, sort of. I'm the department's special deputy," said Nick, wondering how the man even knew he was in the diner, considering he hadn't looked once in his direction.

"Hmm. Well, I think we've seen the girl you're searching for." He shoved a thumb over his shoulder at the other men behind him. "We're framing a house out along Pebble Bay. Noticed we were missing some tools—a hammer, a nail gun, a couple of saws—then saw this kid run into the woods yesterday wearing the kind of clothes described in those notices you put up around the island. That nail gun is a Paslode framing nailer. It's my baby." The man then turned around and walked back to his stool and sat down. "You find her, and you get our tools back," he said without looking back at Nick.

"Sure, and thanks," said Nick.

*   *   *

Nick started the Charger and thumped onto the road, heading in the direction of Pebble Bay and the home under construction. He knew that he was treading outside the purview of his job description as a special deputy, but he justified his decision by telling himself that time was of the essence. Also, official duties put Callahan and Amanda out of reach. He conveniently ignored the fact that he stretched the truth, at least about the *official duties* part.

The annual Taste of Nicolet Island was in full swing, and practically the entire county had converged on the Community Center to sample delectable morsels from the island's eateries and residents. In one of the island's most popular events, professional and amateur chefs competed to titillate the islanders' taste buds to attempt to win the grand prize for the best culinary offering on the island. Callahan attended as a judge, and Amanda ostensibly handled parking and crowd control. She had probably tasted all the pies by now and begun working her way through the samples of chili con carne. Boon-doggle would have been a better description of their activities. Nick could have interrupted them without impeding their service to the islanders.

The house wasn't hard to find. It sat atop an exposed foundation just off the road in a half-acre cleared in the woods. Nick spotted it through the trees and parked the Charger at the start of the dirt trail into the clearing. As he approached the house, he scanned the woods on either side but saw nothing but a jumble of bulldozed vegetation and dirt mounds. He circled the house once, not sure what signs of the girl's presence to look for, before deciding to check inside. He entered through the rear door, which was ajar, and before his eyes adjusted to the dimness of the interior, almost tripped over a stack of drywall on the hallway floor. When he recovered his balance, a figure flashed across the room at the end of the hall. Nick heard rapid footsteps on the room's bare wood floor, and he ran down the hallway toward the sound. As he entered the room, he saw a pair of hands slip from the sill of an open window and heard a dull thud and then the crunch of sand. "Hey, stop," he yelled and raced to the window. He slid through, feet first, leaping to the ground. On landing, he heard a crack; and a searing pain ripped through his left knee. He staggered several feet before he fell facedown into the sand. Nick rolled over on his back and tried to bend his left leg to examine his knee, but the pain almost made him pass out. He then lifted his head as far as he could and looked down at his knee. In the center of an expanding circle of blood, the head of a three-inch nail-gun nail protruded through his jeans. "What the shit?" he bellowed.

Chapter 6

Nick lay on the examination table in Dr. Carl Remy's office while the nurse disposed of needles, bloody gauze, and bandage wrapping and removed the metal tray with the surgical instruments Remy had used to extract the nail. Callahan and Amanda stood at the foot of the table. The look on their faces wasn't exactly one of concern.

"What were you doing out there?" said Callahan.

Nick did not detect a tone of empathy. "Well, I met some construction workers at the Wing and Wheel Café where I stopped for coffee while I waited for the plane to arrive with the package. They're building a house on Pebble Bay and said that someone had stolen some of their tools and that they'd seen a kid dressed like the girl we're looking for around the property." Nick paused.

"And?" said Callahan.

"You and Amanda were busy, and I thought I'd go out and just take a look," continued Nick.

"One of the missing tools wasn't a nail gun, was it?" asked Amanda. Her sarcasm was obvious. No sympathy there either.

"Actually, it was," answered Nick.

Amanda and Callahan exchanged glances. "And, of course, you had the presence of mind to pick up the package," said Callahan, this time with a coal shovel full of reproach.

This was all too much. Nick closed his eyes and sighed. "I'm sorry," he whispered.

"Apparently, you're going to live, so if something like this happens again, you call one of us before you do anything. Got it?" said Callahan.

"Got it," said Nick. "Lesson learned."

The nurse reentered the room with three plastic containers full of pills. "Would you both mind waiting for him in the waiting room. I've got to instruct him on this medication," she said to Callahan and Amanda.

"Make very sure he listens carefully and understands," said Callahan, patting Nick on the shoulder. Nick gave him a wry smile.

In the hallway Amanda turned to Callahan. "Well, we don't know where she is now, but we know where she's recently been," she said and grinned.

Callahan smiled back. "And we know she's armed. All thanks to Nick," he said. "Great police work. I think we'll keep him," he added and laughed at Nick's expense despite himself.

*   *   *

Amanda commandeered the Charger, dropped Nick off for some R&R at the house he rented, and headed for Fallon Lake. A jogger along the lake trail had seen black smoke rising above the trees behind a private beach and called the island's volunteer fire department. Firefighters reached the property in time to extinguish a growing kitchen fire before it became an inferno. The origin of the fire was suspicious as the owners of the house had vacated the property for the winter the week before. House fires on the island were rare. The volunteer fire force kept busy mostly with preventing wildfires caused by campers in the dry summer weeks or by careless vacation-home renters abandoning burning logs in outdoor fire pits.

Amanda had talked to two of the firefighters who had battled the blaze, and both had told her that the fire appeared to have started at the electric stove. No pots or pans were on the stove, and each rejected the possibility that a burner had been left on when the house was vacated. If that were the case, they surmised, the fire would have started earlier, not a week after the owners had left. The control panel had buckled from the heat, and its knobs had melted so it was impossible to tell if a burner had been turned on. The door from a small rear deck to the kitchen was closed and locked when they arrived, as was the front door to the house. The firefighting crew had bashed open both doors. Since no accelerants were evident, they ruled out arson.

Amanda parked the Charger in the side driveway and got a flashlight from the glove compartment. The kitchen entrance jutted off the end of the side drive, so she began her inspection there. The outside entrance to the kitchen had been boarded up as had an adjacent window. Flames had flared up the wall above the door leaving a charred signature in the shape of an ace of spades. Around the window, the billow of dense smoke had deposited a huge bloom of gritty soot.

Amanda continued around to the south side of the house, which faced the lake. She climbed the stairs to the deck and checked the sliding glass door and two large windows along the wall. She found all three closed and locked. The east side of the house had no windows or doors at the first-floor level, but did have two narrow windows at the foundation, both of which opened into the basement. Amanda bent down and shined her flashlight through the first window and into the basement. Four bikes, a kayak, and several cardboard boxes stood against the far wall to the left of the furnace and water heater. She then tried to open the window, but discovered it was locked shut. She approached the second window and pulled on the double pane. It slid open. She crouched down and stuck her leg through the opening to see if she could climb through, but immediately realized that the space was not wide nor high enough for an adult to squeeze into the house. But maybe, she thought, it might be just big enough to allow a young girl to wiggle into the basement.

Chapter 7

"So, you think we have a chicken-stealing, deputy-maiming, house-burning, child escapee on the island," said Callahan, chuckling.

"I don't know whether to think that's funny or just pathetic," said Amanda.

"I definitely don't think it's funny," added Nick, rubbing his knee.

"Humorous or not, if she is on the island, we've got to find her. If she's alone and hiding, she's running from something and needs help," said Callahan. "And it's getting very cold out there. She's too young and unprepared to survive a winter in the wilderness this far north. Anyone got any ideas?"

"If my input still counts for anything, I think I know how to catch her," said Nick.

"How?" said Callahan and Amanda at the same time.

"If she's who we think she might be, then she's going to need medication. When Demarest tackled her, he said he noticed a red patch on her back. Based on that observation and her other descriptors, I refined my search on the missing persons databases of the National Crime Information Center and NamUs to include birthmarks, burns, and rashes. No luck with birthmarks or burns, but rashes turned up one girl fitting the description of our escapee who has a skin condition called eczema and who disappeared from a foster home in Grand Haven, Michigan two years ago. I asked Dr. Remy about eczema, and he said it presents itself in persistent, inflamed, and very itchy patches that sometimes bleed. However, its symptoms could be reduced by over-the-counter steroid creams. My guess is she's stealing them from the first aid aisle at the grocery store. That's where we'll catch her."

"You're back on the team," said Callahan. "If you're right," he added, "and we catch her."

Nick didn't know if he was kidding or not.

*   *   *

"That knee better heal quickly," said Amanda. "It's almost bowling season."

"Bowling season? I didn't know the island had a bowling alley," said Nick.

"It doesn't," said Amanda.

Nick looked confused.

"I'm talking about ice bowling. The best sport on the planet. Its season starts the same time as ice fishing and is almost as popular. If our relationship has a future," Amanda looked at Nick and smiled, "then you are going to learn how to play."

"I can't even visualize how that's done. Is it like curling?" asked Nick.

"Not even close and a heck of a lot more fun. Like ice fishing, it involves alcohol," said Amanda.

"It's beginning to sound interesting," said Nick. "Please enlighten me."

"It's also played at night," continued Amanda. "You pick a frozen lake, usually Butler or Foley Lake, sweep the snow off the ice to form a lane or lanes, and then set up the pins. The pins are the good part. You use empty beer bottles with glow sticks inside. You knock them down with plastic bowling balls. If the bottles break, there's always more empties on hand, especially during a tournament. With a good hurl, those balls will travel a mile on the ice, so the lanes are long, and you must use a hay bale as a backstop. Also, someone's got to be at the end of the lane to reset the pins and roll the ball back. That would be you until you get the hang of the sport. Bowling under the stars on a crisp winter night or during a full moon can't be beat. It's great fun and an island tradition."

"I can't believe I've lived as long as I have and missed such an event," said Nick, shaking his head.

"Oh come on, you're going to love it," said Amanda. "Just like you love me," she said and gave him a sweet smile.

Chapter 8

It had begun to snow, not in flakes but in a fog of infinite tiny crystals that enveloped the island, blinding it in silence and covering its surface like grains of sand. The girl lifted the pine branches that covered the entrance to her makeshift hut and crawled in. Barely more than a lean-to, it sat low and squat, concealed in the bramble between two trees. She had constructed the exterior of intertwined branches and twigs and lined the inside with rags and sheets of cardboard for insulation. On its floor, a sleeping bag lay atop a yoga mat, both of which she had pilfered from one of the houses she had broken into. At the head and foot of the bag, she had stacked cans of food and the glass jars of candles. Inside, she felt safe, even at night when the coyotes came and ringed the hut, more curious than malevolent. And the nail gun was always within her reach. But now she worried. If she left the hut, her tracks could be seen and followed.

Chapter 9

Winters in the upper Midwest nudged and poked and then pushed and pummeled until you either embraced them or resigned yourself to a siege. The ferries were dry-docked, and the weather made scheduled flights to and from the island unreliable and infrequent, so for weeks at a time, there was no way on or off the island. The island offered no respite in the way of malls with their Cineplexes, indoor waterparks, or restaurants. Yet, Callahan marveled at how the islanders dealt with their isolation. They simply didn't see it as such. What the island did offer were pristine ski trails, cathedrals of blue ice shoved by the waves of Lake Michigan high against its beaches, frozen inland lakes perfect for ice fishing and ice bowling, the blinding sparkle of vast stretches of snow fringed with the azure shadows of trees, a lit fireplace at night, the satisfaction of a hardy self-reliance, and the warmth of a community of winter people. That's not to say there wasn't the occasional getaway to Cancun.

Callahan was thinking of all of this as he tried to rock the cruiser out of a snowbank he'd slid into. The first snowfall of the season and he'd managed to embarrass himself with a neophyte's blunder. He'd entered a sharp curve too fast and skidded off the road, almost hitting a tree. He cursed himself and hoped no one would drive by and catch him in this situation. Word of it would spread like wildfire.

No such luck. He watched in the rearview mirror as a pickup truck with a snowplow stopped behind the cruiser and Bud Donahue stepped out. Callahan lowered his window when Donahue approached the cruiser with the rocking gait of a man with bad knees and sidled up to the open window. The rabbit fur on the flaps and peak of Donahue's trapper hat matched the color of his bushy beard and thick eyebrows, and, except for his red nose and blues eyes, it looked to Callahan like a muskrat had wrapped itself around his face. Donahue turned his head and spat into the snow. Then he slowly scanned the length of the cruiser before turning back to Callahan.

"Looks like you got yourself into a bit of a predicament, Sheriff. The usual excuse is that you were trying to avoid hitting a deer in the road. You might want to think about using that one," he said and then laughed aloud. Before Callahan could respond, Donahue said, "I got a chain in the bed of the truck. Come on, let's get you pulled out of here before someone else comes along. I'm on my way to plow out the grocery store's parking lot."

*   *   *

Donahue's truck rumbled away down the road on Michelin winter tires as if it were navigating a Florida interstate instead of packed snow and ice; it disappeared where the road turned toward town. Callahan slowly crunched along in the wheel ruts it left behind in the snow. White powder coated the outstretched branches and tall trunks of bare trees on either side of the road, and, along with the brightness and stillness of the day, gave Callahan the impression that he drifted through a vast reef of frosted coral.

He was enjoying the sensation when the throaty growl of snowmobiles jarred him from his reverie. Two machines leaped over the road in front of him and slalomed at high speed through the trees as he drove through their path seconds later. He was about to disparage the recklessness of teenagers in X-rated language, but as he watched the machines vanish into the trees, he realized that the drivers were grown men—and that they were in pursuit of something.

Chapter 10

A stakeout at the first-aid aisle of the grocery store was out of the question. There was no way to determine if or when the girl might show up, even if Nick had identified the right missing person and she was still on the island. Callahan could not afford to have himself, Amanda, and Nick exchange shifts for days at a time on the remote possibility the girl might eventually arrive. So, he settled for Stephen Broderick, the store's stock person and the son of its owner.

Callahan asked Steve to keep any eye out for the girl as he went about his job. Steve enthusiastically accepted. Callahan now regretted his decision. At eighteen, Steve had decided to defer enrolling at Western Michigan University while he earned enough money to travel to Australia before school started the following year. A mistake because Steve was apparently bored out of his skull, needed glasses, or both. He had called Callahan no fewer than eleven times in two days with sightings of customers lurking in the aisles that he thought fit the girl's description. None of them did, as they all turned out to be female islanders between the ages of forty and sixty-five bundled in winter garb. And none of them had even ventured down the first aid aisle.

Callahan sighed with exasperation as he answered yet another call from Steve.

"Sheriff Callahan, I'm sure it's her this time. She's in the first aid aisle, and she's young. I think. At least she's small. Smaller, anyway." He was whispering so softly that Callahan could barely hear him. "She's grabbed some medicine off the shelf. I think she's going to leave the store. Do you want me to stall her till you get here? I can do that."

"No, no. Absolutely not. Don't do anything except keep an eye on her until I get there. Nothing else. Understand?" Callahan mentally kicked himself again.

"I guess," said Steve. Callahan could hear the disappointment in his voice and prayed that Steve wouldn't take matters into his own hands. He thought of the nail gun.

*   *   *

Steve was waiting at the store's entrance when Callahan arrived. He looked like a panicked traffic cop in the middle of a city intersection at rush hour, his arms windmilling, his head wobbling on his neck, signaling to Callahan. Before Callahan even reached the entrance, Steve ran up to the cruiser, opened the door of the still moving vehicle, and jumped in.

"She headed that way," he said, pointing north down Main Street. "I think she might have dodged onto Pine Street."

Callahan turned the cruiser around and sped out of the parking lot. "What happened back there?" he asked.

Steve shook his head and moaned. "I don't know. She was acting all normal and stuff and then suddenly took off and bolted out of the store. I think she saw me watching her and then calling you. She's fast. I couldn't keep up with her."

*   *   *

After thirty minutes of fruitlessly wandering side streets and stopping to ask people if they saw a young girl running or lurking in the neighborhood, Callahan gave up the search.

Chapter 11

Callahan saw the snowfall as a chance to find the girl. His sporadic attempts to catch her had failed, but, at least, they'd proved that she wasn't squatting in vacant vacation homes. She had to be hiding out in the woods somewhere, and that meant that the snow would reveal her whereabouts. Another snowfall was not predicted for days so any tracks or traces of her presence would not be covered up. Callahan figured that she would avoid any cross-country ski, hiking, or snowmobile trails to avoid being seen. She would stay for as long as she could deep in the woods and evade anyone looking for her. It was now or never.

A massive search was out of the question. Tourist season had ended long ago. Those with summer homes on the island had departed before the first frosts, and the permanent island population had shrunk to just a few hundred. Of those, many were children and older folks, or people with jobs they couldn't leave for long. There simply weren't enough people available to blanket the island in a search for the girl. Callahan also wanted to minimize the number of people searching for the girl to avoid having her tracks inadvertently obliterated by a horde of amateurs, so he hit upon a more targeted approach.

He tasked Amanda with locating three of the best hunters on the island. His aim was to divide the island into three sectors and have each hunter assigned a sector to track the girl. He planned to deputize these individuals, and he, Amanda, and Nick would each accompany a hunter. As small as the island was, the search areas were huge, Callahan expected the hunt to last several days at a minimum, assuming it was successful.

*   *   *

The three men standing in front of Callahan were not quite what he'd expected. Amanda had brought him two hunters and one trapper, and as she introduced each one, his vision of a khaki clad big game hunter with a high-powered rifle slung over his shoulder rapidly vanished.

Steven Dexter was squat with a salt-and-pepper beard and a fixed expression that made him appear that he wanted to be somewhere else and was about to go there. When he shook Callahan's hand, he let go quickly but said he was glad to help and was anxious to get started. Callahan noticed that his heavily stained down jacket had a ripped left sleeve repaired with duct tape that was almost, but not quite, the same color. Callahan had run into him a couple of times at the kayak and bike rental shop that Dexter owned on the bay.

Gary Rea was tall with a gaunt face and leathery skin. Callahan knew him as a local artist with a gallery on Main Street, but he had no idea that he was a hunter. As Rea nodded in greeting, Callahan recalled that most of his art was of wild animals found in Michigan. His paintings were beautiful with the lifelike animals appearing in motion.

Amanda introduced Jeff Donnelly as a trapper. He had a round, red face and a ready smile. He wore a baseball hat with a crown inscribed, *Donnelly Pest Control, Ridding Your Home of Rats to Raccoons since 1992.* Two things struck Callahan about Donnelly: he'd never heard of a modern trapper before, and he wondered about the date on his hat. Donnelly was only in his thirties and would have been a kid when the business started. Callahan figured Donnelly's father had founded the business.

Callahan assigned Nick to Dexter, Amanda to Rea, and himself to Donnelly. Thick clouds mottled in gray filled the sky. Although not predicted, Callahan feared it might start to snow again and cover any tracks. He wasn't wasting any more time. The search would begin immediately. As he ordered everyone off to their designated areas of the island, he hoped that they'd find the girl before the temperature dropped even further.

Chapter 12

Her mother had taught her to survive in the North's unforgiving wilderness: the ways to hunt, trap, and forage; the ways to shelter, clothe, and heal; and the ways to recognize and celebrate the bounty of each season. Her mother had learned these ways from her father, a man the girl never knew, a man who died in a war that was only a name to her. But the grandfather grew alive for the girl in the lessons her mother taught. As the girl mastered the lessons, her grandfather's spirit became strong for her, and she felt his guidance and counsel in all she learned from him through her mother. Now, he was always with her and revealed his presence in the soft curtain of shimmering green that danced above the horizon on crisp clear nights—*waawaate,* the Northern Lights.

The girl opened the blade of the folding knife and cut off a lush pine twig from a fallen branch. She lifted her left foot and held the twig against the sole of her shoe. It extended several inches beyond her toe and heel and several inches on each side of her foot. She cut another twig from the branch the same size as the first. She then leaned against one of the trees supporting her lean-to and tied the twigs to the bottoms of her shoes with twine she had stolen from the grocery store in town. She walked several yards away from her lean-to and looked back. Chunks of snow had been blown from the trees in the forest pocking the snow on the ground. The twigs blended her footprints with the patterns in the snow making her tracks almost invisible.

But if someone were able to pick up her tracks and follow them, she wanted to make the effort slow, confusing, and demanding. She would travel a distance in the snow before veering off to the right or left to form a path from which she would backtrack and begin another trail. Then she would hike farther before forming another divergent path on which she would again backtrack. She would repeat this process again and again. In this way, she created a branching maze of false dead-end trails which would confuse and stall a single pursuer or cause multiple pursuers to separate and lose one another to find her actual path. By then she could be far ahead of any trackers and able to evade them.

Chapter 13

Donnelly chose the state forest in the island's northwest corner as his search area and gave Callahan directions to a trailhead at its southern entrance. As Callahan drove, the sky darkened to a dull gun-metal gray.

"It will snow soon," said Callahan. "That's going to make our search difficult if not impossible."

"Not so," said Donnelly. "It's unlikely to make any difference at all."

Callahan turned and looked at Donnelly, surprised. "But a fresh snow will cover her tracks," he said.

"I'm a trapper not a hunter. We don't need to follow tracks to find her," said Donnelly.

"You're not suggesting that we're going to use a trap to catch her, are you?" said Callahan, imagining a deep pit in the ground for her to tumble headlong into or a spring trap to yank her into the air by her ankles where she would dangle upside down until they found her.

"No, of course not," said Donnelly. "We're simply going to use the right bait." He reached into the back seat of the cruiser, grasped his backpack by a strap, and hauled it into his lap. He unzipped it and retrieved a brown paper bag. "What kind of bait do you think would lure a ten-year-old girl?" he asked.

Callahan eyed the paper bag. Candy, it had to be candy, he thought.

"I know what you're thinking, and it's not candy," said Donnelly, grabbing the bag and dumping its contents onto the seat.

Callahan looked down. Four cell phones lay in a pile beside Donnelly. "What the . . . I don't . . . ," he sputtered.

"Each of these phones is fully charged, loaded with games, and has its location function turned on," Donnelly began to explain. "We'll place them in spots where I believe she's been and will go again. We'll make it look like each has fallen from someone's pocket or backpack while they were hiking or snowmobiling. When she picks one up, which she will—she won't be able to resist—we can then use an app on our phones to locate and follow her as she travels. It's just a short time before she discovers one."

*   *   *

Callahan had to admit that the plan seemed ingenious, but would it work? He had questions: How would they know where to place the phones? What if someone other than the girl discovered a phone and took off with it? What if the girl succumbed to the elements before she found a phone? Shouldn't they also be searching for her to prevent that from happening?

Donnelly had answers: All larger animals get where they need to go by traveling well-worn paths or trails through the woods and forest, he explained. Humans are no different. Since it's difficult and dangerous to make your way through a dense forest, she would either shadow or use the trails when no one was on them. Also, that way she wouldn't get lost. Therefore, he proposed, they would place the phones along certain trails. He further surmised that because everyone has a cell phone now, if others found the phones, they would simply take them to where their owners were likely to recover them—the sheriff's station. That way they would quickly know it wasn't the girl who had one of the phones. Finally, he met Callahan's last concern by stating that by strategically placing several cell phones in the forest, she was more likely to find one quickly and be located faster than through a tortuous hunt through a state forest.

It all sounded convincing to Callahan, especially when weighed with what he had learned from Donnelly about his experience as a trapper. Donnelly worked with state and federal agencies live trapping endangered, threatened, or overpopulated animals to relocate them to safe areas where they would thrive and invigorate declining habitats. He also trapped and relocated animals that endangered humans and livestock. He never killed, was consistently successful, and much in demand.

Yet, as Donnelly had warned, trapping was more art than science; more a matter of increasing the odds of success than reliably hitting the mark.

* * *

They had just returned to the station when Donnelly's phone signaled that their bait had been snatched.

Chapter 14

The girl held the phone in front of her, staring at the lit screen. The scene's multicolored hot air balloons rising into a vivid blue sky above a lush field, made the phone seem like a jewel against the wash of gray surrounding her. She swiped the screen and rows of icons appeared. She recognized almost all of them. She resisted the temptation to immediately open one of her favorite apps. The phone was charged to 98 percent, but the battery wouldn't last forever. She knew that to preserve the charge, she would have to turn the phone off when she wasn't using it and then on again when she needed it. But she was afraid once she turned the phone off, it would lock; and without the pin code, she wouldn't be able to open it again. Her only alternative was to carefully ration her time—unless she could find a charger left in one of the vacant summer homes on the island. She could never go back into town again for what she needed. She had seen the notices describing her and knew they were looking for her.

Chapter 15

"You sure she's in that house?" said Callahan.

"Absolutely," said Donnelly. "She's definitely in there."

Callahan and Donnelly had followed the trace of the girl's path on the app's map until it ended at a two-story home built against the beach-face of a bluff on the east side of the island. The home was new. Its full elevation was visible only from the beach. The second story with the home's main entrance rested atop the bluff; the lower story hidden below. A sturdy wooden deck supported by pillars ringed the second floor along three sides, the longest section facing the lake. The house was large with at least five bedrooms.

If the girl were truly inside, Callahan wondered how she had gotten in. He and Donnelly reconnoitered the house. The entrance door was locked, and all the windows were securely closed, as were the large sliding glass doors on the first and second floors at the rear of the home.

Callahan called the rest of the search team to meet them at the home. Amanda was to pick up the house key from the realtor who managed the property. Callahan stationed Nick on the north side of the home, Amanda on the south side, and Dexter and Rea in the back. Donnelly would stay in front of the house when Callahan entered it. Callahan decided that only he would go into the home. If the girl had the nail gun with her, he didn't want anyone on the team injured.

The house was surrounded. If the girl eluded Callahan and somehow escaped the home, then one of the team would have to catch her.

*   *   *

Callahan opened the front door and called out to the girl. "I'm the county sheriff. We're here to help you. No one is going to hurt you. We just want you safe and out of harm's way. It's getting colder and no one can survive outside for long up here in a bitter winter. You'll be taken care of." He stepped into the entrance foyer and waited for an answer. Nothing. Only silence. He listened for movement inside the home: the creak of a step on the floor, the slide of clothing against a wall, the rasp of breath, the quick squeal of a door hinge. Again, nothing.

Callahan moved out of the foyer and onto to the home's upper floor. The large open space combined a living room, kitchen, fireplace, and entertainment center, illuminated by skylights and two sliding glass doors along the beach wall. If the girl were hiding, she had to be on the lower floor in one of the bedrooms.

Callahan descended the flight of stairs to the lower floor, crouching slightly and bending forward to see below the ceiling before he was fully exposed on the stairwell. He saw a sparsely furnished family room that opened onto the back lawn leading to the lake. Three rooms edged the perimeter of the space. Through the sliding glass doors, he spotted Dexter and Rea standing at the far edge of the yard. They both stared into the home, and as Callahan reached the bottom of the stairs, Dexter gave him a quick wave.

Callahan waved back and started to turn toward one of the rooms when two things happened at once: Dexter and Rea began running toward the house, and a cellphone ringtone blared behind him.

Chapter 16

Had not Callahan been distracted by Dexter and Rea running, he might have turned in time to fend off the blow to his head.

During the few seconds Callahan was stunned, the girl climbed the stairs.

As Dexter and Rea charged toward the house, they had shouted in warning to Callahan. Their cries alarmed Donnelly who left the front of the home and scurried down the bluff toward the commotion. Nick and Amanda also ran to Rea and Dexter, all five winding up in the back yard as the girl plunged out the front door and into the woods.

*   *   *

"What did she hit you with?" asked Remy, as he examined the back of Callahan's head.

Callahan sat on the exam table in Remy's office, slumped over with his head lowered. His posture was not to aid Remy, although it did. Instead, he felt deflated;

and his body language conveyed his mental state. He felt flummoxed, struggling to come to grips with the fact that a ten-year-old girl he'd been trying to save had, yet again, evaded him.

"It was a table lamp, metal, with a heavy base. She hit me with the base of it. What's the damage?" said Callahan.

"Minimal," said Remy. "You'll survive with nothing more than a rather large and sore bump. No fracture and no signs of a concussion. Your speech is coherent, your vision is fine, your balance is perfect; and the skin isn't even broken. Now please leave my office. And take with you the black cloud you brought in here. It's beginning to darken my bright outlook on life."

Remy's irony was not lost on Callahan.

Chapter 17

Callahan's concern for the safety of the girl had now risen to near panic mode. He was convinced that if they didn't find her soon, she would die of exposure. The temperature had fallen below freezing for so long that the lake had started to freeze more than a hundred yards from shore, and the island was ringed in thickening ice. Most of the inland lakes were now frozen over.

The girl had proven herself resourceful, viciously independent, and able to survive alone in the wilderness up to this point. But they were entering a dangerous season, and she could soon lose her struggle to survive.

Donnelly's brilliant but belated idea to call the cell phone to reveal her hiding place in the house had almost worked. Had he thought of it a few seconds sooner, Callahan would have turned fully around and been able to catch her. As it was, she had bashed him on the head and bolted from the home and into the woods where they had found the discarded phone, but not her. Leading the others, Rea had followed her tracks through the woods to where they had suddenly and mysteriously disappeared. Despite an exhaustive effort, he was not able to pick up her trail again. Dexter had expressed what they were all thinking. "That girl has lived in the wild before and been hunted," he said.

Feral had become Callahan's overriding impression of the girl.

*   *   *

"She's not who I thought. I was wrong." Without announcement, Nick appeared at Callahan's office door and made his pronouncement as if he had known Callahan was thinking about the girl.

Callahan waved Nick into his office and motioned for him to sit down. "Well, who is she then?" he asked after Nick settled himself.

"Still don't know," answered Nick, "but she isn't the missing girl with the skin condition. That girl's been found. Turns out, she was grabbed by an aunt in Utah. She'd been hiding out with the aunt until a private investigator found her."

"How did you find this out?" asked Callahan.

"I've been following up and expanding on my initial research of missing persons. Her discovery made the news in her hometown and was on the Internet. The spin on her story is whether the aunt should be prosecuted for kidnapping or hailed as a heroine for rescuing her from abuse in the home. Pretty interesting."

Interesting perhaps, but what really interested Callahan was who their runaway was and what they could learn to help catch her. "Have you uncovered any leads at all on who she might be?" he asked.

"We're at a dead end with an Internet match search. In order to get the necessary information to identify her, we'd have to physically interview everyone who reported a missing girl who would now be ten or eleven years old. That would be impossible. There are just too many missing children in that category. Then, there is the possibility that no one reported her missing. If that's the case, she isn't even in the pool of possible candidates."

"What if she isn't missing; at least, not from this country." Julie appeared in the doorway and flashed a quick apologetic smile when Nick and Callahan turned to her in surprise. "I've been thinking. We've never heard her utter a word. Maybe she doesn't speak English. She's always had her head covered and her face hidden. Maybe she's not from this country at all," she added.

Chapter 18

The girl felt safe again. Her hunters had given up, at least for now, and gone away. The cloak of a moonless night and the invisibility of her snow-covered hut guaranteed she would not be found even if they were still out there combing the woods for her. Evading them had been easy. She had lost weight since being on her own, and her small stature and slight build enabled her to almost float over the snow. Her steps barely made an imprint, and it had been an effort even to make her tracks detectible. When she was sure they were following her trail, she tied branches to the bottom of her boots and tread as lightly as she could. Her prints became invisible as she headed north away from her tracks. After she had gone far enough, she hid beneath a snowbank. She was grateful they weren't using dogs. She hated the dogs, vicious things that relentlessly pursued her, that caused her to panic and run and run until she was exhausted, alone, and lost.

Chapter 19

Donnelly stood at the stove and lifted a gurgling perco-lator from the gas burner. He poured steaming hot cof-fee into his favorite mug and then sat at the kitchen table. Except for the kitchen, his house was dark, empty, and heavy with silence. Normally, his home vibrated with life. But his wife and three-year-old daughter were in Sarasota visiting her parents. He missed them, and should have been despondent; but, just now, he wel-comed the solitude and quiet.

He watched a moment as the steam wafted above the cup, vanishing into the air, before he took his first sip. They had been able to track the girl before they lost her—not far, but far enough for him to learn something important about her. She had fled into the woods and, for a while, kept straight on. But then her path changed, twice. She broke left for a distance and then left again. She had stayed on this last bearing until they lost her tracks.

Virtually every animal he'd ever hunted had the same strategy when chased. They never fled to save themselves. In fact, they wanted to be followed. From beavers to foxes, the ploy was the same: to lead their pursuers away from their kits and lodges or pups and dens. Why should a ten-year-old human be any different? She had been leading them away from something. It was probably her hideout, he thought.

Callahan had given him his cellphone number when they had baited the traps for the girl together. He reached in his pocket and retrieved his cell phone. It was late, but he would call Callahan anyway. He thought of his own daughter. Hadn't Callahan said that time was running out for the girl?

Chapter 20

The girl had climbed the vertical sheets of broken ice that the lake had shoved like playing cards over the beach and had run out onto the field of fast ice that spread from the shore until it vanished into dark water. Shielded by the frozen wall, she had stopped to catch her breath. As her breathing slowed, she felt the lake beneath her feet rise and fall in unison with her breathing, like something alive. She slowly turned full circle. Glow from a partially hidden moon created a vast monochromatic landscape where the boundary between water, ice, and sky were indistinguishable. She could hear the lake under her wheeze and groan as the ice stretched and withered. She took a step back toward the beach and heard a grinding crack. She stopped and stood still, wishing herself weightless above the ice. And for the first time, she was afraid—not of being caught but of dying.

* * *

"This isn't good, Matt." Donnelly had stopped running and called to Callahan who was ahead of him. Callahan halted and turned. They had backtracked her trail and discovered her hideaway. She had seen or heard them coming and had taken off at a run through the woods. They plunged after her, but she was small and fast and maneuvered through the trees and over the snow like a fleeing owl while they stumbled and thrashed further and further behind her.

Callahan walked back to Donnelly. "Why have we stopped? We'll never catch her now," he said.

"She's heading for the lake. If she goes out on the ice, we may lose her for good," said Donnelly.

"She wouldn't do that. Even at her age, she must know that it's too dangerous," said Callahan.

"That's what deer do when chased by dogs or coyotes. They become desperate and swim out into the lake to escape, knowing the dogs won't follow them far into the water. They stay out there swimming until they weaken and drown. In winter they fall through the ice and are dead in minutes. The girl is desperate. She may go onto the ice believing we won't follow because we're heavier and will fall through if we go after her."

"What now then?" asked Callahan.

Donnelly shrugged. "We keep following her, but not at a run. She's panicked. We need her to calm down, to get her wits back."

*   *   *

Callahan and Donnelly trod through the snow along the beach, and every hundred yards they stretched to the top of the ice shoves and shined their flashlights out over the ice. Rather than splitting up and going in opposite directions along the beach, Donnelly had suggested that they stay together. They would start at the point her tracks vanished and then search in one direction before going back and searching in the other. The plan diminished their chances of finding her if she were on the move, but Donnelly hoped that she would lay low on the frozen lake waiting for them to give up and leave. In that case, it would take the two of them to get her off the ice.

Callahan peered over the top of the wall of ice and scanned the beam of his flashlight along the fast ice. Glints and flashes rippled off the clear ice shards that stuck above the snow as the beam roamed further and further out on the lake. The beam passed over a large shard that did not glint and Callahan swung the beam back to it. There was the girl.

"There she is," said Callahan holding the beam steady on the girl.

Donnelly shined his light where Callahan's beam pointed and saw the girl illuminated in the two pale circles of light. She was facing them, standing erect.

"It's okay," yelled Callahan. "We're here to help you. Please come off the ice."

The girl shook her head.

"Please," yelled Callahan again. "It's dangerous for you out there."

The girl didn't move except to shake her head again.

"She's not trying to run," said Donnelly. "I think she might be afraid to move. Maybe the ice has cracked under her."

"We have to get her then," said Callahan, starting to climb over the ice shove. "She can't stay there."

"Wait," said Donnelly, grabbing the back of Callahan's jacket. "I'm lighter than you are. Let me go." Donnelly took off his jacket and then untied the laces of his boots. He pulled his boots off and dropped them in the snow. Then he put his cellphone in one boot and his flashlight in the other. "The lake is shallow for several yards out. After that, it gets deep. She's at the deep part. Follow me out on the ice until I tell you to stop. Then I'll go the rest of the way to her."

Donnelly took off his belt and told Callahan to do the same. He then buckled them together. "If I fall through the ice, lay flat on the ice and stretch out as far as you can. If you can't reach me by hand, then toss the end of the belt to me to grab." Callahan nodded, and they climbed over the ice wall together.

Chapter 21

Nick sat with his feet up on his desk at the station, leaning back in his chair and reading a popular police procedural novel on his Kindle. He was on call on Callahan's orders until Callahan notified him that he and Donnelly were ready to be picked up and driven back to their cars, with or without the girl. He could have waited for Callahan's call at the house he rented, but he somehow felt that he wasn't really on duty. It was silly, he knew, but being at the station helped alter his image of himself from a fumbling dabbler in law enforcement to an earnest neophyte. He had been the whiz kid, the rising star at the NSA and at the university's Center for Domestic Terrorism. He had foolishly assumed it would be the same in law enforcement, but his initial attempts to master the job had been a series of misadventures at best and disasters at worst. And it now made him push too hard and too fast. Amanda had tried to hide it from him, but he sensed her annoyance with his recent missteps as a rookie. His latest caper with the girl and the nail gun had totally unmasked her and Callahan's frustration with his progress and judgment. They both were losing patience, something that terrified him on a personal and professional level.

The novel eased his anxiety as it tugged him into the plot where its protagonist detective began unraveling a crime with what Nick thought were modern detection practices. He hoped he might find some helpful pointers. He'd almost forgotten where he was and why he was there when his phone rang. It so startled him that he dropped the Kindle as he whipped his feet from the desk and sprang from his chair. He grabbed his phone and stammered, "Hello, yes?" before it was fully out of his pocket.

"Would you like some company?" came the answer.

"What?" he said confused.

"Would you like some company?" Amanda asked again.

"Oh, it's you. Uh, I wasn't expecting . . . This is a surprise. It's just that . . . I mean I'm at the station," he said, trying to recover from his confusion.

"Well, that might be an interesting change. Shall I come there or are you otherwise occupied?"

"Yes. Not yes, I mean no. No, not no either. What I mean," said Nick, his voice rising in panic, "is yes, I want your company. That would be great. And no, I'm not occupied, at least not in the way you meant, or I think you meant. Maybe you didn't mean it that way. I'm waiting for a call from Callahan to pick him and Donnelly up. They're still looking for the girl's hideout. He might call before you get here or even shortly after. Maybe you shouldn't come," said Nick, now totally off balance.

"Oh, really. Well, it's not a problem for me. Let's see what happens. I'm on my way," said Amanda sweetly. "And I did mean it the way you thought," she added before hanging up.

Chapter 22

"Stay here," said Donnelly. "I'm going to edge out to her slowly. If I go through the ice, lie flat and toss the end of the belt to me."

Callahan nodded, and Donnelly started for the girl. He'd taken five steps when Callahan heard the crack and Donnelly disappeared. Where he'd stood a second before, bobbing chunks of ice had already filled the hole he'd vanished into.

Callahan squatted and eased on to his stomach. He then began to push himself, slithering toward the hole. He'd slid only a few feet when the ice under him began to give and he stopped. He was just close enough to the hole for Donnelly to grab the belt if he surfaced. If Donnelly didn't reappear within seconds, then Callahan resolved to go under the ice after him. He began to count: 1. . . 2 . . . 3 . . . 4 . . . 5 . . . 6 . . . That was long enough. Callahan had risen to his knees when Donnelly's head shot out of the water and his arms slapped down over the rim of the hole. Callahan dived flat on the ice, stretched out as far as he could, and tossed Donnelly the end of the belt. Donnelly grabbed it, and as Callahan began to pull, the belt slipped from Donnelly's hands. Callahan tossed the belt again, and again Donnelly grabbed it; but even before Callahan began to pull, Donnelly's grip slackened, and he slid back into the water. Callahan started to shove himself toward the hole when the girl appeared in front of him, blocking his way. She crouched and then lay prone on the ice, her body extended to its full length, her outstretched arms reaching for Donnelly, her legs thrust back toward Callahan. She kicked her feet, and Callahan grabbed both her ankles. As she took hold of Donnelly's shirt with both hands, Callahan inched back toward the beach, pulling the girl with him until Donnelly's body lay on solid ice.

*   *   *

Nick's phone rang just as Amanda walked into the station. He turned towards her with the phone at his ear, and she saw the expression on his face turned from attentive curiosity to shock.

She rushed to him. "What's happened?" she asked.

Nick raised his hand to silence her; then grabbed a pen and began taking notes.

Amanda could hear Callahan's voice but couldn't make out what he was saying.

The call ended abruptly. Nick turned to Amanda. "Donnelly's fallen through the ice in the lake. He's in bad shape. Callahan's doing what he can, but he fears Donnelly will die of hypothermia soon if he doesn't get immediate medical help. They're on the beach somewhere along Pebble Bay," said Nick.

"That's too far from town and there's no road that goes directly to that bay. Our volunteer EMTs need to assemble, get on a trail to the bay, and then find them. That might take too long, but we can't get there much faster. What do we do?" said Amanda.

Nick thought for a moment and then tapped into the browser on his phone and entered a keyword search. As Amanda looked over his shoulder, a website instantly appeared. "Keep your fingers crossed and hope this works," he said.

*　*　*

Callahan had removed Donnelly's shirt and his own and cradled Donnelly against his chest to try and warm him with his body heat, his down coat wrapped around them both. The girl had draped her body over Donnelly's legs. Callahan was afraid it wasn't going to be enough. He couldn't feel Donnelly's heartbeat or the rhythm of his breathing.

When the bright speck of light appeared around the point, Callahan and the girl looked down the beach at the same time. Ahead of a helicopter's thudding shudder, the light grew in intensity, blinding them. They shielded their eyes until it was above them, enveloping them in a blazing circle. Heavy air pounded down and blasted the snow around them, and, seconds later, a tethered stretcher clattered to the ground followed by a Coast Guard rescue swimmer.

Chapter 23

"She's sleeping now, thank goodness. She's exhausted, surely emotionally as well as physically." Julie whispered the words as she came out of the detention cell room and padded over to where Matt, Amanda, and Nick were huddled around Amanda's desk. "When she wakes up, I'm taking her home." She spoke directly to Matt and not in a whisper.

"We tried that before and she ran away. I can't risk that happening again," he said.

"I don't care. That poor girl isn't staying in a detention cell, even if it's unlocked and Amanda or Nick is here with her. That's simply not going to happen."

Callahan started to speak, but Julie stopped him. "And, I'm taking her to Remy in the morning for a thorough physical examination. Lord only knows how she is after the way she's been living. Or when someone from Child Protective Services can get here from the mainland."

"That could be awhile," said Amanda. "The airport is closed because this weather is hanging over the island and won't leave."

Callahan gave her an exasperated look. "Okay, but someone has to be with her at all times. We're not letting her out of our sight," he said.

Nick's ringtone sounded, and he grabbed the phone from his back pocket. He looked at the number and then swiped the screen to connect the call. "Yes?" he answered. He listened for a few seconds and then said, "Thanks," ending the call. "Donnelly's conscious and going to be okay," he announced.

*   *   *

Callahan sat in Remy's small waiting room reading an out-of-date hunting magazine when Amanda opened the door leading to the examining room and stood in the doorway. He could tell from her expression that something was wrong. "What's happening in there?" he said.

"The girl and Julie are still with Remy and his nurse, but Remy needs to see you as soon as the examination is over. He wanted me to make sure you don't leave for any reason."

"Did he say why?" asked Callahan.

"She has scars on her legs and back. Remy says they're from burns that have never been treated." Amanda was silent for a moment, and it was obvious to

Callahan that she was trying to control her emotions. Amanda then broke down and cried.

Chapter 24

"Her skin has been burned badly in many places on her body. She's obviously been in a terrible fire. My guess is that she was trapped and somehow escaped, but not before suffering severe burns. I suspect that's why she doesn't speak because there's nothing physical preventing her from talking. It's psychological. Such a trauma could rob her of speech for a very long time. She also refused to write the answers to any questions I asked her, and repeatedly threw the pen I handed to her across the room, so I don't know when or how this happened to her," said Remy.

Callahan sat across the desk from Remy attempting to process what the medical examiner said. "Could it have happened on the island? I mean are her burns recent?" he asked.

"I don't know how long she's been on the island. For the most part, her wounds have healed, but scar tissue indicates that she was burned several months ago. I'd say six or more. It's not a pretty sight, Matt. She suffered, no question," said Remy.

Callahan felt sick.

*   *   *

As a local law enforcement officer, Michigan law made clear his duties in this matter. He was mandated to examine, report, and investigate cases of intentionally injured children. A monster may have done this to the girl, but who, where, and why?

Chapter 25

The gray pall that had settled over the island kneaded itself into dark clumps of low hanging clouds by the time Callahan left Remy's office and nosed the cruiser onto Main Street. It would snow soon with a vengeance, he thought, as he turned onto the coast road heading south. He drove to visit Donnelly's wife who had returned from Florida on news of her husband's hospitalization. No islander would be left in need. He'd learned that soon after his arrival and so was sure islanders were taking care of Donnelly's family while he was in the hospital. Still, he wanted Donnelly's wife to know that she could rely on him if she needed help. Donnelly had volunteered to find the girl and had almost lost his life in the process. Callahan wanted to do whatever he could.

The girl was now in the care—God forbid he should use the word *custody*—of Julie and Amanda. They stayed with her during Remy's examination, and, afterwards, the two of them, especially Julie, dove into ultra-protective mode. Julie literally took his admonition not to let the girl out of sight, minding her like a new mother with a strong-willed toddler at a crowded amusement park. Between Julie and Amanda, the girl did not have a second to herself nor a want for anything. She was obviously a survivor, but Callahan wondered if she could endure such solicitousness. He also felt concerned for the girl's physical and emotional wellbeing, but her condition presented another issue for him: Why had she not sought help and care from anyone for her horrific injuries? Was she was running from something, something even more frightening than suffering and possibly dying from untreated burns? Callahan wanted answers but was at a loss over where to find them.

In the meantime, he sent Nick to search her hideout for clues as to when and how she had arrived on the island. He doubted Nick would find any such evidence, but it was, at least, a beginning.

*   *   *

Nick removed the pine branches covering one side of the makeshift lean-to the girl had constructed and ducked his head in. He turned on his flashlight and scanned the length of shelter. Two sleeping bags, one inside the other, lay on a bed of pine needles. Cans of food, plastic bottles of water, rolls of toilet paper, items of clothing, and various tools (including the infamous nail gun) filled the rest of the interior. Nick suspected the girl pilfered them all from vacant vacation homes. He took several pictures with his phone, and then he removed his backpack, zipped it open and filled it with the cans of food. He figured it would take him at least three trips to carry all the items back to the Charger, which was parked at the trailhead.

Chapter 26

When Callahan returned from visiting Donnelly's family, a battered pickup truck was parked in front of the sign marked *Sheriff* in the station's gravel lot. He parked the Cruiser next to the pickup. Although it was indistinguishable in make, model, color, and condition from a legion of other trucks on the island, Callahan immediately knew the owner. The license plate read *EGGMEON*. Julie and Demarest were having coffee together at the dispatcher's desk when he entered the station. A dozen cartons of eggs sat stacked between them.

"Hi, Matt," said Julie. "Claude here dropped by to see you and brought us these eggs."

"And something else," said Demarest, reaching around the eggs and picking up an object from the desk. He rose from his chair and held it out to Callahan. "Here, take a look at this," he added.

Callahan took the object and began examining it.

"No one has been in that hen house but me, except for that girl we caught. She must have either dropped it or left it there. Heard you've been asking around about her. Thought it might help. You know, it could be some sort of clue as to who she is." Demarest straightened to his full height, raising his chin like a soldier about to be pinned with a commendation medal.

"Yes," said Callahan, picking up on his silent appeal for praise. "Thanks, Claude. Good work. It just might. Do you know what it is?"

"No idea. Thought maybe you would know," said Demarest.

Callahan handed the object to Julie. "Have you ever seen anything like this before?" he asked.

Julie looked at it briefly and then handed it back to Callahan with a quick shake of her head.

"Well, got eggs to deliver. Best be going. Thanks for the coffee, Julie," said Demarest.

Callahan placed the object on Julie's desk and then walked Demarest to the door, thanking him for the eggs.

Julie held the object and inspected it closely as Callahan returned to her desk. "Matt, I didn't want to say anything while Claude was here, but I think I've seen something like this before," she said.

*　*　*

Callahan held the object, twisting his hand to examine both its sides while Nick and Amanda looked on. It was a circle about the size of a jam jar cap and appeared made of bare flexible twigs. The circle was bisected once vertically and again horizontally, creating four segments.

Tightly wound yarn decorated each of the four segments in a different color: white, red, yellow, and black.

"Julie thinks it may be a Native American symbol, but isn't sure of what," said Callahan, handing the object to Amanda.

"That's exactly what it is," said Nick. 'I just Googled it, and it's the exact image of an Ojibwe or Chippewa medicine wheel." Nick then added, "So it's possible our girl is Native American?"

"That's a big leap. There's no way to prove that this belongs to her, and even if it does, that we can conclude she's Native American," said Amanda.

Everyone stood silent for a moment and then Callahan said, "We'll see."

Chapter 27

"What's this all about?" said Callahan.

Nick was on his knees in the detention-cell room bent over a couple of dozen food cans stacked in multiple rows of different levels. He put the can he held on the top of a back row and stood up. "I retrieved these cans from the girl's hideout. When and where the food was canned is embedded in a coded series of numbers and letters printed on the can. To decipher the date and place you need the code, but it's not a secret. The food companies either put it on their websites or give it to you if you email or call them." Nick flashed Callahan a brief triumphant smile and waited for a response.

"And this is leading where?" asked Callahan.

"Oh, yes," said Nick and continued. "Well, using the codes I deciphered the date on each can and then arranged the cans by date with the newest cans in the first row and the oldest cans in the last." Another triumphant smile was met by a still befuddled Callahan.

"Moving on then," said Nick. "I made the assumption that she either stole the cans from the grocery store or from various vacant summer homes on the island. What I've just discovered is that none of these cans is more than four months old. Unless she knew the codes and ate from all the older cans first, that means that she's been on the island less than six months. She wasn't burned here." Nick started to smile then stopped and gave Callahan an apprehensive look.

Callahan gazed down at the pile of cans. "Amazing," he said and patted Nick on the back. "Amazing," he said again, shaking his head as he turned to leave the room. Then he stopped and looked back at Nick. "You did well, very well, reacting to the emergency with Donnelly. Knowing about the Coast Guard air station and rescue team in Traverse City shows you're on top of things here. Donnelly owes you his life. Glad you're on board," he said.

*   *   *

Callahan sat at his desk and stared out the office window through the tangle of bare black branches silhouetted against a backdrop of pale blue. A heavy blanket of clouds that had covered the island was gone, and the temperature had dropped fifteen degrees. The forecast of clear skies for the next four days meant that a service specialist from Michigan's Child Protective Services would arrive on the island by plane in a day or two. That also meant that the specialist would probably take the girl away. Julie was not happy about that possibility and let Callahan know it. She did not want to let the girl go and had even discussed with Callahan the possibility of applying to the Michigan Department of Health and Human Services as a foster family. Where Julie saw care, rehabilitation, and even love, Callahan saw trouble.

There was another matter concerning the girl that troubled Callahan. He had taken the medicine wheel home with him and shown it to her. He hadn't fully removed it from his pocket before the girl snatched it from his hand and clutched it to her chest, bending over and turning her back to Callahan as if protecting it. She hadn't let go of it from that moment on.

Callahan turned away from the window, opened his desk drawer, and rummaged through a jumble of objects until he found a badge from the Sault tribal police. Ralph Tanner, chief of police, had given it to him after he had saved Tanner's life—sort of. If the bomb strapped to Tanner's chest that he had disarmed had been real, he could take credit for doing so.

Since identifying the girl's object, Callahan had learned that the medicine wheel held great significance for the Anishinaabeg, especially the Ojibwe. But the girl's reaction didn't just reveal reverence for and a knowledge of the wheel's significance to a people. To Callahan it seemed to signify much more. Someone she loved had given it to her, and the wheel embodied that love. He suspected it was a relative, perhaps her parents. And if she was Ojibwe, then her tribe would want her back in its care.

Callahan picked up his cellphone, tapped the contacts icon, and scrolled down the list of names until he reached Tanner's number. Then he connected the call.

Chapter 28

"We've found a lone 10-to-12-year-old girl whose been hiding on the island for maybe four months. She's been badly burned and doesn't speak. The burns appear to be intentionally inflicted and not by her. I think she may be Ojibwe but can't be sure. Are you missing any young girls up there, Ralph?"

Tanner grimaced involuntarily. He wasn't being insensitive. It's just that the question seemed so incredibly naive to him. What he wanted to say to Callahan was that in Indian country, children went missing in numbers proportionally much higher than the national average, even considering the underreporting of missing Indian children. A significant number of children were never reported missing, at least not to any state or federal authority. And often, not even to a local authority such as himself. The reasons were many: Parents or relatives didn't want law enforcement rummaging around in their lives, afraid of what might be found; they simply didn't know how to report a missing child; or their lives were too precarious to devote the time and resources to find a child gone missing. Thus, at any given time, he didn't know of all the children who might be missing. Most were found within a few miles of their home; some never were. But he resisted the impulse to tell all this to Callahan. His personal and professional friendship with Callahan wouldn't permit it. He feared such a response would appear snide or sarcastic.

"Matt, I simply don't know what girls may be missing right now. So, you know the drill. Send me some pictures of the girl and any identifiers such as scars, the burns of course, tattoos, height, weight, and so on. I'll have someone ask around. It may take a while. In the meantime, if there's a possibility that she is Ojibwe, I can contact our tribal representative responsible for Indian child welfare. Someone can come down there and investigate to determine whether we or the State of Michigan will have jurisdiction of the girl."

"That would be great, Ralph, but a specialist from the state's Child Protective Services is due here in a couple of days," said Callahan.

"Not a problem. We work with the state all the time to determine if the tribe or the state will take jurisdiction over a child's welfare," said Tanner.

"Just to put you on guard," said Callahan. "It's not likely the girl is going to be much help to either you or the state CPS."

Chapter 29

As Callahan later advised Tanner, he wasn't proved wrong.

Julie had tried her best to prepare the girl for the arrival of the state service specialist and the tribal child welfare representative, explaining in as clear and simple a way as possible where each was from, why they were coming, and how they both wanted to make sure she was well taken care of by a relative or willing family. Yet, the more Julie tried to help the girl understand what would be happening to her, the more agitated the girl became—covering her ears, running from Julie when she approached her, refusing to eat, and eventually barricading herself in her room—until Julie feared she would try and run away again. So did Callahan, and he, Amanda, and Julie had stayed outside her room in shifts until the state service specialist and tribal representative reached the island.

Upon their arrival, things started out well enough. When the state service specialist tried to gently coax her out of her room by speaking through the door, she was met with silence. When the tribal representative used the same method but this time speaking in Anishinaabemowin, all hell broke loose. The girl let out an ear-piercing scream and a violent commotion erupted in the room before they heard glass breaking. Callahan instantly kicked open the door and he and the tribal representative barreled into the room.

The girl stood against the far wall, holding a shard of mirror glass like a long knife, a tee shirt wrapped around it to protect her grip. Her eyes wide in fear, she jabbed the shard toward the tribal representative several times in warning for him to stay away.

That was it for the state service specialist who promptly yielded jurisdiction to the tribal representative who just as promptly contacted the tribal leadership with the recommendation that the girl stay with Callahan and Julie for the duration of his investigation. Callahan and the representative had agreed: the girl was probably Ojibwe. She had understood or at least recognized Anishinaabemowin when spoken to her. And her aggression toward the tribal representative was a signal that she had fled from a life to which she did not want to return.

Now Tanner and the tribe had to figure out who she was and what to do with her. Callahan, on the other hand, had to deal with the girl. But Julie had already decreed what *to deal with* meant.

Chapter 30

The island had no psychologist, psychiatrist, or social worker in residence; but it did have an art therapist. Betsy Neily was Julie's friend and, in this instance, a friend in need. Diminutive, soft-spoken, with a calm demeanor, she was nonetheless like a supple reed: able to withstand the highest winds without breaking. Other islanders besides Julie relied on her strength and healing therapy, and both were needed now. With coaching, Julie had prepared the girl for her first session with Betsy.

"These are all for you," said Betsy Neily. She and the girl sat almost eye to eye across from each other at the dining room table in Julie's home. "You can keep them," she added, pulling an assortment of art materials from a large canvas bag and laying them on the table. When she finished, crayons, colored pencils, markers, gray bogus paper, and oil pastels spread in neat order over the table's surface.

The girl didn't look down at the table but peered through a veil of hair she'd pulled down over her face, keeping her eyes warily on Betsy.

"Well, personally, I like the markers best to start with. They're colorful and fun to draw with," said Betsy. She took one of the larger pieces of art paper and placed it in front of the girl. "Let's start by just scribbling. You can make any kind of marks on the paper you want. You don't have to draw anything. Just scribble away until you want to stop."

The girl lifted her hands from her lap and reached for a piece of paper. Then, with her palm, she rolled a pencil toward her until it teetered at the edge of the table. Before it fell, she grabbed it, raised it above her head, and jabbed the paper; slicing it with the pencil until shreds littered the table. She threw the pencil across the room before returning her hands to her lap.

"That's a start. That's definitely a start," said Betsy unfazed. "We've begun our journey together, haven't we?"

Chapter 31

The island had reached a tipping point. There were now more snowmobiles than cars in the Arranmore Pub's parking lot. And people walked Main Street in snowmobile suits looking like over-bundled school kids from the fifties. Winter's vise grip had choked the breath of summer out of almost everyone. Everyone, except for Stan Lupinski. Stan didn't exactly ignore the season, but he only gave it a passing nod. His attire, even on the coldest days, was a down vest under an open flannel shirt and cargo shorts. Some residents swore they saw him outside shod in flip flops on occasion. He grilled on his back deck all winter, and on sunny days lounged outside on a lawn chair with a can of beer. Stan was an eccentric, but he was also the state's foremost expert on fish species in the Great Lakes, both indigenous and invasive, and a research professor at the University of Michigan.

Callahan stood on Lupinski's porch, knocking on his front door and wondering how to approach him about strange reports from ice fishers on one of the island's inland lakes. Butler Lake, never known for an abundance of fish, had become a veritable bonanza for ice fishing. So much so that a metropolis of ice shanties had sprung up on its surface. Two enterprising locals had even set up stores in their shanties selling spirits, snacks, lunch food, bait, and tackle. But alarms had gone off: at first sporadic, muted, and infrequent; they had now swelled to a continuous blare. The lake water was poisoned. People were outraged and demanded that the villain be found or that the source be located and eradicated.

Lupinski answered the door looking as if he'd just returned from a walk on a Caribbean beach. "Come on in, Sheriff. Have a seat," he said and motioned Callahan into the living room. "You're here about the fish in Butler Lake, I'm guessing. Here, hand me your coat."

"You've heard about the poisoning then," said Callahan removing his coat, hat, and gloves and handing them to Lupinski as he sat in the chair offered him.

Lupinski tossed them onto the couch and then sat down beside the pile. "I've heard about caught fish possibly bleeding from the gills and eyes. And I've heard about a possible die-off, but that hasn't been confirmed," he said.

"So, you don't think the fish have been poisoned," said Callahan.

"I didn't say that because I don't know. I'm a scientist, not a prognosticator. I'd have to perform several tests on the fish and the water first. I will say though that if this is a natural occurrence, then the time and place are very unusual," said Lupinski.

"How do you mean?" asked Callahan.

"You normally don't see fish die in the dead of winter in an isolated inland lake. Die-offs like this one mostly take place in the spring in the Great Lakes," answered Lupinski.

"I need to know if this is a crime or not," said Callahan. "Can you help me?" he added.

"I can and will, but if you suspect an environmental crime, isn't it the bailiwick of the Department of Natural Resources?" answered Lupinski.

"It is, and the department has been notified and is sending a conservation officer to the island to investigate. He or she will be working with me, but I wanted to get the ball rolling before the island is in an uproar over this. Already rumors are spreading that other lakes on the island have been poisoned and that our water sources are contaminated. People are getting scared. They eat the caught fish; they drink the water," said Callahan. "They want to know something is being done now to protect them."

"I'll need permission from the university, but that shouldn't be a problem. As I said, if fish are dying this time of year, then it's odd and should be researched. I'll get right on it," said Lupinski.

Callahan stood up, but Lupinski remained seated and put a hand over Callahan's jacket as he reached for it. "Before you go, I need to ask you a favor," he said.

Callahan straightened up and then sat again in the chair. "Shoot," he said.

"My sister lives in Washtenaw County. Her son, my nephew, will be a fourth-grader next year. For over a year now, he has been enthralled by everything to do with being a sheriff: the cars, boats, uniforms, badges, you name it. My sister can't figure out where this obsession came from. You ever hear of such a thing?" Lupinski gave Callahan a wan smile.

Callahan thought of Amanda. "Actually, I have," he said more to himself than Lupinski.

"Hmm, well my nephew has his heart set on going to the Sheriff's Kid Camp held by Washtenaw County in the summer. Only problem is he, my sister, and her husband are supposed to visit me on the island then. It's the only time all of us can get together due to our busy schedules. So rescheduling is out of the question, but my sister doesn't want to break my nephew's heart." Lupinski shrugged in resignation and then smiled.

The goal of Lupinski's discourse slowly dawned on Callahan. He waited for the punchline, but it didn't come. Lupinski remained silent. Finally, Callahan said, "So you want me to hold a kids' camp here?"

"It's very popular in Washtenaw County. The kids love it, and it's only for two or three days. They learn about law enforcement, 911, first aid, crime scene forensics, or whatever. They're then designated junior deputies," said Lupinski. "Thought it might be a good thing for the kids on the island to do," he added.

"I'll need some time to think about this," said Callahan, beginning to wobble under the scope of the favor.

"No problem, my sister and nephew aren't coming until June 21st, and they're staying for two weeks, so you've got plenty of time to plan," said Lupinski.

Chapter 32

Tribal Police Chief Ralph Tanner smoothed the creases in the lap of his uniform trousers as he stood up from his desk. He turned and examined his reflection in the glass of a citation hung on the wall to his right. He was a big man. There was a lot of him, and he wanted all of himself immaculately presentable. He didn't consider himself vain, but appearances meant something in the face of diminished expectations regarding tribal policing, especially among those well below the bridge. In a few minutes he was due to give a tour to representatives from Lansing. In fact, the tribal police station was one of the most modern and well equipped in the state, and his officers were among the best trained. He made sure of that. Still, prejudices were difficult to overcome, even when proof of false assumptions stood at eye level with the doubting. Tanner knew that public relations was part of his job, but he felt the effort it took drained him of time and energy best directed elsewhere.

Law enforcement applied tribal law within Indian country. As the tribal chief of police, Tanner had to navigate the execution of tribal law within the rambling, shifting, and sometimes faint boundaries of his jurisdiction. It wasn't easy. United States statutes defined Indian country. It included all land within the limits of an Indian reservation, all dependent Indian communities, and all Indian allotments. Judicial interpretation of these statues had also established what were known as informal reservations. Further, Congress could specifically designate land outside these categories for use by Indians and had repeatedly done so.

Also, under the Michigan Indian Land Claims Settlement Act, Michigan tribes could expand the borders of their reservations by purchasing land outside the reservation for the social welfare of their members, which was then held in trust by the US government. Land held under such a trust became tribal land and was designated Indian country.

So broadly speaking, Indian country was any land set aside for the use of Indians by US statute, case law, Congress, or federally sanctioned tribal land purchases. It was this last method that added to Tanner's law-enforcement burden and stretched the use of his personnel to the breaking point. Land had been purchased fifteen miles from the reservation's eastern border for a second casino and gaming facilities.

Tanner had to police the land long distance during construction of the casino, and now that it had opened, he had his hands full with the crowds that came to gamble and drink. He didn't have a single officer to spare to identify a young girl no one had reported missing, who may not be Indian, and, even if she was, probably wasn't from the Indian country he policed. So, he wasn't happy about siphoning his resources to the task. And neither was the young officer standing before him.

"Please, sir. I mean, really? Come on. You know I've been working with the task force on the drug case at the new casino. To do what you're asking will take days, and we're close to discovering how the casino ring is getting the drugs. I can't afford to back away from it now." He held the picture Tanner had given him of the girl between his thumb and index finger as if he were about to drop it into an imaginary trash can.

Tanner had assigned Josh Willis to the Upper Peninsula Safe Trails Task Force to give him experience working with the FBI and state law enforcement agencies as they investigated violent crime, drugs, and gaming violations in Indian country. The task force had discovered and targeted a drug ring running out of the tribe's new gaming facility. Tanner saw in Josh the potential to become one of his best officers, and he wanted that potential realized. "You won't be backing away. The task force can spare you for a couple of days. Put in the effort for that long, and if it comes to nothing, then fine, you're back with the task force," he said.

"And what if I find out who she is? What then, sir?" asked Josh.

"Then we'll talk," said Tanner.

Chapter 33

Officer Josh Willis began his investigation with the schools. None of the 4th through 8th grade teachers or any of the schools' administrative staff recognized the girl. Because she might have been home schooled or visiting relatives on the reservation, he next questioned the directors of the tribe's governing board on the assumption that since they held elective office, they were familiar with most of the tribe's voters. Again, no success. The kids on the tribal youth council didn't recognize her. The Ojibwe language teachers had never seen her in class. The receptionists at the medical and dental clinics of the Medicine Lodge had no recollection of such a girl. Even the clerks in the stores where the kids hung out shrugged their shoulders and shook their heads. If she was Ojibwe, she and her family were strangers to the tribe. As he feared, his time had been wasted. Three days of fruitless effort were enough—more than enough. But he decided to try one more avenue before he reported back to Tanner.

Case Blackwell lived in a small, aluminum-sided ranch house with an attached one car garage. The home had been built in the sixties and showed its age but, except for the yard, had been kept up and was livable. Blackwell eked out a subsistence existence on the proceeds from a sham disability claim and sporadic employment in a smattering of odd jobs. A string of petty crimes had interrupted rather than supplemented this flow of income, jail time being the primary reason. His life's circumstances had made him contrary and, at times, unpleasant. He refused to have a land line or own a cell phone, proudly declaring that if he wanted to talk to someone, he'd do it in person. He spent most of his days lounging around popular hangouts. This proclivity allowed him to know everything that happened in Indian country. As Josh pulled into the driveway, he could hear dogs barking inside the house. Blackwell opened the door wide on the third knock but left the glass storm door shut.

"What you want?" Blackwell demanded.

Josh put the picture of the girl against the glass in front of Blackwell's face. "Have you seen this girl?"

"Why you asking?"

"She's missing. We're trying to find out who she is," answered Josh.

"Where she missing from?"

"Have you seen her?" Josh wasn't going to answer any more questions until he got a straight answer from Blackwell.

"Never. Now you done?"

Before Josh could respond, Blackwell shut the door.

*   *   *

It had vanished in an instant, but Josh had seen it—a flicker of recognition in Blackwell's eyes. He drove the squad car out of the driveway and down the street until he was certain it was hidden and walked across a field to where he could observe the house and not be seen. He waited until the garage door opened and a rusted Chevrolet Corsica with a cracked and dirt-smeared rear window backed out onto the street.

Josh followed the car at a distance as it trailed a cloud of smoke until it turned onto the long tree-lined entryway leading to a single home.

Chapter 34

"There's good news and there's bad news." Lupinski made this pronouncement while he and Callahan stood on a snow-covered boat ramp and overlooked the sheet of ice that was Butler Lake. Two weeks ago, its surface had been jammed with ice shacks. Now only the cross hatchings of tire tracks from the SUVs used to pull the shacks off the lake covered the ice.

"In this business there's always bad news trailing the good. So, lessen the blow. Give me the good news first," said Callahan.

"Viral hemorrhagic septicemia or VHS doesn't affect humans. The virus dies at human body temperatures," said Lupinski.

"What is VHS and why is this good news?" asked Callahan.

"I need to give you the bad news to answer those questions," said Lupinski.

"Okay, let me have it then," said Callahan.

"VHS is a viral disease that freshwater fish can contract. The virus causes hemorrhaging or bleeding in the skin, eyes, and fins. It can be lethal to the fish. The fish in this lake have the disease and shouldn't. It's too cold, and this lake is too isolated from the waters on the mainland where the disease has been found. In other words, it's out of season and way out of town," explained Lupinski.

"Then what's it doing here?" asked Callahan.

"The results of my lab tests were surprising. The fish from this lake appear to have a new strain of the disease, one that can survive in these low temperatures. Right now, though, I only have a guess as to how the virus got here," said Lupinski.

"And what's that?" asked Callahan.

"This disease can spread in different ways, most of which we can determine. This is an isolated inland lake, so the fish didn't swim here from infected waters on the mainland. Also, it's very unlikely that infected water was somehow dumped into the lake. This is a public lake so the Department of Natural Resources stocks it every year. The fish it used this year were from valid hatcheries and tested by the DNR to be disease free. I checked the records. Therefore, it's unlikely that the DNR is at fault. No one else filed for permission with the DNR to legally stock the lake. I checked for that too. So, my best guess is that someone secretly and illegally restocked this lake with fish they didn't know were infected," said Lupinski. He then added, "Think about it. Fishing in this lake has been good every year but not great. However, this year it's off the charts."

"Who would do that?" Callahan wondered aloud.

Lupinski thought for a moment and then said, "Ask yourself who would gain the most by such a stunt."

*   *   *

Callahan needed peace to think so stayed at the lake for a while after Lupinski left. He watched a skein of geese drop from the sky and land on its surface, high stepping over the ice before they began milling around for no reason he could fathom. Puzzles seemed to be the item of the day.

Although it was a possibility, Callahan found it hard to imagine the lake being maliciously stocked with infected fish. So, it had to be unintentional and for a purpose that benefited someone. But who? Offhand, he couldn't think of anyone. Access to the lake was free, and fishing there was not for commercial purposes but for sport. Money didn't seem to be the object. Still, someone had illegally restocked the lake, and it fell to him to find out who and where they got the fish. But first he had to get the word out that the lake had not been poisoned and that anyone who fished there was safe from sickness or disease.

Chapter 35

"What would the likes of Blackwell be doing consorting with the richest Indian around?" said Tanner. "He's not someone Sam Goodfellow would invite to lunch."

"That's what I'm wondering," said Josh. "I'd like a little more time to look into this. Please, sir," he added.

"I thought you were dead set against taking leave from the task force," said Tanner.

"I was. I mean I am. It's just a hunch, a feeling mostly, but I think Goodfellow may know something about this mystery girl. Why else would Blackwell hightail it over to Goodfellow's house right after I showed him her picture?" said Josh.

"Could be lots of reasons," said Tanner.

"You just said it's not likely they're bosom buddies, sir."

"How much time do you want?" asked Tanner.

"Just a few more days. That's all," said Josh.

"Okay, you got 'em," said Tanner. "But no more than a few days."

*   *   *

From the police station, Josh decided to drive straight to Goodfellow's home. It was still morning, and if he didn't catch him there, he hoped someone at the house could tell him where to find him. As he turned off the road and onto the paved tree-lined drive to the house, his perspective on the home's size changed. Its enormity was not obvious from the road, but from a full-on view, the term *mansion* didn't do it justice. Apparently, being the general contractor for a new casino and gaming facilities was a lucrative endeavor.

Josh parked the squad car in the circular driveway, walked to the door, and rang the doorbell. It didn't ring but sounded the beat of ceremonial drumming. Whether meant to be humorous or not, Josh found it rather outlandish. He did not have the same impression of the person who answered the door. She was tall, as tall as he, and she did not peer around a half open door as did most of those he called on in uniform. Instead, she stood erect, braced in the middle of the wide entrance, staring him straight in the eye. She was young, smartly dressed, and touched the edge of beauty. He recognized her immediately.

"Hello, Josh. Haven't seen you since high school. Come in, please." She stepped aside and gracefully motioned him into the house, displaying the poise of a model.

"Hi, Delia. It has been a while," said Josh and walked past her into the living room before turning to face her. She still stood at the door with her back to it. Josh felt the distance between them.

"I could tell by your surprise that you didn't come here to see me. Am I right?" She gave Josh a bright smile.

"I didn't know you were back home. Last I heard you were in New York, or was it LA?" said Josh.

"LA. Working on an acting career." Her smile abruptly disappeared, and Josh decided not to inquire about any acting roles.

"Actually, I'm here to—"

"See me," said Goodfellow, interrupting Josh.

Josh turned to face Goodfellow who had entered the room so silently that he startled Josh when he spoke. "Yes sir, I'm here about a missing girl."

"A missing girl, you say. I don't know how I can help you, but come in and have a seat," said Goodfellow. "Can Delia get you anything? Something to drink? Coffee?"

Josh shook his head. "No thanks."

Goodfellow wore tight jeans and a black tee-shirt that flaunted a taught, muscular physique. His long black hair was pulled straight back from his forehead and tied into a ponytail. From a greater distance, he would have appeared to be in his late twenties or early thirties; but up close, his weathered face and rough skin gave his age away at closer to mid-fifties. Goodfellow motioned Josh to sit on the long couch. It was upholstered in thick brightly colored horse blankets, and Josh couldn't help but stroke them as he sat down at one end to make room for Delia at the other end. But she had disappeared. Goodfellow chose one of the three worn leather-cushioned chairs in the room. It squeaked comfortably under his weight as he settled into it. A huge deer-antler chandelier hovered above them, capping what Josh secretly derided as faux Indian décor. He chastised himself for wondering if Goodfellow had used the same interior decorator for both the new casino and his home.

"So, what's this about a missing girl?" asked Goodfellow.

Josh took the picture of the girl out of his pocket, slid to the edge of the couch cushion, and stretched out an arm to Goodfellow. Goodfellow reached for the photo, glanced at it, and then dropped it on the rough-stone coffee table between them.

"Never seen her. Who is she?"

"We don't know. We're trying to find out if anyone knows her and where she's from," answered Josh.

"Who's interested in finding her?" said Goodfellow.

"Don't know that either. I wasn't told," said Josh.

"Don't you find that odd?" said Goodfellow.

"Not really. Chief Tanner apparently felt I didn't need to know. If and when he does, I'm sure he'll tell me," said Josh, trying to keep his tone polite and professional to cover his pique at Goodfellow's suggestion of incompetence.

"Do you know when she was last seen and by whom? If you have the answers, maybe I could help you. I know a lot of people on and around the reservation."

"That's why I came here," said Josh. "But I can't answer those questions either."

"So, you don't know why someone wants to find her?"

"No," answered Josh.

"Well, I'm sorry I can't help you then," said Goodfellow and stood up as a signal the interview was over. "Good luck in your search. I hope you find her."

As Josh opened the door to leave, Delia appeared, and placed her hand over his on the handle. "One moment, Josh. I wanted to say goodbye. It was good to see you. I hope it won't be as long until the next time." She released her hand from his and then leaned close to his cheek. "I'll be here for a while," she whispered.

Delia shut the door and walked into the living room where Goodfellow was still standing. "That kid is no fool, and he's a good cop. I want you to get to know him better. Find out what he's up to with the girl," he said.

"That's not in the job description," said Delia.

"It is now," said Goodfellow.

*   *   *

Josh sat in the squad car outside the station and looked again at the picture of the girl. His interview of Goodfellow had revealed far more than he expected. The interview had been turned on its head. Goodfellow had become the interviewer not the interviewee. He had asked most of the questions, and they had been too pointed to indicate a simple curiosity. His last question had been especially telling. It telegraphed that he knew the girl and wanted to discover who was searching for her. But why hadn't he said so? Josh decided that the investigation needed to shift from just discovering the identity of the girl to finding out what Goodfellow knew about her and what his connection to her might be. And why he didn't want it known.

As Josh got out of the car to head into the station and report to Tanner on what he suspected, he had another thought: What was Delia doing back on the reservation and living in Goodfellow's home?

Chapter 36

The prolonged presence of the girl in Callahan's home caused escalating tension, but not in the way they had anticipated. She had settled in and now seemed almost a fixture: silent, unobtrusive, low maintenance, and always in plain sight. The problem was Max. He was jealous. And not of Julie's attention to the girl but of their dog's attention to her. The dog was his friend not hers. Max had begun to sulk, and like the girl, he wasn't talking. Julie's entreaties to him to tell her what was wrong went unanswered except for Max turning and stomping away. The dog, for its part, got the same treatment when it tried to engage with Max, which was less often than before the girl's intrusion. Max was becoming inconsolable, and Julie worried. Then things got worse.

"She's gone. She's gone. She's gone." Julie rushed down the hall from the girl's bedroom, brandishing her cell phone in front of her, willing Callahan to answer her call. When he did, she yelled again, "She's gone."

"Are you sure?" asked Callahan.

"I've checked everywhere. I searched outside, calling for her. I've spent the last hour driving all around looking for her. I've just gotten back to the house, and she isn't here. She hasn't returned," said Julie.

"Okay. I'm coming home. I'll be there in twenty minutes," said Callahan.

*   *   *

The girl was more careful this time and better prepared. She waited, hidden in the woods, until she was sure the chickens were asleep. Then she sneaked into the hen house, pulled out the pillowcase she'd tucked inside her jacket, and gently put it over the head of the closest hen. Clutched in her arms, the hen barely made a sound as she scuttled back into the woods.

*   *   *

After Julie's call, Callahan and Nick had spent the rest of the day cruising the island and searching for the girl, asking anyone and everyone if they'd seen her. No one had. Early the next morning, after a sleepless night with a frantic Julie, Callahan was at the station organizing a search party. He'd just managed to shanghai a fifth member of the party, when Julie called. Her tone was not anxious now but vexed.

"She's back in the house, Matt. She has a chicken. She's given it to Max. He won't let go of it. I've had to put the dog outside. You need to come home."

Chapter 37

"No," said Max and turned his back on Callahan, hunching over the hen in his arms.

Callahan paused and thought out his response before addressing Max. He had to remind himself that Max was a young adult with Down syndrome, a condition which those who knew Max only noticed with surprise. "Max," we must give it back. I'm sure it belongs to Mr. Demarest. It's not ours to keep," said Callahan.

"It's not yours. It's mine. She gave it to me." Max shifted the hen to one arm and thrust out the other, pointing to the girl who nodded.

Callahan turned to Julie and gave her an I-did-the-best-I-could shrug.

"Really? You're going to let him keep it. You're kidding, right? We know nothing about the care and feeding of chickens. And where would we keep it?"

"Well, for now we could keep it in the laundry room in a cage up on a shelf. The dog couldn't get to it there. If Demarest agrees to sell it to us, I'm sure he would show Max and the girl how to care for it," said Callahan.

"Yeah," said Max. The hen was resting its head in the crook of Max's elbow as Max stroked its neck.

The girl nodded again.

Callahan leaned close to Julie and whispered in her ear, "Look how happy he is now."

"I don't believe this," said Julie, shaking her head. "And do you have any idea how much the purchase of a laying hen in her prime would set us back, especially one owned by Demarest?" she added.

"No, but we're going to find out," said Callahan.

Julie threw up her hands. "Fine, but if it stays, it's not my responsibility. I want nothing to do with it."

"Deal," said Max.

* * *

Callahan dropped Julie off at the station, and he, Max, the girl, and the chicken headed to Demarest's. The three of them found Demarest at the hen house.

"That's Sadie," said Demarest. Max was standing behind the girl holding the chicken, and Demarest peered around the girl to eye Max. "Where'd you find her?"

"We didn't exactly find her," said Callahan. Demarest looked suspiciously at the girl. "And we didn't bring her here to return her, unless you insist."

"What do you mean?" asked Demarest.

"We'd like to buy her from you," answered Callahan.

"What? No way. She's my prize hen," said Demarest.

"I suspected that," said Callahan.

"I was beside myself when she went missing yesterday."

"I'm sure you were."

"I'm glad you found her, but she isn't for sale." Demarest declared his position on the matter with finality, but he didn't turn away from Callahan as if the conversation were over.

Callahan decided to seize the moment. "I'm willing to give you a good price for her. Above market if necessary," he said. "Cash. Right now." Callahan took his wallet out of his back pocket.

"Hmm. How much?" asked Demarest.

"What do you think is fair?" said Callahan.

Demarest hesitated and then said, "You'd have to take into account the anxiety I experienced over her disappearance."

"Of course," said Callahan.

"Well then, I could part with her for $150. Reluctantly, and there'd be conditions."

"What are they?" asked Callahan.

"First, you can't tell anyone I sold her to you. You bought her from someone else on the mainland. Understand? My chickens aren't for sale, and I don't want it getting around that they are."

"Understood," said Callahan.

"Second, you can't sell or give away her eggs. I don't want any competition no matter how small. You got that?" said Demarest.

"Absolutely," said Callahan. But for $150, we have a condition too."

"What is it?" asked Demarest.

"You have to show us how to care for her."

Demarest glanced at the girl and then looked back at Callahan. "There won't be any more missing chickens? This is the last one?" he said.

"The last one," said Callahan.

Demarest smiled and then held out his hand to shake on the deal. Callahan shook it, and Demarest said, "Follow me into the hen house. I'll give you some seed and show you the basics to get you all started."

Chapter 38

The Nicolet Fisheries and Marketplace occupied a quarter acre sand lot across the two-lane road from the pier where the Manning brothers moored its one fishing boat. The marketplace was a one-story, two-room cinderblock structure with a two-story brightly painted façade, the top half of which announced the name of the enterprise in large blue letters that circled an even larger depiction of a lake trout. In the lower right hand corner, sketched in script designed to look like waves, was *Michael and Benjamin Manning, Owners.* The brothers piled the back room high with fishing nets and gear and sold fish out of a freezer in the front room on the honor system since they were on the lake most of the time fishing. They smoked white fish and lake trout in a smoker in the back.

The brothers were the third generation of island Ojibwe to commercially treaty fish Lake Michigan. They made most of their money not from the freezer but from selling fresh and smoked fish to restaurants and grocery stores in Charlevoix, Petoskey, and Traverse City. The brothers fished in all seasons, including the winter when their battered, steel-hulled, turtle-back tug could break though the ice in the bay. Their income was enough to keep them afloat, so to speak.

Nick arrived at the marketplace early, not to buy the market's popular smoked fish before it sold out, but to catch the brothers before they left to fish. He found them on the pier about ready to cast off. They weren't happy to be waylaid, and neither were the gulls that screamed and flapped in a chaotic cloud over the boat.

"We've not got time for this unless you want to come out on the lake with us. We could use another hand." It was the older brother, Michael, who spoke to Nick. The younger brother, Benjamin, continued to ready the boat.

"No thanks. This won't take long. You heard about the Ojibwe girl hiding on the island?"

"Sure. Everyone here has," said Michael.

"We're trying to find out who she is and how she got here," said Nick.

Benjamin stopped working on the pier and stepped into the boat through the open side hatch.

"And you think we can help you?" said Michael.

"I thought you might be able to," said Nick.

Michael bent down to unleash a bow line and then stood, holding it until the engine shuddered and exploded to life. He jumped onto the deck as the boat backed away from the pier and shouted to Nick over the engine chug and the screech of the gulls. "That's rich. You really believe because we're Indian we know every Indian around here and everything about them?"

As Nick watched the boat head out of the bay, he mentally kicked himself in disgust. The brothers had expertly double teamed him in dodging his question and then made him feel guilty about asking it. Brilliant.

*   *   *

Nick returned to the fish market that afternoon to confront the Manning brothers. This time with Amanda but not about the girl. The Mannings had dumped the fish heads and entrails from their business at the tip of a spit on a dirt road north of the market. However, the spit was no more. High lake levels had swallowed it, and now the brothers were dumping fish guts nearer the road. Too near for the owners of the four houses the road serviced. They complained that the smell was overpowering, and that the huge pile of viscera attracted vermin of all sorts. The homeowners' protests to the brothers fell on deaf ears, and now they demanded that the sheriff do something. Callahan sent Amanda and Nick out to have a look and assess the validity of the owners' complaints. The grievances' legitimacy became apparent long before they arrived at the dump site. The robust stench traveled even in the frigid air. Nick had driven only a short way down the dirt road when they both began to gag.

"Okay, that's enough. Let's turn around," said Amanda.

"You bet," said Nick.

On the way back to the station, Nick brought up his morning contact with the Manning brothers and the suspicion it created.

"So, you think the brothers brought the girl to the island on their fishing boat?" Amanda laced her question to Nick with a dose of skepticism.

"Well, maybe. It's only a hunch but think about it. How else would she get on the island virtually unnoticed? It's unlikely she stowed away on the ferry. The crew is careful about who gets on and off the boat. And she certainly didn't fly to the island. She's a minor, alone, and without money," said Nick.

"True. But she could have been smuggled in one of the cars the ferry takes to the island or hidden in one," countered Amanda.

Nick thought about that for a moment. "Yes, but how would she get to the ferry dock in Charlevoix from anywhere on the mainland, especially from a reservation in the Upper Peninsula? She's only ten. She couldn't hitchhike safely, and it's too far to walk, but the Manning brothers' fishing boat goes up there."

"But that still doesn't eliminate the possibility that someone drove her to Charlevoix and then hid her in the car while it was loaded onto the ferry," said Amanda.

To answer her, Nick fell back on the incident underlying his hypothesis. "They obviously didn't want to answer my questions. I think they know the girl or know something about her, and for some reason, they're not willing to give that information up," he said.

"The brothers are fishermen and keep to themselves. That's their nature. They'd be close-mouthed with anybody." Amanda wasn't buying Nick's hunch.

Chapter 39

Delia hung her down jacket on the restaurant coat hook and stuffed her gloves into its pockets. Then she slid into the booth beside Josh, moving close enough so that their hips touched.

"Glad you could take a break for lunch. You must be busy at your job with the police," she said.

"Busy enough. But I didn't want to miss the chance to see you and get caught up. I was surprised when it was you who answered the door at Mr. Goodfellow's," said Josh, trying to be amicably curious rather than prying, which he was.

Delia didn't miss his real intention. "Yes, I imagine you were. I should explain."

"No. That's not what I meant. I— "

Delia stopped him with the raise of her hand. "It's fine," she said. "I want you to know. It's not what it looks like."

"I didn't assume anything," said Josh, not fooling himself or her.

Delia gave him a sideways glance that said *Sure you didn't.* "I went out to LA after two years of community college. Did the usual: Took acting lessons, waitressed, spent endless hours, days, and eventually years auditioning for acting gigs. Landed a spot in a few commercials. But I realized the break I'd hoped for wasn't going to come when my agent stopped returning my calls. That's when Sam offered me a job at the casino. So, I took it. I'm now in training for the assistant manager's position at the casino's hotel. I start tomorrow."

"Oh," said Josh not sure whether to commiserate or congratulate. Delia made the decision for him.

"I don't regret giving Hollywood a try. I learned a lot, made friends, and had some fun. But, in truth, I'm glad to be back. LA culture, even its weather, the heat and the fires, wasn't for me. I realized that I was enduring not flourishing." Delia smiled and shrugged. "I needed a change."

"Well, I'm glad you're back. Shall we order now?" said Josh.

"You bet. I'm famished," replied Delia.

Josh waved to the waitress.

Delia playfully elbowed Josh in his ribs. "In case you're wondering, Goodfellow is an old family friend. He offered me a place to stay until I'm settled," she said.

Josh was wondering and didn't want to admit it, but his awkward silence gave him away.

"Now tell me about yourself," she said.

*   *   *

Josh felt reluctant to talk about himself, but with Delia's gentle prodding he'd loosened up and opened up. The heavy parts of his life, the ones he didn't talk about, lost their weight under her sincere curiosity, lifting easily: his enlistment in the army and tours of duty in Afghanistan with the military police, his wasted years after his discharge and the death of his parents, his struggle with PTSD, and the lifeline Chief Tanner threw him that saved him. He'd never talked this way with anyone, and in retrospect, he was starting to regret it. Was his easy trust in her justified, or was he a victim of all those acting lessons? He barely knew her, but he had exposed himself in a way that at first felt natural, even compelling, but now made him feel vulnerable. However, there was another aspect to their meeting that troubled him. When Delia had told him of her new job as the assistant manager of the casino's new hotel, he had considered the possibility of recruiting her as an inside source for the joint task force's investigation into the casino's drug ring. He had to admit that he was attracted to her and wanted to see her again. But was his motive to groom her as a source or to develop a personal relationship? It couldn't be both.

Chapter 40

Delia busied herself with learning the intricacies of hotel management: handling customer and employee relations; hiring, scheduling, and supervising employees; managing purchasing and inventory; attending to the upkeep of the facility; and superintending hotel events. Her days were full, but in the rare downtime afforded her, Josh managed to cross her mind.

She hadn't suspected things would click for them, but they had. Almost from the first moment with him, she felt comfortable and at ease. Halfway through lunch, she knew he was someone with whom she could be herself. LA had been different. There, she was always pretending, even when not auditioning or performing in commercials—always trying to impress with a false persona, a fixed smile and boosted breasts as part of her uniform at the upscale bistro where she waitressed. She had come to hate herself. But Josh had, for an instant, made her like herself again. She wanted more of that feeling.

Delia chided herself that she mustn't rush things and hazard spoiling any chance she had with Josh. But Goodfellow still wanted an answer from her about the tribal police's interest in the girl, and he wanted it now. He made it clear without saying so that her job depended on her efforts to find that answer. She and Josh had been so involved with getting to know each other that she had completely forgotten to press him on the Indian girl. She was sick of pretending but could she stomach one more charade? Just one more, she told herself.

Chapter 41

The girl's evolution from ward to family member tran-
spired so naturally and with such grace that Callahan almost didn't grasp what had occurred and what it meant
for Julie. Julie had taken over the task of shepherding
the girl to make sure she didn't run away again. That
meant that the girl was rarely out of her sight. She took
her everywhere, including to the station. While Julie attended to her jobs as dispatcher and station manager,
the girl watched: at first mute, wary, and sullen. But
through Julie's gentle invitations and a growing trust on
both their parts, the girl began to help with minor tasks
at the station and then with responsibilities at home.

The girl's participation in Julie's life gave her a sense
of belonging and caused Julie to see her as far more than
a charge. Closeness and shared daily experiences formed
a bond between them that, despite the girl's inability or
unwillingness to speak, allowed them to communicate
beyond words. Max treated the girl as a sibling, and the
dog welcomed her as a member of the pack. In everybody's mind, there were no longer the four of them. Now

there were five. But the girl would eventually have to leave them, and Callahan realized that Julie had blinded herself to that eventuality.

Callahan sat in his office pondering this development when Lupinski called him.

"I've checked the other lakes on the island. They're clean. The virus is only in Butler Lake," he said.

"Can it be contained there?" asked Callahan.

"It can if we get the word out that there's to be no more fishing on Butler Lake and you enforce that edict. In effect, we need to quarantine the lake. Also, no fish caught there can bc used as bait fish on any other lake on the island. That's imperative."

"I'll get right on it," said Callahan.

"Matt, one more thing," said Lupinski.

"What is it?"

"Since the virus is only in Butler Lake, it's looking more and more like it was illegally stocked with contaminated fish. I'd bet that someone who lives on or near that lake might have had a hand in it. Who else would have an interest in upping the catch on that particular lake and no other?" said Lupinski.

"I'll check into that too. Thanks, Stan," said Callahan, ending the call.

He got up from his desk and walked to his office doorway. Julie and the girl were huddled together over some papers on Julie's desk. He stood in the doorway watching them as Julie chatted over the papers and the girl leaned next to her listening, both comfortable in each other's company. The girl noticed Callahan first and tapped Julie on the shoulder. When Julie looked up and saw Callahan, she asked," Do you need something, Matt?"

"Yes. Yes, I do," he said. "Can you find out for me who owns the vacation and year-round homes surrounding Butler Lake?"

Chapter 42

As Amanda walked along Main Street toward the Donegal Motel, she marveled how the cover of snow on the frozen bay shone blue under the morning sun and how it would blister to a blinding white before noon. The promise of an open sky and a windless day should have heralded a record turnout for the island's annual Winterfest and ice fishing tournament. But the crowds were absent, and the normally jubilant atmosphere was missing. Amanda could feel the disappointment that pervaded the town.

The tournament's Butler Lake venue and the lake's sudden record catches of pike, the prize fish, guaranteed a huge draw. But the venue had moved to Foley Lake, a smaller body of water with a dwindling fish population. As a result, the anticipated turnout of island contestants had also dwindled. And it wasn't just the islanders who enjoyed the fest and tournament. These events usually drew a crush of people from the mainland, all of whom needed places to stay. But news of the Viral Hemorrhagic Septicemia virus on the island had scared away visiting contestants and festival participants. Tourists cancelled reservations for rooms at the island's three motels and for local Airbnbs. A low turnout meant less essential income for the island merchants. The rumor that someone stocked Butler Lake with contaminated fish had mushroomed, and demands for retribution peaked. Callahan asked Amanda to question the owners of homes on Butler Lake, one of whom also owned the Donegal Motel.

As she reached the motel, Amanda saw the owner about to mount his snowmobile and rushed towards him. When he spotted her approaching, he put on his helmet, straddled the machine, and started it. Amanda stepped in front of him and held out her arms to block him from leaving. "Whoa. Hold on, Mr. Friel," she shouted over the engine's throaty idle. Friel stopped the engine and removed his helmet. White hair fell around his ears and over his forehead. He brushed the hair from his face but didn't look at Amanda.

"We've been looking for you. You're a hard person to find," said Amanda.

"I've not been hiding. I want you to know I'm not re-sisting you. I knew you'd get to me eventually."

"This might not be the best time, but—"

"There's never a good time for something like this, es-pecially now," said Friel, interrupting Amanda.

"No, no, of course not, but it's important I ask you a few questions," said Amanda.

"Yes, I know it is. They're required." Friel shrugged his shoulders in a sign of acceptance.

"Yes, it's my duty. We're inquiring about the contaminated fish in Butler Lake," said Amanda.

Friel glance up at Amanda. "Shouldn't those questions come later?" he asked.

"I was hoping I could ask them now," said Amanda.

"I thought you would take me to the station first," said Friel.

Amanda relented. "Sure, perhaps it's best if we continue this at the station later. How about after the tournament? I know you're busy with the festivities."

"That's very kind of you," said Friel and started the snowmobile. "I assure you, I'm not going anywhere. I wouldn't do that. I'll be right here after the fest." As he put his helmet on, he turned toward Amanda and said something she couldn't hear over the noise of the engine. Then he twisted the throttle and motored out of the motel's parking lot.

Amanda headed back down Main Street toward the school where Callahan wanted her to inquire about using its facilities for a sheriff's summer youth camp. As she walked, she replayed her interaction with Friel. It troubled her, but she couldn't peg the reason. They'd seemed to be participating in two different conversations that somehow didn't quite sync. It was as if each had grabbed a different meaning from a parallel dialogue. But what did Friel think she meant? Hadn't she made it clear? She almost reached the school when it came to her. "Oh my

God. He thought I was there to arrest him," she blurted out to herself.

Chapter 43

Callahan stood behind his desk as Daniel Friel lowered himself into the chair facing him. Friel adjusted his posture to that of a new cadet at mess in a military academy: back erect, feet flat on the floor, hands on knees, and head up; his chin held high. His long, thin, white hair draped his scalp like dew-heavy spider webs. He was sweating even though he had removed his jacket. Amanda sat next to him and turned her chair towards his.

Callahan sat down. "You sure you don't want a lawyer, Mr. Friel? It would probably be a good idea," he said.

"No, no. I've thought long and hard about this. I should have done this sooner. I'm sorry I didn't. As I told Amanda, I want to confess. I'm waiving my rights, and I don't want a lawyer. I'm not causing any more trouble for anyone." Friel raised his head even higher. "It was me who stocked Butler Lake with those fish. I didn't know they were contaminated, but that doesn't matter. I can't make it up to everyone who lost money because of me, and I'm not going to ask everyone for forgiveness. I'm going to take the punishment I deserve. It's the right thing to do."

"I appreciate your sentiments and resolve, Mr. Friel, but before we go there, I'm curious. Why did you stock the lake when it had already been stocked by the state?" asked Callahan.

"I've actually been doing it for the last couple of years. I'm ashamed now, but I acted out of greed, pure greed. I'd seen what happens when lakes get a reputation for great fishing, especially ice fishing. Opportunities arise to pull in a good profit. It was me who set up those bait and tackle stores on the lake. Also, I thought if Butler Lake was chosen for the ice fishing tournament, my profits would go through the roof. I could rent out my motel rooms and the bedrooms in the two homes I own on the lake to contestants from the mainland. That money would see me through until tourist season. I also thought everyone could profit, not just me." Friel lowered his head and hair slid onto his face. He let it hang there. "But everything turned out wrong and people got hurt. I couldn't live with myself anymore unless I came forward and confessed."

"Are you aware of the penalty for illegally stocking a lake?" asked Amanda.

Friel turned towards her. "Yes, I looked it up, and I can quote the DNR regulations: 'The penalty for stocking fish into public waters of the state without a permit is a misdemeanor, punishable by imprisonment for not more than 90 days, or a fine of not more than $500.00, or both.' I'm willing to take full responsibility and serve my time," he added.

"Well, Mr. Friel, you might want to take full responsibility, but you may not be the only culpable party in this mess," said Callahan.

"What do you mean? I was the only one who stocked the lake other than the DNR," said Friel.

"Where did you get the fingerlings?" asked Callahan.

Friel looked stunned. Then he said, "I don't want to get anyone else in trouble. That's not what I want at all."

"It's vitally important we know the source of the contaminated fish. The contagion mustn't be allowed to spread," said Amanda.

"Who did you buy the fish from?" said Callahan.

Friel's fingers began to flutter over his knees as he nervously tapped them. He sighed once, then again, before shaking his head. "No, I can't," he said.

"Accepting punishment is only going halfway," said Amanda. "If you really want to do the right thing, then you have to go all the way. Tell us who gave you the fish. You owe this island that."

Friel's body seemed to deflate as he sunk down into the chair. "The Manning brothers. I bought the fish from them," he said.

*　　*　　*

Callahan watched out the window of his office as Friel drove away from the station. Then he stood and stretched. "True or false? Which is it?" he asked.

"I don't know what you mean," said Amanda, confused.

"A true confession or a false confession?" answered Callahan.

"What? Are you serious? It never crossed my mind that he came here to falsely confess. Why on earth would he do that?" said Amanda.

"A surprising number of people make false confessions for any number of reasons. They might have been coerced or threatened; they could be covering for someone else; they may be consumed by guilt for something else they did and were never punished for; they might even think they did commit the crime; or they have a mental disorder that compels them to confess to crimes they didn't commit. It's unlikely Friel fits into any of these categories, but there's something fishy about this—pun intended," said Callahan. Amanda groaned.

"So, let's don't rush into charging Friel yet until we've investigated a bit more. I'd like to start with the Manning brothers," said Callahan.

Chapter 44

Tanner trusted conclusions underpinned by facts: objective, immutable, quantifiable, observable, acknowledged. True, an amalgam of facts could lead to differing interpretations; but, if he applied sound reasoning and used proper methods of deduction, the results were rarely preposterous. Not so with hunches. In his long career in law enforcement, too many hunches had proven wrong. Hunches had wasted time, gobbled up resources, and tarnished reputations. He no longer put any stock in them. Yet, that's what Josh was asking him to do. On the flimsiest basis—facial expressions on the one hand and misplaced curiosity on the other—Josh suspected that others were interested in the girl, and for reasons that did not include her best interests. Why else would they not disclose her identity when they knew who she was? At least, that was Josh's hunch.

The kid had good instincts. Tanner had to hand him that. And, along with Callahan, Josh had helped save his life not that long ago. He owed them both. The task-force could spare the kid for a while longer, and Callahan needed his help in finding out who the girl was. He decided to go with his gut and not his head on this one and grant Josh's request to broaden the investigation. He hoped he wouldn't regret it.

*　　*　　*

Josh decided to turn things around. Instead of showing the girl's picture to people on and off the reservation, he would show the girl pictures of the two people he suspected recognized her. Maybe she knew one or both of them. He thought it was worth a try.

The drive from Sault Ste. Marie to Charlevoix should have taken just over two hours but unpredicted snowfall slowed him down. By the time he reached the Charlevoix airport, he'd spent almost four hours on the road. But he wasn't complaining. The weather had cleared, and Island Air still had a flight scheduled to the island.

Nick met him at the airport when he landed.

*　　*　　*

"You'll be staying at my place," said Nick as he and Josh walked from the small terminal to the parking lot. "I rent accommodations in a large vacation home right on the edge of the bay. It's a comfortable and even spacious attic efficiency. The view's fantastic, but the real bonus is that I have the run of the house for all but a few weeks in the summer when the family who owns it is there for vacation. As part of the rent, I look after the place the rest of the time. You'll have your pick of the five other bedrooms. Here's my car."

"Sounds great," said Josh. He tossed his backpack into the back seat. As he buckled his seatbelt, he asked, "When can I see the girl?"

Nick started the car but didn't back out of the parking space. He twisted toward Josh. "She's at Callahan and Julie's house. They're taking care of her until Tribal Child Welfare and police can locate her relatives or find a foster home for her. Everyone's pretty sure she's Ojibwe. She apparently understood Anishinaabemowin when the tribal child welfare representative spoke it to her. But she did not want to go to the reservation. She was terrified of being taken away. That's why she's still here. Have you been told that she's been traumatized and doesn't speak?"

"Yes, Chief Tanner filled me in on a bit of her background. Do you know what happened to her?" asked Josh.

"No, except that she has burn scars all over her body. We don't know how she got them, but it looks like it didn't happen on the island. She had been living here in the wild for months until we found her. But the burns were older. We believe they were inflicted before she got here," said Nick.

"Inflicted? You think someone deliberately burned her?" Josh looked shocked.

"We're not sure, but some of the burn marks look that way," answered Nick. "And that's why Julie is very concerned about how you approach the girl. She insists that you do it slowly and with care. She wants you to meet the girl at home, briefly at first and then again until she thinks the girl feels safe in your presence and is willing to look at the pictures you brought. It may take a few days."

"Wow," said Josh and then nodded. "Sure, I understand. That's fine."

"Great, let's get you settled in, and then we'll head to O'Malley's for dinner. It's within walking distance of the house. My treat," said Nick. Then he added, "Amanda's meeting us there."

*   *   *

Revelers from the festival and animated fishermen swapping stories about their catches should have jammed O'Malley's. But they didn't. Nick, Amanda, and Josh had no trouble finding a table next to the fireplace—a coveted spot, usually taken for the evening. The atmosphere inside, generated by a smattering of glum patrons focused more on drinking than conversation, reflected the mood of the island.

"It's usually livelier here," said Nick, "but most everybody is at home licking their wounds."

"What happened?" asked Josh.

"The annual winter fest and ice fishing tournament were busts," said Nick.

"Yes," Amanda added. "There are few year-round jobs on the island, and the islanders rely on fall and winter events that attract mainlanders to supplement their incomes from the short summer tourist and construction season. The loss of that income has been a blow to the island."

"Don't be fooled by the large vacation homes," continued Nick. "The islanders build them but don't own them. Most can't afford to."

Josh was about to speak when five elderly gentlemen entered the pub, greeted the bartender, and then ambled to the table in front of the fireplace, which had a reserved sign on it. Each carried a book. Before they sat down, one of them came over to the snug. He smiled and nodded to Nick and Josh and then said to Amanda, "Amanda, dear, how nice to see you. May we join you by the fire? We'll be discussing a rather interesting book, and some of us hold rather strong opinions regarding its author and content. The talk may become rather heated. I hope we won't disturb you three."

"Not at all, Mr. Dugan. What are you reading?" said Amanda.

"*Say Nothing,* by Patrick Radden Keefe, a veritable tome about the Troubles in Ireland."

Amanda nodded, but Nick and Josh stared at him with blank looks of incomprehension.

"Jesus, Mary, and Joseph," Dugan roared. Then he smiled and shook his head in mock dismay. "Can you lads be that ignorant? Amanda, do us all a favor and educate these two eejits on recent Irish history before this island quakes and sinks into the lake." He turned and left, still smiling and shaking his head until he'd taken his seat with the other men.

"They're a remarkable group of octogenarians," Amanda said to Josh and Nick. "They're the Assembled Hibernian Order of Literary Elders, a mouthful and an island institution. The five of them started the group in their fifties and have been meeting here every month without fail for over thirty years to tear into books, and sometimes tear them up. They're gentlemen of strong opinions."

"Apparently so," said Nick. He nudged Josh and pointed over to the round table of seated men. Each member wore a Kelly-green tee shirt with the acronym of the group's name emblazoned on the front and flanked by opposite pointing arrows. They read:

← A * * HOLES →

Amanda waited until the two of them stopped chuckling and refocused their attention on their own table. Then she said, "Before their discussion gets too animated, there's something I want you to look at, Josh." She took a folded piece of paper out of her jeans pocket and handed it to him. "This is a drawing of a figure the girl did yesterday after her session with her therapist. She's drawn it in several sessions, and each time it has become a more developed image. It began with a prompt from her therapist to draw a human figure. It's strange looking, rather frightening, almost human but not quite. Her therapist thinks the image manifests the girl's fears and may originate in her culture, maybe as a myth or something. Her therapist feels that if she knew what the figure was, it might help with the therapy. She asked me to show it to you. Do you have any idea what it might be?"

Josh unfolded the paper and stared at it for a moment. Then he carefully refolded it and handed it back to her. "I know exactly what this is," he said. "I need to see the girl as soon as possible."

Chapter 45

Amanda sat in her pajamas on the side of her bed and studied the drawing the girl had made: the one that Josh had said depicted the Wendigo. Halting strokes from a child's hand stabbed through or weaved over one another, faint threads and heavy smudges mingled and crawled along the page; lines faded and reappeared like stitches—all imperfectly contained within the broken flow of a silhouette. Yet, the overall effect was not amateurishly charming but jarring. The girl had drawn a gaunt, long-limbed, half-human cadaver: clawed, lipless, hollow-eyed, fanged, poised like a set steel trap. So real did the image appear that it seemed about to spring in fury at its observer. Amanda wondered what horror could embed such a nightmare in a young girl's psyche.

She placed the drawing in the drawer of her nightstand and slid under the covers, pulling them up a little higher than usual. She reached for the table lamp to turn it off and then decided against it, at least for a while longer. She didn't consider herself superstitious or gullible or prone to the creeps. But . . .

Josh's description of the Wendigo had been chilling. Amanda had never heard of the creature, which both surprised and shamed her. Here she was, surrounded by Ojibwe and Odawa bands and tribes, but knew little of their history and culture. She was grateful that Josh had not judged her and Nick's blind ignorance but patiently explained the Wendigo. He described a cold, cannibalistic, part human monster that inhabited the Northwoods and sought out and feasted on human avarice and selfishness, stealing its victim's heart; or a spirit that possessed greedy humans, turning them into murderous cannibals of insatiable want. A cautionary mythical creature, Josh had said, but nonetheless believed to be real by many, and not just Ojibwe children, whose parents scared them into good behavior by tales of the monster's atrocities. He admitted, without embarrassment, that as a tribal policeman, he had heard of savage and inexplicable deaths convincingly attributed to the Wendigo. The Wendigo was out there somewhere, and if the girl had seen it and been the victim of its evil, it needed to be hunted down.

Amanda turned out the light and, in the dark, remained awake, listening for the noises in the woods outside her bedroom window.

Chapter 46

Julie was adamant. The girl needed more time to be emotionally ready for Josh's visit, at least another day. She hoped to ensure that the girl fully understood the purpose of the visit and her part in it, that it was a sincere effort to protect her. She wanted her to know that she was not going to be taken away until everyone was sure she would be safe.

Since Josh now would be on the island until Julie signaled that the girl was ready to be interviewed by him, Nick planned to bring Josh along when he questioned the Manning brothers about Friel's accusation against them. Callahan had assigned him that task. Josh had been surprised when Nick told him about Friel pointing his finger at the brothers. He knew of the brothers' work with The Great Lakes Indian Fish and Wildlife Commission and the Inter-tribal Fisheries and Assessment Program to help manage the health of treaty fishery resources. Josh doubted the brothers would have procured game fish for stocking without a health inspection or test. And he had told Nick so.

*   *   *

"Didn't realize it was a crime not to know an Indian girl. You here to arrest me?" Michael took a fish filet off the scale on the counter and stuffed it into a plastic freezer bag. He wrote the weight on the bag and tossed the fish into an open cooler on the floor beside him.

"No, I'm not here about the girl," said Nick. "Just here to ask you and your brother a few questions about a different matter."

"Then why are you here?" Michael addressed Josh.

"I'm on the island working on something with Deputy Randolph," answered Josh, nodding toward Nick. "It has nothing to do with the two of you. I'm just along for the ride," he added.

Nick could see through the open back door of the fish house where Benjamin fussed with the smoker, preparing it for another load of fish. Nick nodded toward the back door. "You want to call your brother in here?"

Michael wiped his hands on his blood-stained apron and cocked his head over his right shoulder. "Benjamin, the law's here. Better come at a run."

Benjamin slid a rack of fish steaks into the smoker and turned and walked into the fish house. When he stepped beside his brother, he dipped his head in greeting to Josh but ignored Nick.

"So, what's this about?" asked Michael.

"Well, I'll get right to the point. Tom Friel is accusing the two of you of supplying him with fish for stocking that turned out to be sick with VHS," said Nick.

The two brothers turned to each other in obvious surprise and then looked back at Nick, both glaring. "That's total bullshit," said Michael.

"What's bullshit? That you didn't sell him sick fish?" said Nick.

"The whole thing is bullshit. We didn't sell him any fish for stocking. I don't know what the hell he's talking about," said Michael. Benjamin nodded and looked as if he were about to come across the counter at Nick.

"Then why would he say something like that?" said Nick.

"How the hell would we know? Maybe he's confused or has something against us. Anyway, he's wrong," said Michael.

"Fine," said Nick. "We'll look into this more."

"You do that," said Michael.

"One more thing," said Nick. "You've got to find another place to dump your fish waste. People are complaining about the smell. I've experienced it myself, and its overpowering."

"We should be the ones complaining about a stink," said Benjamin and slammed his fist on the counter.

Michael placed a hand on his brother's shoulder and said to Nick, "We'll do what we can."

Chapter 47

The girl sat at the dining room table with her hands in her lap, her head up, and her eyes on Josh. She wore a green flannel shirt and blue corduroy slacks, her choice from the clothes Julie had bought her. As Josh seated himself across from her, she raised her hand to curl her hair over her right ear and then quickly dropped it in her lap again as if she had done something wrong. Her eyes darted to Julie who stood with Callahan at one end of the table. Julie smiled and then nodded in Josh's direction. The girl's eyes softened, and she returned her attention to Josh. She had met Josh briefly two days earlier when he'd come to the house at Julie's suggestion for an initial get-together. He had introduced himself, said why he had come to see her, and chatted about himself: his duties as a tribal policeman, where he lived, where he went to school, what he did for fun. He stressed again and again that he was not there to take her to the reservation. She had reacted to none of it. But now, although expectant, the girl did not appear nervous or frightened of him.

Josh placed an envelope on the table and took out five pictures, all mug shots of men of about the same age. He placed them one by one in a row in front of her and then asked her to look at them. The girl lowered her eyes for a moment and then looked back up at Josh. Her expression had not changed.

"Do you recognize any of these men?"

The girl shook her head.

"Please," said Josh, "look again. Just to be sure."

The girl did not look again but remained staring at Josh.

Josh gathered up the photos and then arranged another five pictures in front of her. "How about these men? Do you recognize any of them?"

Again, the girl stared down at the photos for a second and then brought her gaze back to Josh.

"Okay," said Josh. He collected the five photos and then took the last five from the envelope. When he arrayed these in a row, he asked her to look down again.

She lowered her eyes and then leaped from her chair with a piercing, primal scream. Josh jolted in his chair, knocking it backwards, almost falling. Callahan and Julie stood stunned as the girl screeched, her arms thrashing the air and her body writhing as if being gnawed by some animal. They rushed to her. Julie reached the girl first and grabbed her, pulling her to her chest. The girl tore herself away and snatched one of the photos, ferociously shredding it and clawing at its pieces as they scattered around her. Callahan tried to restrain her, but she fought against him as if her life depended on escaping.

*   *   *

The girl had shredded the mug shot of Case Blackwell. More like attacked it, thought Josh as he waited in the small terminal to board the next plane off the island. Callahan had to restrain the girl as Julie tried unsuccessfully to calm her until Dr. Carl Remy arrived and sedated her. Josh left the house after the girl fell asleep. So, there it was. Blackwell had recognized the girl as Josh had suspected, and the girl had certainly recognized Blackwell. But how were they connected, why was the girl so frightened of him, and how did Blackwell's relationship with Sam Goodfellow figure in all of this? The girl still wasn't talking. That meant that the answers lay with Blackwell. But he wasn't talking either.

Chapter 48

The day was unusually warm for one so deep in winter, and the snow fell in heavy flakes, some as big as cotton balls, that splattered against the cruiser's windshield as Callahan drove through the curtain of slush. The wipers slapped in decreasing arcs, clumping the snow into ridges of ice that rose higher and higher until the wipers jammed to a halt. Callahan had to stop twice already to shovel the accumulation off the cruiser. The wet snow refused to be swept away. But the icy mess wasn't Callahan's only frustration. Friel and the Manning brothers occupied his thoughts as he drove to the brothers' fish market. So far, only a razor-thin line divided black and white in the case. No gray area existed between Friel's accusation and the Manning brothers' denial. That was unless Amanda turned up evidence that Friel's confession was a hoax or the product of an inflamed mind, which he thought unlikely. Often, it was in the gray areas where the truth hid and, with deft probing, could be found. For now, he'd make no judgment about the truth, but test if Friel or the brothers could substantiate their statements. He'd decided to start with the brothers.

The brothers' pickup truck rested alongside the fish market collecting snow. Callahan parked next to it. As he did, Michael stepped onto the store's narrow wooden porch. "We're closed. No fish today. Weather's too bad to go on the lake," he called out to Callahan.

"Not here for fish, unfortunately," said Callahan, exiting the cruiser. "I'm investigating the Friel matter."

"The Friel bullshit, you mean." Benjamin now also stood on the porch.

"Mind if I come in?" Callahan waited for an answer while the brothers eyed him in silence, snow beginning to stick to his watch cap and the shoulders of his jacket. Finally, Michael nudged his brother back into the store and motioned for Callahan to come in.

A pass-through counter divided the one-room interior into a narrow entryway and a larger area dominated by a long steel table. Lockers, basins, and two glass-paneled freezers lined the walls behind the counter. Benjamin had raised the countertop hatch and Michael and Callahan walked through to the workspace.

"The coffee's fresh. Want a cup?" asked Michael.

"That would be great," said Callahan. "Just black would be fine," he added.

Michael poured coffee into two ceramic cups and handed one to Callahan, keeping the other for himself. "Sit yourself down," he said, pointing to a bare wooden table in one corner of the room with two folded metal chairs. "I imagine this will take a while."

"Maybe not," said Callahan. He placed his cup on the table, unfolded one of the chairs and sat down. Michael did the same. Benjamin had stationed himself at the counter, leaning on it and facing Callahan with his arms folded. Benjamin was short, maybe five six or seven but barrel chested and muscular. Michael was tall, over six feet like Callahan, and when he had handed Callahan the coffee, he had stood eye to eye with him. Callahan had the impression that Michael was sizing him up.

"So, Friel is incorrect when he said you sold him the fish for stocking?" Callahan spoke across the table to Michael.

"The bastard outright lied," said Benjamin.

"Fair enough," said Callahan, still addressing Michael. "If you didn't supply the fish, then who do you think did?"

Michael flashed a glance at his brother who lowered his head and turned slightly away. "No idea," he said.

Callahan raised his coffee mug to his lips and took a sip, gazing over the rim at Michael. He had answered too quickly, too emphatically. The brothers must have speculated on the source of the contaminated fish. It was inconceivable to Callahan that they hadn't. They knew everyone who fished commercially on upper Lake Michigan and all the fisheries in Michigan's Upper Peninsula. And if they didn't participate in it, they at least had some knowledge of trafficking illegally harvested commercial and sport fish. That meant they either knew of or could discover the identity of those who avoided the cost, paperwork, and state scrutiny associated with the rigorous fish pathogen testing requirements for stocking. Callahan set his mug back down on the table.

"Why would Friel pick the two of you to accuse?" said Callahan.

"Same answer, no idea," said Michael.

"Maybe he's covering for someone and we're a convenient scapegoat. Why don't you ask him?" added Benjamin.

Callahan stood. He'd get no farther with the brothers, but before he left, he wanted to warn them not to take matters into their own hands. "I know your reputation is at stake here and perhaps your business. I understand your concern. We're trying to get to the bottom of this without things getting worse for everyone. If you find anything out, I'd appreciate the help." A nod from Michael gave him hope that he had gotten the hint.

Chapter 49

Julie and Callahan dodged each other as they glided around the kitchen preparing their portion of dinner: Callahan lined marinated fish in a baking dish and shoved it into the oven, and Julie gathered cucumbers, lettuce, and tomatoes from the fridge for a salad, scattering the ingredients next to a cutting board on the kitchen island. Max and the girl sat on the living-room couch watching an episode of Max's favorite TV series. The chicken cuddled next to Max softly warbling, while the dog snoozed, curled up on the girl's lap.

Julie should have been enjoying the scene of domestic tranquility, but she wasn't. Despite efforts to suppress it, Julie's internal turmoil over the girl frequently bubbled to the surface. This was one of those times. She began slicing a tomato a bit too vigorously. "We're not letting anyone take her away from us, no matter what reason they give, Matt. Not until we're sure she'll be safe and protected. I won't let that happen." She stopped slicing and put the knife down. "You saw her reaction to the mug shot. She's terrified of that man. Josh says he's living on the reservation. There's no way I'm going to let her go to where he is, or might be, no matter what safety assurances we're given. I want her here by us. We've got to find out why she's afraid of him and do something about it, Matt."

Callahan finished setting the oven timer and turned to Julie. "Tanner and Josh are working on that, and no one has any plans yet to take her anywhere. So, you mustn't worry."

"But I am, Matt. What if that Blackwell person comes to the island looking for her?"

"I've taken care of that. Tanner and Josh are keeping her whereabouts secret, even from the rest of the tribal officers and staff. And Island Air is letting me know everyone who flies to the island. It's the only way to get here now." Even as he said this, he knew Julie wasn't buying it.

"Don't patronize me, Matt. Pardon my French, but that's just bullshit. News that the girl is with us has already reached the reservation through that tribal child welfare representative, and who knows how far it has spread. We have to assume that her whereabouts is widely known."

"Tanner is being mindful of the girl's safety. He's got Josh working fulltime on the Blackwell connection." Callahan checked the oven timer and said, "Better finish that salad. The fish is almost done." He was reaching for an oven mitt and spatula when his phone rang. He fumbled for it on the counter and answered it.

"Friel has been attacked and beaten." It was Amanda. "He's in bad shape and at the medical center now with Remy. I'm with them, but you'd better get over here."

*   *   *

Remy had just finished suturing a jagged gash to Friel's forehead when Callahan arrived at the medical center's small surgery room. "He's got a broken nose, a fractured forearm, and two lacerations, one in the back of his skull and one on his forehead. Looks worse than it is. He'll live," said Remy.

"It was the damn Indians that done it. They snuck up on me, the cowards." Friel's weak voice hissed like air escaping from a punctured tire, and Callahan had to lean down to hear him.

"You saw your attackers?" said Callahan.

"First, they whacked me on the back of the head. Like I say, they were cowards. But I got a look at them both when I fell to the ground. I landed on my back. Then they hit me some more. Or one of them did."

"You could see their faces?" pressed Callahan.

"They were wearing ski masks, but I'm sure it was them. They ran when I started screaming for help."

"Can you describe their height and weight; what they were wearing?"

"Damn it. I know those brothers. It was them. One was tall, the other short. They wore coats and jeans. That's all I can remember."

"What did they hit you with?"

"Just the one hit me; the tall one. Could have been a bat or a board. It was heavy. I know that."

"Did they say anything?"

"No, but I could smell fish."

Remy coughed to get Callahan's attention and then sliced the edge of his hand across the front of his neck as a sign that the interview was over.

"Sorry this happened," said Callahan. "We'll get to the bottom of it."

"You'd better," whispered Friel.

*　　*　　*

Callahan and Amanda paused under the entrance portico before leaving the medical center. Two corner floodlights illuminated the small parking lot in an oasis of dim yellow light that struggled to push back the darkness. Eerie orange mounds of plowed snow seemed to smolder along the fringes of the lot. The scene chilled Amanda and made her anxious to leave, but Callahan wanted more information from her about the attack. "How did he answer your questions? Any discrepancies?" he asked.

"His story changed some with you. He only told of one attacker when I questioned him. He seemed certain it was Benjamin, although he said he wore a ski mask. And the bit about the fish was a new addition with you."

"Did he tell you when this happened?"

"He said he left O'Malley's after a couple of beers about 6:00 or 6:30. He wasn't sure, and then went to the motel to pick something up before he went home. The attack happened outside the motel."

"Did he tell you how long he was at the motel."

"Yes. He said it couldn't have been more than a few minutes."

"How alert was he when you questioned him?"

"The same as when you arrived."

"Interview him again tomorrow and see if any more details emerge. I'll question the brothers."

*   *   *

Amanda followed the beams of her headlights through the dark as if spiraling through an unlit tunnel. The woods along the unpaved snow-packed road to her home seemed to press in on her as she drove, narrowing her visible world. The tires shuddered over the rough surface, causing the steering wheel to shake as the car wobbled and skidded. She was driving too fast and knew it, but she wanted to get home. She felt alone and strangely frightened. The girl's case had ramped up in a way that unnerved her and increasingly made the familiar alien. She peered into the faded limits of the beams, struggling to discern the weave of the road, when the headlights suddenly flashed back on her, exploding against the windshield in a blinding sweep. She slammed on the brakes, sending the car whirling until it jolted onto the shoulder and slid against a tree. The car stalled, facing the way she came, and up ahead she could see the opaque glow of the animal's eyes through the trees. A deer. She had almost hit it when it leaped in front of the car. If she had, she thought, it would have crashed through the windshield, thrashing with razor-sharp hooves behind flying shards of glass. She was shaking and then sobbing.

*   *   *

When Amanda had stopped shaking, she drove to Nick's house. She did not want to be alone that night. The next morning, she woke up in bed beside him. Nick had his arm around her as she lay on her side, and she could feel the warmth of his breath on the nape of her neck. She could tell from the rhythm of his breathing that he was awake.

"How you feeling? You slept like a rock," he said.

"Better now." She rolled over and gave him a kiss. He brushed her hair away from her face and kissed her back.

"I let you sleep in, but it's late and we have to get to the station," he said. "I'll make coffee and eggs while you get dressed."

Amanda pushed the covers off and sat up. "I'm sorry I showed up so late last night like some mongrel puppy whimpering for a handout. I just couldn't be alone. I needed you."

Nick climbed out of bed and walked to the bedroom door. He stopped and turned to her. "You don't have to apologize for anything," he said. "You know how I feel. We could make this a permanent arrangement and not have to sneak in the odd night. I imagine pretty much everyone on the island knows we're sleeping together anyway."

"Not everyone. My parents may suspect, but they don't *know* and I don't think they're ready yet."

"I'm not going to go there," said Nick. "I've got eggs to prepare."

Amanda watched him saunter through the living room and into the kitchen. He wore nothing and looked gorgeous. She wished now that she had awoken earlier.

Chapter 50

Callahan waited on the pier as the fishing boat chugged toward him following the channel cut through the ice in the bay. Its hull sagged deep in the water and Callahan figured that the brothers had made a good day's catch. The boat slowed until its forward movement almost stopped and then it turned and drifted sideways into the pier, bumping it with a jolt that almost knocked Callahan off balance. The brothers jumped from the boat and secured the mooring lines before Michael acknowledged Callahan.

"We've got nothing for you. Like I said the last time, we've no idea who he got the fish from." He talked as he and his brother began preparing the boat to offload the fish.

"Friel was attacked and beaten last night. He's at the medical center," said Callahan.

The brothers stopped working and faced Callahan.

"And you think we did it," said Benjamin. It was a statement, not a question.

"That's what Friel is saying," said Callahan.

"And you believe that bastard," said Michael.

"I'm not here to arrest you. That should tell you something. But I want direct answers. No equivocations. Where were you both last night between six and seven o'clock?"

"We closed up the market about five, and then I drove my brother to his house, had dinner with him and his wife, and went home," said Michael. Benjamin nodded.

"What time did you get home?"

"I don't know for sure. We live close, maybe five minutes from each other," said Michael. "Probably around seven."

"Can anyone else back that up?"

Michael shook his head. "I live alone. Divorced," he said.

*   *   *

Before returning to the station, Callahan decided to see if the brothers had found a more remote spot to dump their fish waste, away from complaining homeowners. He drove to where the spit had been, but before he got there, two clues told him the brothers had complied with his demand: no gulls hovered in a noisy cloud above the road ahead, and no noxious odors assaulted his olfactory cells. The former dumping site was bare.

Chapter 51

Liam Rafferty was an old friend of Julie and an island legend for his fiddle playing. In his late seventies, he persisted as a catalyst for impromptu gatherings of musicians in homes and pubs on the island where they played sets of reels, jigs, and hornpipes into the early morning hours. Rafferty had won the Irish National Fiddle Championship for the first time in his teens and appeared on the Tonight Show with Johnny Carson after his fourth win, giving the island a rare instance of national recognition. His sessions gathered not only musicians but those who enjoyed listening to traditional Irish music, which included almost everyone.

In recent years, the crowds had become so large that Rafferty had revived the tradition of House Parties, first established by the island's Irish settlers. These occasions for music, dancing, and singing formed the early islanders' prime source of entertainment. The new House Parties provided a venue for the island's musical talent, including choral groups, classical trios and quartets, chamber orchestras, and *céili* and rock bands. They'd become such a popular pastime that they now took place in the Catholic church hall, the school gym, or the community center. They provided good *craic,* as the Irish say, and got the islanders out of their homes and together during the dark stretch of winter.

Julie loved them and had convinced Callahan to accompany her, Max, and the girl to one on the weekend. The island chamber orchestra would be performing the music of Bach, Hayden, Brahms, and Joplin followed by show tunes sung by the high school choir. The evening would end, as always, with a virtuoso performance by Rafferty, who also served as master of ceremonies.

Music lovers filled every seat in the community center's theater auditorium, and folding chairs had been set up along the walls to accommodate the overflow. The orchestra musicians busied themselves tuning their instruments while Rafferty adjusted the height of the mic as the last of the attendees trooped in.

As Callahan entered the auditorium, Rafferty descended from the stage and approached him. Fine-boned and still agile with sharp features eroded by weathered skin, his movement was almost birdlike. He grabbed Callahan's elbow and pulled him close, bending to his ear. "Sheriff, might I have a word with you after the show?" He spoke quickly, his voice low and his tone conspiratorial. "It won't take but a minute. Will you wait for me in the hall, please?" Then he hurried back to the stage before Callahan could answer.

*   *   *

Julie, Max, and the girl had thoroughly enjoyed the show, Max and the girl clapping and smiling through the show tunes, and all cheering in a standing ovation after the finale. Callahan felt glad of it, especially for the girl. He too had enjoyed the evening, more than he had expected. So much so that he'd forgotten about his meeting with Rafferty. Rafferty caught up with him as he exited the auditorium. He motioned for Callahan to follow him. Callahan told Julie that he'd meet her at the cruiser and then trailed Rafferty to a corner of the entry hall.

"What is it?" asked Callahan.

"A night ago, at the Arranmore Pub session, there was talk among the musicians." Rafferty paused.

"Yes?" said Callahan.

"The establishment serves the players rounds of beer on the house, if they draw a big enough crowd. They also buy their own, so a few tongues were wagging by the end of the evening." Rafferty paused again, obviously enjoying the moment.

"And?" said Callahan.

"And Friel has been blabbing, saying the Manning brothers sold him contaminated fish and then beat him up for saying so. He's also bad-mouthing you. Says you've done nothing about it and won't because of that Indian girl with you and Julie. Looked to me like some agreed with him. Maybe it's just talk, but I didn't like the feel of it and thought you should know about it. For Julie's sake too," he added.

"I appreciate this," said Callahan. "Let me know if you hear anything else."

Rafferty touched his index finger to his forehead in a quick salute. "Will do, Sheriff," he said.

Chapter 52

The brothers sailed into the commercial fishing port of Naubinway just after 4:00 am. The first fishing boats were leaving the harbor, visible only by their bouncing tangle of green and red running lights before they spread out into the lake. The brothers had motored several hours through the night to reach the remote village on the shoreline of Michigan's Upper Peninsula at the very top of Lake Michigan. As Michael piloted the boat through the broken ice, Benjamin scanned the harbor for the man they were to meet. He spotted him standing on the cement pier along the harbor's edge. Barely a shadow under the lamp light from a tall, weathered pole, the man waved an arm to attract them. He held a backpack over his shoulder with his other arm.

As the boat ground against the pier, the man leaped to the gunnel, grabbed Benjamin's outstretched hand as the boat dipped, and jumped through the open side hatch and into the boat. Benjamin held the man's arm until the rocking of the boat subsided, then he let go.

The man dropped the backpack beside him and waited until the engine rattled to a halt before he spoke.

"You were supposed to keep the girl with you. Keep her until you were told different. But you two fucked that up. Jesus, you couldn't babysit an eleven-year-old?"

"It wasn't babysitting, and you don't know how clever she is," said Michael.

"Cunning," interrupted Benjamin.

"Yeah. She got us to trust her and then she slipped away from us," continued Michael. "We spent weeks trying to track her down. You know that. When we found no trace of her, we thought she must have died in the wilderness. Then we heard she'd been found."

"And that's why you're here. You know she's alive and where she is. Now you get her back. She's to be taken elsewhere. When you have her, I'll tell you where." The boat rolled in the bow wave of a departing tug and bumped the pier. The man staggered and grabbed for something to steady himself, nearly falling. The brothers had barely swayed.

"That's impossible," said Michael. "She's under the protection of the sheriff. She's living with him and his girlfriend. Either the girlfriend, the sheriff, or one of his deputies is with her all the time. Plus, we're on the sheriff's radar now. An islander accused us of selling him contaminated fish and then got beat up and said we did it."

Benjamin added, "A while back, one of the deputies came by toting a picture of the girl and asked us if we knew who she was. He didn't suspect us then of knowing about her, he was just asking. But what if the girl has somehow told the sheriff about us? There's no way we could even get close to her."

"If the sheriff knew about your connection to the girl, he would have done something by now. For some reason, she's keeping quiet about you."

"Then let's keep things the way they are," said Benjamin.

The man shook his head. "We can't. That ship has sailed, to use a phrase." he said. Neither brother smiled. "Look, when the girl was hiding on the island, only the three of us knew where she was. Everything was fine. But, now, the tribal police up here are sniffing around about her. Her whereabouts is or will soon be common knowledge. We can't have that. We have to act soon. We have to know what her father discovered and hid before others find out."

"So, we add kidnapping to an assault charge?" said Michael.

"We were to keep the girl hidden, no matter the risk. You've understood that from the beginning." The man reached down and picked up the backpack. He unzipped it and took out two cloth-wrapped parcels. He handed one to each of the brothers. "Take these, you may need them."

Michael clutched the cloth and hefted the parcel, weighing it. Then he slowly lowered his hand to his side, still gripping the unwrapped package. "Has it come to this?" he said to the man.

"It came to this when the girl was found," said the man.

Benjamin folded back the top layer of cloth on the parcel he held. Beneath it was a Glock pistol and two loaded clips.

Chapter 53

They'd exchanged numbers at the restaurant, but he hadn't called or texted, and it had been long enough that she was certain he wouldn't. She would have to kick start a relationship if there was ever going to be one between them. Delia began a text to Josh, finished it, read it three times, and then deleted it. Too brazen, almost demanding, she thought. She started over, this time softening the tone and easing into the invitation to meet with cheery news about how her job was going and asking about his. Too long and chatty this time. On rereading, it came across as lame, even cloying. She deleted it. She tried again. This attempt was even worse, sophomoric and pleading was her verdict. Delete. Finally, she settled on:

> *Hi, I'd like to see you again. I'm free for lunch tomorrow. How 'bout it?*
> *D*

She took a deep breath and tapped *send*. She hadn't even placed her phone back on her desk when it dinged. The text from Josh read:

Sounds great. Where and what time?

*   *   *

She'd decided against the hotel restaurant. Although up-beat with good fare, the crowd and noise at lunchtime nixed it for her. She'd chosen Emilio's, a small, storefront eatery a mile from the hotel. Quiet, unassuming, popular with the locals, attractive, and with an eclectic menu, it fit the bill—she hoped. Josh waved to her from a table along the wall when she walked in.

Delia was halfway to the table when what had been a nagging tug at her consciousness crystallized into a re-solve. Perhaps it was seeing him at a distance, sitting there smiling, youthful, vulnerable, even in his uniform. Maybe she was tired of pretense, of not always liking herself, but she decided she would be honest from the start with this man—no BS.

Josh stood when Delia reached the table. Before he could speak, she motioned for him to sit, but stayed standing herself. "I texted you because I wanted to see you again. Truly, that's the only reason. But there's something you should know. Goodfellow wanted us to meet up. He wanted to use me to find out why you're in-terested in the Indian girl. He threatened me with my job if I didn't go along with him. I'm not going to do it, but I wanted you to know. There, I've said it. If you want me to leave, I will."

Josh's smile faded and he pushed his chair back as if trying to distance himself from her.

"I'll leave," she said and began to turn around.

"No, don't," he said. "Please, sit down."

When Delia had seated herself, Josh scooted closer to the table and leaned toward her. "You didn't have to tell me that," he said. "You could have not pressed me about the girl, and I would have been none the wiser. Why did you do it?"

"I know it might sound odd, especially since we hardly know each other, but I just didn't want something like that between us, even if you weren't aware of it. I wanted it out in the open and then gone," Delia held her breath waiting for Josh to reply.

"The fish tacos here are fantastic. Shall we order?" he said.

*   *   *

They had spent much longer at lunch than either had expected. And both had agreed they wanted to see each other again. Outside the restaurant, before they separated, Josh said to her that he didn't want her to get into trouble with Goodfellow, and that she could tell him that they believed the girl was a runaway of several months and had been traumatized; that she could not or would not speak or otherwise communicate; and that they were trying to discover her identity and the circumstances of her trauma. He added that her ongoing psychological counseling appeared promising and that they were hopeful she would soon regain her speech. He wasn't being totally honest with her either about his motive for confiding in her or about the information he volunteered. He rationalized that he could kill two birds with one stone without wounding his conscience. Delia had given him an unexpected opportunity in his investigation: to covertly discover Goodfellow's response to such news and maybe a clue to his connection to the girl.

Chapter 54

To Nick, the logic was unassailable. The counter arguments simply collapsed under the weight of the obvious. The Manning brothers had brought the girl to the island on their boat from the UP. No way could the girl have gotten to the island by herself from there, and no way could she have been brought here any other way unnoticed by anyone on such a small, remote wedge of land. She had been spirited away, but why? No one seemed to want to entertain that question or accept that conclusion. He suspected it was because they both originated with him.

He also suspected that he might be a bit paranoid. Admittedly, he was having trouble adjusting to his new status as low man on the totem pole. In every previous phase of his adult life, the NSA, the University of Michigan, and the university's biological and environmental station, he had been the expert, used to having his counsel sought and his conclusions accepted. Not so now. Now, he believed he was looked upon as raw, unseasoned, untested, which in many ways he was, but in many he wasn't. Worse yet, he felt that his conduct often elicited exasperation, even bemusement. Even from Amanda. And he got the shit assignments, the most recent of which he was attending to.

At ninety-six, Mrs. Sweeney lived alone in a two-story cottage eight miles from town, and took care of herself—mostly. Callahan made sure that someone checked in on her at least twice a week and called ahead of time to see if she needed anything brought to her. This task had fallen to Nick, and it was one he didn't mind and did cheerfully. But he wasn't on a charity run today. Today, he performed the sheriff's statutory duty of animal control. This chore he did mind. Somehow, it always seemed to involve blood, guts, and puke inducing stench.

Mrs. Sweeney had called the station and in her raspy nasal twang declared an emergency. Nick was dispatched to the scene.

Nick knocked on her door and on hearing her high-pitched invitation to enter, he let himself in. She never locked her door and never gave the wood-burning stove in the corner of her living room a rest. The stove was in overdrive, and Nick guessed it had blasted the temperature past ninety degrees. He immediately began to sweat. Despite the heat, Mrs. Sweeney wore a thick flannel shirt, fur-lined leather slippers, jeans, gloves, a scarf, and a knit watch cap. A half dozen cats surrounded her, languidly draped on every upholstered surface in the room.

"Did you see him? Oh, it's just horrible. Horrible. Poor, poor Jimmy. You must help him, please." She shuffled up to Nick, pulled on the collar of his jacket and dragged him to the window overlooking her deck. "There he is. See him? In the snow under that tree." She pointed with a gloved hand. "He's too old to be outside. He knows better. He's been with me for eighteen years. I can't lose him now."

All Nick saw was a patch of disturbed snow where, to him, it looked like a branch of the tree had fallen. "I'll go out and take a look," he said.

He was halfway to the site when he could see what had happened. A white owl's talons had gone completely through the cat's back. But the cat had twisted up, clawed the feathers from the owl's neck, and sunk its teeth into its throat. The struggle had been violent, bloody, and fatal for both. The scene had a strange effect on Nick as he stood, staring at it. Perhaps, he thought, it was witnessing the last moment of a mortal dance frozen in snow or the contrast of the owl's magnificent beauty with the old cat's mange. Whatever the cause, he sensed that the cat had left a testament, one declaring that he was unwilling to cower in a secluded corner of a house waiting for death, but instead wanted to be in his element, doing what nature had intended him to do: hunt and die in a manner worthy of his species. Nick had never felt that he belonged on the island more than he did in that moment.

*   *   *

"Jimmy's gone," said Nick. "I'm sorry. I'll bury him for you. Just tell me where."

Mrs. Sweeney nodded and then turned away from Nick and wiped her eyes. "Out back is fine if the ground isn't too frozen. If it is, there's a wooden box with a lid against the wall outside. Put him in there until it's warm enough so the coyotes don't get him," she said. As Nick was about to leave, she faced him and said, "I heard you were looking for a little girl. Did you find her?"

"Yes, we did," said Nick,

"That's nice. A little girl would come around occasionally and then she stopped. I wondered what happened to her and if she was the one who you were looking for."

"What? What do you mean when you say she came around?"

"I saw her a couple of times through the window hiding in the woods. I don't think she could see me. After that, I began leaving her candy on the deck railing. She started taking it, but I never saw her do it. It'd just disappear. I knew it was her, though, and not the squirrels because she would sometimes leave me cans of food or wood for the stove as a thank you. But after those two Indians came round, she never came back for the candy."

"You mean the Manning brothers, the fishermen?" asked Nick.

"Yeah, it was them two, I think. They came through the woods in the back, like her. It was strange. I've never seen anyone back there but the girl and them. I saw the Indians more than once though. If you ask me, from the way they were acting, I thought they were looking for something or someone. Maybe her. And like I said, after them, she never came back for the candy. Is she okay?"

"She's fine," said Nick. "Why didn't you tell us this before?"

"Didn't know you were looking for her until recently. Don't see anyone much but you or Amanda, and neither of you said a little girl was missing."

Chapter 55

Callahan swiveled his chair toward his office window and leaned back, resting his legs on the corner of his desk. He locked his fingers together behind his head and took a deep breath. He needed to think, and he did it best in what he christened his ponder pose. This was as close to yoga as he ever got.

Nick was being persistent—all the way to the frayed edges of Callahan's patience. Nick believed that the Manning brothers knew more about the girl than they let on, which was nothing at this point. But that could change with the girl's help, and Nick was pushing hard for permission to approach her. Callahan thought he had made it clear that approaching the girl wasn't in the cards. Not after her reaction to Josh and the mug shots. Julie had been adamant: no way would she allow the girl to be subjected to that kind of probing again. Investigations be damned. The weight of the scales tipped in Julie's favor on this one. Nick would have to find another way.

But Nick's stubbornness, as annoying as it had become, forced Callahan to reassess his judgment regarding the girl. Looking back, he now recognized that what he perceived as their comfortable familiarity with the girl had become for Julie much more. If he now ignored their bond or pushed against it, how would his and Julie's relationship be tested? If he considered the bond inviolate, how would that affect his professional responsibilities to the girl and others? These thoughts piled up in a noisy collision, such that he didn't hear Amanda enter his office. She startled him when she spoke.

"A penny for your thoughts."

Callahan swung his legs off the desk and sat up.

"My grandmother used to say that when she caught me daydreaming," said Amanda.

"Not sure they're even worth a penny," said Callahan. "What's up?"

"The Manning brothers have an alibi."

"You don't say. When did they spring this on you?" said Callahan with palpable skepticism.

"They didn't. Shelby Berry is a friend of mine. She knows Charlotte, Benjamin Manning's wife. They work together summers at Martha's This and That Shop on Main Street. We bumped into each other this morning, and I used the opportunity to ask her about Charlotte and subtly inquire about the Manning brothers. Charlotte knits and makes beautiful scarves, which she sells, and Shelby had asked her to knit one for her. Charlotte had called her to say she was finished and Shelby could come and pick it up."

Callahan squirmed in his chair and sighed.

"Hang on. I'm getting there," Amanda responded and continued. "Well, it turns out that Shelby knocked on Charlotte's door at 7:30 on the evening of Friel's beating. Shelby and her husband were returning home after dinner at The Arranmore Pub. She knew the time because she had just called the babysitter to say they were making a quick stop on the way home and would be a few minutes late, and . . . "

Callahan whirled his index finger as a sign to wind things up.

"Okay, okay, I'm almost done," said Amanda and hurried on. "Well, when Charlotte opened the door, Shelby saw both brothers in the house at the dining room table. She remembered because she was embarrassed to have interrupted their dinner. So, there you go, neither of the brothers beat up Friel." Amanda waited for Callahan's response.

"You tell the Mannings they're off the hook. I'll deal with Friel," he said.

*   *   *

Callahan called Friel and arranged to meet him at his home. The house, perched atop a high wooded dune, was accessible by a switch-back paved drive plowed of snow. Trees had been cleared to provide an unobstructed view of Butler Lake through an enormous picture window that spread almost the entire length of the wall facing the water. As Callahan made the first switch in the drive, the late morning sun reflected off the glass and momentarily blinded him.

Friel waited outside and directed him to back the cruiser along the south wall of the house. "Makes it easier to head back down," he said as Callahan stepped out of the cruiser. "Come on in."

Friel ushered Callahan into the house and shut the door. "Did you arrest them?" he said without offering Callahan a seat.

Callahan turned and faced Friel. "No, and that's not going to happen."

Friel's body stiffened and his face hardened. "What do you mean that's not going to happen?"

"They have a solid alibi. It wasn't them who attacked you. We're working to find out who did."

"Bullshit. They're lying, and if you believe their crap, you're either naïve or stupid."

Friel had raised his voice in agitation. Callahan decided to use logic to try and calm him down. He kept his voice modulated. "They didn't give us an alibi. We discovered it independent of them. The alibi and the fact you couldn't positively identify who attacked you gives us no cause to arrest them." Logic didn't work. Friel's agitation jumped to full blown rage.

"You crooked bastard. You're protecting them because of that Indian girl with you. I knew it. Who the hell else would do it?" he screamed. "They beat me up because I told you they were the ones who sold me contaminated fish. And I bet you let them know it. It's you who is responsible for this, and I'm going to see that you pay, Callahan." Friel gesticulated wildly and spit his words. His face had contorted into an ugly, belligerent mask.

Aggressive postures in most animals make them appear larger and more intimidating. But in Friel they diminished him. He appeared small and pathetic, like a hooked fish writhing and flopping on the splintered planks of a pier. But for his vitriol, Callahan might have pitied him. "I'm leaving now, and I suggest you get out of my way," he said.

So immersed was Friel in his tantrum that he looked surprised when Callahan spoke, as if he'd forgotten he was there. He ceased bellowing and moved away from the door.

Callahan started to leave and then stopped and faced Friel. "If you're thinking about stirring up trouble for the Mannings or anyone else in order to deflect attention from your own criminal conduct, you might want to seriously reconsider that course of action," said Callahan.

"Is that a threat?" stammered Friel.

"Just sound advice," said Callahan as he left.

Chapter 56

Case Blackwell's life was shiftless, hapless, and possessed of the undercurrent of nascent chaos of those who live from hand to mouth. That's why Josh was surprised when Blackwell's life suddenly took a fortuitous upturn. Josh uncovered that every Thursday Blackwell drove to a strip club on the outskirts of Saint Ignace, stayed until closing, and then checked into a motel with one of the strippers. That took money, money that did not come from a spurious disability check or cleaning gutters. No one had reported thefts of large sums of money or valuable property to the tribal police, so Blackwell apparently hadn't stolen to supplement his income. And he had not secured permanent employment. Someone was paying him on the sly. But who and for what? Josh decided to drive down to Saint Ignace. Before he left, he withdrew from his bank one hundred dollars in tens and fives.

The Lion's Lair was a barn-shaped ramshackle structure across from the municipal airport and edging the frontage road along Interstate 75. A looming billboard with a come-hither blond nymph announced *YOU ARE HERE.* As Josh entered the door of the Lair, a turnstile and a three-hundred-pound behemoth ensconced behind a velvet covered counter stopped him. "There's a twenty-buck cover, pal. Plus, you buy a drink inside."

Josh took his police ID out of the back pocket of his jeans and showed it to the behemoth. "I just want to ask a few questions," he said.

'I don't give a flying fuck if you're a cop or not, especially a pretend one from the reservation. It's still a fucking twenty bucks and a drink inside." The behemoth spoke from a shaved head the size of a watermelon and through a muddy mustache that bristled from his upper lip and drooped down below his jowls. His eyes and teeth were the same yellow.

Josh took two tens out of his wallet and gave it to the man. The behemoth nodded for him to go through the turnstile. "Who can answer some questions for me about one of your customers?" said Josh when he'd gone through.

"Depends on what you're asking and why," said the behemoth.

Josh took a picture of Blackwell out of his wallet and showed it to the man. "It's about this guy," he said. "And it's about a possible child abduction."

The behemoth took the picture and examined it. "A child abduction, you say? Hmm." He handed the picture back to Josh. "See that girl at the end of the stage serving drinks, the one in the gold-spangled g-string? Try her.

And get one thing perfectly clear. What these girls do after they leave here is none of my business, literally. You get what I'm saying?"

"Yeah, sure," said Josh. He started to walk away but the behemoth clamped a paw on his shoulder and stopped him. "Oh, and you take up her time, that's another twenty bucks." The behemoth extended an upturned palm the size of a steak platter to Josh. Josh placed a ten and two fives in it. This investigation was getting expensive, and the thought crossed his mind that he should have brought more than a hundred bucks with him.

*   *   *

The place was empty except for four customers, older men, with their knees jammed against the edge of the stage, ogling a lone pole dancer's grinding undulations to a thudding rhythm as roving lights washed over her body. Josh figured that just past noon was not the peak time for titty bars. The girl came to his table as he sat down.

"What are you drinking?" she asked.

"A Coke."

"That's eight dollars. Same as every other drink. You sure you don't want something stronger?"

"No thanks. A Coke's fine," he said and tossed a ten-dollar bill on her tray.

"Suit yourself," she said. "Be back in a moment."

The girl was short and thin with breasts impossibly large for her stature. The skin stretched so tight over them that Josh thought it would split with each breath she took. In the dim light beyond the stage, it was difficult to gauge her age. As she turned, her back ignited in a dazzle of deep reds, blues, greens, and yellows from the tattoo of a parrot, one wing of which spread up her back and over her shoulder, the tip of a teal feather just touching her right arm. Watching her leave, Josh marveled how the image seemed to cloak her nudity more than if she wore an evening dress.

When she came back to his table, she set the drink in front of him, and started to walk away, the two dollars in change still on her tray.

"Just a second. I'd like to talk to you," said Josh.

The girl stopped and then turned around. "Sure, if you buy me a drink," she said.

"Fine, whatever you're having." Josh gave her another ten-dollar bill. "Please, sit down."

The girl complied and scooted her chair closer to Josh. He placed the picture of Blackwell on the table and slid it in front of her. "Do you know this man?"

The girl shoved her chair away from the table and stood up.

"Wait," said Josh. "Your boss said it was okay to talk to me."

The girl looked at the behemoth and Josh saw him nod.

The girl slowly lowered herself back into the chair. "You a cop?" she asked.

"Yes. I'm with the tribal police in Sault Ste. Marie."

"Why are you asking if I know him?" she said.

"I'm investigating a possible child abduction and—"

The girl tensed and her eyes widened. "Oh my God. Did he snatch a kid? Jesus. I have a kid of my own. Oh God." She began to scream. "Is he dangerous?"

"Please calm down. We're not accusing him. We're just conducting an investigation, trying to find out who may be involved," said Josh.

"Did you find the kid? Please tell me you did."

"The kid is fine now."

The girl relaxed and slumped back in her chair. She took a deep breath and after a long moment said, "How can I help?"

*   *   *

Josh returned to Sault Ste. Marie the next afternoon one hundred bucks lighter but with information about Blackwell. The girl had been a big help. Blackwell had come to the club lugging cash, which he had flung freely in the direction of all the girls until one in particular caught his fancy. Pixie—that was the stage name the girl had given herself—was the lucky one, if you considered snaring an otherwise worthless miscreant providential, thought Josh. Pixie obviously did. The strip club circuit in the Upper Peninsula was not the road to riches. She needed the money and she needed Blackwell alive and healthy to get it, so she told him that he should not be so conspicuous with his newfound wealth as some very bad types were beginning to take an interest in him. She suggested that he discretely concentrate its distribution in a single direction—toward her. She apparently made it so worth his while that Blackwell had wanted her to run away with him. He was to get some really big money soon, he said, and had to disappear for good. She had heard crap like that before and didn't believe him. She wanted to know where the money was coming from first. He would only say that he was to do a job for someone and then vanish. That's why she became so upset when she thought Josh was investigating a child abduction. Then Blackwell had run out of cash, and she had told him to take a hike. Josh had left a forty-dollar tip on the table.

In Josh's mind the only job that required the hired to disappear permanently was murder. And the only way to assure the permanence of that disappearance was to, in turn, murder the hired. The promise of money to go on the run clouded the mind of the ignorant and desperate. Blackwell perfectly fit the bill. Plus, if he disappeared, no one would miss him or even care where he went.

It was imperative that Josh get to Blackwell and stop whatever was going to happen.

Chapter 57

"Give me the gun." Michael stood on the pier blocking his brother's path to the boat.

"I think I'd best keep it," said Benjamin and shouldered his way past his brother.

Michael grabbed him by the arm and jerked him back so that they faced each other. "Give it to me now," he snarled, still gripping his brother's arm.

Benjamin pulled himself free. "No. Now, get out of my way." He shoved his brother with both hands and lurched past him.

Michael staggered backwards, almost falling. He reached out, seized the collar of his brother's jacket, and pulled. They both lost their balance and tumbled to the pier landing on their backs. Michael clambered on top of his brother and pinned his arms, holding him down. Benjamin bucked and tried to twist his body free, but Michael bore his knee down into his brother's groin. Then he lowered his face within inches of his brother's. "Listen to me," he spat, "don't be a fool. We can't be caught with the guns. We need to hide them until we have a solid plan, a plan that works to keep her and us alive."

Benjamin plunged his forehead into Michael's nose causing him to bellow and rear back. "You're the fool," he rasped. "The guns are our best chance to keep all our hearts beating. Why do you think we were given them? We're on our own now. No one has our backs anymore. It's just us. Now get the fuck off of me."

Michael released his grip. He stood up and extended his hand. "Take it," he said. Benjamin hesitated, but then grabbed it. Michael pulled him to his feet. "Things haven't reached that level. Not yet. Come on," he said and jabbed Benjamin's shoulder in a mock punch. He forced a smile. "Let's get to the boat."

They began walking together down the pier, but Benjamin hung back a step. "Things reached that level when we lost her and Callahan found her," he said.

"We can still take care of that. It's not too late," said Michael.

"So, you already have a plan?"

"Maybe."

"And what does this 'maybe' involve?"

"The drugs."

Benjamin halted, grasped his brother's shoulder, and spun him around. "The drugs? No way. No fucking way. You mess with the drugs and we're all dead."

"Hear me out. Then we decide how we use the guns," said Michael.

Chapter 58

The tracks were fresh: well defined in the snow and not iced over. The hunter could tell from them that the deer was large. He had followed the animal for almost a mile until it had stopped in a clearing to feed. The hunter watched from a crouch downwind as the eight-point buck stomped the snow to expose the browse beneath. Then he rose in a single motion, nocked an arrow, and clipped the release to his bow's string. As he raised the bow, the deer stopped feeding, turned in full profile, and lifted its head as if presenting the perfect target. The hunter's heart began to race. He couldn't miss now. He took a deep breath to slow his heart, slowly exhaled, and then brought the bow to a full draw, leveling the forty-yard pin sight inches behind the deer's shoulder. His finger had just touched the trigger of the release when the deer suddenly ducked, spun, and scrambled into the trees, vanishing. Damn, he cursed aloud. Some sonofabitch got to the deer before him. A fraction of a second sooner and the animal would have been his, he moaned to himself. "Hey, asshole," he yelled. "That deer was mine."

"You hear me?" he yelled again when he got no answer. He trudged through the snow to the spot where the deer had been. Nothing but silence and an empty wood. Then he glimpsed something ahead at the edge of the clearing, half buried in the snow. From a distance, it looked like carrion; some large animal that had been picked over by turkey vultures. Maybe the deer had been spooked by it and not shot by another bow hunter, he thought. Curious, he decided to take a closer look.

As he approached, its identity became less rather than more defined the closer he got, more confusing in its contours. It wasn't until he was almost upon it that he recognized its true form and he reeled back in horror. It was a man or what was left of him.

He was nude and on his back, the snow around him blood splattered. His arms and legs were splayed so that he seemed to be leaping in macabre celebration. The skin of his face had been surgically scored in strips, then peeled away from the skull and left draped over the neck. His eyes bulged above a lipless rictus. The upper arms and thighs had been skinned in the same manner. Thin flaps of flesh hung over the lower arms and calves like the leather fringes of a jacket. Equal portions of muscle from both thighs had been sharply sliced away, exposing bone. The hunter turned away and retched. These mutilations had been done with precision. They had been slow and deliberate, excruciating beyond imagination but not deadly. But in stark contrast, the man's chest had been violently smashed and cracked open, exposing a ravaged cavity. His heart had been torn out.

Chapter 59

"It's Blackwell." Chief Tanner stood beside Josh at the table in his office as they both perused the spread of photos of the body. "The fingerprints are a match with those in our file on him."

"Who could have done this?" mused Josh.

"That's not the question being asked in the community. It's not *who* but *what*. That hunter took pictures on his cell phone. He showed them around and talked up what he'd seen. His story spread like fleas on a dog and inflamed the imaginations of those with susceptible minds. He's triggered a mass hysteria. Word has swelled that a Wendigo feasted on the body and took its heart because evil is abiding here. It's coming for others now to devour the sinful. Everyone is scared stiff and afraid to talk. Even the nonbelievers are skittish. We're not likely to get any leads on this for a long time," said Tanner.

Josh shuffled the order of the pictures, examined them, and then said, "Maybe that's exactly what whoever did this wanted to happen, sir." Tanner gave him a quizzical look. "They want everyone silenced in fear.

What happened to Blackwell will happen to them if they don't keep mute." he added.

"If they don't keep mute about what?" asked Tanner.

"That's what we have to find out, sir," said Josh. "That and who did this."

*   *   *

As near as could be determined, considering the freezing temperatures, Blackwell had been killed about forty-eight hours before he was discovered by the hunter. Hystcria about the Wendigo had burgeoned in much less time. It was full blown when Josh returned to Sault Ste. Marie. He didn't hold with the notion of the Wendigo as a physical being, a living manifestation of an avenging evil that fed upon and stole the hearts of the wicked. But he did believe that the Wendigo presented itself in the world. He believed that evil could possess the heart and devour the living; that evil feasted upon itself. And he believed that the work of evil, when exhibited in plain view to expose its terrible capacity, engendered paralyzing fear; and that such fear allowed evil to spread. Josh suspected that Blackwell had been sacrificed to seed that terror. The perpetrators had to be found. But his first concerns were for the stripper and the girl on the island. Blackwell's blighted hand had touched each in different ways. He had confided to the stripper. The girl had recognized his photo and been terrified. Josh was convinced she had witnessed something Blackwell had done: something horrific. The two were now marked.

Somewhere in the woods, the Wendigo sniffed the air for fresh blood. Josh's first call would be to the Lion's Lair; his second to Callahan.

Chapter 60

Lately, Friel had been bellying up to the bars at O'Malley's and the Arranmore Pub, the two wintering watering holes on the island, more often than the island's inveterate drinkers. But banishing vaporous fits from a grueling winter with amiable discourse and alcohol was not his purpose. He came to sow discord. He sought recruits to an army of rabble rousers sympathetic to his grievances, to wit: Callahan's refusal to arrest the Mannings for battery and for illegally selling fish for stocking the lake. He hadn't attracted a battalion, a company, or even a platoon, but he had gathered a sizeable squad with the assertion that Callahan gave the Mannings a pass because of the Indian girl living with him. At best, Callahan was professionally negligent or, at worst, criminally liable for his refusal to enforce the law. As Friel had hoped, the argument gained traction among those with a seething prejudice against Native Americans, and those who objected to authority of any kind as an impediment to their God-given freedoms. He now had his militia of malcontents in the living room of his home, preparing to send them into battle.

Down coats hung from every hook, buried the settee, and littered the floor in the coatroom off the entrance hall to Friel's house. His minions crowded the living room seated shoulder to shoulder on the couch, in folding chairs, and on pillows thrown on the rugs. A wood-burning stove in a bricked corner of the room comfortably warmed the house, but body heat from the throng had already raised the temperature. Everyone had a bottle of beer in hand, and two ice-filled coolers of beer bordered each end of the coffee table. Bowls of peanuts and potato chips rested within easy reach of all. If an army traveled on its stomach, then Friel made sure this one would be well sated.

"Let me start off by thanking everyone for coming," said Friel. He stood, framed by the doorway to the kitchen, facing his audience.

"You bet, man. Glad to be here," said someone across the room. Everyone else mumbled in agreement.

"Law on this island isn't equally enforced," Friel continued. "It's—"

"— used as a hammer against some of us." someone interrupted.

"Against most of us," another added.

"Damn right," chimed in two others.

A guy on the couch got to his feet and leaned into the assembly, raising a fist. "Callahan's a fucking prick. The way he runs the law here you'd think you were in a fucking prison," he said, staring everyone down, daring a challenge.

"Unless you're a damned Indian or a friend of his; then you can do whatever you damn well please." This declared through a derisive grin by a geezer leaning his chair against the wall.

"Who invited those fishermen here anyway?" asked the man next to him, shaking his head in exaggerated dismay.

"It ain't our island anymore is it?" someone shouted.

"Hell no," several responded in a chorus of assent.

Friel was ecstatic. He had tapped into a pent-up source of bile, which was spewing forth like a geyser before his very eyes. Things were going far better than he expected.

Then someone yelled, "What are we going to do about it?"

And that was the question Friel had been waiting for.

"This is the modern age." Friel flapped both hands in front of him to signal silence. "We've got at our fingertips tremendous power. You all have email, or a Facebook or Twitter account, I expect. If you don't then get them. These are our weapons. Our legitimate grievances won't just bounce off these four walls and land in our ears. People will hear us loud and clear everywhere. No one can shut their ears to us. We can get justice and our island back." Friel looked around the room. He saw vigorous nods, hi-fives, and heard a few *amens*. "Look what Callahan justice got me." Friel turned his head to the side and lifted it, exposing the jagged line of stiches on the side of his forehead. Then he pulled up his shirt. Deep purple and gray bruises creeped from his ribs to his chest like a stalking animal.

Damns and *sonofabitches* peppered the room.

"I confessed my wrongs and manned up to receive my punishment," Friel continued. "I shouldn't have illegally stocked Butler Lake. But when I did my duty as a citizen and unmasked those who sold me the contaminated fish, this is what it got me. And the ones who did this to me are being shielded from justice by Callahan." Friel paused and then said, "The truth will bring back the right kind of law to our island. So spread the truth to everyone you know, here and on the mainland: The Mannings sold contaminated fish and poisoned our lake, and when I turned them in, they almost killed me, and our sheriff did nothing about either."

The reaction to his exhortation came immediately.

"We know how to take care of this. Don't we boys?"

"Damn right, we do."

"Hell yes."

Friel let the temperature rise and the beer flow.

Chapter 61

GET OUT NOW AND GO WHERE YOU BELONG

Nick and the Manning brothers faced the south wall of the Fish Market studying the words scrawled in fresh red paint on the weathered cinderblock. Nick had driven the snowmobile directly from the station to the Market when Julie received the call from Michael. It had begun to snow heavily as he left the station, and behind Nick and the brothers, the machine's tracks were already covered.

"Found this early this morning when we came to take the boat out fishing," said Michael.

"Any idea who might have done it?" asked Nick.

"Don't think it was anyone originally from the island, else they would've known our family has lived here for four generations. This is where we belong," said Benjamin. He emphasized the last words.

"Anything like this ever happened to you before on the island?" said Nick.

"Nope," said Michael.

"Any speculations on why someone did this?" continued Nick.

"Nope to that either, unless it was Friel. He's the only one we know of who has a beef with us," replied Michael.

Benjamin chuffed and then snarled, "That crazy bastard."

"I don't know," said Nick. "This may smack of something beyond Friel. Something ugly." He noticed the two brothers exchange glances.

Nick removed his gloves and took his cell phone out of his jacket pocket. He took several pictures from various distances and angles. Wet snow had begun to stick to the wall. Then he slipped his phone back into his jacket and got out his pen knife. He opened it and scraped some paint off the wall and spread it on a page of his notebook with the blade. "We need to find out what this is about and end it. In the meantime, let us know right away of anything that is suspicious or worrisome," he said as he put his notebook away.

"Your concern is touching, deputy; but we can handle this ourselves if we need to."

A combative tone infused Benjamin's words, and Nick felt he was being put on notice. He carefully framed his response. "It's a small island. Keeping the peace is important. Let us take care of this, please," he said.

Chapter 62

Edward Chen sat across the desk from Callahan. He was tall and lanky with toffee-colored skin, short-cut raven hair, and piercing, intelligent eyes, but with an engaging smile which prevented him from being intimidating. Even sedentary, he radiated an excited energy. He looked more like a high school senior than the newly appointed editor of the island's newspaper, the *Nicolet Ledger*. At least that's how he appeared to Callahan, who recently admitted to himself that he had entered that stage of his life when all thirty-somethings looked like teenagers.

"So, how are you surviving your first winter on the island?" The question was meant to commiserate rather than inquire, but Chen didn't take it that way.

"I'm doing great. Thought I would dread it, but I don't. Just the opposite. I'm enjoying it. Who knew? I'm from LA originally. Before this assignment, I'd only seen snow but once, and that was when I drove over the Rockies my senior year in college. Now, I've got myself two dogs who love the snow as much as I do, and we spend most of our time outside together. That's them howling from my truck in front of the station."

"Well, when we get an unbroken chain of days like today, it can get even veteran islanders down," said Callahan still singing a sympathetic note.

"Are you kidding? The dogs and I wish we had more great days like this." Chen extended his arm toward Callahan's office window. "Just look."

Callahan did. It was snowing with the wind blowing so strongly that the flakes pinged against the glass. He could only wonder at Chen's enthusiasm for what he considered climatological Armageddon.

"I'm anxious to try out a new pair of snowshoes, so I'll get right to the point of why I wanted to meet with you," said Chen.

"Shoot," said Callahan, smiling.

"Stan Lupinski came by the *Ledger* the other day and informed me that your office is going to establish and run a kids' camp this summer. He thought it a great idea: informative and fun for the kids and something their parents would favor. I called the county board president and he's solidly behind the idea; a bit vague on the funding though. Anyway, I'd like to publish a story about it," said Chen.

Callahan's smile vanished. "Well, I . . ." He hadn't given the idea a second's thought since tossing it to Amanda. In fact, he'd totally forgotten about it. He'd hoped that Lupinski's push for a sheriff's summer camp on the island for his nephew would weaken with time.

He now realized that hope was in vain. Lupinski had just brought in more muscle.

"So, what have you got for me? A calendar? An agenda? A schedule of classes? Equipment needed? Age groups? Field trips? Are lunch or snacks provided? When and how do parents register their kids? Cost?" Chen paused and gazed at Callahan expectantly, his notebook in hand.

"Well, I . . . Umm . . . " Callahan felt himself slipping into that nightmare world where a ghoulish proctor stared down at him from a high desk as he sat alone in a strange classroom to take his final exam in a course he'd never attended. Then he punted with a sudden inspiration. "We plan to model it on the one in Washtenaw County; modified, of course, to fit the uniqueness of our island." He hoped he'd correctly remembered the county Lupinski had mentioned. "We're still working on the details but can get them to you soon."

"Great," said Chen. "I'll do a preliminary article announcing the camp's establishment, get some local perspectives on it, some history and background on sheriff kid camps in other counties, ideas and reactions from children—those sorts of things—and then follow up with the details when you have them. How does that sound?"

"Perfect," said Callahan to Chen. "Shit," he said to himself. Now he would actually have to do the damn thing. The only mental picture he could conjure of the project was the kids' TV show *Bozo's Circus* in Chicago, and he was the clown. He hadn't joined law enforcement for this.

As Chen left the station, Julie appeared at his office door. "You've got a call waiting from the tribal police in Sault Ste. Marie. Better take it. It's Josh, and he says it's important."

*   *   *

Josh's call had been succinct, almost perfunctory, except for the urgency it conveyed. Blackwell was dead: horribly tortured; then murdered. The stripper Blackwell had been seeing and who Josh had interviewed did not show up for work after dropping her three-year-old daughter off at her sister's. She was now missing. Chief Tanner informed the tribe's child welfare people of possible danger to the girl because of her connection to Blackwell and recommended that she stay on the island for now. They had agreed. So far, he had no leads to the source of danger to her, only the prospect.

Chapter 63

Callahan hung up the phone on his office desk. The call from O'Donnell was unpleasant but not unexpected. As an inveterate politician and head of the island's board of commissioners, O'Donnell kept attuned to the slightest vibration of public sentiment on any subject.

Friel and his anti-Callahan delegation of rabid rednecks—O'Donnell's description—had besieged his office demanding that he force Callahan to arrest the Manning brothers for assault and for selling contaminated fish for seeding. Friel bragged that his delegation was just the tip of the iceberg; that many, many more islanders were fed up with Callahan's job performance. The one encouraging aspect to the call was that O'Donnell stressed that he would never interfere in any way with Callahan's performance of his duties. He called only to alert Callahan. Callahan believed him.

Callahan left his office and walked up to Amanda at her desk. "How is your investigation into the creditability of Friel's confession going?" he asked.

Amanda looked up from some papers she had been reading. "Well, it's interesting. First of all, I've found absolutely no evidence to verify the confession. There's no one he confessed to other than us; no witnesses to his seeding the lake; no documents of any kind that he could provide. The Mannings, of course, deny they sold him contaminated fish. Their denial has creditable weight in light of their heavy involvement in managing the health of treaty fishery resources. They're well respected for that. Right now, there's absolutely nothing to show that his confession is anything more than BS. But here's what's interesting: Two summer houses that were for sale on Butler Lake sold this past spring to two related families. One sister and her husband bought one house and another sister and her husband bought the other. The sisters and their husbands love fishing. That's why they purchased those homes on the lake. Several of their friends, who also love fishing, visited the houses over the summer. But here's the clincher. Their residences on the mainland are near lakes that have been found to contain fish contaminated with VHS. Talking to the sisters, they told me how surprised they were that the virus had spread so far. They didn't expect it to be in an island lake like it was in interconnected lakes on the mainland."

"So, you're thinking they or their friends may have brought the virus here by accident?" said Callahan.

214 ~ RUSSELL FEE

"That's a possibility I'm considering. But I need answers to more questions before I can confirm it," said
Amanda.

"Then I guess we don't arrest Friel just yet," said Callahan.

"Not yet. Not until we can find some independent evidence that he actually did it. And that's another thing
I've been thinking about," she said. "What if Friel is accusing the Mannings of beating him up to convince us
that he did seed Butler Lake with fish they sold him?"

"You mean he's trying to prove to us his own guilt,"
said Callahan.

"Exactly. But why?" said Amanda.

*   *   *

Callahan went back to his office and shut the door. He
needed to think through the issue with Friel and didn't
want to be disturbed. He settled into his desk chair,
linked his hands behind his head, and turned toward the
window—his ponder pose.

Amanda's supposition that Friel's claims against the
Mannings were attempts to establish his own guilt,
somehow didn't ring true to him. If Friel wanted to atone
for his harmful conduct, there were better ways of doing
so than seeking to serve time in jail. Self-punishment
in this instance seemed futile. But what if they were
examining the facts from the wrong direction? What
if they had everything backwards? What if Friel's con-

fession was intended to convince others of his charges against the Mannings, not the reverse? Maybe, it was the Mannings he wanted incarcerated; and he was willing to falsely accuse himself and them of crimes to do it. Friel's whipping up of public outrage against them and support for their arrests made this motive more plausible. Still, Callahan wasn't sure if his reasoning was any better than Amanda's, but he decided to run it by her before he left the station.

*   *   *

Amanda had been intrigued by Callahan's take on Friel's confession and his accusations against the Mannings. While her perspective didn't reveal a coherent motive, Callahan's did: Friel wanted to destroy the brothers' reputations by framing them for crimes they didn't commit. His feverish efforts to procure their arrests and to gin up antagonism towards them, pointed in that direction. But why? Especially if it besmirched Friel's own reputation. But did it really? Friel looked more and more like a victim at the hands of the Mannings and a hero for admitting his own wrongdoing and seeking atonement for it. Amanda didn't believe Friel about the Mannings attacking him or about selling him contaminated fish. So, she asked herself, what did he have against them that would explain his conduct?

Chapter 64

Nick got the call to go to the scene. When he arrived, the jittering flash of the ambulance lights flickered around two paramedics who kneeled beside a body, working unhurriedly through the routine protocols for the dead. The Gibney boy and his parents were also there, as well as two other people who stood behind the three of them.

"My boy found him," said the father. "He came running home and brought us here straight away. These are my neighbors." The father jerked his head to the back of him. "I asked them to come with us."

"The snowmobile was on its side, and he was under it, face down," said the boy, looking up at Nick with the search for approval in his eyes. "I only shook his shoulder some to get him to speak to me. But he was limp and all and wouldn't talk. That's when I ran to my parents."

The father stepped beside his son and put his arm around him. "We called the paramedics the second we got here, same time we called the station," he said.

One of the paramedics stood and motioned Nick over to him. Nick excused himself from the Gibneys, asked them to stick around until he could talk to them some more, and walked to the body.

The paramedic stepped away from the body and turned his back to the Gibneys. When Nick reached him, he grasped Nick's arm and pulled him closer. "Good you're here," he said and then dropped his voice to just above a whisper. "That's Daniel Friel. He's dead. This is your job now," he said,

"You think this was a hit and run?" asked Nick, having suspected from the scene that it was an accident.

"I doubt it. But Doctor Remy can tell you more about his death. What we can tell you is that he's been stabbed at least five times. We're pretty sure that's what killed him."

"What's happened here?" said Edward Chen as he aimed his camera at the body. Neither Nick nor the paramedic had heard him approach.

*   *   *

The immediate outcry on social media shocked everyone in the station. The scowls and cold shoulders Callahan, Amanda, Nick, and Julie began receiving also came as a blow. But the vitriol caused the anxiety. The message to them was clear: They were responsible for the death of a prominent islander. They had refused to arrest the ones who had first attempted to kill Friel. Now he was dead, and the Mannings were still walking free. The island needed new law enforcement—pronto.

Chapter 65

Carl Remy finished dictating his notes of Friel's post-mortem, removed his surgical gloves, and removed his cell phone from his back pocket. He scrolled through his contacts until he came to Callahan; then he tapped the green receiver icon and waited for the call to connect.

When Callahan answered, Remy said, "Okay, here's the scoop so far. Friel died of multiple sharp-force entries. In other words, he was stabbed five times in the chest and neck with a sharp instrument. Most likely a knife with a tapered seven-inch narrow blade. The skin opened cleanly when punctured. A blunt or dull instrument would have torn the skin. And all five wounds go deep, each measuring the full seven inches. The blade sliced cleanly into bone so it was very sharp. Judging by the length, sharpness, and narrowness of the blade, I'd say it was a fishing fillet knife. And Friel has no defensive wounds. His hands and arms don't have a single scratch or bruise on them, no skin or hair under his fingernails, etc.

"All this tells me several things. Since Friel was stabbed in the chest and neck, he was facing his assailant. Because there are no defensive wounds, he probably knew his assailant and didn't fear him or her, or he was caught by surprise. Further, Friel's assailant stabbed him with a downward plunge rather than jabbed him with an upward thrust. All the wounds in the upper chest and neck penetrate downward at an angle of about 30 degrees. That indicates that his assailant was tall, at least six feet or more, judging from Friel's height. Probably a man. Also left-handed. All five wounds are clustered on the right side of Friel's chest and neck. Oh, and he'd been dead less than an hour before the Gibney boy discovered him."

Chapter 66

She sensed the change: the subtle rise in tension, the sudden appearance of vigilance disguised as everyday caution, worry cloaked in a forced calmness. She had experienced them all in her home just before the monster came for her parents. It was coming now. Callahan and Julie knew it. It wanted her, but it would take them too. She could never let that happen. She wouldn't let it happen. To save them, she had to leave. To save herself, she had to disappear—again.

*   *   *

The only sound was the soft squeak of her boots on the snow. No other sounds. Just silence below the low, heavy clouds that curtained the stars high above her and made the woods dark and close. She tried not to think about what she was leaving behind. The weight of it would slow her, would weaken her resolve, would make her vulnerable when she most needed her strength and wits to survive. But she had become soft living with Julie and Callahan. She could no longer clear her mind and sharpen her focus at will. In the dark and silence, memories besieged her. Like black flies, they swarmed and bit. The ones of her parents stung the most, then those of Julie, Max, and Callahan. Still she pressed on through the woods.

She didn't notice when the clouds disappeared and the sky opened. She wasn't aware when a new wind split by the trees spiraled around her. She didn't feel the falling temperature begin to hone the air to a razor's edge. It was the sudden cracking and snap of tree limbs that awakened her. Then she noticed the cold, the bitter piercing cold that had seemed, moments before, only a chill that nipped at her face.

*　　*　　*

"Oh my God. She's gone." Julie stood at the door to the girl's bedroom holding on to the frame with one hand to support herself. Her other hand clutched her chest. "Matt, she gone," she yelled.

Max got to the bedroom first. "Where did she go?" he asked.

Callahan came running down the hall from their bedroom, still in his pajamas. "Are you sure?" he said.

"I've looked everywhere. Her boots, jacket, and backpack are not in her closet. It looks like some of her clothes have been taken too. She's left us, Matt."

"Nick's on duty at the station. Amanda is at home. I'm calling both of them to meet me here. We're going to look for her. We'll find her like we did before," said Callahan, trying to be reassuring. But from the look on Julie's face he was failing.

"Matt, they're predicting record lows for the next three days. I've checked. It's minus twelve outside, and the temperature is dropping. She'll freeze to death out there."

* * *

She'd never been so cold. She tried stamping her feet and clapping her hands, but the feeling in them wasn't coming back. She'd long ago lost the feeling in her face. If she kept walking until the sun came up, she would be okay she told herself. Keep moving to keep warm. When day broke the temperature would rise. But the shaking started: shivers at first and then she couldn't control the quaking that overtook her body. If she just kept moving. But she was so tired. Maybe a short rest. Just a short one. She stopped and lay down in the snow. When she did the shuddering of her body ceased. As she lay still, she started to feel warm, almost hot. She covered herself in snow, sweeping it over her. A short sleep was all she needed. She closed her eyes and the world stopped.

She floated in an infinite void soothed by a beautiful song. So beautiful and so familiar. Then she recognized the voice of the singer. It was her mother. And her mother was calling to her. She tried to get up but couldn't. Her body seemed frozen to the ground. Her mother wouldn't find her unless she stood up or called out. She tried to scream but snow filled her mouth and froze her words. Her mother was alive and searching for her. She thought her mother was dead. She had seen her lifeless body. But she must have been wrong. Her mother had lived and was coming for her. She had to call out to her. She must. With all her strength she screamed, screamed for her mother. And then she felt her mother's arms around her, lifting her from the snow, higher and higher.

*   *   *

Edward Chen's cellphone blared the National Weather Service's warning signal for the fourth time since he awoke. Historic low temperatures were predicted for the area, and the service continued to warn everyone to keep inside. Chen stuffed the phone in the upper pocket of his coat. No way was he going to follow that injunction. When the island achieved climatological history, he wanted to experience it firsthand. He had to be out in the weather. The dogs picked up on his excitement and howled to be let outside. As he opened the door, he too let out a howl.

The dogs raced ahead of him on the trail as he followed on his snowmobile. His face was masked, and goggles shielded his eyes. An 800-fill goose down snowsuit, boots with a cold rating down to -60°, and polar-fleece-lined, multiple-insulation-layered gloves completed his protection against weather that could otherwise kill him. The air temperature was minus twenty-two degrees. The windchill index? Unimaginable.

The dogs suddenly leaped from the trail and darted into the trees, braying as they ran. Chen braked, and as the snowmobile clawed to a stop, he dismounted and charged after them, high-stepping and stomping through the snow as best he could. The braying ceased and was replaced by yelping. The dogs had stopped sprinting, and he could see them up ahead worrying over something in the snow.

When he reached the dogs, one of them had the arm of a pink down jacket in its teeth and was pulling at it. The other had shoved its snout into the snow where it had dug. When it lifted its head, Chen saw the face of the girl. From that point on, all he could remember was grabbing the girl's arm, throwing her body over his shoulder, and running, running as fast as he could.

Chapter 67

Callahan, Julie, and Chen all rose from their chairs in the clinic's waiting room as Remy entered. He hadn't gone two steps beyond the door when they clustered around him. They all began to speak at once, creating a jumble of incoherent questions about the girl's health. Remy stepped back and raised his hands for silence.

"She's going to live. She was entering the final stages of hypothermia when you found her, but you got her here in time." Remy nodded to Chen. "She's lucky. We're set up here for severe cold weather trauma. She's getting the works and warming up nicely. She's receiving a warm saline solution intravenously and through catheters in her chest and abdomen. A breathing tube up her nose is warming her airways with humidified oxygen. She's also suffering from frost bite in her feet, hands, and face, but she's not going to lose any digits. It will take time, but she'll be okay." Remy paused and then said, "She's found her voice, Matt. She talking, in whispers and with great difficulty; but she's made one thing perfectly understandable. She wants to talk to you."

*   *   *

"Hi."

The single syllable, uttered barely loud enough to hear, had the impact of a high-swung sledge hammer. The girl's silence had defined her for Callahan. He had not seen her muteness as a debility, but, paradoxically, as a strength. Her ability to communicate and survive well without words had made her seem capable and wise beyond her years. In retrospect, Callahan realized he had been projecting, unconsciously substituting his own interpretations, conjectures, and conclusions for her unspoken ones. But now, hearing the one word in the soft, tremulous voice of a young girl, he saw her as she was: immature, vulnerable, and frightened.

"Tell me your name," he said.

"Emma." She tried to smile but winced at the attempt.

"Emma, I've so many questions for you, but you need to get better first."

Emma shook her head. "No," she whispered. "It's coming for me. It killed my parents, and it will kill you and Julie too."

"What is coming, Emma?"

"The Wendigo. My father took something valuable and hid it, something the Wendigo wants. I know where it's hidden."

"What did you father take?"

"Emma shook her head again and then closed her eyes. "I don't know," she said.

Chapter 68

Like blood coagulating in an open wound, the water scabbed with ice over the bay and closed it off from the lake. The island was now icebound.

The brothers faced each other from either side of the worktable in the fish market.

"We can cross on snowmobiles. The ice goes clear to the mainland and should be thick enough." Michael leaned forward as if to catch Benjamin's answer sooner.

Benjamin chuffed and shook his head. "You don't know that for sure. You could be talking suicide," he said.

"We'll take that risk. Time's run out for us." Michael leaned back and stood straight.

"And if we fall through the ice with the girl, then what?" Benjamin persisted.

A fillet knife lay flat on the table in front of Michael. He spun it and waited as its revolutions slowed and then stopped. "We can't think that way," he said. "We've got to succeed. Like us, they can use the ice to get on and off the island fast. They don't need a boat. This is when they'll come for the girl."

"And Callahan?"

"We deal with him."

"You're talking suicide again."

"No. Not suicide. Survival."

Chapter 69

Delia looked at the tilting pile of papers on her desk and then at the endless stream of emails on her computer screen—and smiled. She was thrilled with the work of hotel management and couldn't get enough of it. She couldn't thank Goodfellow enough for offering her the job and for his patient schooling in every aspect of the business: every aspect but two. He maintained control over purchasing and maintenance, with the promise that eventually she would take over these tasks from him. In the meantime, he handled all matters connected with those sides of the operation. She'd not thought this odd but simply accepted that these areas involved a higher level of understanding and needed someone with richer experience in hotel management. Her time would come.

But something she came across by accident piqued her interest and then stirred a concern in her. An invoice for toilet paper had erroneously reached her. The invoice had to be incorrect. The amount of toilet paper purchased so far exceeded the projected needs of the tribal hotels that she wondered where there was enough space for the rolls to be stored. She'd forwarded the email to Goodfellow with a note expressing her concern for an obvious mistake. She had not heard back from him, so had tried to put it out of her mind. She had almost forgotten about the invoice until she and Josh were together again.

"Missed you," she said.

"Missed you too," said Josh.

Delia gave Josh a quick kiss and then slid into her chair at their table. Emilio's had become their haunt where they met for lunch or coffee whenever their busy schedules permitted, which for each of them wasn't enough.

"How's work going?" asked Josh. He both wanted to know and didn't want to know, but understood how much Delia enjoyed her job and liked telling him about it. He liked seeing her happy.

"Great. I'm still learning so much. And as I've said a hundred times, I love working with all the people there. But there is something you could give me your opinion on."

"What's that?" asked Josh.

Delia recounted the details of her discovery of the toilet paper purchase, her bafflement by the quantity, and Goodfellow's failure to get back to her. She wondered what she should do, if anything.

Josh gave Delia a reassuring smile and then said, "Goodfellow's probably taking care of it and either doesn't see the need to follow up with you or simply got busy and forgot. I wouldn't worry about it. Now, how about planning our weekend?" he added.

*   *   *

As Josh drove back to the police station from his lunch with Delia, he thought through the disingenuousness of his answer to Delia's question about the hotel's supply purchase. If the purchase invoice was evidence of a pattern, then Delia's discovery might be a matter of concern for her. If so, he did not want her pursuing the matter. However, he decided he would inform the task force of what she'd stumbled upon. It had the hint of money laundering, and money laundering hinted of drugs.

Chapter 70

Goodfellow was all smiles when Delia entered his office at the casino. He stood behind his desk and motioned for her to sit in one of the two plush chairs in a decorative corner of his sprawling office. He waited for her get comfortable and then took a seat in the other chair. The smile never left his face as he crossed the room.

"I've got some good news for you, and think it will be good news for me too. But that depends upon you," he said and paused, waiting for a response.

Puzzled, Delia responded with the proverbial quizzical surprise. "Really?" She had expected that Goodfellow's summons involved her discovery of the inflated receipt for the hotel's toiletries.

"Yes," said Goodfellow. "You've made tremendous progress here. You have talent and all the right instincts. You're a natural for the hospitality business."

"Thank you," said Delia, still confused about where this was going.

"No, I should thank you. Talent as well as loyalty are hard to find. And you have both. I'm going to be selfish

234 - RUSSELL FEE

here and trade on them in the hope that you'll accept my offer."

"What offer?" asked Delia.

"The manager of the reservation's first hotel is leaving. I want you to take over his position," said Goodfellow.

"But I . . . I don't . . . It's only been . . . ," stammered Delia.

"I know. I know. You don't think you have enough experience. I expected you to feel that way. But don't worry. I've had experience with the kind of person who makes a first-rate manager, and I'm convinced from what I've seen that's you. Please say yes," said Goodfellow. "I'll triple your salary," he added.

"Thank you," said Delia, stunned.

"Then you accept?"

"Well, yes," said Delia.

"Wonderful." Goodfellow hesitated and then stumbled to begin his next words to her. "Umm, there's one condition though. Just one. How shall I put this? I hope you haven't become too friendly with that policeman," he said.

"What do you mean?" asked Delia taken aback by the sudden switch.

"Please don't misunderstand me. The last thing I would want to do is interfere in someone's private life. But sometimes, in this particular line of work, a person's private affairs can affect the business."

"What are you asking me?" said Delia.

Goodfellow's importuning changed from a fumbling apology to an ultimatum. "Stop seeing that policeman. The two of you together at the hotel, the casino, and around town have made some of our better customers uncomfortable. They'd prefer that our employees are discrete from the authorities. I don't question their reasons, but I have to respect their wishes. Appearances matter."

Chapter 71

Julie's voice crackled over the cruiser's radio. Callahan grabbed the mic and acknowledged the call.

"Matt, the Mannings want to meet with you at their fish market as soon as you can," announced Julie.

"What about?" Callahan responded.

"They wouldn't say, except that's its important and for your ears only. That's all I could get out of them."

"Are they at the market now?"

"They just called from there."

"Fine. I pass there on the way to the clinic. Call them back and tell them I'm on my way now."

"Will do," said Julie, signing off.

*   *   *

Callahan climbed the three steps to the market's narrow porch. As he did, he noticed through the storefront window Benjamin rise from a stool and say something to someone in the room. Callahan knocked on the door. Michael opened it wide and nodded for him to enter.

Callahan stepped into the cramped space separated from the work area by the customer counter. Beyond the counter, the room was empty. "Where's your brother?" he asked.

Michael slipped past Callahan to his left and stopped at the countertop hatch. He turned, reached back, and braced himself against it with his hands. "Benjamin will be along in a minute," he said, and grinned below rigid eyes that flicked once away from Callahan to a spot behind him.

Callahan heard a hollow thud and twisted toward the sound. Benjamin stood, just feet away, with his back to the closed door, blocking Callahan's exit.

Callahan's limbs pulsed as he braced himself, and he instinctively raised his hand to his holstered weapon. The brothers had flanked him and closed him in.

Michael pushed off the counter and leaned into Callahan's face. "Easy, Sheriff. No need for that. When we're done here, I hope you agree. If not . . ."

"What's going on?" said Callahan.

Michael stepped back and opened the countertop hatch. "Come in and have a seat. We'll talk, and you'll hear us out. And when you have, you will not make the mistake of trying to arrest us."

*   *   *

Josh parked his car in the Charlevoix Municipal Airport lot and lugged a stuffed duffle bag through the terminal's gabled entrance. He'd be staying a while on the island, and the bag contained a sufficient assortment of appropriate clothing. Its bulk also included the weight of his body armor. He purchased a ticket and then found a seat to wait out the thick overcast before his plane could fly.

As a boy, Josh had been enthralled by the stories of spirits the surviving elders in his band had recited. Those stories had resonated deep within him and, like lazy seeds, had germinated in his teens and sprouted in his adulthood. They now enriched his life in ways he was beginning to understand.

The *enlightened* considered as superstitious those who believed in the spirits, or manitous, but Josh regarded such dismissiveness as ignorance or a failure of vision. The manitous existed in story, but they were nonetheless real. For they still sustained, nourished, protected, and admonished the Anishinaabeg. The old stories had new meanings for those who listened: lessons and guidance to help navigate through a wondrous but perilous life in a changing world. They also held clues to discerning the spirits and recognizing their presence in the modern world.

The spirit of the cannibalistic and grasping Wendigo was now embodied in voracious CEOs and their corporations that poisoned the air and water, denuded the earth, and subjugated workers to accumulate vast wealth for the few. For them, like the Wendigo, no amount was ever enough. They literally fed on the weak and vulnerable.

Josh believed in the girl's fear of the Wendigo. Callahan had called Tanner and informed him of the girl's near-death experience and of her regaining her speech. Her first words to him had been a warning—a warning about the Wendigo. The spirit of the Wendigo had loomed over Indian country, resulting in death and disappearance. But now it was on the move and headed for the girl and Callahan. The girl knew where something it craved was hidden.

*   *   *

The two brothers sat across the worktable from Callahan, both positioned like Sphinxes: forearms resting forward on the burnished steel, palms flat, heads erect, peering straight ahead at Callahan, their enigmatic expressions masking all emotions. Michael spoke first.

"The girl's mother was our cousin," he said.

"She, her husband, and Emma lived in Canada," interjected Benjamin.

"They lived off the reservation on a remote plot of land in a home the husband built himself. They lived simply at the edge of the wilderness by choice. The husband made a decent living as a surveyor."

Benjamin shook his head. "That's why what he did doesn't make sense."

"A few months ago, our cousin called us," Michael continued.

"She was frightened," interrupted Benjamin.

"She was terrified. Especially for Emma," continued Michael. "Her husband worked for the outfit that built the roads to the new casino. He surveyed the land before construction."

"He confided to our cousin that he had found something, something that the Casino owners would not want made public. He told her he had hidden the evidence of his discovery," said Benjamin.

"Yes, and he planned to blackmail the owners with what he knew," said Michael.

"Our cousin feared for herself and her family and begged us to come and get Emma and take her to safety before her husband confronted the casino owners. She felt Emma would be safe on the island with us," said Benjamin, stepping into Michael's narrative again.

"She pleaded with her husband to back away from his scheme, but he refused," added Michael.

Both brothers paused a moment as if simultaneously taking a breath. In the interval, Callahan felt the dysrhythmic beat of the broken wind against the walls of the market. Then Michael continued with his story.

"When we got to their home it was burning. The whole house was aflame," he said.

"We kicked in a window, and I jumped through it. Our cousin and her husband lay on the floor, dead, but not from the fire," said Benjamin. "I called for Emma and searched for her as best I could, but the heat and smoke became too intense. I had to get out fast."

"The house collapsed a minute later," said Michael.

Callahan waited for the brothers to continue, but neither did. "What did your cousin's husband hide?" asked Callahan.

"She wouldn't tell us," said Benjamin.

"Did she tell you where he hid it?"

"No. She refused," said Michael.

The wind rattled the windows and stirred the air in the room as each man waited for the other to speak. While the silence grew, the brothers' focus on Callahan sharpened like linebackers before a snap: tense, expectant, predatory.

Callahan's body stilled and his gaze steadied on Michael. Then his eyes flicked to Benjamin.

Benjamin shot to his feet, knocking his chair over. As it clattered against the wall, his hand darted behind his back. In a single motion, Michael grabbed his arm, twisted up from his chair, and body-shoved him against the wall. He held him there with his forearm jammed against his neck. "Easy now," he said. "The sheriff here is going to hear us out. Isn't that right, Sheriff?" He withdrew his arm from his brother's neck. Then he reached down, righted his brother's chair, and signaled for him to sit. Benjamin hesitated a moment and then complied, his body coiling down like a spring under slow pressure.

"You want that to happen, then you both place your weapons on the table and slide them to me." Callahan raised his arms from his lap to above the rim of the table. He held his gun in his right hand. It was pointed at Michael.

Benjamin glanced at Michael who lifted his down vest and did a complete turn. "As you can see, Sheriff, I've no weapon," said Michael. "However, my brother may not have taken my advice before meeting with you. If that's so, he'd best take it now."

Benjamin reached behind him and brought his gun up to the table. He pushed the gun to Callahan, touching it only with his fingertips.

"We know what you're thinking," said Michael. "That we took Emma because she can tell us what her father hid so we can collect from the casino. You suspect we kidnapped her and that's why she escaped from us and stayed hidden. You believe if she hadn't gotten free of us, she might not be alive."

"You're batting a thousand," said Callahan. "You didn't take her to a hospital for her burns. You didn't deliver her to the tribal child welfare agency. You didn't report the fire as a possible arson to the police. You didn't come to me about her until now, months after she's been on the island."

"We expected this," said Benjamin.

"It looks bad, we know," said Michael.

"Then why are you telling me this now?" asked Callahan.

Chapter 72

Nick had driven to the airport to pick up Josh, Julie was at the clinic with Emma, and Callahan was on his way to the Fish Market to meet the Manning brothers. So, Amanda was alone at the station when the call from Sheila Doyle came in.

"They came back last night. This is the second time this month. There's never been this much activity from them before. You've got to see." Her voice was low for a woman's and sounded conspiratorial when she spoke, as if she was confiding in you and only you. She was tall with bobbed hair, deliberate in her movements, wore oval glasses, and was articulate and well versed in astronomy and astrophysics which gave her an academic air and imbued her declarations with credence. People believed her, at least initially. However, it didn't take long before most suspected that something was amiss. Because Sheila was an ardent promoter of conspiracy theories about alien landings, complete with a website, blog, and Twitter and Facebook accounts.

"Sheila, I'm alone at the station and can't come out now. I have to stay here," said Amanda, trying to convey an unyielding stance.

"But you have to before the evidence is lost. You've got to see it for yourself. I've taken photos and a video, but I need independent corroboration from someone in authority. This is too important not to have it. Please, you must come now."

Amanda picked up a pencil on her desk and stabbed the word *INSANE* on the notepad beside it. Then she scribbled across the letters until they were illegible. "Okay," she said. "But I have to get someone to relieve me before I can leave the station."

*   *   *

Amanda parked the Charger at the trailhead where Blue Spruce Road ended. The trail wound about a mile through the woods to the island's southwest shore where Sheila Doyle's cabin perched on a bluff facing the lake. She would have to hike the trail to the cabin. Amanda now regretted that Nick and Josh readily agreed to come directly to the station from the airport to spell her before going to Nick's apartment.

Doyle had picked the remote site to be as far away from light as possible in order to observe the full night sky through her numerous telescopes on the deck that surrounded the cabin. Thirty miles from the mainland and twelve miles from the nearest cluster of lights on the island, she could observe the Milky Way. It was the spot on the island where numerous UFO sightings were reported—mostly by her. Fortunately, Doyle's scores of snowmobile runs packed the trail snow tightly, so the trek to the cabin went easily.

When Amanda came out of the woods into the clearing fronting the cabin, Doyle waited for her by her snowmobile. "Get on," she said. "I'm taking you there right away."

Doyle took off, plunging into the woods, dodging tree trunks, diving under low branches, sailing over steep depressions, and careening at a speed Amanda feared guaranteed certain death. When they stopped, it was so sudden that Amanda almost lurched over Doyle. "We're here. C'mon, take a look," Doyle said, dismounting the machine.

Amanda followed Doyle to a spot about twenty-five yards ahead of the snowmobile where Doyle halted and then pirouetted in a three-hundred-and-sixty-degree sweep with her arms outstretched. "Behold," she said.

All around, trees bent outward, as if pushed by a gale-force whirlwind, some smaller ones even knocked to the ground.

"Look closer," said Doyle.

When Amanda did, she saw that the lower branches of most of the trees were singed. Something had burned them. And at her feet, dry earth spread into an almost perfect circle. The snow had melted and gouges pocked the dirt.

Doyle walked up to Amanda. "They landed here last night. I saw the ship's flashing blue lights through the snowfall and heard the throbbing hum of its engine. They've come to the island again. They're among us."

*　　*　　*

Amanda maneuvered the Charger into a 180-degree skidding turn and headed north on Blue Spruce Road. As she drove along the snow-packed surface, she debated with herself on whether she had just witnessed the aftermath of an otherworldly event or evidence of an earthly phenomenon. The answer, of course, depended on who asked the question. She understood that most people saw only what they were prepared to see. The deeper they immersed themselves in a subjective viewpoint, the narrower their perspective. Sheila Doyle's perspective had shrunk to a pinpoint and blinded her to anything outside that narrow focus. To her, what she witnessed in the woods could never be anything other than an alien landing. Amanda hoped that her experience and training allowed her to be objective and open-minded, not accepting or rejecting outright the unorthodox or novel. But she wasn't fool enough to believe that it was anything more than hope. To some things, she too was blind.

With her phone, she had taken almost two dozen photos of the scene and would decide who could provide a professional opinion on what had occurred in the woods near Sheila Doyle's property.

Chapter 73

Callahan's question about why the Manning brothers now shared their story signaled only a slight willingness to listen further, but enough to scatter the tension in the room. The brothers visibly relaxed.

"We found Emma," said Michael. "We'd seen a car heading away from the burning house when we got there. It's a remote rural area, and there's only one road for many miles and few travelers. We decided to head after the car when the house collapsed. We caught up with it and followed far behind with our lights out. Eventually, it turned off the road and into the woods. We followed it on foot until we came to where they'd pulled up next to a hut. We went in. Two men had her. One man escaped us; the other did not. We have blood on our hands."

Michael paused and lowered his eyes from Callahan. His wrists rested on the table; his fingers closed as if holding open the pages of a book. When he spoke again, his words were measured as if the text was difficult to read. "It's blood we had to spill to save Emma and ourselves. But who would believe us if we were discovered as the killers? Who would believe we didn't kidnap her? That's why we haven't come to you before now." Michael raised his head and steadied his eyes on Callahan's. "We didn't kill Friel, but there's the threat that we'll be arrested for his murder. That's what people here are screaming for. That's what we fear you'll do, to appease them. If that happens, we cannot protect Emma. There's no one but us. Us and now you."

"Did you know the men who grabbed Emma?" asked Callahan.

"We didn't know the men then," said Benjamin.

"You now know who they are?" asked Callahan.

"We know the one who escaped us," said Benjamin.

"His name is Case Blackwell," said Michael. "He's dead."

"I know," said Callahan.

The brothers turned to each other with questioning looks and then focused their attention back on Callahan. "It wasn't us. We didn't kill him," said Benjamin.

Callahan slouched back in his chair and twisted his body so that he sat in profile to the brothers. He shook his head and then spoke so softly that the brothers weren't sure if he was addressing them or thinking aloud to himself. "Why should I believe any of this?" he said.

"Because we're admitting to you that we killed a man and jeopardizing our liberty and maybe our lives to protect Emma. We're trusting you, Callahan. We may be fools, but the risk to us is worth it for Emma's sake," said Michael.

"And you need us," said Benjamin.

Callahan lowered his gun from the table and holstered it. Then he shoved Benjamin's gun, sliding it across the table towards him. Callahan watched as Benjamin grabbed it with his right hand. "And why would that be?" he said.

Benjamin answered. "Something has been going on right under your nose that you know nothing about. Something big that involves Emma and now involves you."

"Drugs are run up the lake by freighter from Chicago to where we wait for the shipments in the water three miles off the northwest end of the island. From there we take the shipments to Naubinway and offload them in fish barrels. We don't know the identity of who delivers the drugs, who takes delivery from us in Naubinway, or where the drugs go from there. Our instructions come in encrypted, self-erasing texts. The last shipment we received was huge, worth maybe millions. We kept it and hid it. Not for the money but as leverage to negotiate for Emma's life, ours, and our families." Benjamin paused and then Michael spoke.

"Six months ago, while we were fishing, armed and masked men from a yacht boarded us. The only one who spoke told us that they knew we had the girl. If we kept her silent and delivered the drugs when ordered she could live. If we refused, they would kill her and us. As long as we had her with us and did as we were told, Emma was safe. But then Emma ran away. We're not sure why. When you discovered her, it was only a matter of time before they knew we no longer had her. We couldn't protect her and keep her silent. They would come for her and kill her and us. So, we took the drugs, and then we waited for someone to contact us. It didn't take long."

"We were approached by two men here on the island—foreigners. We were told that if we refused to hand over the drugs immediately, we'd be shown the consequence of our refusal. After that, if we continued to refuse, we'd not be given a second chance," added Benjamin.

"We refused," finished Michael.

Callahan stood, clasped his hands in the small of his back, and arched his spine. The bones in his neck snapped as he lifted his head. "That's one hell of a mess," he said.

"So you believe us," said Benjamin.

Callahan bent over the table, placing his hands flat on its surface. His eyes slid from the face of one brother to the other. "Do I have a choice? I should arrest you and turn you in to the federal authorities. But if I do that, what happens if you're telling the truth?"

"Emma dies. Arresting us doesn't help anything. If we don't tell them where the drugs are hidden, they'll kill her and maybe others they think she told about what her father had taken. They'll kill her anyway to silence her. With us free, we can bring them to you. It's all true, Sheriff. You can turn us in later, but now you have to stop this and put an end to it."

Chapter 74

Carved from rock resisting the grinding retreat of a glacier that dug the great lake in which it floated, the narrow island sat low in the water off the north end of the big island which was Nicolet County. Uninhabited for a century, it sheltered an Odawa and Ojibwe cemetery—a sacred place of the Anishinaabeg. The Manning brothers stood among the pines and hemlocks on a bluff overlooking the bleached wooden remnants of spirit houses that lay crumpled in the burial ground's glacial till. Not far from where they stood, they had buried the barrels containing the drugs. They waited for the emissaries of the drug ring to come to retrieve them.

High above them in the dark, two drones manned by federal agents scanned the island's perimeter and the ice shelves jutting from its shores—searching. A swat team stood by in a ready helicopter on the mainland just minutes from the island. It too waited.

The signal would come from the Mannings' satellite phone when those who wanted the drugs were on the island.

*   *   *

Callahan had placed himself, Amanda, Nick, and Josh to cover all avenues of approach and to allow each to cover the other if fired upon. Callahan and Amanda each carried a Sig Sauer .40 caliber pistol and a Mossberg 590A pump action shotgun. Nick and Josh each carried 9mm. Glocks and AR-15 semi-automatic rifles. Although well-armed, Callahan counted on stealth and cover rather than armament to accomplish their mission.

*   *   *

"They've made contact with the brothers by text, sir. They're on the island."

The joint task force swat commander turned to the drone pilots. "Do you see them?"

"No, sir," they responded in unison.

"Could you have missed them?"

"Not likely, sir," said one of the pilots. "The island's not that big. We can see the whole of it. And the two of us have had eyes on it continuously. No movement by persons or means of transport of any kind—none."

"Agreed, sir," said the other pilot.

The swat commander weighed waiting longer for a possible sighting and risking lives if they didn't get there in time. Then he made his decision. "Something's wrong.

Contact the brothers. Tell them we're coming," he ordered.

*   *   *

Through the phosphorescent green glow of the night vision binoculars, the man watched the light vanish behind the shade of an east window of the house and the ghostly torso of a woman reappeared in the kitchen.

"The girl's in bed in the east room. The woman's fussing about in the kitchen. There's no sign of anyone else in the house," he whispered to the man prone in the snow next to him. He spoke English but with a thick Eastern European accent. He was much older than the man next to him.

"No cars in the driveway or anywhere else on the property," said the man in the snow.

The man with the binoculars rolled over on his back and flashed twice with a pen light into the woods behind him. In moments, two other men emerged from the trees at a crouch and sprawled beside them. Each armed with an M4A1 carbine, the four men huddled in the dark at the edge of the woods circling the open area around the custom log cabin. The light from the cabin's windows illuminated the porch and spread several yards out into the snow, fading before it reached the woods.

"Do we make it quick and charge the door?" whispered one of the men.

"We go one at a time at the intervals I signal," said the man with the binoculars. "We cover the man on the move until he's in place. I want a man on each end of the house and a man behind me when I go through the door. I'll take care of the woman, and the man with me grabs the girl. The other two make sure no one comes. There are no surprises. Understand?"

The men nodded.

"Good," he said and jabbed the man next to him with his elbow. "Now, text the Indians that we're on their island and coming to meet them."

The leader tapped the shoulder of the man to his right and wobbled his hand in the direction of the west side of the house. The man rose and darted into the open area at the front of the cabin. As he ran, his weapon followed the sweep of his head from side to side. The leader then motioned for the man on his left to take his position at the east end of the porch.

When both men had signaled the *all clear,* the leader and the last man with him raised themselves out of the snow and, in single file, approached the cabin's door.

Halfway there, the kitchen window went dark, snatching the light from half the porch. The two men halted and crouched down, scanning the kitchen window for a face, their weapons ready. They heard footsteps beyond the door and then silence. They rose again and climbed the steps to the porch, placing each foot flat with deliberate slowness, dampening the weight of their footfalls on the snow covering the stairs. On the porch, the leader reached for the doorknob and twisted. When it didn't turn, he stepped back, aimed his weapon at the lock and fired.

Metal shards and wood splinters showered the living room, ripping through chair cushions and embedding in walls as the door blasted open. When the leader lunged into the cabin, Amanda rolled from the inside wall, jammed her shot gun into his stomach, and fired.

The man's body bent double and rocketed backwards into the man behind, splattering him with gore and slamming him to the porch floor. The downed man scrambled to his feet and lifted his rifle. Callahan stepped out of the cabin and pumped two rounds through him. As his body backslid down the porch steps, the two outside men began sprinting to the woods, their automatic weapons burning the air with dozens of rounds. Nick and Josh gunned them both down before they reached the trees.

Chapter 75

The bodies of the four men lay in the hospital morgue in Charlevoix awaiting possible identification by the FBI through photographs, fingerprints, and DNA. The Manning brothers faced prosecution for transporting drugs across state lines, the circumstance of their transgression and cooperation with authorities promising to mitigate any sentencing. Julie was on her way back to the island from Charlevoix with Emma and Max where they had been under the protection of Sheriff Markos and his deputies. The cabin's door had been repaired, the furniture replaced, the porch scrubbed. Everything wrapped and tied in a bow. Only, it wasn't.

The men had come for Emma, not the drugs, as Callahan had thought. The value of what she knew was greater to someone than the vast profits to be made from barrels of poison. The *what* and the *who* were still unknown after the attack on Callahan's home and the attempt to snatch Emma. And the question of who killed Blackwell and Friel remained unanswered.

Emma provided the first piece of the puzzle, correctly placed and accurately aligned to slide perfectly into its allotted position. Her father had hidden in plain view what he had stolen, displayed for all to see if they knew where to look. The second piece came from Amanda, but without placement and orientation and from an unlikely source.

*   *   *

Ralph Tanner approached the front desk of the Ojibwe Cultural Center and Library in Sault Ste. Marie and stood before the smiling face of a young woman. Before he could speak, she said, "You must be Chief Tanner. We've been expecting you. Please wait a second while I get Ms. Darrow, our executive director. She wanted me to let her know the minute you arrived." The young woman darted from behind the desk and disappeared through a doorway along the back wall.

As Tanner waited, he casually surveyed his surroundings. He took them in, and the whitewater rush that cascaded through his mind when he was on duty slowed to the trickle of a creek, and the brittle grip on his body released. The earth tones of the room's colors, the glow of recessed lighting, and the muted illumination of the glass display cases swathed the center in a calming radiance. The comfortable arrangement of transportation, clothing, tools, habitats, and pottery displays beckoned him to an unhurried stroll through Ojibwe history in Upper Michigan. Tanner felt ready to accept the invitation when Aubrey Darrow materialized in his vision. For an instant he pictured her as one of the museum's lifelike native figures, until she spoke.

"*Boozhoo.* It's so good to see you, Ralph. When I got the message, you were coming, I wanted to be here myself. What is it we can do for you?" Her voice was soft and as unrushed as the center's atmosphere.

"It's good to see you too, Aubrey. I'm here because you may have something I'm interested in," he said.

"I certainly hope so. Our purpose is to stimulate and satisfy the interests of all who want to learn more about Ojibwe history and culture. I'm glad you finally got around to visiting us. It's your first time, I believe." Her smile blunted the obvious jab, but not by much.

"Well, yes, I know. I should have come sooner, but actually this visit is professional, not personal." Tanner pushed his embarrassment behind a hasty explanation.

"You're not here to arrest anybody are you?" Her smile diminished slightly. "Not me I hope." It brightened again.

"I'm looking for something you may have received recently. It may have been mailed."

"What is it?"

"I'm not sure. It might have come to you anonymously with or without instructions on how it should be handled by the center."

"We're very careful about the artifacts we receive. We make certain they weren't scavenged or pilfered from a sacred site or purchased illegally. If we can't verify their authenticity and provenance, we contact the federal authorities. To my knowledge we haven't received any artifacts within the past several months."

"This may not be an artifact. It could be a picture, or a document, or a recording. I'm sorry to be so vague, but the only information we have is that whatever it is was sent here."

"Hmm. I can check our records to see if we've received something of that sort. I can't recall anything offhand. I can do it now if you have the time to wait. Hopefully, it won't take too long."

"That would be fine. I'd appreciate it."

"Great. Then please look around. Enjoy."

Tanner walked the main room of the center, stopping to inspect the different exhibits until he came to one of particular interest to him. He stared through his reflection in the glass panel of the display case to an unfurled birch bark scroll—the *Wiigwaasabak*—depicting the centuries-old story of his people's migration from the Atlantic coast to the Great Lakes. Entranced, he jumped when Aubrey Darrow tapped him on the shoulder.

"I'm sorry," she said. "I didn't mean to startle you, but I've found something I want you to see. It may or may not be what you're searching for." She held an 8x10 envelope in one hand and a folded document in the other, which she handed to Tanner.

Tanner unfolded the paper and spread it on the glass top of the display case. It revealed what appeared to him to be a satellite photo or aerial relief map. He'd seen something like it before but couldn't remember where. The source and location of the map or photo had been cut away.

"The note which accompanied that is in this envelope." She held up the envelope to Tanner, and he noticed that it had no return address. Then she continued. "It says only that the survey is of historical interest to the Ojibwe and asks us to secure it in our library. We didn't connect its relevance to Ojibwe history, but we catalogued and archived it as geological subject matter because it shows the topography of the area. We've kept it until we get around to researching it."

"Is the note signed?" asked Tanner.

"No."

"Can you copy this for me, and the note too, please?"

"Absolutely. Is it what you were looking for?"

"It just might be," answered Tanner.

Chapter 76

Amanda had sent the pictures of Sheila Doyle's alien landing site to Stan Gibbons, the meteorologist of WPBN-TV in Traverse City, surmising that severe weather rather than Martians created the scene. As she'd hoped, he had analyzed the photos and formed a solid opinion about them. It wasn't quite what she expected when she received his call.

"I figured I'd better call you rather than emailing. Your pictures warrant discussion," he said.

"You mean the jury is still out on this one?" said Amanda.

"Well, not exactly. At first blush, I was tempted to agree with you that weather events caused the evident disturbance. Perhaps *upheaval* would be the better term. I wanted that to be the case because my desire for a meteorological news scoop swamped my scientific objectivity."

"What do you mean?" asked Amanda.

"The bent trees, broken branches, the pattern and area of destruction, the bare earth where there should have been snow, all of it, indicative of a tornado's touch-down. But the conditions that create a tornado are al-most unheard of this late in winter. In fact, they're so rare that there have been only three recorded occur-rences of winter tornados in Upper Michigan in the past forty-five years. And all three were of weak intensity and so brief that they could have gone unnoticed."

"So that eliminates a tornado," said Amanda.

"Pretty much, but not quite," said Gibbons. "When you add the burned branches into the mix, you could be talking lightning. Lightning might have caused the singe-ing of the tree branches. But you'd have to have thun-dersnow for that to happen. Thundersnow is a winter thunderstorm with snow instead of rain. Lightning, of course, causes the thunder in thundersnow. They're rare but more common in the upper Great Lakes than else-where. Not as rare as tornados, but you could live a long time up here and never experience one.

"So, you'd need both a tornado and a thundersnow to create the damage I saw?" asked Amanda.

"Exactly. There is some evidence that a tornado can occur with thundersnow, but the possibility seems as-tronomically small. In any case, I checked the records for the time period you gave me, and there were no thunder-snows in your area."

"So, any ideas on what happened?" asked Amanda, stunned that the answer might actually be an alien land-ing.

"Actually, yes. I showed your pictures to my assistant. Before he studied meteorology, he flew attack helicopters for the army in Afghanistan. In flight training, he practiced hard landings in all types of terrain and weather. He also had to make a couple in combat conditions—one in the mountains in winter. He saw in your photos evidence that something large, heavy, and hot slammed down from above and then lifted off from the ground. Maybe a turbine or jet engine helicopter."

"Holy shit," said Amanda before she could stop herself.

"My sentiment exactly but without the adjective. I was hoping to report on a meteorological event for the record books. Oh well, *c'est la vie*," said Gibbons.

Chapter 77

Delia had agonized over where and how to approach Josh about Goodfellow's ultimatum. She was willing to walk away from the casino and hotel for the sake of their relationship. But what about Josh? His reaction would tell her everything she wanted, but also feared, to hear about their relationship. Would he also want their relationship to continue and deepen, or would he let her take the job on Goodfellow's condition and end their relationship? For better or worse, she had resolved that his response would decide their future. After LA, she'd sworn she would never relinquish control of her life to anyone, especially a man. Yet now, one man was forcing her to allow another man to make a fateful decision for her. She'd been sick to her stomach and unable to sleep for days.

*   *   *

Josh took another bite of his Reuben sandwich and watched as Delia pushed the greens around the plate of her seared tuna salad with her fork. She'd eaten nothing since they'd been served, and he was almost finished with his lunch. Their talk had essentially been about nothing.

"Not hungry or is something troubling you?" he finally asked.

Delia lifted her head and looked so long at him without speaking that he began to feel uncomfortable.

"There's something I have to tell you," she finally said.

"This sound ominous. Should I stop eating?" he joked.

"Please. Just listen. I've been offered a promotion," said Delia.

"Wow, that's great," said Josh. "For a minute, I thought this actually was going to be ominous."

"Hear me out. Goodfellow offered me the manager's position at the reservation's first hotel. It comes with triple my current salary," said Delia.

"Congratulations," said Josh. "That was fast."

"Goodfellow praised my talent and instincts. He was very complimentary. He said I'm ready for the job," said Delia. "But then he dropped a bombshell. The job also comes with a condition."

"What's the condition?" asked Josh.

"I have to stop seeing you."

"What?"

"We can't see each other anymore."

Josh put down his sandwich and leaned back in the booth. "Am I hearing this right?" he asked. "Are you saying we're finished?"

"No. No. I'm not saying that. I'm not," said Delia beginning to panic.

"Then what are you saying?"

"I'm just telling you the condition Goodfellow placed on my accepting the promotion. And I'm asking should I take it? Do you want me to take the job?" she almost shouted.

Josh retreated to silence, and Delia knew she had blown it. It had all come out wrong and spun out of her control. She had no idea how to fix it now. She waited for Josh to speak, afraid to say anything more.

Josh broke the silence with, "Did Goodfellow give a reason for that condition?"

"Yes. He said certain customers of the casino and hotel were uncomfortable with my being seen with you."

Josh thought for a moment and then said, "He's grooming you."

"What do you mean?" asked Delia.

"I should have warned you when you first told me about that receipt you found. I thought then that you tripped over what may have been evidence of money laundering at the hotel," said Josh.

"You're kidding," Delia responded with genuine surprise.

"I don't think I'm wrong," said Josh. "What Goodfellow's doing convinces me. He's pulling you in with enticements and praise; establishing an indebtedness to him and demanding loyalty. He'll then anchor you to the job with a higher and higher salary and trusted responsibilities before he initiates you into the scheme. By then, you won't be able to leave."

Delia shook her head. "I didn't see this at all," she said. "I wasn't the least bit suspicious, at least not until his demand about us."

"I'm warning you not to take the job, but it's your decision," said Josh.

"Is my welfare the only reason you're warning me?" asked Delia.

Josh reached across the table and took both her hands in his. "No. I'm looking out for mine too. You must know how I feel. I don't want us to end," he said.

Chapter 78

Tanner turned the squad car into the lot behind the two-story gabled building of Block and Rutledge Surveyors and parked in the space with *Customer* hand-painted on a post. A weathered flight of stairs led up to a second story entrance, but Tanner decided to walk around to the street entrance. He trudged through the murky slush of an alley to the sidewalk, where, to his relief, someone had shoveled the snow. When he opened the door, a bell chimed; and a short, squat man in jeans and a down vest that covered a faded, short-sleeved t-shirt stood up from a polished wooden table stretching across the back of the room. He had the hairiest arms Tanner had ever seen.

The man waved Tanner in. To get to the table, Tanner had to edge his way between several desks fixed with architect lamps and piled high with papers surrounding large computer monitors.

The man extended his hand in greeting, and, as Tanner took it, the man said, "Sorry, we're kind of cramped here for space. But you came at a good time. Could have been even more crowded, but everyone's out in the field except me. Have a seat. By the way, I'm Sal Rutledge. I own the place. You must be Chief Tanner. The uniform gave you away." Rutledge spoke in the halting cadence of someone about to tell the punchline of a joke. His smile even anticipated the laugh.

Tanner smiled back. "Always does," he said. "But please, call me Ralph."

"Sure thing. What can I help you with, Ralph? You said on the phone something about an aerial or satellite photo of some land?"

"Yes." Tanner reached into a large envelope and took out the survey. He handed it to Rutledge. "I'd like you to take a look at this to identify the area it includes, if you can, and also tell me if you notice something unusual about it, or anything else you think is noteworthy. I'm sorry to be so vague, but we believe this may be important in one of our investigations, but we're not sure why yet."

Rutledge spread the survey out on the table and began examining it. In a few moments, he looked up at Tanner. "This is an aerial survey or aerophotogammetry. This type of survey is typically used in construction and development projects. The area projected here is local and rendered as a 3D model. Nothing unusual about that. And there's nothing remarkable about the landscape except maybe this," he said. He pointed to a spot on the survey and made a circle with his index finger. "Do you see here what appear to be three elevated areas of the landscape? They're very faint but visible."

So far so good, Tanner thought. This guy wasn't trying to overwhelm him with his expertise but simply attempting to make himself clear and understandable. Tanner nodded as he looked down the thick matt of hair on Rutledge's arm to the tip of his finger.

"Well, they shouldn't be there," continued Rutledge. "They don't fit with the surrounding terrain. They're also the same size and shape and are parallel to each other. That suggests they're earthworks of some sort. There are no other fabricated objects or features in this survey."

"They're pretty large. Could they be waste dumps or landfills? It looks like the earth was recently dug up and then filled in," said Tanner, peering closer to the survey.

"I don't think so," said Rutledge. "If you were standing on the ground near them, you probably wouldn't notice them. They appear raised in this aerial survey because of the photo imaging and software used to make a 3D rendering, even of elevations undetectable at or near surface level. Whatever they are, they're old. Probably very old. Time has covered them. But they've been covered over by something else since this survey was done."

"What?" asked Tanner.

"The road to the new casino runs right through them," said Rutledge.

Chapter 79

A gift. Forty-five degrees. Mid-February and a tease to winter's end. The warmth a yeast, converting the winter's languor to excited energy. Before the sun was fully up, people were out in shorts and sweatshirts celebrating their good fortune. The heartier ones wore flip flops, if only on the shoveled walks of Main Street.

Callahan decided to begin the day by walking Main Street around the bay from the Catholic church to the lighthouse and back. He needed the exercise, but that need had not driven his decision; another had. Father Martin Boucher had answered his early morning call and waited for him in the Church parking lot. A French-Canadian Franciscan priest, Boucher had been sent to the island by his order as a young man to temporarily fill in for a retiring pastor. Now pushing sixty, he had been on the island so long that he was convinced that his order had forgotten him. An oversight that the islanders were more than happy about, especially Callahan. Boucher had become his close friend and confidant.

"Ah, such a day. It reminds us that the soul is immortal, *oui*?" Boucher hailed in greeting.

Callahan granted him a glance but not a reply.

"If we but have faith, we are restored to life, *non*?" Boucher tried again.

A young man approached them in a sweatshirt emblazoned with 906 and gave them a thumbs up as he passed. They each raised an open hand in return salute.

"I need your advice," said Callahan.

"*Certainement*," said Boucher.

"It's the girl. The one who's living with Julie, Max, and me—Emma."

"The Indian girl," said Boucher.

"Yes. She can't stay."

"Is this about the islanders linking her with your not arresting the Manning brothers?"

"No. I'm not making myself clear. I mean, she can't be with us forever."

"Of course not," said Boucher.

"But it's what Julie wants—for her to be with us forever. Julie sees her as a daughter. Max thinks of her as his sister. Hell, when I give the dog a command, he now looks at her for permission before he obeys. It can't happen. She should be placed with an Indian family. But Julie refuses to listen to any talk of Emma leaving us."

"Ah, I see. And Emma? How does she feel?" asked Boucher.

"She's a child. She has no say in the matter."

"But she has feelings, *non*?"

"We haven't asked her. As I said, Julie has locked the lid down on this issue. No discussion—period."

"And what do you desire?"

"My desire can't be considered. She must be placed with an Indian family. And she should be, regardless of how any of us feel now."

"So, you're telling me that your heart should be captive to your logic."

"No, I'm saying that it's her tribe's policy in placing a child with a family for adoption or foster care to give first priority to an Indian family and members of the tribe. That's in keeping with the Indian Child Welfare Act and her tribe's Child Welfare Code. And that is how it must be. She has to keep in touch with her culture."

"Ah, *préférence*."

"Preference?"

"Oui, préférence. You say *priorité*, but I hear *préférence*. It is the preference of her tribe to place her with an Indian family, *bien sûr*. Other choices might not be preferred but are made necessary. *Non*?" said Boucher.

"The tribe's code does permit placement with a non-Indian family in some circumstances, but, as you say, it is not preferred. I'm sure there are many willing families in the tribe that would take priority over Julie and me. In case you have forgotten, we're not married. So, Julie's fear of losing Emma is real," said Callahan.

Boucher responded with an *Oh* and then slowed his pace to a stroll. Callahan followed, and they walked that way in silence until they reached the marina where

Boucher stopped. The docks were empty except for the ever-present gulls. A couple without gloves or knit hats sat on the bench at the marina's entrance having coffee. Boucher turned to face Callahan. "Perhaps Julie's fear of losing Emma is not her only fear," he said.

"What are you getting at?" said Callahan, slowly stretching out the question.

"Do you not think Julie has learned of the tribe's policy? Of course she has. She knows that being married improves her chances of keeping Emma. And she is smart. She also understands that while it would not guarantee keeping Emma, it would be a promise of keeping you."

"We're living together, and things are fine between us. What are you talking about?" said Callahan.

"She has been abandoned once when her husband left her after Max was born. You cannot be like the big bird that sticks its head in the sand," said Boucher.

"An ostrich."

"*Oui*, an ostrich. She needs your commitment, Matt. Lift your head out of the beach."

"But she hasn't said anything about . . . She hasn't asked me to . . . " Callahan couldn't say the word.

"Now you're being like the monkeys. Your hands are all over your face."

Callahan frowned. "You mean *see no evil, hear no evil, speak no evil?*"

"Those are the ones. You are blind and deaf. Julie is afraid of hearing the word *No*. She is afraid of pushing you away. She does not want to be abandoned again."

"This is more than I bargained for," said Callahan.

"What did you expect of me when you called?"

"I don't know, maybe just to bend your ear."

Boucher reached up and touched the side of his head.

"It's an expression," said Callahan. "It means to—"

"I know," said Boucher. "You had need of me to lend you my ears."

"Yes. I guess I did," said Callahan.

Chapter 80

Tanner leaned against the tractor and watched as slices of earth were lifted from the pit and then fingered apart as they were deposited on its rim.

He had assembled a team of three, not including himself: Josh and two experts from Northern Michigan University's forensic anthropology research department, Ashley Denton and Pierce Malloy. An archaeologist, Dr. Denton specialized in the archaeology of the ancient Americas. As a taphonomologist, Dr. Malloy studied the effects of extreme climate and harsh environment on human remains, especially the fossilization of bones. Both were young and fit and used to the vigorous field work their disciplines demanded. Both had jumped at the opportunity Tanner had presented to them. He had a hunch about the earthworks seen in the aerial photo, and the two scientists would either confirm or disprove his suspicion.

The four huddled together in a field fifty yards from the shoulder of the road that led to the casino and waited as the tractor's backhoe broke through the frozen topsoil and dug down to the softer earth below. Then Josh, Denton, and Malloy began taking turns digging with shovels and sifting through the removed soil. The first bones and object fragments appeared before they were shoulder deep. A foot further down, when Denton's blade lifted the skull from the dirt, they stopped.

Denton climbed out of the pit and handed her shovel to Tanner. She brushed the dirt off her jeans and then said, "For verification, we'll check the age of the bones and dig later for more artifacts that may be found here. But right now, it's pretty clear that this is an Indian burial mound or what's left of it."

"The university will notify the tribe of what we've found and hand over these bones and artifacts to it," added Malloy. Then he looked at the road and shook his head. "There's no way those bastards didn't know what they were plowing through," he said.

Chapter 81

Callahan drove to the far northeast end of the island and stopped where he could see the full sweep of the point that curled like a scythe into the lake. He'd heard that two bald eagles had been sighted there, and he hoped to get at least a glimpse of the magnificent birds. On his last visit to this spit of land in September, he had witnessed the spectacle of hundreds of gulls roiling the water with slashing dives on migrating bait fish. Their piercing screeches rang in his ears for hours. Now the point was swaddled in a peace only winter brought. It was what he craved.

As Callahan adjusted the focus of his binoculars, two huge birds rose in unison from behind the trees and soared over the point, not once moving their out-stretched wings. As they began to circle over a pool in the ice, the ringtone of his cell phone sliced into the quiet, and the caller ID flashed *Peter Dempsey*. Callahan muttered an expletive, but reached for his phone in its mount on the dashboard. This call had to be taken. Gratitude and friendship demanded it. As head of the FBI's

Detroit Office, Dempsey had become not only a valued colleague but a close friend—a friend who had risked professional suicide to save Callahan's life.

"You've pissed off some very mean people," said Dempsey when Callahan connected the call.

Callahan didn't have to guess where Dempsey was heading. "You identified the four dead," he said.

"Well, three of them," said Dempsey. "They're from Chicago's Bulgarian mafia. It's not a big outfit, but growing, mainly by eliminating the competition. The older guy was its primo assassin. You blew away a notorious hitman, Matt. The Bulgarians are not pleased."

"They were coming for Emma. Why?" asked Callahan.

Callahan could feel Dempsey's shrug in the brief silence before he said, "Our Chicago office knew the Bulgarians ran drugs through Chicago, but didn't know where the drugs were destined for. Now we know they funneled them into Michigan. We also know how. But why they were after the girl and not the buried drugs is a puzzle."

"So, what now?" said Callahan.

"Do you believe the two brothers didn't know who they were drug mules for?" asked Dempsey.

Callahan surprised himself with an immediate answer. "Yes. Yes, I do," he said.

"Then we double down on the Safe Trails Task Force's efforts to find who's taking delivery of the drugs at the Indian casino and from whom. That could be our link to the Bulgarians—maybe," said Dempsey. He paused and then added, "One more thing, Matt. Keep a head's up. These Bulgarians don't forgive or forget. You might say it's their business model, and they want that message broadcast loud and clear. My guess is they're not done with the girl, you, or the Manning brothers. They've a score to settle. Understand me. If they get the girl, they've sent their message to you and the brothers. Be careful."

*　　*　　*

The eagles had disappeared when Callahan replaced the phone in its mount. He picked up the binoculars from the seat and slung them around his neck before shouldering open the door and sliding out of the cruiser. He walked from the road, high stepping through the snow over a ripple of low dunes until he reached the narrow beach that edged the point. From there, he began to make his way along the sand-dusted ice, his arms grabbing for invisible braces when his boots slipped on the glaze. Twice, he almost fell. The grueling march over the ice and the sporadic wrenching of his muscles in an effort to keep his balance exhausted him, and he stopped halfway to the tip of the point to rest. He stared out over the frozen surface of the lake that stretched solid to where the ice undulated with the rolling waves beneath it, and then beyond, to the huge chunks that floated like icebergs in the open water. The view and the effort to reach the point made him feel at once

282 - RUSSELL FEE

both in awe of and defeated by the island. As he caught his breath, he thought how these conflicting emotions somehow mirrored the current stage of his life. He was awed by the blessings the island had given him in Julie and Max, and a job with purpose. But he felt beaten down by the threat that purpose brought to those closest to him. He understood now that he couldn't stop the malevolence that invaded his life from spreading to them. His recent conversation with Boucher had been troubling but also eye-opening. Not committing fully to his and Julie's relationship was being unfair to her and selfish. But that commitment had to come with a pledge to everyone's security: hers, his, Max's and Emma's. To make that pledge, he could no longer be sheriff.

Chapter 82

It hadn't been much to work with: tall, left-handed, smelled of fish (if the same person who beat up Friel was the one who later killed him). The killer was likely a man. The Gibney boy, when interviewed, had told Nick that he had heard two men arguing before he discovered Friel's body. Almost everybody on the island fished year-round, but only four men worked enough with fish to capture their smell: the two Manning brothers, Stan Lupinski (perhaps), and George Cannon. Of the four, Cannon was the only southpaw. And he was tall, well over six feet. He also left the island in winter for weeks at a time to cut and package fish from the Atlantic and Pacific coasts, the Great Lakes, Chile, and Europe at Inland Seas Wholesale Fish Distributors in Detroit. It was a long shot, but Nick wanted to follow through and interview Cannon anyway. For all he knew, Cannon was off the island when Friel was murdered. It was more than likely, but he needed to check it out.

Cannon was in Detroit when Nick called the Cannon home, but his wife, Edna, said she wanted to speak with

Nick right away, and in person. She wouldn't tell him what about over the phone.

Edna had made coffee, and she and Nick sat at her dining room table with two matching mugs. She wore jeans and a loose-fitting sweatshirt so long in the arms that it hid her fingers when she held her mug to take a sip. She kept the mug at her lips for a few seconds as she looked at Nick. Then she lowered the mug, and said, "I've been prepared for this. I expected you might come—the sheriff, I mean."

"You've been expecting us?" said Nick, confused.

"Yes. I'm ready to talk. I'm scared, but I can't live like this anymore. I need you to protect me," she said.

"Protect you? From whom?" said Nick.

"My husband, of course. Who else?" Edna looked down and pinched the front of her sweatshirt, tugging it away from her chest. Then she brushed it once with a flick of her fingers.

"Has he threatened you?" asked Nick.

"Yes. The beatings aren't—weren't—enough for him."

"Oh, that's awful," said Nick, not sure of what else to say. Then he added, "You need a restraining order."

Edna smiled. "No," she said, "you need to arrest him. He murdered Daniel."

"Daniel? You mean Daniel Friel?" said Nick, stunned.

"Yes. Daniel and I were having an affair. George suspected. He beat me and then beat up Daniel. That didn't stop us. I told George I was leaving him for Daniel. That's when he beat me again and then murdered Daniel." Her lips tightened and she raised her head, tilting it back until her chin pointed up. "I'm done being scared of him," she said.

"You're sure he killed Friel?" said Nick.

"He told me he did and that if I ever left him, he would come after me and kill me too. And I have proof he killed Daniel. You have to protect me from him, please."

Chapter 83

Nick called Callahan from the Charger before he left the Cannon house and drove to meet him at the Adult Day-care Center, where Callahan was dropping Max off for his shift there working as an aide. Callahan was waiting for Nick in the lobby when he arrived. Nick pointed to two chairs at a small table in the corner of the room away from the receptionist's desk, and they both sat down.

"So, what have you got for me? It sounded important," said Callahan.

"It definitely is," said Nick. "I did some research, digging around really, on tall, male, left-handed islanders, whose jobs involved fish. Sounds crazy and like a long shot, I know; but it led me to George Cannon—Mrs. Cannon, actually. I just finished interviewing her. And guess what? Cannon is violent, a wife beater. He discovered that Friel and his wife were having an affair, and he beat up Friel to stop it. The affair didn't end, and the night Friel was murdered, Mrs. Cannon told Cannon she was leaving him. He beat her and left the house. When he returned, he had blood on his gloves and the left sleeve of his coat.

"The Gibney boy discovered Friel's body at almost the same time Cannon got home. Cannon burned the gloves and coat in their wood burning stove that evening. Mrs. Cannon watched him do it. She said that he wore that coat loading and unloading fish from the trucks where he worked. There were tiny flecks of blood on the collar of Cannon's shirt that he didn't notice. Mrs. Cannon discovered them and hid the shirt. I bagged and tagged it as evidence. But here's the clincher: Cannon admitted killing Friel and threatened his wife with the same if she ever left him. All this may sound like a wife trying to rid herself of an abusive husband, but if that's Friel's blood, then bingo, we have proof of his murderer."

As Callahan was about to speak, Max entered the lobby at the side of a woman pushing a wheeled walker. He gently kept his hand below her upper arm as she shuffled behind the walker, gripping the handles with fierce concentration to keep her balance. Halfway across the room, Max smiled and waved to them.

Callahan and Nick waved back, and when Max and the woman had finally passed through the lobby, Callahan said to Nick, "That's remarkable. Excellent work. Incredible instincts. You may have solved your first murder. We'll have a DNA analysis done on the blood. For now, I want you and Amanda to go back to Mrs. Cannon tomorrow and question her again to see if her answers are consistent and to have Amanda as a witness. In the meantime, I'll find out when Cannon is due back on the island. Pending the result of the DNA analysis, we'll arrest him for assaulting his wife when he lands at the airport. If the blood is Friel's, we'll also charge him with murder. Again, good work."

Nick nodded and then said, "Thanks, but there's still something that bothers me about Friel. Why did he accuse the Mannings of beating him up? He must have known it was Cannon. Cannon would've made sure Friel knew to stay away from his wife. So, why did Friel want the Mannings to take the rap for the beating?"

*   *   *

As Callahan drove to the station, he marveled at Nick's exponential growth as a deputy. He acknowledged that he was grateful for it for two reasons: First, Cannon's indictment would exonerate the Mannings and squelch the public uproar over his refusal to arrest them for Friel's murder. And second, he could leave his office in capable hands with Amanda and Nick.

Chapter 84

Tanner was not surprised by the upheaval that swept through Indian country like a tsunami, nor was he filled with sympathy for the person about to be swallowed by the onrushing wave. Sacred land had been deliberately defiled. Goodfellow had turned his back on his own people in an act of unimaginable perfidy and greed. He had closed his eyes to the desecration of their ancestors' spiritual resting place and had allowed their bones to be scattered and crushed.

Tanner was now convinced that Goodfellow had been the person blackmailed by the girl's father and therefore was connected to the woman and her husband's murder. The girl's mother had told her cousins, the Manning brothers, about her fear for her family because of her husband's plan to blackmail the casino with what he had discovered. Tanner had uncovered the husband's discovery of the burial mounds and the means by which he carried out his scheme. But was any of this sufficient evidence against Goodfellow? The brothers were confessed drug runners and their story hearsay—their creditability diminished by their criminality, and the source of their evidence dead. Plus, Tanner had nothing to directly connect Goodfellow to the blackmail other than as general contractor for the construction and manager of the tribe's gaming facilities. He would be the one to approach. Not enough to hang his hat on, thought Tanner. The girl, Emma, could now speak. But what might her trauma still prevent her from telling them?

As the denunciations magnified, Tanner watched in disgust as Goodfellow writhed and whipped like a pinned snake. At first, he hid behind denials and finger pointing, but as the news agencies dug deeper, the backpedaling began: the road crews hadn't known what they were digging up; the crews had known but didn't inform the subcontractors; the crews had informed the subcontractors who had not informed the contractor; and, finally, the contractor had known but had not informed Goodfellow.

Tanner's disgust verged on pity when Goodfellow steadfastly portrayed himself as the epitome of innocence even as he squirmed against the onslaught of condemnations. He had become a pariah and a prisoner in his own home, unable to leave because of the angry crowds that surrounded it. But then the tribal governing body had ordered the offending road closed, blocking travel to and from the new casino and hotel. Cash flow slowed to a trickle. That's when Goodfellow's calls to Tanner had begun. Tanner refused to return any of them, letting him flail—until now.

"I know you've been avoiding me, like everyone else," said Goodfellow when Tanner answered his call. His voice was hollow, drained of its veneer of cockiness.

"There's nothing I can do for you, Sam," said Tanner.

"You can get these maniacs away from my house," said Goodfellow.

"From what I'm told by my officers, they've done no damage to your property, they've kept their distance from your house, and there have been no rowdiness or physical threats," responded Tanner.

"They're here twenty-four hours a day. They're disturbing my peace. I can't sleep or even leave the house," said Goodfellow.

"They're peaceably assembling in protest," said Tanner. "Like I said, there's nothing I can do."

"Bullshit. And what about that roadblock?"

"What about it?" said Tanner.

"You can order it stopped," said Goodfellow.

"Not my call. You have to take that up with the tribal directors," said Tanner.

"Don't be a fool, Ralph. The money from the casino and hotel pays your and your force's salaries. You could convince the directors to open the road. They respect you. They listen to you."

"I have a busy day. This call's over."

"No, wait," said Goodfellow. "I want to make this right. I can make it right. But the casino has to stay open. Otherwise, I'm a dead man."

"What are you talking about?" asked Tanner.

"Meet with me and I'll tell you," said Goodfellow.

Chapter 85

Goodfellow insisted that he and Tanner meet in private, just the two of them. The police station and his home were out of the question. Tanner suggested that they meet at a small campground two miles north of the casino. The grounds would be empty of campers and they could park at one of the interior sites. Tanner arrived fifteen minutes before their agreed upon time of six, and it was now almost seven. He suspected that Goodfellow was having difficulty leaving his home undetected and decided to give him another fifteen minutes of wait time before leaving. Five minutes into the wait his phone rang.

"Chief," said Josh, "it's Goodfellow. He's dead. His car was found nosed into a snow bank. Sir, the accident didn't kill him. His body was mutilated; his chest torn open and his heart missing."

Chapter 86

O'Malley's would have to do. The island didn't offer a Michelin three-star in the offseason (or at any other time), but the burgers and pizza at O'Malley's surpassed excellent: and Callahan had asked the bartender to hold a table at the fireplace for him and Julie. He'd ordered flowers from a florist on the mainland to be delivered by air to O'Malley's and arranged on their table, and had instructed the bartender not to come to their table until he signaled to him that they were ready. That took care of cuisine, atmosphere, and the necessary privacy. The rest was up to him, and he feared he wasn't up to the task—romance being the tricky ingredient in the recipe.

"This is really lovely, Matt. But what's going on?" said Julie.

Callahan reached across the table and took Julie's hands in his. "First, let's turn off our phones. I have something important to say, and I can't be interrupted."

"That sounds ominous. I'm not about to get dumped, am I?" Julie chuckled and then got serious. "Am I?"

"No. No. How could you even think that? I mean . . . What I want to—"

"But what about the kids at home? What if they have to call us?" Julie interrupted.

"Max knows to call Amanda if he can't reach either of us, and our phones will only be off for a few minutes." This wasn't the start Callahan had pictured. "They'll be okay. Please."

Julie put her phone on the table and turned it off. "Okay, now you," she said.

Callahan did the same and then took a deep breath. "Our relationship is important to me—very important."

"I know that, Matt," said Julie. "It's important to me too."

"And that's the point," said Callahan, relieved. "Something so important to us both has to be nurtured, protected, even celebrated. I realize that now. It can't be taken for granted. It has to be preserved. What I mean is..." He took another deep breath.

Julie looked around her and took it all in: the flowers, the fire, the silent phones, Matt's nervousness. "Matt, are you proposing?" she said.

Callahan hesitated and then said, "Yes."

"Well then, my answer is yes."

"I love you," said Callahan. "Can we order drinks now?"

Chapter 87

A sentinel. A watcher. A herald. An emissary. She was all of these. Sheila Doyle unfolded the thick wool blanket and draped it over her lap. It and the down parka and gloves she wore would keep her warm for the next few hours in the chair as she kept vigil, bent over the eyepiece of the telescope on her deck. She'd trained her scope on the Pleiades, the Seven Sisters, the star cluster of their origin. They would come again and soon, out of the heavens in the night sky. She only need be patient, alert, and ready. It was just a matter of time and opportunity before she was believed.

As she observed the cluster, the southernmost star detached itself and grew larger and brighter as it descended in a slow swoop towards her. This was it. They were on their way, and she knew where they would land. She would be there waiting for them. But Amanda must be there too as a witness. She stood up, the blanket falling to her feet, and rummaged through the deep pocket of her parka for her phone.

*   *   *

Amanda and Nick were comfortably paired on her couch, stocking feet resting on her coffee table, and halfway through a Netflix Original and a bottle of red wine when Amanda's phone lit up and the ringtone sounded. She glanced at the screen. "It's Sheila Doyle," she said to Nick. "Should I answer it?"

Nick reached for the remote on the table and paused the show. "Go ahead," he said. "It might be important." But his look said *Yeah, right.*

"They've come back. I knew they would. They'll be landing soon. You must be here with me," said Sheila Doyle when Amanda answered the call.

"Who?" said Amanda. "Who has come back?"

"The aliens, the extraterrestrials. You've got to be here with me when they land. Someone has to greet them."

"Sheila, what are you talking about?" said Amanda still confused.

"Their ship is just above the lake, flying toward the island. I can see its lights, just like last time. They're heading for the place we saw together. The one I showed you."

Amanda turned to Nick. "Oh my God. I know what's happening. Get your gun. We're leaving now." Then she spoke back into the phone. "No, Sheila. It's not what you think. They're not who you believe they are. They're men coming to the island in a helicopter, and they're dangerous. Stay at your cabin. Don't go to them." Amanda was shouting now.

"You're wrong. So very wrong. I'm going. I have to be there when they land," said Doyle. Then the call went dead.

*   *   *

Amanda wrenched the cruiser off the paved coast road and onto the iced gravel of the road that led to Doyle's cabin. The cruiser fishtailed and then skidded as she tried to maintain speed. "Call them again, both of them. One of them has to answer," she barked to Nick.

"I keep dialing but only get their voice mails. You've heard me, I've left several messages."

"Well, keep trying."

"I am. I am."

"We've got to get through to them. We've got to."

*   *   *

Doyle crouched and covered her head, shielding herself from the roar and blast from above her. A blinding light seared the ground around her and then vanished along with the noise and confusion. She stood and peered into the sudden darkness as she listened. "I'm here," she said. "I'm here for you. Don't be afraid." She sensed more than saw movement to her left and then heard the crunch and rustling of steps. "Stay. Don't leave. Please," she called. "I've been waiting for you."

*   *   *

"This is it," whispered Amanda. "This is the place she showed me; where she thought a spaceship had landed." She and Nick had their guns drawn, and Nick swept his flashlight around the perimeter of the clearing. He stopped when the beam framed the worn souls of two small boots, heels touching, forming a V balanced in the snow at the far edge.

"Oh, God, no," said Amanda, and they both rushed to the spot.

Shelia Doyle lay on her back, her head resting below a crimson halo in the white of the snow, a small red hole in the center of her forehead.

Chapter 88

Max turned the puzzle piece first one way then the other before he picked it up from the kitchen table. "I know where this one goes," he said, holding it in front of his face.

"Where?" said Emma.

"Right here," he said and placed it over an open space, pushing down with his thumb until it snapped together in a perfect fit with the surrounding pieces. "See?" he cheered.

Two paws appeared at the edge of the kitchen table followed by an inquiring snout. Emma reached for a chip from the bowl on the table and gave it to the dog.

"You're too good at this," she said, smiling.

"I like puzzles," said Max.

"Me too," said Emma and reached for a puzzle piece from the scatter on the table. As she scanned their completed portion of the puzzle, the dog began pawing at her lap. "Here," she said, offering him another chip. But the dog refused and ran to Max, pawing at his lap instead.

"I guess he only wants you to feed him," she said, but when Max held out a chip, the dog backed away and began to bark.

"Maybe he needs to go outside," said Max.

"Okay, I'll get his leash," said Emma. She pushed her chair back from the table and started to stand when the dog leaped at her chest and knocked her back into the chair. It then raced to the kitchen window where it stood beneath it quivering and emitting a low growl.

"Max, something's wrong. Turn out the lights and stay here. I'll switch off the light in the living room and be right back."

Emma entered the living room with the dog at her heels growling and flicked the light switch, plunging the room into darkness. She turned back toward the kitchen, and in the dark, Max's silhouette shown in the ice-blue glow of the stove's digital clock. Behind him, the deep blackness outside the window stirred. It all came back to her then. She'd seen this before, this very thing, and knew what was going to happen to them.

"Max," she yelled, "we have to get out of the house, now."

Emma grabbed Max's hand and pulled him after her into the utility room and to the back door of the house. As she unlocked and opened the door, Max reached up to the chicken's cage on the shelf above the dryer and opened it.

"We have to take the chicken too," he said.

"No," she said and yanked Max with her out of the house, the dog right behind them.

Emma led them into the trees behind the house. They ran headlong, falling over logs buried in the snow and cutting and scraping their faces on branches, invisible in the dark. But the night and the open woods gave them cover, room to flee, and evade. In the house she knew they were trapped. But she and Max had escaped without coats, hats, gloves, or even boots. And Max was shivering. They stopped and hid.

"I'm cold," whispered Max.

"I know," said Emma. "But we can't go back until we know it's safe." She rubbed his hands trying to both warm and calm him, afraid that before much longer it would be the cold that defeated them. She had to get them help fast.

She was about to stand when the figure of a man rose out of the snow in front of them and the dog leaped over her shoulder and charged toward it. She heard the dog yelp and saw its body flip in the air and land motionless in the snow.

Max screamed and ran to the dog before Emma could stop him. The man grabbed Max, yanked him to his feet, and held him off the ground, his arm locked around Max's neck as he searched the woods with the gun in his other hand. "Show yourself or I choke the life out of him while you watch," he said.

Emma stood up. "Let him go," she yelled.

The man dropped Max to the ground and swung the gun at Emma, leveling it at her with both hands.

Emma squeezed her eyes shut, waiting for the muzzle blast she wouldn't hear. Instead, there came a squawk and a piercing scream, and when she opened her eyes, she witnessed the man clawing at a thrashing mass of feathers on his face, the chicken flapping and screeching, its feet dug deep into his flesh. The gun lay in the snow at the man's feet.

Emma dived for the gun, grabbing it as she slid between the man's legs face down in the snow. She rolled on her back in time to see him pry the chicken loose from his face and reach for her. She held the gun steady and fired.

*   *   *

Amanda, Nick, and Callahan and Julie arrived at the house at the same time. All four heard the gunshot and started running toward the noise. The dog appeared out of the trees first, limping, followed by Emma and Max together.

Chapter 89

Tanner's mood, if not celebratory, was at least uplifted by the current state of policing in his jurisdiction. Based on a tip to Josh, the task force uncovered prodigious overbilling by the casino and hotel, especially for construction materials in the building of the road to the casino. The invoices all went to businesses connected to the Bulgarians in Chicago. The mob had its claws deep into Goodfellow and was using the casino and hotel to launder drug money from its operations in the Upper Peninsula. The guy that Emma shot was cooperating with the task force, so multiple convictions were more than likely. Thankfully, she didn't kill him, but Tanner couldn't vouch for his quality of life or Emma's aim. Her frantic shot had cut short the guy's manhood, so to speak.

Tanner had called Josh into his office to congratulate him on his excellent work, both independently and with the task force, but his purpose quickly shifted to two matters that were troubling him.

"We have absolutely no leads or evidence of any kind involving the killings of Blackwell and Goodfellow," said Tanner. "It's odd and frustrating. No prints, DNA, weapons, witnesses, hair samples, fiber samples. Nothing, absolutely nothing. And the identical way they both died, it's almost as if they were murdered by . . ." Tanner's voice trailed off into silence, and he looked away and shook his head as if trying to rid himself of a thought.

"An avenging spirit? A manitou?" offered Josh, ending the quiet.

Tanner turned to Josh and held his gaze. "I don't hold truck with the old stories. Gave that up by high school," he said. "And such superstition only hinders police work." Tanner paused again and then uttered, "Still, it makes you wonder. It does make you wonder."

Josh stood before Tanner and let his boss's doubt ripen in the lingering stillness.

Chapter 90

Callahan sat at his desk and read again the ten-page report Amanda had prepared, and the knot of resignation squeezed tighter in his gut. He could no longer evade the inevitable. The islanders demanded action and did not take no for an answer. A Sheriff's Summer Youth Camp was going to happen, no matter what. He had to accept reality. Sometimes in life's circus you were the lion tamer and sometimes the clown. However, things could be worse, he thought.

The letter from the tribe had arrived in the morning, and Julie was overjoyed. The Manning brothers would not be prosecuted, and with their future on the island secure, the tribe had approved Emma's adoption by Benjamin and his wife. Emma would stay on the island where she could share Julie, Callahan, and Max's lives, but also be one with her family and tribe. It was a solution gratefully embraced by all.

His wedding was nearing, and afterwards, he and Julie would be off to Hawaii for a honeymoon. From one island to another, Callahan mused.

When they returned from Kauai, he would make it official. He would not run for sheriff in the upcoming election. He would campaign for Amanda. An islander born and bred, she was sure to win as his successor. She had proven herself more than qualified and had an excellent and up-and-coming deputy in Nick. The island would be well served and protected by both of them.

The days grew longer now, and with the increasing light came the promise of warmth and color. The planets had aligned in what had been a universe spinning in chaos. Callahan could glimpse the future, not blinded by the swirling mayhem that had enveloped his island in winter. Soon the island would be bustling with tourists and the summer residents that kept it alive, and he and Julie could settle in to its rhythms and savor the peace they both craved.

THE END

Author's Note

I sincerely hope you enjoyed the read. Your rating or review of this novel on Goodreads or the online site where you purchased the print or ebook edition would be a great help to potential readers and an even greater help to the author. Please consider it and thank you.

Russ Fee

About the Author

Russell Fee was born in Indiana but grew up in Washington D.C. and London. After graduating from the College of William and Mary, he served in the army as an intelligence officer and then became a trial lawyer in Chicago, litigating civil rights and civil liberties cases, before becoming a teacher.

A Dangerous Season is Russ's fourth novel and the third book in his Sheriff Matt Callahan Mystery Series. Kirkus Reviews described the first book in the series, *A Dangerous Remedy,* as "A well-written mystery about a unique community imbued with a palpable sense of place . . . well-plotted and highly enjoyable." The second book in the series, *A Dangerous Identity,* won the Chicago Writers Association's Book of the Year Award.

Russ and his wife are dual citizens of the United States and Ireland. They now live in the Upper Midwest, which they love.

Also by the Author

Fiction
The Sheriff Matt Callahan Mystery Series:
A Dangerous Remedy, Book One
A Dangerous Identity, Book Two

Russell Fee writing as Russell Ó Fiaich
Who You've Got To Kill

Poetry
A Dash of Expectation

Acknowledgements

I am indebted to two fine books by Basil Johnston for insight into Ojibwe culture, heritage, and traditions: *The Manitous* and *Ojibway Heritage.*

I am also indebted to the following people, many of whom read multiple drafts of the manuscript and all of whom provided invaluable feedback: John Morris, Robert Karrow, Gary Strokosch, Jonathan Alpert, and Don Debruin. I am grateful to each of you.

Heartfelt thanks this time go to my good friend and fellow author, James Elsener, who did a fantastic job of editing and who pointed me in the right direction whenever the writing took a wrong turn.

My thanks once again to Dr. Michael Kaufman for technical assistance with the medical and trauma scenes and for making sure I had a polished manuscript before publication.

And a special thank you to Aubrey Hall, my niece and an art therapist, who inspired and guided the scenes involving art therapy.

Finally, as always, my greatest thanks to Joan—editor and helpmate supreme.

Lightning Source UK Ltd.
Milton Keynes UK
UKHW010456090223
416681UK00008B/2353

9 781949 661569

Istanbul
& the Aegean Coast

TOP 10 ATTRACTIONS

Bosphorus by ferry. A trip along the famous strait, with lots to see on the way. See page 65.

Süleymaniye Mosque. The finest Ottoman building in Istanbul. See page 47.

Kariye Museum. One of the world's greatest monuments to Byzantine art. See page 51.

Grand Bazaar. The largest covered market in the world, with 4,000 shops. See page 45.

Ephesus. One of the best-preserved ancient sites in Turkey and the top historical attraction along the Aegean coast. See page 81.

Basilica Cistern. Part of the city's Byzantine-era system of underground reservoirs. See page 43.

Janissary Band concert. Reviving days of Ottoman glory in spectacular fashion. See page 60.

Topkapı Palace. Richly adorned home of the sultans and their harem. See page 34.

Hagia Sophia. Completed in AD537 and still one of the world's greatest architectural wonders. See page 30.

İstiklal Caddesi. At the heart of the lively, European-style New City. See page 58.

A PERFECT DAY

9.00am **Breakfast**

Enjoy a Turkish breakfast in your hotel or a local café – lots of fresh bread, white cheese, honey, and gallons of black tea.

1.00pm **Süleymaniye Mosque**

Walk up historic Divan Yolu, following the tram line to this immense mosque. After you've gazed inside Sinan's masterpiece, visit the tombs of Süleyman and his wife Roxelana, in the peaceful rose-strewn graveyard, then eat tasty *fasülye* beans for lunch in the outdoor café.

11.30am **Archaeology**

Stroll to the Archaeology Museum and marvel at the Babylonian-era frescoes, the mammoth marble statues and the interior of Mehmet II's tiled Pavilion.

2.30pm **Grand Bazaar**

Enter the bustling 500-year-old bazaar, the world's largest covered market, to explore narrow alleyways crammed with treasures. If you need a break from shopping, head to the Old Bedesten, its historic heart, for a cappuccino in a choice of smart little cafés.

10.00am **Hagia Sophia**

Walk up the steps to the gallery of this architectural wonder for a closer look at the 13th-century mosaic of 'Christ Pantocrator', flanked by the Virgin Mary and John the Baptist.

IN ISTANBUL

5.30pm Galata Tower for panoramic views

Cross Galata Bridge, past lines of fishermen. Walk uphill to Galata Tower, or take the tiny funicular from Karaköy to Tünel. Ascend the sturdy tower for a fantastic panorama.

8.30pm After dark

Head to busy Nevizade Sokak for a lively *meyhane* (tavern) to feast on fresh fish, or take your pick along İstiklal Caddesi for Thai fusion or good old Turkish home cooking. Then take the elevator up to ever-so-trendy 360 Istanbul, for rooftop cocktails and dancing.

4.00pm Eminönü

Walk down the trading streets to busy Eminönü, to the Egyptian (Spice) Market and Yeni Camii (New Mosque). Buy *lokum* (Turkish delight), peruse the outdoor stalls, then try a *balik ekmek* (fish sandwich), filled with fish straight from the fishing boats.

7.00pm Sundowner in Tünel

Walk up Galipdede Sokak, a narrow street of music shops, with traditional instruments hanging in the windows, to Tünel, a bohemian nightlife area filled with café-bars and tucked-away wine bars, perfect for an aperitif. Browse bookstores along İstiklal Caddesi or rummage for discounted designer clothes in İş Merkezi.

CONTENTS

INTRODUCTION

Istanbul is one of the world's most venerable cities. Part of the allure is its setting, where Europe faces Asia across the waters of the Bosphorus, making it the only city in the world to bridge two continents. Here, where the Black Sea blends into the Aegean, East and West mingle and merge in the cultural melting pot of Turkey's largest metropolis. Oriental bazaars co-exist with European shops and malls; kebab shops and teahouses sit alongside stylish brasseries; sleek glass-fronted office buildings and hotels alternate with Ottoman minarets along the city's skyline; traditional music and Western pop, bellydancing and ballet, Turkish wrestling and football all compete for the attention of the *İstanbullu* audience.

This is the only city in the world to have been the capital of both an Islamic and a Christian empire. As Constantinople, jewel of the Byzantine Empire, it was for more than 1,000 years the most important city in Christendom. As Istanbul it was the seat of the Ottoman sultans, rulers of a 500-year Islamic empire that stretched from the Black Sea and the Balkans to Arabia and Algeria.

Strategic Location

Istanbul's historical significance is due to a strategic location at the mouth of the Bosphorus. From this vantage point the city could control the ships that passed through the strait on the trade route between the Black Sea and the Mediterranean, and the overland traffic from Europe to Asia Minor that used the strait as a crossing point. In the words of the 16th-century French traveller Pierre Gilles: 'The Bosphorus with one key opens and closes two worlds, two seas.'

Iznik tiles in the Harem section of Topkapı Palace

Talking Turkey

The name Turkey relates to both a country and Christmas or thanksgiving dinner. Is there some relationship? The succulent birds we enjoy at these festivals originated in the Americas. Turks call a turkey a 'hindi' though. Certainly, the Moghul Emperor Jahangir had a painting of a turkey – perhaps he imported them and exported them to Turkey and thus to Europe.

That strategic advantage is no less important today than it was 2,500 years ago, when a band of Greeks first founded the city of Byzantium on this spot. Ankara is the official capital of modern Turkey, but Istanbul remains the country's largest city, most important commercial and industrial centre, and busiest port, accounting for more than one-third of Turkey's manufacturing output. The Bosphorus is one of the world's most active shipping lanes, and the overland traffic is carried by two of the world's longest suspension bridges.

Urban Contrasts

The city has long since spread beyond the 5th-century Byzantine walls built by Emperor Theodosius II and now sprawls for miles along the shores of the Sea of Marmara on both the European and Asian sides. In 1507 this was the world's largest city, with a population of 1.2 million. That figure has now passed 12 million and is still growing, swollen by a steady influx of people from rural areas (more than half the population was born in the provinces). These new arrivals have created a series of shanty towns around the perimeter of the city. Their makeshift homes, known as *gecekondu* ('built by night'), take advantage of an old Ottoman law that protects a house whose roof has been built during the hours of darkness. The slums are eventually knocked down to make way for new tower blocks – a new suburb is created, yet another shanty town springs up beyond it, and Istanbul spreads out a little farther. In addition, run-down neighbourhoods are being spruced up by the council, with subsequent leaps in property values that force out poorer residents.

At the other end of the social spectrum are the wealthy *İstanbullus*, who live in the up-market districts of Taksim, Harbiye and Nişantaşı, where the streets are lined with fashion boutiques, expensive apartments and stylish cafés. Members of this set are the lucky few who frequent the city's more expensive restaurants and casinos, and retire at the weekends to their *yalı* (restored wooden mansions) along the Bosphorus. But most of Istanbul's inhabitants fall between these two extremes, living in modest flats and earning an average wage – lower than in the rest of the Europe – in the offices, shops, banks and factories that provide most of the city's employment.

Young people drinking in a back street in Beyoğlu

Although small Armenian, Greek Orthodox, Jewish and Catholic communities survive, the majority of *İstanbullus* are Muslim and adhere to the principles known as the 'Five Pillars of Islam' – to believe with all one's heart that 'There is no God but Allah, and Mohammed is his Prophet'; to pray five times a day, at dawn, midday, afternoon, sunset and after dark; to give alms to the poor and towards the upkeep of the mosques; to fast between sunrise and sunset during the month of Ramadan; and to try to make the pilgrimage to Mecca at least once.

Islam in Turkey is, on the whole, an open, welcoming brand of the religion, where the visitor is made to feel at home (able to go into mosques, for example). The secular society created by Atatürk is clearly visible in the contemporary culture and fashion followed by both men and women. However, there is creeping conservatism among the poor, more traditional population, who look to Islam to solve their economic problems and who generally support the ruling AKP party that has been gradually drifting apart from the secular state installed by Atatürk.

Principal Attractions

Just as the Bosphorus separates Asia from Europe, so the inlet called the *haliç* (Golden Horn) separates old Istanbul from the new. The main attractions for the visitor are concentrated in the historic heart of old Istanbul. Three great civilisations have shaped this part of the city – Roman, Byzantine and Ottoman. Though little remains from Roman times, the city's Byzantine legacy includes Hagia Sophia (Aya Sofya in Turkish, the Church of the Divine Wisdom), one of the world's greatest buildings; the magnificent mosaics of St Saviour in Chora; and the impressive Theodosian Walls. The Ottomans built countless mosques, the finest being Süleymaniye Camii, built by Turkey's greatest architect, Sinan.

Muslim women in chador at the Eyüp mosque complex

Inside the Byzantine Hagia Sophia

But the most popular tourist sight is Topkapı Palace, home of the Ottoman sultans, where the riches of the Imperial Treasury and the intrigue of the Harem draw thousands of visitors each year.

From the belvedere in the palace treasury, where the Sultan used to gaze down upon his fleet, you can look across the mouth of the Golden Horn to the modern district of Beyoğlu, where multistorey hotels rise beyond the turret of the Galata Tower. Round the corner, by the Bosphorus, is the 19th-century Dolmabahçe Palace, while beyond stretches the span of the Bosphorus Bridge, a concrete symbol of the city, linking Europe with Asia. Down the centuries the city has been open to influences from both East and West, and this cross-fertilisation of ideas has created one of the world's liveliest, most engaging and hospitable cultures. It is neither European nor Oriental, but an unparalleled and intoxicating blend; it is, quite simply, uniquely Istanbul.

A BRIEF HISTORY

Byzas, the legendary founder of Byzantium, was the son of the sea god Poseidon. His maternal grandfather was Zeus. In around 660BC, the oracle at Delphi told him to settle an area opposite some blind people who had established a town on the eastern shore of the Bosphorus. They must have been blind not to have noticed the advantages of such a site: surrounded by water on three sides, it not only occupied a perfect strategic location, but was an ideal spot for trade. Topkapı Palace, transport hubs and bazaars occupy the same position today.

Ancient ruins at Priene

Centuries earlier, Jason and the Argonauts, seeking the Golden Fleece, had rowed through the Bosphorus following a pigeon, and escaped the clashing rocks, which threatened to kill them. The rocks never clashed again. Could this myth have grown from an earthquake, which are common here?

The shores of the Aegean are equally fabled. The Trojan War stemmed from the love of Paris for Helen of Troy. The ancient Greeks took the fall of Troy, as recounted by Homer, as the starting point of their history.

Aegean Cities

The Mycenaean Greeks who conquered King Priam's Troy

soon lost their homelands. Power changes forced successive waves of immigration: the Ionians and others settled on the Turkish shore. While Greece went into a 'Dark Age', civilisation blossomed here. By the 8th century BC the 12 main city-states of Ionia, including Ephesus, Priene and Miletus, had formed what was known as the Pan-Ionic League. Science, philosophy, architecture and the arts flourished, and the Ionians founded further colonies.

Ford of the ox

The name Bosphorus stems from Greek mythology: the king of the gods, Zeus, fell for Io, but his wife Hera wasn't pleased. Poor Io was turned into a cow, goaded so sorely by a gadfly that she swam the Bosphorus, the ford of the ox.

In the 6th century BC coastal city-states fell to the Persians, who incorporated them into their empire. Athens supported a revolt, which was quickly subdued. Athenian involvement provoked the Persian King Darius to invade the Greek mainland. He suffered a succession of defeats: the famous Battle of Marathon in 490BC and the loss of the Persian fleet at the Battle of Salamis 10 years later.

As a result of the Persian Wars, cities along the Aegean coast were encouraged to join the Delian Confederacy, paying tribute to Athens in return for protection against the Persians. Athens demanded this source of easy money and dissent soon grew among the member cities. There followed the Peloponnesian War (431–404BC) after which Sparta led the confederacy. The Persians, sensing weakness in the ranks, launched another offensive, resulting in the Aegean coastal cities coming under Persian control in 387BC.

Alexander the Great

Meanwhile, King Philip II of Macedon dreamed of driving the Persians out of northern Greece and unifying the entire

Greek world. He thought Byzantium was well positioned and attempted to take it in 340BC.

Philip's dreams were surpassed by his son, Alexander the Great, who lived for only 33 years (356–323BC). In 334BC, aged 22, he led his army across the Hellespont (now the Dardanelles). He paused at Troy to make a sacrifice at the Temple of Athena and pay homage to his hero Achilles, before going on to defeat the Persians. Having conquered the Aegean and Mediterranean coasts of Anatolia, and subdued Syria and Egypt, Alexander took the great prize of Persepolis, the Persian capital, before advancing into India. He built the greatest empire the world had yet seen, although it lasted only 10 years.

After Alexander's death, his empire was divided among his generals. The conflict between them left the Turkish Aegean and Byzantium open to acquisition by Rome.

Enter the Romans

Attalus III, the last of the Attalid kings, a dynasty dating from 264BC, ruled a prosperous city-state, Pergamon, on the Aegean. When he died in 133BC, his subjects discovered that he had bequeathed his kingdom to the Romans. Thus Pergamon became the capital of the new Roman province of Asia. Under Emperor Augustus, Rome ceased to be a republic, and, in 27BC, became an empire. There followed a long period of

The Crescent Moon

Philip of Macedon launched his raid on Byzantium in the dead of night. But the goddess of the moon, Hecate, illuminated the scene and foiled Philip's plot. This divine intervention was commemorated by the striking of coins bearing her star and crescent. Some say that is why the crescent moon became an important symbol, later passed on to the Ottomans and, subsequently, to the Islamic world.

peace and prosperity known as the Pax Romana. Asia Minor (the Roman name for Anatolia) was incorporated into the Roman Empire. The advent of Christianity threatened the Roman establishment because it rejected the old gods and denied the divinity of the emperor.

Theodosian Walls

The journeys of St Paul the Apostle (AD40–56) led to the founding of numerous churches, notably the Seven Churches of Asia addressed in the Revelation of St John – Pergamon, Smyrna, Ephesus, Thyatira, Laodicea, Sardis and Philadelphia.

City of Constantine

Meanwhile Byzantium had developed as a city-state, much like the cities of the Aegean. It, too, fell under the sway of Athens, Sparta, Persia, Alexander and Rome. It tried to regain its independence from Rome, but proved too small and weak, and was conquered by Emperor Septimius Severus in AD196. He had the city razed to the ground, but then saw the advantages of its strategic location, and began a programme of enlarging and strengthening the old defensive walls.

Weak and decadent emperors saw the Roman Empire decline into anarchy. In AD286 Diocletian sought to reverse the decline by splitting the administration of the empire in two. His policy succeeded for a time, but following his abdication in AD305, the empire continued to weaken, harassed by invaders and troubled by internal strife.

Constantine the Great (who was a convert to Christianity) reunited the empire. He chose Byzantium as his new capital to emphasise the break with heathen Rome. The city was inaugurated with great ceremony in AD330 and, in honour of the emperor, was renamed Constantinople. Constantine added new city walls, following a plan he claimed to have been given by Christ in a vision, and commissioned many monuments, including a grand central forum decorated with a triumphal column. The 'New Rome' soon achieved a pre-eminence in the Christian world it would retain for 1,000 years.

In 392 the Emperor Theodosius proclaimed Christianity to be the official religion of the Roman Empire. On his death in 395 the empire was split once more, between his two sons. The Western Empire, ruled from Rome, fell in 476, but the Eastern, or Byzantine Empire, became one of the longest-lived empires the world has ever known, lasting from 395 to 1453. The greatest of the Byzantine emperors was Justinian (527–65), who extended the boundaries of the empire into Spain, Italy and Africa. Together with his wife, Theodora, he encouraged the arts, reformed the legal system, and commissioned the building of the magnificent basilica, the Hagia Sophia (Aya Sofya).

Hagia Sophia mosaic

Crusades

Following the death of the Prophet Mohammed in 632, Arab armies, united under Islam, took Egypt, Syria and Palestine from the Byzantines; Constantinople was besieged from 674 to 678, but survived because of its defences. North Africa and Italy were lost. Troubled times were only lightened by a brief golden age under Basil II (976–1025) before further invasions by the Seljuk Turks came to wrest large parts of Asia Minor from Constantinople's control. Christian holy places were threatened and pilgrims bound for Jerusalem attacked.

Emperor Alexius Comnenus had sought help from the Christian West to recover his lost territory, but got more than he bargained for as the 'barbarian' Franks of the First Crusade rampaged across the region and finally captured Jerusalem in 1099 (massacring Muslims and Jews as well as local Christians in the process). However, the Second

Crusaders sack Constantinople

and Third Crusades were a disaster for the Christians. The Fourth Crusade, launched in 1202 and partly inspired by Venetian jealousy of Byzantium's trading power, became an excuse to plunder Constantinople itself. Thus, the city that had held out against so many attacks by the infidel became subjected to mindless pillaging by fellow Christians. Constantinople was recaptured in 1261, but the city had been shattered and its great monuments were stripped of gold, silver and precious works of art. The place was never the same again.

Ottoman Rule

The Turks in Anatolia rallied under the banner of Sultan Osman Gazi, who defeated the Byzantines in 1300. By the 15th century, the whole of Anatolia and Thrace, except for Constantinople,

Süleyman the Magnificent

was under the control of these Osmanli (or Ottoman) Turks. The Byzantine emperor at the time, Manuel II (1391–1425), attempted to appease his enemies by allowing a Turkish district, mosque and tribunal within his city, and by courting Turkish goodwill with gifts of gold, but to no avail. The young Ottoman Sultan, Mehmet II, who reigned from 1451 to 1481, set about cutting off Constantinople's supply lines. The huge fortress of Rumeli Hisarı on the Bosphorus was built in just four months in 1452.

The Byzantines tried to protect the Golden Horn from enemy ships by stretching a huge chain across its mouth. They strengthened the city walls that had saved them so many times in the past, and waited for the inevitable onslaught. In April 1453 the Sultan's armies massed outside the walls, outnumbering the Byzantines 10 to one. The siege lasted seven weeks. The Ottoman admiral bypassed the defensive chain by having his ships dragged overland under cover of darkness. The final assault came on 29 May 1453, when the Ottoman army surged through a breach in the walls. The last emperor, Constantine XI, fell in the fighting, and by noon that day Mehmet II and his men had taken control of the city.

After allowing his soldiers three days of pillaging, he restored order, acting with considerable leniency and good sense. Henceforth he became known as 'Fatih' (Conqueror), and his newly won capital was renamed Istanbul. Mehmet ordered that Hagia Sophia be converted into a mosque; on the following Friday, he attended the first Muslim prayers in what came to be called Aya Sofya Camii (Mosque of Aya Sofya).

Mehmet laid claim to all the territories previously held by the Byzantines. Expansion continued and during the reign of his great grandson, Süleyman, the Ottoman Empire reached its greatest and most celebrated heights. Süleyman the Magnificent, aged 25, ascended the throne and ruled for 46 years (1520–66), the longest and most glorious reign in the history of the Ottomans. Istanbul was ornamented by the new rulers with elegant, richly decorated buildings, mosques and palaces, public buildings and fountains. This was the period of the master architect, Sinan, whose most famous work is Süleymaniye Mosque.

Imperial expansion continued and by the mid-17th century the Ottoman Empire stretched from the eastern end of the Black Sea to Algeria, taking in Mesopotamia, Palestine, the shores of the Red Sea (including Mecca and Medina), Egypt, Anatolia, Greece, the Balkans, Hungary, Moldavia, the North African coast, the Crimea and southern Ukraine.

Decline and Fall

Such far-flung territories made effective rule impossible, and years of decadence, bitter family infighting that led to the

Sinan

Sinan (1489–1588) was the most celebrated Ottoman architect. Before taking up the profession (at the age of 49), he worked as a construction officer in the Janissary corps of the army. He designed hundreds of buildings, but is best remembered for his mosques, which include the Sehzade and Süleymaniye mosques in Istanbul and the Selimiye Mosque in Edirne. The basic template for his designs was Hagia Sophia (completed AD537), but he refined the use of domes, half domes and buttresses both to maximise interior space and to achieve the best natural lighting on the richly decorated interior surfaces.

Atatürk

premature deaths of most of the Ottomans with leadership qualities, and intermittent wars caused the sultanate to fall into irreversible decline. The failure of the siege of Vienna in 1683 highlighted the weakening. The Istanbul court was still elegant: Ahmet III presided over festivities from 1703 until he was deposed in 1730. Gradually the sultans moved further and further into European control, bringing in foreigners to advise on, then run, every aspect of the empire.

The massacre of the Janissaries (the elite corps of the Ottoman army) in 1826 opened the door to change, ridding the court of its standing army. It is estimated that 10,000 were slain. Ottoman garb was replaced by Prussian blue uniforms, the Ottoman Topkapı was replaced by the rococo Dolmabahçe Palace. But attempts at reform came too late; by 1876 the government was bankrupt. Sultan Abdül Hamid II (1876–1909) tried to apply absolute rule, and succeeded only in creating discontent among a younger generation of educated Turks who were increasingly interested in Western ways of government and social organisation. The Galatasaray Lycée (French Academy) and Anglophone colleges were turning out men with dreams of democracy who formed an underground group known as the 'Young Turks'. In 1909, their revolt removed Abdül Hamid and replaced him with his brother, Mehmet V.

There followed the Balkan Wars, and World War I, which Turkey entered on Germany's side. In the Gallipoli campaign of 1915, the Turks, led by General Mustafa Kemal, defeated the Allied attack on the Dardanelles. At the end of the war, the Treaty of Sèvres stripped the Ottoman Empire of its lands, which were divided between the Allied powers.

Atatürk and the Turkish Republic

In 1920, Mustafa Kemal (Atatürk, see box) was elected president of the Grand National Assembly in Ankara in defiance of the Sultan's government in Constantinople. A war leader and popular politician, he set about turning defeat into victory as he ruthlessly liberated Turkey of foreign invaders and its more troublesome people, such as the Armenians. He had the task of abolishing the sultanate without antagonising religious elements (the Sultan was also the caliph, leader of the Islamic world). In 1922, Mehmet VI, last of the Ottoman sultans, finally went into exile.

From 1925 to 1935, Mustafa Kemal transformed the country. He secularised institutions, reformed the calendar, adapted the Latin alphabet for the Turkish language, emancipated women, outlawed Dervishes and improved industry and agriculture. He was enormously popular with the common people, and after he died in 1938, thousands lined the railway track to salute the presidential train as it carried him from Istanbul for burial in Ankara, which in 1923 had been made the capital of Turkey. It was a clean break with the past. Diplomats abandoned the Rue de Pera, which was renamed İstiklal Caddesi (Avenue of Independence).

Name change

Mustafa Kemal introduced the Western idea of surnames (Turks had previously had a single name). Everyone had to choose a family name, which was handed down to their children. For himself he chose Atatürk, Father of the Turks, an appropriate name, as he single-handedly created the modern Turkish state.

Istanbul lost revenues and status, and the city was left with its imperial past and an uncertain future.

Istanbul – at Last

The 1930s were the romantic 'Orient Express' years celebrated by foreign writers at the Pera Palas Hotel, but the subsequent decade was depressing, blighted by corruption and depopulation.

Since the war, Turkey has had mixed fortunes both economically and politically, with the military often on hand to safeguard Atatürk's legacy from economic and social disorder and from militant Islamist forces. But Istanbul has ploughed on regardless, and since the 1960s, when major transport and restoration schemes were set in motion, its revival has been spectacular. The city has re-established itself as the hub of the nation's cultural life and the powerhouse of its economy, with the largest companies and banks, the main national newspapers, television networks and advertising agencies all having headquarters here.

Clean and efficiently run, Istanbul is back in the top league of world cities, and certainly won't be bowed by the terrorist attacks to which it periodically falls victim. Since becoming European Capital of Culture in 2010, Istanbul's profile has risen immensely in the fields of tourism and the arts, and it also boasts one of Europe's most successful economies during the global recession. In 2013 the government's plans to develop Istanbul's Ghezi Park triggered a sit-in protest which was brutally suppressed by the police, leading to violent clashes. As a result, over 3.5 million Turks stood up in defence of freedom of press, expression and assembly.

Turkish flag, Blue Mosque

Historical Landmarks

c.660BC Byzantium founded by Byzas the Greek.

330 Constantine makes Byzantium the new capital of his empire.

395 Death of Theodosius I; final division of Roman Empire.

527–65 Reign of Justinian the Great.

532–37 Construction of Hagia Sophia (Aya Sofya).

726–843 Iconoclastic Crisis divides the empire.

11th century Seljuk Turks invade Asia Minor.

1204–61 Crusaders sack Constantinople and occupy the city.

1326 The Osmanli Turks capture Bursa; the Ottoman Empire is born.

1453 Mehmet II (Mehmet the Conqueror) captures Constantinople and makes it his capital, renamed Istanbul.

1520–66 Reign of Süleyman the Magnificent.

1683 Ottoman Empire reaches its greatest extent.

18th century Ottomans lose territory to European powers.

1909 Young Turks depose Sultan Abdül Hamid II.

1915 The Turks under Atatürk defeat Allied attack on the Dardanelles.

1922 The sultanate is abolished.

1923 Turkey becomes a republic; Atatürk elected president.

1938 Death of Atatürk.

1952 Turkey joins NATO.

1973 Bosphorus Bridge completed.

1999 Huge earthquake hits the Istanbul area, killing around 20,000.

2003 Erdogan becomes prime minister.

2004 Turkey bans the death penalty.

2005 State TV broadcasts its first Kurdish-language programme; Negotiations on joining the EU begin.

2010 Istanbul is European Capital of Culture.

2013 Police attacks protesters at Gezi Park; 11 people are killed and more than 8,000 wounded.

2014 Recep Tayyip Erdoğan becomes Turkey's president.

2015 Parliamentary elections.

WHERE TO GO

Modern Istanbul is split in two by the narrow, sinuous strait known as the Haliç (Golden Horn), an estuary of the Bosphorus. The city mood varies: Sultanahmet, heart of the Old City, has distinctive architecture – there's so much history on show, you feel you are in the Orient. Towards the city walls, Fatih is conservative and poorer; Balat and Fener, although run-down, hold treasures of Istanbul's Greek, Armenian and Jewish history. Across the Galata Bridge, the feeling is more cosmopolitan, but with hints of a naughty, *fin-de-siècle*, Art Nouveau history. Taksim Square is much like any main city square, full of traffic and people in a hurry; Beyoğlu is the hip, bohemian area with nightlife and entertainment aplenty. The Asian side of the city, contrary to stereotypes, is more modern, organised and residential.

This guide takes Eminönü as the starting point for tours of Istanbul. It is possible to reach almost all the attractions from this point using public transport. Eminönü is the terminus for the *feribot* (ferries); nearby Sirkeci Station is the European railway terminus, where the Orient Express used to steam in, trailing romance. Travellers today are mostly suburban commuters, and there is a good restaurant and a small museum detailing its romantic past. (Asian trains leave from the Haydarpaşa Station across the Bosphorus.)

Take the tram

A sleek tram runs past the Dolmabahçe to Eminönü, across the Galata Bridge, through Sultanahmet, past the Grand Bazaar, the hotels of Laleli and Aksaray, and on to the city walls at Topkapı bus station (not to be confused with the famous palace of the same name). It is a handy way of getting from one sight to another.

Mosque domes at sunrise

THE OLD CITY (STAMBOUL)

Eminönü

Istanbul's most popular tourist attractions are concentrated in the Sultanahmet district, but before setting out there are sights to be seen in **Eminönü**. At rush hour the waterfront becomes a bedlam as commuters pour off the ferries from the modern, European side or from the Asian side. The air is loud with blasts from ships' horns, and the water boils white as vessels jostle for a vacant berth. Smaller boats equipped with stoves and frying pans bounce around in the wash, while their crews, seemingly oblivious to the violent, churning movement of their floating kitchens, dish up fried-fish sandwiches to hungry local people standing on the quayside. Adding to the activity, and competing for passing trade, are the vendors with carts from which they sell grilled corn cobs, pickles and fried mussels.

The wide square opposite Galata Bridge is dominated by the **New Mosque** *(Yeni Camii)*. Commissioned in 1597 by the Valide Sultan Safiye, mother of Mehmet III, it was not completed until 1663, making the Yeni Camii the youngest of Istanbul's classical mosques.

The Spice of Life

At the Spice Bazaar in Eminönü, sellers once sat cross-legged on carpets, ready to seize pestle and mortar for pounding potions both efficacious and fanciful, optimistically prepared to cure anything from lumbago to lovesickness through to highly complicated cases of combating the Evil Eye. Nor were they all charlatans – some of the market's herbal remedies are still available, even though they no longer contain such rare ingredients as ambergris, dragon's blood or tortoise eggs.

The large archway to the
right of the mosque is the
entrance to the famous **Spice
Bazaar** ❶ (www.misircar
sisi.org; daily 8am–7.30pm)
also known as the Egyptian
Bazaar *(Mısır Çarşısı)*. It was
opened a few years before
Yeni Camii, and its revenues
originally paid for repairs to
the mosque complex. Inside,
the L-shaped building has an
array of shops, its air heady

Inside the Spice Bazaar

with aromas of ginger, pepper and cinnamon, although these
days it is dominated by tourist-friendly souvenirs, jewellery
and fabrics, plus plenty of apple tea and *lokum* (Turkish
Delight). The dried fruits, cheese and fresh produce in the
stalls outside are far better quality. Nearby streets are filled
with local people shopping for household items.

If you leave the Spice Bazaar by the gate at the far end of
the first aisle and then turn right, you will find **Rüstem Paşa
Mosque** ❷ *(Rüstempaşa Camii)*, with its minaret soaring
above the narrow backstreet. This is one of Sinan's smaller
works, and one of his most beautiful. The interior is almost
completely covered in İznik tiles of the finest period, with
floral and geometric designs in blue, turquoise and coral red.

Sultanahmet
The summit of the first of the Old City's seven hills is occupied by **Sultanahmet**. This was the site of the original
Byzantium, founded in the 7th century BC, and of the civic
centre of Constantinople, capital of the Byzantine Empire.
Here, too, the conquering Ottoman sultans chose to build
their most magnificent palaces and mosques.

Hagia Sophia

Of the few remains of the Byzantine city, the most remarkable building is **Hagia Sophia ❸** (also known as Aya Sofya; www.ayasofyamuzesi.gov.tr; Tue–Sun 15 Apr–Sept 9am–7pm, Nov–Mar 9.30am–5pm). For almost 1,000 years, this was the greatest church in Christendom, an architectural wonder built by the Byzantine Empire to impress the world.

It is thought that a Christian basilica was built here in AD325 by Emperor Constantine, on the site of a pagan temple. It was destroyed by fire in AD404 and rebuilt by Theodosius II, then burnt down again in 532. The building you see today was commissioned by Justinian and completed in 537, although many repairs, additions and alterations have been made over the centuries. The dome was damaged by earthquakes several times, and the supporting buttresses have coarsened the church's outward appearance.

The finest materials were used in its construction – white marble from the islands of the Marmara, *verd antique* from Thessaly, yellow marble from Africa, gold and silver from Ephesus, and ancient red porphyry columns that possibly came from Egypt and may once have stood in the Temple of the Sun at Baalbek. The interior was covered with golden mosaics, lit by countless flickering candelabras.

The last Christian service ever to be held in Hagia Sophia took place

Sultanahmet at night

on 28 May 1453, the day before Constantinople fell to the Turks. Mehmet the Conqueror immediately converted the building to an imperial mosque, and built a brick minaret at the southeast corner. The architect, Sinan, strengthened the buttresses and added the other three minarets during the 16th century. Hagia Sophia served as a mosque until 1935, when Atatürk proclaimed that it should become a museum.

The entrance path leads past the ticket desk to a shady tea-garden outside the main portal, which is surrounded by architectural fragments from the 5th-century church built by Theodosius; an excavated area to the left of the door reveals

The cavernous interior

a part of this earlier building. You enter the building through the central portal, across a worn and well-polished threshold of *verd antique* and under a 9th-century mosaic of Christ Pantocrator, into the long, narrow narthex, running to right and left. Note the beautiful matching panels of marble, and the vaulted gold mosaic ceiling. As you continue through the huge bronze doors of the Imperial Gate, your eyes will be drawn skywards by the upwards sweep of the dome. The scale is overwhelming: the dome is around 31m (100ft) in diameter, and floats 55m (180ft) above the floor – the same height as a 15-storey building.

The sensation of space is created by the absence of supporting walls beneath the dome. It was the great achievement of the architects Isidorus and Anthemius to transfer the weight of the dome to the pillars using semi-domes, arches and pendentives to create the illusion of an unsupported dome.

The original decoration has long since disappeared. Eight huge medallions, bearing the Arabic names of Allah, Mohammed, two of his grandsons and the first four caliphs, and a quotation from the Koran in the crown of the dome, are remnants of Hagia Sophia's 500 years of service as an imperial mosque, as are the elaborate *mihrab* and *mimber* in the apse. But a few Christian **mosaics** survive – above the apse is the Virgin with the infant Jesus, with the Archangel Gabriel to the right.

The best mosaics are in the galleries, reached by a spiral ramp that starts at the north end of the narthex. By the south wall is the famous **Deesis**, an extraordinary 13th-century mosaic showing Christ flanked by the Virgin Mary and St John the Baptist. On the east wall are two images showing Byzantine emperors and empresses making offerings to Christ on his throne (to the left) and to the Virgin and Child.

At the east end of the galleries, two small columns and a circle of green marble mark the spot where the empress sat during services; on the floor of the nave below, a circle of col-oured stone, right of centre, is the **Opus Alexandrinum**, the place where the Byzantine emperors were crowned.

As you leave by the door at the south end of the narthex, turn round and look up to see a beautiful 10th-century **mosaic** of an emperor and empress offering symbols of Hagia Sophia and Constantinople to the Virgin Mary and Child.

The beautiful İmaret building (soup kitchen) of Hagia Sophia, built in 1743, now houses the **Carpet and Kilim Museum** (Halı Müzesi; www.halimuzesi.com). It has a fine collection of historic carpets, some dating from the 14th and 15th centuries, displayed in three halls: former dining room, kitchen and bakery.

Across from the entrance of Hagia Sophia is **Hürrem Sultan Hamamı** (www.ayasofyahamami.com; daily 8am–10pm) also known as Roxelana's Bath, a bathhouse built by Mimar Sinan in 1556 for Roxelana, favourite wife of Süleyman the Magnificent.

Weeping Column

Inside Hagia Sophia, look for the Weeping Column (Column of St Gregory), which has a thumb-sized hole covered with a brass plate; insert your thumb then turn it 360° and your wishes, allegedly, come true. The moisture is said to be beneficial for eye diseases

Topkapı Palace (Topkapı Sarayı)

Between Hagia Sophia and the tip of Saray Burnu is the walled enclosure of **Topkapı Palace ❹** (www.topkapisarayi. gov.tr; Wed–Mon mid-Apr–Oct 9am–6.45pm, Nov–mid-Apr 9am–4.45pm, the Harem and Hagia Irene operate the same hours but have a separate charge; online bookings www.muze.gov.tr/buy_e_ticket; is included in the Istanbul Museum Pass http://museumpassistanbuldistributor.com), the former residence and seat of government of the Ottoman sultans. Begun in 1462 by Mehmet the Conqueror, it was extended by each succeeding sultan until it became a miniature city, which included mosques, libraries, stables, kitchens, schools, the imperial mint, treasuries, barracks, armouries, government offices and audience halls. At its height it supported a population of nearly 4,000.

Sultan Abdül Mecit moved into the newly built Dolmabahçe Palace in 1853 (see page 62), and by 1909 Topkapı was completely abandoned. In 1924 it was converted into a museum, and has been undergoing a continuous programme of restoration

Topkapı – the Film

Fans of 'exotic' locales will appreciate Jules Dassin's *Topkapı* (1964). The film has some wonderful scenes of Istanbul, including the old wooden houses that used to be such a feature of the city – and some of which still stand, in various states of repair – around Topkapı Palace. The star was Dassin's wife, Melina Mercouri. In the film, she gets her boyfriend (Maximillian Schell) to assemble a team to pull off a heist – stealing the emerald-encrusted Topkapı dagger. The action is terrific, and there's a lengthy sequence featuring the traditional Turkish sport of oil wrestling. The film is enhanced by the presence of Peter Ustinov, who won an Oscar for his performance as a bumbling Brit, and Akim Tamiroff, as a foul-mouthed, drunken cook.

ever since. It is the city's most
popular tourist attraction, and
deserves at least several hours
to do it justice. If pushed
for time, the essentials are,
in order of importance, the
Harem (get there early), the
Treasury and the Pavilion of
the Holy Mantle.

The palace is laid out as
a series of courtyards linked
by ceremonial gates. You
enter through the **Imperial
Gate** (built in 1478) into
the wooded gardens of the
First Court. On the left is the

Tower of Justice

Byzantine church of **Hagia Eirene** (Divine Peace), rebuilt
together with Hagia Sophia after being burnt down in 532.
This area was also known as the **Court of the Janissaries**,
after the crack military corps that served as the sultan's body-
guard and used it as an assembly ground (the name derives
from the Turkish *yeni çeri*, meaning 'new army'). It originally
contained the palace bakery, the armoury and the mint. In
the far right-hand corner is the ticket office, which originally
served as a prison. The fountain is called the Executioner's
Fountain because here he rinsed his sword and washed his
hands after carrying out his orders; examples of his handiwork
were displayed on pikes at the Imperial Gate.

Pass through the turreted Gate of Salutations (*Babüsselam*),
better known as the Orta Kapı, or **Middle Gate**. Only the sultan
was permitted to ride through this gate on horseback; all others had to dismount and bow. It leads into the Second Court,
also known as the **Court of the Divan** because the Imperial
Council (the Divan) governed the Ottoman Empire from here.

Doorway into the Harem of the Topkapı Palace

Five avenues radiate from the inside of the gate. To the right lie the **Palace Kitchens**, housing a collection of European crystal, Chinese porcelain, and Ottoman serving dishes and cooking implements. Straight ahead is the ornate Gate of the White Eunuchs (*Babüssaade*), which leads into the Third Court. The avenue on the left leads towards the pointed **Tower of Justice** (*Adalet Kulesi*), at the foot of which lie the Council Chamber and the Grand Vezir's Office.

Here, too, is the entrance to Topkapı's main attraction, the **Harem**. The Harem housed the private quarters of the sultan, his mother and his wives and concubines. Its network of staircases, corridors and courtyards linked the sumptuously decorated chambers of the royal household, and harboured a claustrophobic world of ambition, jealousy and intrigue. You enter by the **Carriage Gate**, where the women mounted their carriages. The only adult males allowed in the Harem were the Black Eunuchs, who were in charge of security and administration. Their quarters opened off the narrow **Courtyard of the Black Eunuchs**, beyond the gate. Windows in the colonnade on the left give a glimpse of their tiny rooms; sticks hanging on the walls were used to beat miscreants on the soles of their feet.

A long, narrow corridor lined with shelves (for trays of food) leads to the Courtyard of the Women Servants, from which you enter the **Apartments of the Valide Sultan** (the sultan's mother, the most powerful woman in the Harem). Her domed sitting room is panelled with 17th-century Kütahya tiles, and decorated with scenic views. A raised platform framed by two columns contains divans and a low dining table. The door on the left, beyond the hearth, leads to the valide sultan's bed-chamber, with a gilded bed canopy and ornate floral faïence in turquoise, blue and red. A small adjoining prayer room has scenes of Mecca and Medina.

The right-hand door leads to the **Apartments of the Sultan** himself. First you pass the entrance to the royal bath chambers, designed by Sinan and richly ornamented in marble. There are paired but separate chambers for the sultan and the valide sultan, each having a changing room, a cool room and a hot room. The sultan was bathed by elderly female servants, then dried and pampered by groups of younger handmaidens.

Next, you enter the vast and splendid **Imperial Hall**, with three marble fountains, and a canopied throne from which the sultan would enjoy the music and dancing of his

Forbidden Fruits

The harem occupies an important place in Western fantasy. In fact, the word is derived from the Arabic *haram*, meaning forbidden, and it was the place where the sultan and the women lived. Many women in the Islamic world, especially wives and mothers, had power and influence over their menfolk, but the harem women included 'odalisques', the slave girls who gripped the imagination of writers and artists from Mozart and Balzac to Renoir and Picasso. Many famous artists produced paintings of girls they imagined, but there is little reality in the image. While Matisse was painting his odalisques, Atatürk was proclaiming the Turkish women's right to vote (eventually passed in 1934). When Picasso inherited the fascination from Matisse and began to paint odalisques, Turkish women had equal rights in many areas, including education, and had had the franchise for 30 years.

Return to sender

The Persian emperor, Nadir Shah, sent the Ottoman emperor a jewelled throne. To return the compliment, Istanbul dispatched the Topkapı dagger. But en route for Persia, the emissaries discovered that Nadir Shah had died, so they sensibly decided to hang onto the dagger and take it back home with them.

concubines. The even more splendid **Salon of Murat III** has inlaid floors, flowered İznik tiles, carved fountains, canopied sofas and a superb domed ceiling, designed by Sinan. On the far side a door leads to the Library of Ahmet I, with cupboard doors and shutters inlaid with mother-of-pearl and tortoiseshell, which in turn opens into the dining room of Ahmet III, better known as the **Fruit Room**. This tiny room is covered all over with lacquered paintings of flowers and fruit in rococo style. Ahmet III was known as the 'Tulip King', and celebrated each spring with a tulip festival in the palace grounds.

The exit from the Harem opens into the **Third Court**, otherwise reached through the Gate of the White Eunuchs. Inside the gate is the ornate **Throne Room** (*Arz Odası*), where the sultan received foreign ambassadors. Head down to the right to the **Treasury**, which contains an astonishing selection of artefacts and relics, chief among them the golden Topkapı Dagger, with three huge emeralds set in the hilt and a fourth forming the lid of a watch hidden in the handle; and the Spoonmaker's Diamond, an 86-carat, pear-shaped diamond set in a gold mount encrusted with 49 smaller diamonds. Exhibits include gilded thrones studded with precious stones, a pair of solid-gold candlesticks set with 666 diamonds (one for each verse of the Koran), and reliquaries containing the hand and part of the skull of John the Baptist.

Across the courtyard is the magnificently decorated **Pavilion of the Holy Mantle**, which houses relics of the Prophet Mohammed (including hairs from his beard) and is therefore a place of great religious importance for Muslims. The **Fourth Court** contains a number of pretty pavilions and terraces, and a restaurant and cafeteria with fine views of the Bosphorus.

Archaeological Museums

Leaving the palace, a steep, narrow cobbled lane with well restored Ottoman houses leads to the Fifth Court, which contains these excellent museums (www.istanbularkeoloji.gov.tr; Tue–Sun 9am–7pm, Nov–Mar till 5pm; single charge for all three; another entry by Gülhane tram stop). The **Archaeological Museum ❺** (*Arkeoloji Müzesi*) is made up of three sections, housing one of the world's great collections, with galleries devoted to Cyprus, Syria and Palestine, the Phrygians, Troy and Anatolia, from the Palaeolithic to the Iron Age, as well as the classical era. Its main attraction is the magnificent collection of sarcophagi from Sidon (in modern Lebanon), especially the Alexander Sarcophagus, decorated with scenes of hunting and battle.

The Archaeological Museum

The **Museum of the Ancient Orient** (*Eski Şark Eserleri Müzesi*) displays objects from ancient Near and Middle Eastern civilisations, including Babylonian ceramic panels from the Ishtar Gates at the time of King Nebuchadnezzar (605–562BC), Hittite stone sphinxes from Hattuşaş, the world's earliest known peace

Justinian's saviour

The Empress Theodora first appeared on stage at the Hippodrome as a dancing girl in a circus troupe. But perhaps her biggest role here came in January AD532, when she faced down an ugly riot between the rival Green and Blue political factions, known as the Nika Revolt. Buildings were set on fire and a new emperor proclaimed. As Justinian prepared to flee the city, the indomitable empress exhorted the troops to rally to his defence. Thirty thousand rioters were killed and the empire was saved.

treaty, the Treaty of Kadesh, signed between the Hittites and Egyptians in 1269BC, and the oldest recorded set of laws, the Code of Hammurabi (1750BC).

Built in 1472 for Mehmet the Conqueror, and decorated with turquoise and blue tiles, the most eye-catching building in the square is the **Tiled Pavilion** (*Çinili Köşk*). It houses a valuable display of ceramics going back to Seljuk times.

Hippodrome

The long arc that stretches southwest from Hagia Sophia is known as the **Hippodrome** ❻ (*At Meydanı*), and in Byzantine times that's exactly what it was. Inspired by the Circus Maximus in Rome, it was built in AD203 as a stadium for chariot-racing and other public events. Later it was enlarged by Constantine the Great and could hold an audience of 100,000.

The Hippodrome was the setting for the ceremony that proclaimed Constantinople as the 'New Rome' in AD330, following the division of the Roman Empire, and soon became the civic centre of the Byzantine capital, decorated with imposing monuments and flanked by fine buildings. Unfortunately it was destroyed when the city was sacked during the Fourth Crusade, and left stripped of its statues and marble seats. In the 17th century its ruins were used as a quarry for the building of the Blue Mosque. Only its outline, a few brick vaults and three fine ancient monuments, survive today.

The north end of the *spina*, or central axis, is marked by an ornate domed ablutions fountain, given to the city by Germany's Kaiser Wilhelm II to commemorate his visit in 1900. At the opposite end rise three remnants of the original Hippodrome. The **Egyptian Obelisk**, brought to Constantinople by Theodosius in AD390, had been commissioned by Pharaoh Thutmose III in the 16th century BC. What you see is only the top third of the original – it broke during shipment. The reliefs on the pedestal show Theodosius and his family in the Hippodrome presiding over the raising of the obelisk. The **Serpentine Column** consists of three intertwined bronze snakes; they originally supported a gold vase, but the snakes' heads and the vase have long since disappeared. It is the oldest Greek monument in Istanbul, commemorating the Greek victory over the Persians at Plataea in 479BC (it was brought here from Delphi by Constantine the Great). A second, deeply eroded stone obelisk is known as the **Column of Constantine Porphyrogenitus**, as an inscription on its base records that the emperor of that name (AD913–59) had it restored and sheathed in gilded bronze plates.

Egyptian Obelisk

Blue Mosque

The six minarets of the **Blue Mosque** ❼ (daily, but

closed at prayer times – best visited early in the morning; free but donations are appreciated) dominate the skyline of the Hippodrome. Known in Turkish as *Sultanahmet Camii* (Mosque of Sultan Ahmet), it was built between 1609 and 1616 for the Sultan Ahmet I, after which it became the city's principal imperial mosque because of its proximity to Topkapı Palace. To savour the full effect of the architect's skill, enter the courtyard through the gate that opens onto the Hippodrome. As you pass through the portal, the facade sweeps up in front of you in a fine crescendo of domes. (Go out through the door on the left of the courtyard to reach the entrance for visitors, which leads to the mosque proper.)

Once inside you will see how the mosque earned its familiar name. The very air seems to be blue – more than 20,000 turquoise İznik tiles glow gently in the light from the mosque's 260 windows, decorated with lilies, carnations, tulips and roses. Four massive columns support a dome 22m (70ft) in diameter, and 43m (142ft) high at the crown – big, but not quite as big as Hagia Sophia, the design of which obviously influenced the architect. The *mihrab* and *mimber* are of delicately carved white marble, and the ebony window shutters are inlaid with ivory and mother-of-pearl. The painted blue arabesques in the domes and upper walls are restorations; to see the originals, look at the wall beneath the sultan's loge.

A rival for Mecca?

A mosque with six minarets is unusual. Apparently, the sultan wanted to outshine Hagia Sophia but in doing so, he fell foul of those who felt that he was trying to vie with Mecca (which had six), and so he paid for a seventh minaret for Mecca.

The Blue Mosque stands on the site of Constantine's palace, a treasury of 500 halls and 30 chapels. All that remains is the 6th-century mosaic floor, now housed in the Büyük Saray Mozaikleri (Museum of Great Palace Mosaics; www.ayasofyamuzesi.com.tr; Tue–Sun 9am–5pm, in summer till

Inside the Blue Mosque

6pm), reached via the **Arasta Bazaar** (www.arastabazaar.com), a small shopping mall of high-quality craft and jewellery shops.

Across from the Hippodrome and the Blue Mosque is the **Museum of Turkish and Islamic Arts ❽** (*Türk ve İslam Eserleri Müzesi*; Tue–Sun 9am–5pm; www.tiem.gov.tr), newly reopened after a long renovation. The collection, housed in the former palace of Ibrahim Paşa, the son-in-law of Süleyman the Magnificent, includes illuminated Korans, inlaid Koran boxes, carpets, ceramics, and Persian miniatures.

Yerebatan Sarnıcı

Across from the tram lines from Hagia Sophia lies the entrance to one of Istanbul's more unusual historic sights – the **Basilica Cistern ❾**, also called the Sunken Palace (*Yerebatan Sarnıcı*; daily 9am–5.30pm; www.yerebatansarnici.com). This amazing construction is part of the city's ancient system of underground reservoirs, which was fed by water from the Belgrade

Yerebatan Sarayı

Forest. The cistern measures 140m (460ft) by 70m (230ft); its vaulted brick roof is supported by a forest of columns topped by Corinthian capitals, 336 in all, set in 12 rows of 28. It was built under Justinian in 532 and used during the Byzantine era, but forgotten thereafter until 1545 when a Frenchman discovered that residents drew water from wells in their homes. He got into the cistern and it was brought back into use as the water supply for Topkapı.

Çemberlitaş

Divan Yolu is the street with tramlines leading uphill from Sultanahmet. It was (and still is) the main road leading to the city gates in Byzantine and Ottoman times. Just off the road, on Klodfarer Caddesi, the **Binbirdirek Sarnıcı** (Cistern of 1001 Columns; daily 9am–midnight for sightseeing; free beverage included in the ticket price; www.binbirdirek.com) is an even older 4th-century cistern, with 224 columns – not 1001, in spite of its name.

The next tram stop is called **Çemberlitaş** (Hooped Column) after the stone pillar that rises to the right of the road. Also called the **Burnt Column**, it was charred and cracked by a great fire that ravaged the district in 1770 (the iron hoops help to reinforce the column). Constantine erected it in AD330 to mark the city's new status as capital of the Eastern Roman Empire. Parts of the cross and the nails with which Christ was crucified are reputed to be sealed in the column's base.

Built by Sinan, the **Çemberlitaş Hamamı** (*Vezirhan Caddesi*; 6am–midnight; www.cemberlitashamami.com) is still in use today as a Turkish bath and well worth a visit.

The Grand Bazaar

Behind the Burnt Column rises the Baroque exterior of the **Nuruosmaniye Camii**, dating from 1755. Walk towards it, then turn left through an arched gate into the mosque precinct and follow the crowds into the bustling **Grand Bazaar ⑩**. The *Kapalı Çarşı* (Covered Market; http://kapalicarsi.com.tr) of Istanbul is the world's largest covered bazaar, with more than 4,000 shops, as well as banks, cafés, restaurants, mosques and a post office, crammed together in a grid of 66 narrow streets that total 8km (5 miles) in length. It's all protected from summer sun and winter rain by a multitude of domed and vaulted roofs. Mehmet the Conqueror built the first covered market on this site in 1461. It has been rebuilt several times after destruction by fire and earthquake.

Inside the Grand Bazaar

Most of the streets follow a pattern and are well sign-posted. From the Nuruo-smaniye entrance, stretching towards the **Beyazıt Gate**, is the main street, lined with jewellers' shops. On your right is the entrance to the 16th century **Sandal Bedesten**, with brick vaults

The evil eye

You'll see many shops selling *nazar boncuk* – glass discs with a distinctive pattern of blue, white and black concentric circles, also sold in the form of jewellery, key-rings and general knick-knacks. These are considered a talisman to avert the evil eye and bring good luck.

supported on stone pillars. It is quiet for most of the week, but comes alive during the auctions held here at 1pm on Tuesday, Wednesday and Thursday. In the centre of the bazaar is the **Old Bedesten**, where you can find the best-quality gold and silver jewellery, brass and copper ware, curios and antiques.

The Beyazıt Gate, at the far end of the main street (*Kalpakcılar Başı Caddesi*), leads to a street of bargain clothing stalls. Turn right, and first left up the steps to the **Book Market** (*Sahaflar Çarşısı*), a tiny, historic courtyard, popular with students.

Beyazıt

The next tram stop, **Beyazıt**, brings you to **Beyazıt Meydanı**, a vast, pigeon-thronged square below the entrance to Istanbul University (www.istanbul.edu.tr). Site of the Roman Forum Tauri (Forum of the Bulls), it has been one of the city's main gathering points for 2,000 years. It's a busy square, full of students, children and vendors, as well as the many pigeons.

The east side of the square is dominated by the beautiful **Beyazıt Camii**, built in the early 16th century by Sultan Beyazıt II, son of Mehmet the Conqueror. It is the earliest surviving example of classical Ottoman architecture, inspired by Hagia Sophia. Opposite the mosque is the arched gateway to Istanbul University and the 50m (148ft) **Beyazıt Tower**, built in 1828 as a fire-lookout point and still in use. On the west side of the square is the Calligraphy Museum (closed for restoration at time of writing), part of the old *medresse*.

Süleymaniye Mosque

The outline of the **Mosque of Süleyman the Magnificent** ⓫ (*Suleymaniye Camii*), rises from a site above the Golden Horn (near the north gate of Istanbul University). Deemed the finest Ottoman building in Istanbul, the mosque is a tribute to the 'Golden Age' of the Ottoman Empire, and to the two great men of genius who created it – Sultan Süleyman I and his chief architect, Sinan. Süleyman, known in Turkish as Kanuni (The Lawgiver), reigned from 1520–66, when the empire attained the height of its wealth and power.

Süleymaniye Mosque and its complex of buildings were built between 1550 and 1557. Legend has it that jewels from Persia were ground up and mixed in with the mortar for one of the minarets, and that the incredible acoustics were achieved by embedding 64 hollow clay vessels facing neck-down in the dome. It is also said that Süleyman, in awe of his architect's

Friday prayers at the Süleymaniye Mosque

achievement, handed the keys to Sinan at the inauguration ceremony and allowed him the privilege of opening it.

You enter through a courtyard, colonnaded with grand columns of granite, marble and porphyry, with a rectangular şadırvan (ablutions fountain) in the centre. The interior is vast and inspiring, flooded with light from the 16th-century stained-glass windows. The mosque is square in plan, about 58m (172ft) on each side, capped by a dome 27.5m (82ft) in diameter and 47m (140ft) high. The tiles are original İznik faïence, with floral designs; the woodwork of the doors and shutters is delicately inlaid with ivory and mother-of-pearl.

The impressive interior of Süleymaniye Mosque

Both Süleyman and Sinan are buried nearby. The **tombs** of the sultan and his wife Roxelana lie behind the mosque in the walled garden, where roses and hollyhocks tangle among the tall grass between the gravestones, and sparrows swoop and squabble in the fig trees. Sinan's modest tomb, which he designed himself, stands in a triangular garden just outside the northern corner of the complex, capped by a small dome.

A walk around the terrace beside the mosque, which affords a fine view across the Golden Horn, gives some idea of the size of the complex with its attendant soup kitchen and caravanserai,

school and library, now housing restaurants and archives. The
hamam is back in use.

Towards the City Walls

The tram continues towards the city walls, passing Laleli and
Aksaray, where there are many hotels, and out to the suburbs.
There are a number of worthwhile sights between Süleymaniye
Mosque and the city walls, but they are scattered and require
a long walk or bus or taxi rides. Away from the main roads,
these neighbourhoods contain a maze of backstreets, muddy
lanes and cobbled alleys. If you choose to walk, there are some
good large-scale maps available. The odd, old wooden house
that has survived the city's numerous fires leans creaking across
the crumbling bricks of some forgotten Byzantine ruin.

One of Sinan's early buildings, in memory of Prince
Mehmet, Süleyman the Magnificent's son, who died in 1543
aged 21, is the imposing Mosque of the Prince (*Şehzade Camii*),
overlooking a park that is spoilt by traffic noise.

Aqueduct of Valens

Spanning the park and the six lanes of the busy thoroughfare
Atatürk Bulvarı are the impressive remains of the **Aqueduct
of Valens** (*Bozdoğan Kemeri*). Constructed in the 2nd century AD, it was rebuilt by Emperor Valens in the 4th century, restored several times by both the Byzantines and the
Ottomans, and remained in use up till the 19th century.

If you follow the line of the aqueduct away from the city
centre, you soon reach the vast complex of the **Mosque of
the Conqueror** (*Fatih Camii*), perched on top of the city's
Fourth Hill. It was the first imperial mosque to be built following the Conquest of Constantinople in 1453, and its *külliye*
(mosque complex), the biggest in the whole of the Ottoman
Empire, included a hospital, alms houses, a mental asylum,
visitors' accommodation and a number of schools teaching

Valens Aqueduct

science, mathematics, history and Koranic studies. Built by Mehmet the Conqueror between 1462 and 1470, the complex was almost completely destroyed by an earthquake in 1766. Only the courtyard and its huge portal survived; the rest was rebuilt. The tombs of the conqueror and his wife are in the walled graveyard behind the mosque. Wednesday sees a lively street market selling everything from vegetables to umbrellas and underwear.

Farther out, dominating the Fifth Hill, is the **Mosque of Selim I** *(Sultan Selim Camii)*, dedicated to the father of Süleyman the Magnificent. Its dedicatee was known as Yavuz Selim (Selim the Grim), but the mosque is one of the loveliest in the city, with sparse, tasteful decoration of beautiful İznik tiles in turquoise, blue and yellow, and richly painted woodwork. Its dramatic situation overlooking the Golden Horn commands a sweeping view across the picturesque districts of Fener and Balat.

Kariye Museum

The brightest jewel in Istanbul's Byzantine crown is the former Chora Church, now housing the **Kariye Museum** ⓬ (*Kariye Müzesi*; www.ayasofyamuzesi.gov.tr; Thur–Tue 9am–5pm, till 6pm in summer; due to restoration works some parts of the museum may be closed). Opened as a museum in 1958, this small building, tucked away in a quiet corner, is one of the world's greatest monuments to Byzantine art. 'Chora' means 'in the country' because the first church to be built on this site was outside the city walls. It was later enclosed within the Theodosian Walls, but the name stuck.

The oldest part of the existing building, the central domed area, dates from 1120. The church was rebuilt and decorated early in the 14th century under the supervision of Theodore Metochites, an art-lover, statesman and scholar who was a friend and adviser of Emperor Andronicus II Palaeologus. Sadly, Metochites was reduced to poverty and sent into exile when the emperor was overthrown in 1328. He was allowed to return in 1330 provided he remained a monk at Chora, which he did, living the last years of his life surrounded by the magnificent works of art he had commissioned.

Metochites left the central portion of the church intact, but added the outer narthex and the parecclesion (side chapel). The wonderful mosaics and frescoes, dating from 1310–20, are almost certainly the work of a single artist, now unknown. Their subtlety of colour, liveliness of posture, and strong, lifelike faces record a last flowering of Byzantine art before its descent into decadence. The church was converted into a mosque in 1511, but fortunately it was not substantially altered. The mosaics were covered with wooden screens, some windows were boarded up, and a minaret was added.

The **mosaics** are grouped into four narrative cycles depicting the lives of Christ and the Virgin Mary, along with portraits of various saints, and large dedicatory panels. The mosaic above

Byzantine beauty at the Kariye Museum

the door leading from the narthex into the nave shows the figure of Metochites, wearing a huge hat, offering a model of his
beloved church to Christ. Each tiny tile is set at a different angle
to its neighbours so that the reflected light creates the illusion
of a shimmering, ethereal image. The **frescoes** are all in the
parecclesion, which stretches the length of the building and was
used in Byzantine times as a funerary chapel. The artist's masterpiece is the *Anastasis* (Resurrection) in the vault of the apse,
showing Christ pulling Adam and Eve from their tombs, while
the figure of Satan lies bound and helpless beneath his feet.

Fifteen minutes' walk from the museum, and marking the
summit of the Sixth Hill, is the **Mihrimah Sultan Camii**,
built by Sinan in 1565 for Süleyman's favourite daughter. Next
to the mosque are the **Theodosian Walls**, pierced here by the
Adrianople Gate *(Edirnekapı)* where Mehmet the Conqueror
entered the fallen city in 1453. The double walls, built in the 5th
century during the reign of Emperor Theodosius, stretch 6.5km

(4 miles) from the Sea of Marmara to the Golden Horn. They were defended by 96 towers and had numerous gates. Much of the inner wall and several of the towers are still standing. Seven gates are still in use. It is possible to follow the walls as there are roads alongside them and in some places you can walk on the actual wall. The state of repair varies from section to section, and there is a great deal of painstaking renovation work being carried out.

Yedikule

At the Marmara end of the Theodosian Walls, far from the city's other sights but easily reached by bus or taxi, stands **Yedikule** (Seven Towers; Thur–Tue 9.30am–4.30pm). The ancient fortress encloses the **Golden Gate** (*Altınkapı*), the triumphal arch of the Byzantine emperors, which existed before the walls were built and was incorporated into them. In 1470 Mehmet the Conqueror further strengthened the ancient portal by building three towers of his own, linked by curtain walls to the four Byzantine towers flanking the Golden Gate. During Ottoman times the fortress was used as a prison and a treasury.

Eyüp and The Golden Horn (Haliç)

The **Golden Horn** is an inlet of the Bosphorus, penetrating 7.5km (4.5 miles) into the hills behind the city. It forms a natural harbour, and in Ottoman times was the site of the Imperial Tershane (Naval Arsenal), capable of holding 120 ships. It later became an industrial area, but the factories and shipyards have given way to

Inside the Mihrimah Sultan Camii in Üsküdar

Service at Eyüp mosque

hotels and tourist attractions. Millions have been spent on improving the water quality.

Hourly ferries depart from the upstream side of Galata Bridge for the half-hour trip along the Golden Horn to the suburb of **Eyüp**, which contains one of Islam's most sacred shrines. **Eyüp Sultan Camii** ⓭ marks the burial place of Eyüp Ensari, the standard-bearer of the Prophet Mohammed. He died in battle while carrying the banner of Islam during the Arab siege of Constantinople (674–8). Following the conquest in 1453, his grave was rediscovered, and Mehmet the Conqueror erected a shrine on the spot, followed in 1458 by a mosque, the first to be built in Istanbul. Thereafter each sultan, on his accession, visited Eyüp Camii to gird himself ceremonially with the Sword of Osman, the first Ottoman sultan. The original mosque was destroyed by an earthquake in 1766; the present building dates from 1800. The **Tomb of Eyüp Ensari**, behind the mosque, is decorated with gold, silver and coloured tiles, and is protected by a gilded grille. Remember that this is a sacred place – dress respectfully and remove shoes before entering (women should cover their legs, upper arms and hair).

Covering the hillside behind the mosque is a vast cemetery littered with turbanned headstones. A path and cable car *(teleferik)* lead up to the **Pierre Loti Café**, named in honour of the 19th-century French writer who lived in the neighbourhood, and wrote romantic novels about life in Istanbul. The café enjoys a splendid view down the Golden Horn to the distant domes and minarets of Stamboul. The *teleferik* gets busy on summer evenings and at weekends.

A short bus ride from Eyüp is **Santralistanbul Museum of Energy** (*Silahtar*; Tue–Fri 10am–6pm, Sat–Sun 10am–8pm; www.santralistanbul.org; free except guided tours), a restored Ottoman-era power station, now a superb arts venue with contemporary exhibitions and a restaurant.

On the opposite side of the Golden Horn, at Sutluce, is a children's favourite, **Miniaturk** (*İmrahor Caddesi*; daily 9am–7pm; http://miniaturk.com.tr). Its miniature buildings and monuments have been selected to reflect the variety of landmarks in the Ottoman Empire. A little further south (accessible by bus), the **Rahmi M Koç Museum** (*Hasköy Caddesi*; Tue–Fri 10am–5pm, Sat–Sun 10am–6pm, summer 10am–8pm; www.rmk-museum.com.tr), housed in an old iron foundry on

Pierre Loti

Louis Marie Julien Viaud (1859–1923) was a French naval officer whose travels took him to various places in the East and the South Seas. They provided a background for a steady stream of novels, about one per year, written under the pseudonym Pierre Loti. His books were once popular and highly regarded, but are now largely forgotten among English-speaking people.

Aziyadé, part autobiography and part romance, recounts his travels to Constantinople and his love affair with the green-eyed Circassian harem girl, Aziyadé. The book shows a passionate nature, and a man's dreams and melancholy in Constantinople in the last days of the Ottoman Empire. The café at Eyüp is where Pierre Loti is best remembered, but there's an eponymous restaurant and hotel in Sultanahmet.

the south side of the Golden Horn, is a fascinating private collection of scientific, technological and transport items, from an 1898 steam car to a 1940s US submarine as well as masses of smaller instruments, toys and hands-on things to play with. Not the obvious Turkish 'sight' but well worth visiting.

THE NEW CITY (BEYOĞLU)

The north shore of the Golden Horn was traditionally the quarter where craftsmen, foreign merchants and diplomats made their homes, beginning in the 11th century when the Genoese founded a trading colony in the district of Galata. Following the conquest, European ambassadors built their mansions on the hills beyond Galata, a place which came to be called Pera (Greek for 'beyond'). Foreigners from the entire Ottoman Empire flooded into Galata and Pera, attracted by the wealth and sophistication of the capital. As the area became crowded, the wealthy foreign merchants and diplomats moved farther along the 'Grande Rue de Pera' (now İstiklal Caddesi), forming a focus for the 19th- and 20th-century expansion of the modern, European-style part of Istanbul, known as Beyoğlu.

St Stephen's church

On the south side of the Golden Horn, between the ferry stops of Fener and Balat, stands the Church of St Stephen of the Bulgars. This is an unusual building, for the neo-Gothic structure and decorations are made entirely of iron. The sections were cast in Vienna and shipped down the Danube and across the Black Sea. It was built for Istanbul's Bulgarian community in 1871, and is still used for worship.

Galata and Pera

The mouth of the Golden Horn is spanned by the **Galata Bridge ⓮**. The first bridge here was a wooden structure, built in 1845. It was replaced in 1910 by

the famous old pontoon
bridge with its seafood
restaurants, which served
until the present one was
opened in 1992. The bridge
is thronged with fisher-
men and a waving forest
of rods occupies every last
piece of space. As you walk
across the bridge, your eyes
are drawn naturally to the
pointed turret of Galata
Tower. Sometime during
the 11th century, a rough
bunch of coastal traders and
drifters from every port in
the Mediterranean began to
settle on the northern shore
of the Horn, in the mari-
time quarter which became
known as Galata.

Galata Tower

To avoid the steep climb up the hill beyond Galata Bridge
take the **Tünel**, the world's second oldest (and probably shortest) underground railway, built in 1875. The trip to the top
station (Tünel) takes just 90 seconds. To reach Galata Tower
from here, follow the signs back down the hill.

Galata Tower ⓯ (*Galata Kulesi*; observation deck daily
9am–5pm, till 7pm in summer) was the keystone in the colony's defences. Its age is uncertain, but it seems to have been
built in its present form in 1349, at the highest point of the
walls. With an open viewing gallery and restaurant at the top
(open till late; belly dancer shows at 8pm, book in advance), it
offers fine views over the city, and across the Golden Horn you
can count the minarets and domes of Old Istanbul's skyline.

Near the tower is modern art research centre SALT Galata, which attracts the local art crowd.

Up the hill on Galipdede Caddesi are shops selling books and musical instruments. There's also the **Galata Mevlevihanesi** ⓰, the former Whirling Dervish Hall, where Sufis whirled from 1491 until Atatürk proscribed their practices in 1924. The centre is now the Museum of Divan Literature (www.galatamevlevihanesimuzesi.gov.tr; daily 9am–5pm, till 7pm in summer), where manuscripts and a selection of instruments are preserved in glass cabinets. Public performances of the order's distinctive whirling, trance-inducing dance, are held Sundays at 5pm. The centre is also home for a community of cats, who bask on the graves in the peaceful courtyard.

Dervishes at prayer, Galata Mevlevihanesi

Just up the road, restored 1920s trams clang their way along **İstiklal Caddesi** ⓱ (Avenue of Independence), once lined with the palatial embassies of foreign powers. The mansions have been downgraded to consulates since the capital was transferred to Ankara in 1923, and modern shops and restaurants have sprung up. The street is now pedestrianised, and has some of the city's smartest cafés and many international chain stores. At Galatasaray

Square, where İstiklal Caddesi bends to the right, an elegant wrought-iron gateway marks the entrance to the 19th-century **Galatasaray Lisesi**, the Franco-Turkish *lycée* (secondary school) that educated many of the great names in modern Turkish history. Just behind it is another of Istanbul's great historic hamams, the **Tarihi Galatasaray Hamamı** (Turnacıbaşı Sokak 24; daily 7am–10pm for men, 8am–9pm for women; www.galatasarayhamami.com).

Tram on İstiklal Caddesi

Past the square on the left is the entrance to **Çiçek Pasajı** (Flower Alley; www.tarihicicekpasaji.com), a high, glass-roofed arcade lined with bars and restaurants. The opposite end of the arcade leads into the **Balık Pazarı** (Fish Market), a block of narrow streets lined with small restaurants and stalls selling fish, fruit and vegetables, and a local speciality snack – *midye tava* (fried mussels on a stick). Go back to Galatasaray Square, and left at the British Consulate along Meşrutiyet Caddesi, and you will reach the beautifully restored **Pera Palas Hotel** (www.jumeirah. com). Established in 1892, it provided accommodation for Orient Express passengers and displays highlight its historic ephemera. Agatha Christie stayed in Room 411 when writing *Murder on the Orient Express*. Room 101, the suite used by Atatürk, has been kept as a museum. The old Bristol Hotel is now the **Pera Museum** (Meşrutiyet Caddesi 141; Tue–Sat 10am–7pm, Sun noon–6pm; free Fri 6–10pm and for students on Wed; www.peramuzesi.org.tr), housing the Kiraç family collection of Kutahya tiles and European portraits of life at the Ottoman imperial court. Not far, at İstiklâl Caddesi 136, a 19th-century townhouse has been transformed into the three storey ultra-modern exhibition space **SALT** (www.saltonline.org; Tue–Sun noon–8pm, Sun till 6pm), with an English-language bookshop and a panoramic restaurant.

Taksim and Beyond

Beyond Çiçek Pasajı, the side streets off İstiklal Caddesi are the focus for Istanbul's raunchier nightlife. Buzzing bars and cafés are always springing up here, especially at the Tünel end. Look out for great live music venues from techno to jazz. The street ends at **Taksim Square** *(Taksim Meydanı)*, the heart of modern Istanbul, lined with hotels. The governmental proposal to build a shopping centre on the site of Gezi Park, the only green space in this area, provoked social protests in 2013 and the rise of the movement Occupy Gezi. The **Atatürk Cultural Centre**, once the city's largest concert hall and fine example of modern Turkish architecture, closed in 2008 for renovation and has not reopened since.

At the far end of the square Cumhuriyet Caddesi leads past the Hilton Hotel for a good kilometre (0.75 mile) to the **Military Museum** ⓲ *(Askeri Müzesi*, Tues–Wed and Fri–Sun 9am–5pm). The exhibits include a section of the massive chain that the Byzantines used to stretch across the mouth of the Golden Horn to keep out enemy ships, as well as captured enemy cannon and military banners, the campaign tents from which the Ottoman sultans controlled their armies, and examples of uniforms, armour and weapons from the earliest days of the empire down to the 20th century. The main attraction is the concert given by the **Janissary Band**

(Mehter Takımı), a revival of the Ottoman military band that accompanied the sultans' armies on campaigns and led victory processions through the conquered cities. The colourful uniforms are exact replicas of the originals.

Taksim Square also leads to the shopping districts of **Çukurcuma** (southwest) with antiques dealers and cafés and **Teşvikiye** and **Nişantaşı** (north), home of designer labels. Created by famous writer Orhan Pamuk, the **Mazumiyet Müzesi** ❶⓽ (Museum of Innocence; Tue–Sun 10am–6pm, Thur till 9pm; free; www.mazumiyet

Janissary Band drummer

muzesi.org), shows Istanbul life as it was in the second half of 20th century.

The Bosphorus Shore

Karaköy Square *(Karaköy Meydanı)*, at the northern end of the Galata Bridge, is home to the local fish market and is a great place to begin a walk through the old docks area where the cruise-ship terminus is located. A couple of tram stops northeast is **Istanbul Modern** ❷⓪ *(Meclis-i Mebusan Caddesi Liman Sahası*; www.istanbulmodern.org; Tue–Sun 10am–6pm, Thur till 8pm), housed in a former customs warehouse on Karaköy pier, which has a permanent collection of modern Turkish paintings, sculpture, photography,

The ornate Dolmabahçe Palace, near Beşiktaş

video and sound installations, as well as a room for touring exhibitions. There is also an art-house cinema and a chic first floor café-bar with superb views.

Dolmabahçe Palace

Take the tram to Kabataş and along to **Dolmabahçe Palace** ㉑ (*Dolmabahçe Sarayı*; www.millisaraylar. gov.tr; daily except Mon and Thur, 9am–4pm, may close earlier if the daily ticket quota of 3,000 is exceeded; guided tours only). Sultan Abdül Mecit (reigned 1839–61) decided that Topkapı Palace was too old-fashioned. He commissioned a vast new palace on the shores of the Bosphorus, on the site of a park that had been created by filling in an old harbour (*dolmabahçe* means 'filled-in garden'). Completed in 1853, the palace was intended as a statement of the sultan's faith in the future of his empire, but instead it turned out to be a monument to folly and extravagance. Its construction nearly emptied the imperial treasury, and the running costs contributed to the empire's bankruptcy in 1875.

The guided tour is in two parts – first the **Selamlık** (public rooms) and **Throne Room**, then the **Harem** (private apartments). Highlights of the *Selamlık* include the vast Baccarat and Bohemian crystal chandeliers, 36 in all, and crystal balusters of the main staircase, the sultan's bathroom, two huge bearskins (a gift from the Tsar of Russia), Sèvres vases, Gobelin tapestries and carpets, and the vast bed used by the 'giant sultan', Abdül Aziz. The Throne Room is huge and lavishly decorated.

Further along the waterfront, the **Naval Museum** ㉒ (*Deniz Müzesi*, Iskele Caddesi, Beşiktaş; Tue–Sun 9am–5pm, in summer also Sat–Sun 10am–6pm; www.deniz muzeleri.tsk.tr) is a reminder that the Ottoman Empire was one of the world's great sea powers. This is a fascinating repository of naval memorabilia, from charts and the personal records, clothes and belongings of Turkish sailors to the splendidly ornate Ottoman royal barges. Outside the museum is the statue and tomb of 16th-century admiral Barbarossa.

Just 2km (1.5 miles) beyond Dolmabahçe you can escape from the city among the wooded walks of **Yıldız Palace and Park** (www.millisaraylar.gov.tr), once the hunting grounds of the sultans. The ornate **Şale Köskü** (Chalet Pavilion; Tue–Wed and Fri–Sun 9am–5pm), now an interesting little museum, was built by Abdül Hamid II in 1882 for the sultan's guests, but the paranoid Abdül Hamid moved in himself until he was deposed in 1909, living a solitary life as a carpenter. Nearby, **Malta Köskü** is another restored royal pavilion, hat has been converted into a café, with a terrace looking over the treetops to the Bosphorus.

The End of a Dynasty

It is appropriate that Dolmabahçe Palace, the main financial drain that contributed to the downfall of the empire in 1875, was witness to the final act of the empire.

When Atatürk's government abolished the sultanate in November 1922, Mehmet VI, the last representative of the dynasty that had ruled the Ottoman Empire for six centuries, was ignominiously smuggled aboard a British warship anchored off Dolmabahçe, to spend his last years in exile. Atatürk died in the palace on 10 November 1938 at 9.05am, the hour at which all the palace clocks were stopped.

The Maiden's Tower

ACROSS TO ASIA

You can head from the hustle and bustle of Eminönü or Beşiktaş across the water to Asia. **Üsküdar** lies opposite, at the eastern shore of the Bosphorus. The ferry passes **Kız Kulesi** ㉓ (Maiden's Tower), perched on a tiny island about 200m/yds offshore. The name is derived from a legend about a princess confined by her father to protect her from the fate foretold by a dire prophecy: that she would die from the bite of a serpent. Ironically, the princess was eventually bitten by a snake that arrived in one of the baskets containing supplies. Originally a 12th-century Byzantine fort, the present tower dates from the 18th century, and has served as a lighthouse, customs office and control tower. It is now used as a restaurant and café (www.kizkulesi.com.tr) with shuttle boat services from both sides of Istanbul. In Byzantine times a huge chain could be slung between here and the Saray Burnu Peninsula to close the mouth of the Bosphorus. The ferry leaves you at Üsküdar's main square, Iskele Meydanı. Note the **İskele Camii**, designed by Sinan in 1548 for Mihrimah, daughter of Süleyman the Magnificent, and the **Yeni Valide Camii** from the early 18th century. West of the square is Sinan's **Şemşi Paşa Camii** (1580) on the waterfront.

Üsküdar was known as Scutari by Europeans, and Scutari is traditionally associated with the name of Florence Nightingale. During the Crimean War (1854–6) the English nurse set up a hospital in what is now the enormous **Selimiye Barracks** (*Selimiye Kışlası*), situated in the district of Harem to the south of Üsküdar. A small corner of the building is kept as a **museum** (daily 9am–5pm) in her memory – the exhibits include the famous lamp, which led to her being called 'The lady with the lamp'. Down a lane off Tibbiye Caddesi, the **Commonwealth War Graves Commission Haidar Pasha Cemetery** (*Commonwealth Harp Mezarligi Haidarpaşa*) is a tranquil, beautiful spot. There is a huge memorial to the Crimean War, and the dead from that war (mostly victims of cholera) and the two world wars rest in immaculate graves, with men from the UK and the Indian subcontinent lying side by side.

LOCAL EXCURSIONS

Along the Bosphorus

The **Bosphorus** (*Istanbul Boğazı*) is the narrow strait linking the Black Sea to the Sea of Marmara, and separating the European part of Turkey from the vast hinterland of Anatolia. The winding channel is 30km (18 miles) long and about 2km (1.5 miles) wide, narrowing to 750m (2,450ft) at Rumeli Hisarı.

The strait, once navigated by Jason and the Argonauts in their search for the Golden Fleece, and crossed on a bridge of boats by the Persian army of King Darius in 512BC, en route to battle with the Scythians, is today busy with commercial shipping, ferries and fishing boats. Its wooded shores are lined with pretty fishing villages, old Ottoman mansions, and the villas of Istanbul's wealthier citizens. It is spanned by two impressive suspension bridges. The first bridge to link Europe and Asia was the **Bosphorus Bridge** (*Boğaziçi Köprüsü*) at Ortaköy, opened in 1973. It was followed in 1988 by the **Fatih Sultan Mehmet Bridge** at Rumeli Hisarı. Further north construction on the Yavuz Sultan Selim Bridge began in 2013.

The sleek Bosphorus Bridge

The **boat trip up the Bosphorus ㉔** (many sailings daily from private and public companies) from the pier at Eminönü is worth every penny. The ferry weaves back and forth between Europe and Asia, calling first at Beşiktaş and then a string of attractive villages. You can remain on the boat for the round trip, or stop for lunch at Anadolu Kavağı, or disembark anywhere and return by bus or taxi. Plenty of private companies offer shorter cruises if you are pressed for time; there is also a nonstopping 90-minute evening cruise in summer.

The public ferry heads north, past Istanbul Modern

and Çirağan Palace, now a luxury hotel, stopping at **Beşiktaş** where you can visit Dolmabahçe Palace, the Naval Museum and Yıldız Park. From here you pass beneath the Bosphorus Bridge. Beneath its western end is **Ortaköy**, with a waterfront mosque. The village is a pleasant place, with shops, art galleries, bookstalls and cafés. Just beyond the bridge, on the Asian shore, is **Beylerbeyi Palace** (www.millisaraylar.gov.tr; daily except Mon and Thu Tues–Wed and Fri–Sun 9.30am–74pm), a sultan's summer residence and hunting lodge built in 1865.

If you continue past the rich suburbs of **Arnavutköy** and **Bebek**, famed for their wonderful *yalıs* (ornate wooden mansions on the waterfront), you will soon reach the massive fortress of **Rumeli Hisarı** (Thur–Tue 9.30am–4.30pm). It was built at the command of Mehmet II in 1452 in preparation for his last assault on Constantinople. Its walls enclose a pleasant park with an open-air theatre that occasionally hosts folk-dancing and concerts in summer. On the opposite shore is the smaller and older fortress of **Anadolu Hisarı** (closed to the public), dating from 1390. South of the fort is the ornate rococo facade of the **Küçüksu Pavilion** (*Küçüksu Kasri*; Tues–Wed and Fri–Sun; 9am–5pm; www.millisaraylar.gov.tr), an Ottoman summer-house built on a favourite picnic spot known as the Sweet Waters of Asia.

Beyond the Fatih Sultan Mehmet Bridge the boat stops at **Kanlıca** on the Asian shore, a village famous for its yoghurt, which you can sample at one of the waterside cafés. The upper reaches of the Bosphorus are lined with picturesque fishing villages – **Tarabya**, **Sarıyer** and **Rumeli Kavağı** – where you can enjoy a meal at one of many seafood restaurants. In Sarıyer you can also visit the **Sadberk Hanım Museum** ㉕ (Buyukdere Piyasa Caddesi 27; Tues–Sun 10am–6pm, until 10pm on Wed and Fri; www.sakipsabanciimuzesi,org), a fabulous private collection covering the period from 500BC to Ottoman times, housed in two 19th-century villas. Well-presented displays of gold jewellery, embroidery, costumes and Anatolian figurines help make this one of the finest small museums in Turkey.

Last stop is **Anadolu Kavağı** on the Asian side, a picturesque place overlooked by a Byzantine castle, where the ferry leaves you for a couple of hours or so.

Arnavutköy mansions

The Princes' Islands

An hour's ferry trip to the southwest of Istanbul lies the bucolic retreat of the **Princes' Islands** ㉖, known to the Turks simply as Adalar, 'The Islands'. This archipelago of nine islands in the Sea of Marmara has been inhabited since Byzantine times by monastic communities, and was a place of exile for deposed rulers. The Emperor Justin II built a palace on the largest island in the 6th century; it soon came to be known as Prinkipo, the Prince's Isle, and the name later spread to cover the whole group. Today the islands' pretty beaches provide a perfect weekend retreat for the people of Istanbul. Cars are banned, and all transport is by foot, bicycle or *feyton* (horse-drawn carriage).

Check at the ferry terminal for times of ferries, leaving from Eminönü and Beşiktaş; also check terminals for inter-island trips. The biggest and most popular island is

Büyükada (Big Island), with a pleasant town, a picturesque monastery and the modern **Museum of Princes' Islands** (*Adalar Muzesi Hangar*; Aya Nikola Mevkii; tel: 0216-382 6430; www.adalarmuzesi.org; Tue–Sun 10am–6pm). You can take a tour of the island on a *fayton* – to find the 'taxi rank', walk uphill from the jetty to the clock tower in the square and turn left. You can also walk to most places, including a steep uphill hike to **St George's Monastery**, where there are iron rings in the marble floor of the chapel that were used to restrain the mentally ill, who were once brought here, hoping to be cured by the waters. There is a simple, delightful restaurant in the monastery's outdoor courtyard. The ferry also calls at the islands of **Kınalıada, Burgazada** and **Heybeliada**, so it's possible to visit two in one day.

Belgrade Forest

This is an area north of Istanbul and west of Sarıyer that was once more or less a nature reserve kept for royal hunting. There was a village called Belgrade founded by Süleyman the Magnificent, who moved people from the other Belgrade into the area to look after the reservoirs and aqueducts that provided Istanbul's water, so there are scattered remains of all this activity. Nowadays, people use the forest for picnics and exercise, so it is popular during summer weekends.

Black Sea

There are some small, pleasant resorts accessible from Istanbul, with sandy beaches and clean air. They can be reached by *dolmuş* or minibus. **Kilyos**, about 35km (22 miles) from the centre of Istanbul on the European side, is reached via Sarıyer. The beach (the private stretch is worth paying for) is long but the sea has some dangerous currents. The ruins of a Genoese

Feyton driver on Büyükada, largest of the Princes' Islands

castle can be seen but not visited as the area is in use by the military; however, there are some good walks. On the Asian side, there's transport from Üsküdar to **Sile**, which takes about an hour. Sile is fairly quiet during the week, but becomes the Brighton of Istanbul at the weekend. It has high cliffs and good fish restaurants.

OVERNIGHT EXCURSIONS

There are places of special interest that can be visited from Istanbul, but are sufficiently distant to require at least one overnight stop. They include the historic cities of Edirne, Bursa and İznik, and in winter there's a ski resort at Mount Uludağ, south of Bursa. Troy and Gallipoli are also very popular, and visiting them usually involves an overnight stay in **Çanakkale**, a seaside resort with hotels, restaurants and amenities, which also has a good Archaeological Museum.

Gallipoli

The **Gallipoli Peninsula** ㉗ *(Gelibolu Yarımadası)*, on the north side of the Dardanelles, was the scene of one of the most notorious military campaigns of World War I. The Allied assault, involving Australian, British, New Zealand and French forces, aimed to capture the peninsula and control the narrow strait of the Dardanelles, thus securing an ice-free sea passage to supply arms to Russia and open a front against the Germans.

The first landings took place on 25 April 1915, and met with fierce resistance from the Turks, under the command of General Mustafa Kemal. The Allies only managed to gain a toehold on the peninsula, and then deadlock ensued, with almost nine months of static trench warfare. The cost in human lives was severe, with 160,000 Allies and 86,000 Turks killed and some 250,000 wounded. The Anzacs (Australia and New Zealand Army Corps) saw some of the worst fighting and suffered the heaviest casualties; the beach where they landed has been named **Anzac Cove** *(Anzak Köyü)* in their honour.

The whole peninsula is a memorial, with plaques describing the campaign's progress, and monuments to the soldiers of the Allied and Turkish armies. Start either at the New Zealand Memorial at Chunuk Bair to take in the sweeping view of the battlefield or at the monumental **Çanakkale Epic Presentation Centre** in Kabatepe (Çanakkale Destanı Tanıtım Merkezi; daily 9am–4.45pm), opened in 2012, to watch a multimedia

'Our sons as well'

'There is no difference between the Johnnies and the Mehmets to us, where they lie side by side here in this country of ours. You, the mothers who sent their sons from faraway countries, wipe away your tears; Your sons are now lying in our bosom and are in peace after having lost their life on this land. They have become our sons as well.'
The words of Atatürk on a memorial at Gallipoli

presentation of the battle. Each war cemetery is signposted, and all are beautifully tended, planted with flowers and scented with fragrant hedges of rosemary. A memorial service attended by families of Turkish and Anzac veterans as well as other visitors is held each year on Anzac Day (25 April).

Troy

The exact location of the legendary city of **Troy** (daily 8.30am–5pm) remained a mystery until an amateur archaeologist with a passion for Homer began excavations in 1871. Heinrich Schliemann found his fabled city, and discovered 'Priam's treasure', a cache of gold. He smuggled it back to Germany, but it vanished during World War II, only to make a dramatic reappearance in Moscow in 1993.

Archaeologists have now uncovered nine superimposed cities, from Troy I, an Early Bronze Age settlement (3000–2500BC) to the Hellenistic and Roman metropolis, known as Ilium Novum, which stood here from 334BC to AD400. American scholars identify the level known as Troy VIIa as King Priam's city, and place its destruction around 1260BC. Certain eminent Turkish archaeologists disagree, instead opting for the preceding level, Troy VI.

The Trojan Horse

Most people know the story of the Trojan War as Homer told it. It all started when peace-loving King Priam's son, Paris, was inveigled by a trio of jealous goddesses into abducting the most beautiful woman in the world, Helen, wife of Menelaus, king of Sparta.

The ensuing war between Greece and Troy lasted 10 years and cost the lives of great heroes such as Hector and Achilles. The end came when the Greeks tricked the Trojans into accepting a gift of a huge wooden horse within their walls – it was filled with armed men who sacked the city and left it in ruins.

The Aegean coastline

The site, near the village of **Hısarlık**, is marked by a large replica of the famed wooden horse. For those who have enjoyed Homer's *Iliad* and *Odyssey* it is a magical place, where the stones are haunted by the spirits of Helen and Paris, Achilles and Agamemnon.

AEGEAN COAST

Turkey's Aegean coast offers an unparalleled combination of natural beauty and historical interest. This was one of the most densely populated parts of the ancient world, with many famous cities to its name – Troy, city of the *Iliad* and the *Odyssey*, and Smyrna (İzmir), the birthplace of Homer; Sardis, home of the wealthy King Croesus; Ephesus, where St Paul preached the gospels; and Halicarnassos, birthplace of the historian Herodotus. The ruins of two of the Seven Wonders of the World – the Temple of Artemis at Ephesus and the Mausoleum of Halicarnassus – are also to be found here.

Set amid these historic sites are many beautiful beaches and pretty fishing villages, and a number of modern holiday resorts, notably Kuşadası and Bodrum. The main city is İzmir, which has an international airport; there are other airports at Bodrum and Dalaman, where most package tours arrive.

İzmir and the Northern Aegean

Known to the Greeks as Smyrna, and to the Turks as *Güzel İzmir* (Beautiful İzmir), Turkey's third-largest city sprawls around the head of the finest natural harbour on the Aegean coast. **İzmir** ❷⓿ was founded in the 3rd millennium BC on the north shore of the bay, and reached a peak during the 10th century BC, when it was one of the most important cities in the Ionian Federation – the poet Homer was born in Smyrna during this period. After the Lydian conquest in the 6th century BC the city lost its importance, but was refounded by Alexander the Great on the slopes of Mount Pagus (now Kadifekale). Under the Greeks and Romans it became one of the principal centres of Mediterranean trade.

King Aegeus

The Aegean is named after King Aegeus, whose adopted son, Theseus, went off to kill the Minotaur, helped by Ariadne, who loved him. He deserted her, and so taken up was he with his adventures, he forgot a promise to change the black mourning sail from his ship for a white one. As his ship sailed home, Aegeus, seeing the black sail, thought Theseus was dead and threw himself to his death in the water.

When the Ottoman Turks took control in the 15th century, İzmir grew wealthy as a merchant city, handling Smyrna figs and Turkish tobacco from the farms of the interior, and allowing the establishment of European trading colonies. It prospered as a port until the close of the Greco–Turkish War in 1922, when it was almost completely destroyed by bitter fighting and fire. Rebuilt around the site of Alexander's city, it is

Konak Meydanı

once again a bustling port and industrial city, the third largest in Turkey, but almost no trace remains of its former glory.

The heart of the city is **Konak Meydanı**, a square distinguished by two famous monuments. The **Clock Tower** *(Saat Kulesi)*, dating from 1901, is the unofficial symbol of İzmir. Nearby stands the tiny **Konak Camii** (mosque), built in 1756 and decorated with colourful Kütahya tile panels. On the hill to the south of the square stands the **Archaeological Museum** (Tue–Sun 8.30am–noon, 1–5pm, Jun–Sept until 6pm), whose superb collection of antiquities includes statues of Poseidon and Demeter that once stood in the Agora of ancient Smyrna. The nearby **Ethnographic Museum** *(Etnografya Muzesi;* Tue–Sun 8.30am–noon, 1–5pm, Jun–Sept until 5.30pm) recreates such treats as the interiors of traditional local houses, an Ottoman pharmacy, a bridal chamber, a circumcision room, and exhibits on the manufacture of the 'evil eye' amulets and camel wrestling. Inland from the Konak

Trajaneum at Pergamon

Mosque is İzmir's **bazaar**, one of the best in Turkey.

North of Konak Meydanı, **Atatürk Caddesi** (also known as the **Kordon**) runs along the waterfront to the ferry port at Alsancak, 3km (2 miles) away. A horse-drawn *fayton* will take you on a tour, which passes through **Cumhuriyet Meydanı** (Republic Square), the centre of modern İzmir, surrounded by glittering luxury hotels and palm-fringed promenades. Nearby is the **Kültür Parkı**, a huge, shady pleasure garden, venue of the annual İzmir International Fair. Uphill, through the huge bazaar, lies the **Agora** (daily 8am–5pm; summer 9am–7pm), one of the few remaining traces of İzmir's ancient history. This colonnaded square, built during the 2nd century AD, was once the city's bustling marketplace. At the top of the hill is the imposing medieval fortress of **Kadifekale**. This was the ancient Mount Pagus, where Alexander the Great commanded his generals Lysimachus and Antigonus to found a new city back in the 4th century BC. However, no trace remains of their original fortifications.

Pergamon

The modern city of Bergama is 171km (107 miles) north of İzmir, towered over by the ruins of **Pergamon ㉙**. The **Bergama Archaeological Museum** (daily 8am–5pm; summer

9am–7pm) is in the centre of the modern town, housing a large collection of material from Stone Age to Byzantine times.

At the height of its power, in the 2nd century BC, Pergamon (daily 8am–5pm, summer until 7pm) was one of the most splendid cities on the Aegean coast. Its acropolis was capped with magnificent buildings, and it had a library of over 200,000 volumes (the Pergamenes are credited with the invention of parchment). Its ruins, high above the modern town of Bergama, are still impressive.

The **acropolis** was built on a set of terraces. On the left of the entrance ramp is the open space once occupied by the **Temple of Athena**, close to which are the remains of the **Pergamene Library**. Its contents were eventually given to the beautiful Cleopatra as a gift from Mark Antony, and went to enrich the famous library of Alexandria.

Beyond the library is **Trajaneum**, the city's most splendid building, its glittering white marble columns, now partly restored. It was erected during the 2nd century AD in honour of the deified emperors Trajan and Hadrian.

Below the Temple of Athena is the steep *cavea* of the **theatre**, set in a shallow depression in the hillside. Nearby is the base of the **Altar of Zeus**, built to commemorate the defeat of the Gauls by the Romans in 190BC. This was once decorated with a remarkable frieze depicting the Battle of the Gods and Giants, one of the finest existing examples of Hellenistic sculpture, which now resides in Berlin's Pergamon Museum.

Visible on the plain below is the **Asclepion**, one of the ancient world's leading medical centres, rivalling similar establishments at Epidauros, Kos and Ephesus. Dedicated to Asclepius, god of healing, the Asclepion provided

Legacy of slavery

İzmir has a sizeable black community, the Turkish-speaking descendants of slaves from the Sudan, who were brought to Turkey in the 16th to 19th centuries.

hot baths, massages, dream interpretation, primitive psychiatry, and draughts of water from a sacred spring (found to be mildly radioactive). Galen (AD130–200), the most famous physician in the ancient world after Hippocrates, practised here.

The entrance to the Asclepion is along a colonnaded street, the Sacred Way, which leads to the **medical precinct**. Here you can see the remains of the library, the theatre and the treatment rooms. In the middle of the square is a pool fed by the sacred spring.

Sardis

The site of **Sardis** (daily summer 9am–7pm, winter 8am–5pm, but access is easy at other times) is usually visited from İzmir, though the nearest accommodation is Salihili which is just 9km (6 miles) away. Sardis, the former capital of ancient Lydia, is 100km (60 miles) east of İzmir, on the road to Uşak and Afyon.

Sardis was once the wealthiest city in the world, under the famous King Croesus (reigned 560–546BC), hence the expression 'rich as Croesus'. During his reign, the Lydians invented coinage, producing the first-ever coins of gold and silver, stamped with the royal emblem: a lion's head. The gold was washed down from the hills by the River Pactolus; the Greek historian Herodotus relates how flakes of the precious metal were trapped in the fleece of sheepskins spread in the streambed, perhaps giving rise to the legend of the Golden Fleece.

Intent on expanding his empire into Persian-held territory, Croesus consulted the oracle at Delphi. It told him that if he attacked the Persians he would destroy a great empire. He attacked anyway, and was crushed – the empire he destroyed was his own. The monuments you see today date from Roman and Byzantine times.

The principal ruins of Sardis are in two parts. On the left side of the main highway you will find the **Gymnasium complex**. From the car park you follow a line of **ancient shops** to a gate at

Sardis Gymnasium

the far end, which leads into the **synagogue**, whose floor is richly decorated with mosaic patterns. The gymnasium itself, a huge open square, is dominated by the magnificently restored **Marble Court**, lined with ornate marble columns and niches that once held statues. The arched gateway leads to a large swimming pool and the ruins of a Roman and Byzantine **baths** complex.

In the nearby village, a road leads south for 1km (0.75 mile) to the imposing **Temple of Artemis** (separate charge) begun during the reign of Alexander the Great, and abandoned, unfinished, following the ascendancy of Christianity in the 4th century. The enormous structure had a peristyle of 52 columns, of which two still stand at their full height. A 5th-century Byzantine church hides behind the columns at the far end.

Çeşme

A six-lane toll motorway leads 80km (50 miles) west of İzmir to the small resort and ferry port of Çeşme, where boats cross daily to the Greek island of Chios, a mere 12km (7.5 miles) away. The town was a quiet spa and beach resort (its name means 'drinking fountain') until the motorway's arrival brought it within comfortable commuting distance of the city; now it is set to become a bustling seaside suburb of İzmir, and a terminal for international ferries from Italy and Greece.

The town is dominated by an Ottoman **fortress** (daily 9am–7pm, 8am–5pm in winter), built in the 16th century. Beside the fortress lies a 16th-century **caravanserai**, or inn, which has been converted into a luxury boutique hotel. On the main shopping street, among the many carpet and jewellery shops, you will find an attractive and interesting art gallery housed in the ancient Greek basilica of Ayios Haralambos.

There are a few other sights to see – the main attractions are the golden-sand **beaches at Ilıca**, home to several **hot springs**. The warm, sulphurous waters (around 35–50°C/95–122°F) are said to be good for rheumatism and respiratory complaints.

Kuşadası and Environs

Situated on a small promontory, **Kuşadası**, meaning 'Island of Birds', is one of Turkey's liveliest and most popular holiday resorts. The town, 80km (50 miles) south of İzmir, has a large yachting marina, and serves as a port for Mediterranean cruise ships. Attractions here include some pleasant beaches, a vibrant nightlife mainly geared to British and Irish holiday-makers, and the nearby ruins of Ephesus.

Whitewashed houses climb the hill above the harbour, where ferries depart daily for the Greek island of Samos, and lively bars and restaurants line the streets of the old quarter. The busy **bazaar** clusters around the walls of a 17th-century *caravanserai*, now converted into a hotel; across the street, seafood restaurants skirt the quay of the old harbour.

Beyond the modern ferry port, a 350m (1,050ft) causeway connects Kuşadası to **Güvercin Adası** (Pigeon Island), which is topped by a 13th-century Byzantine castle and ringed with gardens and colourful cafés.

A *dolmuş* (minibus) service links the town to the busy Ladies' Beach *(Kadınlar Plajı)*, 3km (2 miles) to the south, and there are also beaches at **Pamucak** and more peaceful ones in the **Dilek National Park** *(Dilek Yarımadası Milli Parkı*; www. dilekyarimadasi.com), 25km (15.5 miles) from town.

Efes (Ephesus)

Ephesus 30 is 17km (10.5 miles) inland from Kuşadası, and is usually visited on a trip from there, although the closest town is **Selçuk**, a small place 19km (12 miles) northeast of Kuşadası. Selçuk has taxis, restaurants, hotels and some lively bars, and the **Ephesus Museum** (Tue–Sun 8am–4.30pm) has an exceptional archaeological section, including the famous 'many breasted Artemis'; and a fine ethnographical section. There are also several

Kuşadası, a lively and popular resort

Ephesus Amphitheatre

noteworthy monuments in and around town, including the 6th-century **Basilica of St John**, on Ayasuluk Hill, which supposedly marks the site of the Apostle's tomb. Above it is a fortress dating back to Byzantine times. Downhill you will find the impressive **Isa Bey Mosque** (1375), and beyond is a solitary column marking the site of the once-great **Temple of Artemis**.

Ephesus itself is one of the best-preserved and most visited of Turkey's ancient cities (daily summer 8am–7pm, winter until 5pm). Its marble streets and monuments have been extensively excavated and restored, and it is easy to transport yourself back to Roman times.

Ionian Greeks from the island of Samos settled in Ephesus around 1000BC. The site was associated with the worship of the Anatolian mother-goddess Cybele, who became merged with the Greek Artemis. The great Temple of Artemis, one of the Seven Wonders of the World, was erected in her honour. The city was ruled in turn by the Lydians, the Persians and the Attalid kings of Pergamon, until 133BC, when Attalus III bequeathed his kingdom, and Ephesus with it, to the Romans. Ephesus was one of the most important cities in the new province of Asia, with a population of 200,000, and grew wealthy on the proceeds of trade. But its greatness was linked to its fine harbour, and when this silted up in the 3rd century AD, the city went into decline. The site was rediscovered by the British archaeologist J.T. Wood in 1869. Many of the ruins you see today date from the Roman period, between the 1st century BC and the 2nd century AD.

Most guided tours begin at the **Magnesian Gate** and head downhill along the main street. The first buildings inside the gate are the well-preserved **Odeum** (council chamber), with its semi-circular seats, and the **Prytaneum**, where archaeologists found the two statues of Artemis, now on display in the Selçuk Museum. The marble-paved **Street of the Curetes**, its stone rutted by ancient cart wheels, leads through the Gate of Hercules to the remarkable **Temple of Hadrian**, with an arched doorway capped by the head of Tyche, the goddess of fortune. At the corner of Marble Street, on the right, are the **Baths of Scholastica**, which also included a brothel.

Rising up ahead is the imposing facade of the **Library of Celsus**, built in AD110 by a Roman consul as a memorial to his father. Beautiful statues of the four virtues – Episteme (Knowledge), Sophia (Wisdom), Ennoia (Thought) and Arete (Valour) – adorn the niches between the columns.

Marble Street leads from the library to the **Great Theatre**, the probable setting for the riot of the silversmiths described in the Bible (Acts 19:24–41). Its vast *cavea* provided seating for 25,000 people, and still accommodates the crowds who gather for performances during the annual International Festival of

Mary's House

Legend has it that St John the Apostle brought the Virgin Mary to Ephesus around AD37–48. Situated in the Bulbul Hills just south of Ephesus, the Meryemana (Mary's House) is where she is thought to have passed the last years of her life. It was discovered during the 19th century by priests from İzmir following instructions given by a German nun, Anna Katharina Emmerich, who had seen it in a vision. There is now a chapel occupying the site, which has long been a place of pilgrimage, but the building's foundations may date from the 1st century. Whether you're religious or not, it's a lovely walk into the pine-scented hills.

Petrified waterfalls at Pamukkale

Arts and Culture (see page 100). From the top rows of seats you can enjoy a grand view of the Arcadian Way, the city's colonnaded main street, once lined with fine statues, and lit by oil lamps at night.

Pamukkale and Hierapolis

One popular excursion from the Aegean resorts is to the spectacular travertine terraces of **Pamukkale** ➌ (Cotton Castle; daily sunrise–sunset), above the town of **Denizli**, about 200km (125 miles) inland from Kuşadası.

This remarkable natural formation has been created by mineral-rich hot springs cascading down the hillside and depositing layers of calcium carbonate. The resulting pools, terraces and 'petrified waterfalls' of dazzling white travertine are one of Turkey's most famous sights. The ruins of ancient **Hierapolis** lie scattered on the hillside behind the terraces, adding historical interest to natural beauty. The **Antique**

Pool is a therapeutic, restorative spring whose waters will float you above a picturesque jumble of broken columns and Corinthian capitals.

A trip to Pamukkale also usually includes a visit to the site of the ancient city of **Aphrodisias** (daily 8am–5pm, summer until 7pm). The city, dedicated to the worship of Aphrodite, goddess of love, was famous for its superb sculpture. The ruins, which are still being excavated, include one of the best-preserved stadia in Turkey, 228m (748ft) long, with seating for 30,000, and the remarkable Sebasteion, a porticoed gallery of sculpture dedicated to Aphrodite and the Roman Emperor.

The hotels are all in the village of Karahayıt, on the plateau nearby, which has multi-coloured travertines, hot springs and spas and excellent, ridiculously cheap cotton clothing.

South of Kuşadası

Between Selçuk and Bodrum lie three important archaeological sites that can all easily be seen in one day.

Priene (8.30am–sunset), once one of the most active ports in the Ionian Federation, now stands about 5km (3 miles) inland, due to the silting up of the River Maeander. It enjoys a beautiful location on a higher terrace overlooking the plain, backed by the steep crag of the acropolis. The theatre, *bouleterion* (council chamber) and agora are worth exploring, but the main attraction is the great **Temple of Athena**. Alexander the Great, who passed through the city in 334BC, paid for its completion; five of the original 30 columns have been restored to their full height.

The silt of the River Maeander has also stranded the once-mighty city of **Miletus** (daily 8am–5pm, summer 9am–7pm). Its harbour, from which Milesian ships set forth to found more than 100 colonies during the 7th and 8th centuries BC, is now a frog-filled marsh. Some idea of its former glory can be gleaned from the ruins of the agora, theatre and the Baths of Faustina.

Beaches and hotels

There are no good beaches in Bodrum itself, but you have the choice of taking a boat trip from the harbour to one of the many coves that line the peninsula to the west. Most of the hotels that claim to be in Bodrum are actually in one of the many heavily developed villages on this peninsula, including Turgutreis, Gümüşlük, Yalıkavak and Türkbükü.

No city ever stood at **Didyma**, just the colossal **Temple of Apollo**, one of the largest and most elegant temples in the ancient world. Only two columns still stand, but the forest of massive marble stumps gives some idea of the grandeur of the original building. People would travel great distances to consult the oracle of Apollo, seeking advice on business issues, marriage and military campaigns. When the Persians destroyed Miletus in 494BC, they also razed the Temple of Apollo at Didyma. Its reconstruction was begun by Alexander the Great (his victory over the Persians at Gaugamela in 331BC was predicted by the oracle), and continued for centuries, but the temple was never completed – some of the columns remain unfluted.

Bodrum

The picture-postcard resort of **Bodrum**, dubbed the St Tropez of Turkey, occupies the site of ancient Halicarnassos, famed as the city of King Mausolus, whose tomb was one of the Seven Wonders of the World, as well as the birthplace of Herodotus, the 'Father of History'. Little remains of Halicarnassos, however, and the town's main attractions include its laid-back, Bohemian atmosphere, a beautiful double bay backed by whitewashed houses, and the magnificent **Crusader Castle** that dominates the harbour. The attractions of Bodrum, however, have not gone unnoticed – it gets very crowded during the summer.

The **Castle of St Peter** (www.bodrum-museum.com; Tue–Sun 8am–6.30pm, in winter closes earlier) was built in the 15th century by the Knights of St John, who used stone quarried from the ruins of the Mausoleum of Halicarnassos. It fell to the Ottomans in 1523, and its various buildings now house a fine collection of antiquities, including a fascinating **Museum of Underwater Archaeology**. Among the highlights are the medieval Glass Wreck, the Kas-Uluburun Shipwreck, the Late Roman Shipwreck and the Hall of the Carian Princess with a royal tomb from about 360BC. The **towers** offer splendid views across the town and harbour. In the **English Tower** the banqueting hall has been restored, and you can read the graffiti carved in the window niches by homesick knights.

Castle of St Peter, Bodrum

The site of the **Mausoleum** (same hours and website as Castle), the tomb of King Mausolus, is set a few blocks in from the harbour. It was begun around 355BC at the behest of the king (the word 'mausoleum' is derived from his name) and remained standing until at least the 12th century. By the time the Crusaders arrived in 1402 it was in ruins, destroyed by an earthquake. Today, nothing remains except the foundations. An exhibition hall displays several versions of how the building may have looked.

WHAT TO DO

SHOPPING

Istanbul's markets and bazaars offer some of the world's most interesting – and challenging – opportunities for shopping. A huge variety of handmade goods finds its way into the city from towns and villages all over Turkey, much of it of very high quality – wool and silk carpets, kilims (flat-weave rugs), *cicims* (embroidered kilims), leather goods, ceramics and pottery, copper and brassware, and jewellery.

The principal shopping area in Istanbul is the Grand Bazaar, with more than 4,000 shops crammed beneath its roof. Running downhill from here is Uzunçarşı Caddesi, lined with hardware shops, which leads to the Spice Bazaar, the best place to buy *lokum* (Turkish Delight). Across from Beyazit square are the backstreets of Laleli, the place to look for low-priced clothes, especially leather jackets. Shopping isn't confined to the market. For more modern up-market shopping, try the stylish boutiques of Nişantaşı and Teşvikiye, near Taksim Square, or head west for international designer brands to the Galleria shopping mall by the marina at Ataköy or east to the Kanyon Mall in Levent. There are also plenty of smart shops along İstiklal Caddesi. For craft shops, antique dealers and bijou galleries, try Çukurcuma in Galatasaray, or Ortaköy on a Saturday or Sunday. For leather go to Zeytinbürnu, halfway to the airport.

Bargaining

Unless you're in a fixed-price shop, bargaining for handicrafts and souvenirs is a way of life, especially in the Grand Bazaar. If you are buying more than one of anything, try and bring

Pencil boxes made of bone on sale at the Grand Bazaar

the price down even more. Shop around (especially if it's a major purchase) and find out how much shopkeepers ask, then offer about half what you are prepared to pay. (Fixed-price shops, especially for carpets, are a good way to gauge prices.) The owner will feign amazement at your insulting low offer, you will plead poverty, and add that you can get it cheaper elsewhere. Good-natured banter continues until you reach a mutually acceptable price. Large purchases can take several glasses of tea and a good half-hour's discussion. Never begin bargaining for something you don't intend to buy, and never quote a price you are not prepared to pay. Traders are often aware that tourists are uncomfortable bargaining, so they simply offer a 'best price'. This is the least they'll be able to accept and there's no point discussing it as their profit margins are slender. Items on sale in the resorts are not always of the best quality.

What to Buy

You need an export licence to take a genuine antique out of the country, and this involves getting a certificate. If you buy an old-looking item, even if it's clearly fake, get a *fatura*, an invoice, from the dealer stating the piece's value and when and where it was made, because the customs people may need convincing. A reputable dealer will organise a certificate for you.

Carpets at the Grand Bazaar

Carpets and kilims. No two carpets are identical. Patterns and symbols have significance, conferring good luck and protection from the evil eye. Carpets and kilims from different regions of Turkey differ in design and colours, and even more so when they are from overseas, as is increasingly the case.

Carpet prices reflect the age, rarity, quality of materials and dyes, and tightness of weave. The number of knots in a square centimetre ranges from 20–30 for a coarse wool carpet to 100–200 in a silk carpet. The amount of work is reflected in the price. Natural dyes cost more than synthetic ones. It is worth doing your homework, and asking a few pertinent questions will make the seller less likely to fob you off with an inferior

Copper and brassware

item. Kilims are rugs that are woven, rather than knotted. A *cicim* is a kilim with embroidered decoration.

Ceramics and pottery. The kilns at İznik near Bursa produced the best ceramic tiles ever, and these are now collector's items. You'll have to make do with polychrome tiles, bowls and vases, some of which copy the traditional designs but are affordable.

Copper and brass. Hand-beaten pieces are available in the shops of the Old Bedesten in the Grand Bazaar and on Bakircilar Caddesi, behind Beyazıt Square, where braziers, shoeshine boxes, lamps, candlesticks, coffee grinders and samovars are ready to buy. Coppersmiths may even make items to order or engrave a purchase.

Leather and suede. Handbags, wallets, belts, jackets, trousers, coats and skirts are all bargains. The leather is generally good quality but sometimes the stitching is poor, so check on the workmanship before you commit yourself. Clothing and shoes can be made to order, but good-quality work takes time.

Jewellery. The best place to look for quality jewellery is Old Bedesten in the Grand Bazaar. Some cheaper items can be found in Kalpakcilar Basi Caddesi (the main street of the bazaar). Gold is sold by weight, and prices are posted daily. There's a surcharge for workmanship. Genuine sterling silver is hallmarked. Beware of cheap imitations with fake stones and silver plating, especially in shops in resorts. For contemporary local designer jewellery, browse the tiny shops in Çukurcuma, or in Nişantaşi.

Clothing. Turkey is one of the world's largest suppliers of cotton and cotton clothing, including many big-name brands. Good-quality cotton clothing is excellent value, while the resorts often have great designer boutiques. You can pick up great bargains of 'slight seconds' of designer gear at rock-bottom prices in Iş Merkezi on İstiklal Caddesi.

Books

For English books about Turkish culture and history, try Homer Kitabevi, 12A Yenicarsi Caddesi; Galatasaray; Pandora Kitabevi, 3 Büyükparmakkapi Sokak, off Istiklal Caddesi; Robinson Crusoe 389, 195A Istiklal Caddesi, Galeri Kayseri, Divanyolu 58, Sultanahmet and Greenhouse Books, Hilmi Paşa Caddesi No.21/B.

Other items. In the resorts sponges of all shapes and sizes can be found. A speciality of Bodrum is handcrafted leather sandals. You might consider buying a sheesha pipe, a nargile, the kind smoked by old men and trendy students in Turkish cafés, or a highly decorated chess or backgammon board. There are beautiful meerschaum pipes and figurines, too.

The Book Market (Sahasar Çarsısı) by the Grand Bazaar

You can't leave without a *nazar boncuk*, the evil-eye amulet. If ever you find it cracked, it's done its job and you need a replacement. Prayer beads, traditional musical instruments and puppets also make good souvenirs.

ENTERTAINMENT

Nightlife

In Istanbul, nightlife is to be found on İstiklal Caddesi and the surrounding streets, around the Taksim and Beyoğlu area and along the European shore of the Bosphorus, especially at Ortaköy. There isn't much revelry in the old city, so if you prefer a quiet supper and early bed, that's the place for you. Of course, there are rip-off joints, where you will be charged an astronomical amount and forcibly relieved of your wallet if you don't pay up, but these are outnumbered by places

A night out on Nevizade
Street, off İstiklal

which are good value. (Men travelling alone should resist the temptation to join a 'new friend' at his favourite bar or club; reports of pricey scams are still around.)

Istanbul has a thriving bar and club scene, with venues to suit every taste with DJs, live bands, dance music and rooftop cocktail bars. Aside from Turkish contemporary music, everything from jazz and rock to house and hip-hop is on offer, in some club or other. Turkey is somewhat ambivalent about gay life, but there are gay clubs and bars.

Nightlife is a feature of the Aegean resorts – bars pump out music, live or otherwise, with Turkish or English lyrics. There is probably something for everyone among the ubiquitous English and Irish pubs and other bars, and the live entertainments. Turkish evenings and other treats are available.

Clubs and Bars

Although Islamic, Turkey is far from 'dry' and Istanbul's nightlife is some of the best and most varied in Europe. Most of it centres around Beyoğlu. In stylish rooftop bars like **360 Istanbul** (8/F Misir Apt, 163 İstiklal Caddesi; www.360istanbul. com) and **5. Kat** (3 Soganci Sokak, Cihangir; www.5kat.com) you can sip cocktails with the beautiful people while gazing at the city's panorama and the Bosphorus. Alternatively, join local bohemians drinking cold beer at **Arsen Lüpen's terrace** (Mis Sokak No:15/4) with its superb views; or enjoy ingenious shots at trendy Tektekçi (Akarsu Sokak No.2/1) which is a perfect place to meet friends and start the evening.

Babylon (Şeybender Sokak, off Asmalimescit; http://babylon.com.tr) is one of Istanbul's best clubs for live bands from around the world, and top-class international DJs. If you prefer techno music and electronic sounds, try the very busy **Indigo** (1–4 Arkasu Sokak, off İstiklal Caddesi; www.indigo-istanbul.com).

If alfresco clubbing is your scene, you will like the summer-time outdoor clubs at Ortaköy, which attract local socialites and wannabes; phone to get on the guest list at **Anjelique** (5 Salhane Sokak, Muallim Naci Caddesi; www.anjelique.com.tr) and perhaps at **Reina** (44 Muallim Naci Caddesi; www.reina.com.tr).

Turkish Music

Turkey has developed its own exuberant pop scene, with influences coming from folk rhythms, traditional tunes, the tango (which was at one time popular) and Arab and Western pop music. Timeless, well-known Turkish pop stars are Mustafa Sandal, Nilufer and Sezen Aksu, and Tarkan who has achieved

Belly Dancing

This ancient art is thought to have its origins in Africa. It is a popular entertainment for local people although mainly for tourists, and the best dancers are famous, often appearing on Turkish TV.

A belly dance is not just a performance, it's an invitation to join in – any Turkish gent worth his salt will be up shimmying on the dance floor at the earliest opportunity. Even if you don't join in, you can show your appreciation by moistening a bank-note and sticking it on the dancer's forehead. Some local men prefer to tuck it into her bra or waistband. Most major dinner and belly-dancing shows are geared to tour groups.

superstar status – although it's rare to see these megastars in concert in Turkey.

You're likely hear traditional *fasil* music in bars and restaurants, especially the restaurants in Nevezade Sokak where wandering musicians play for diners. The side streets off İstiklal Caddesi, near the Taksim end, often have live shows in the local bars; check the boards outside for listings.

Classical Music and Cinema

While the Ataturk Cultural Centre remains closed for renovation/refurbishment/demolition (depending on who you ask), classical ballet and opera have transferred to the Kadiköy Süreyya Opera House, Bahariye Caddesi, Kadiköy. The Istanbul International Music Festival (www.iksv.org), held from mid-June to mid-July, hosts musicians and performers from all over the world in various venues. Jazz is popular in Istanbul, and many bars and clubs have live bands performing at weekends; some specialist venues have jazz nightly.

There are many cinemas on İstiklal Caddesi (including Beyoğlu Cinema), which show mainstream movies although some of the older cinemas are gradually being shut down. Look for the word 'orijinal' on the poster – this means that the film will be shown in its original language, with Turkish subtitles; otherwise it has been dubbed.

SPORTS

Spectator Sports

Football is Turkey's favourite sport and there are three internationally famous Istanbul teams: Galatasaray, Fenerbahçe and Beşiktaş. Most years one of these teams wins the Turkish Superlig, although Bursaspor surprised everyone by winning it in 2010. Check the local newspapers for home fixtures;

Inönü Stadium, overlooking Dolmabahçe Palace, and home to Beşiktaş, is the most accessible and attractive venue,

The British media in particular has previously given much coverage to the perceived hostility of Turkish fans; however, trouble between fans is rare and the stadiums are heavily policed.

Unique to Turkey is the centuries-old national sport of oil wrestling *(yağlı güreş)*, with tournaments held in the summer. The largest and most famous is Kirkpinar, held in June near Edirne, 230km (143 miles) northwest of Istanbul. The competitors, wearing only a pair of leather breeches, coat themselves in olive oil and perform a ceremonial procession before getting to grips with their slippery opponents and flinging each other around, to the delighted cheers of thousands of spectators.

Oil wrestling is the national sport

An even more exotic spectacle is camel wrestling *(deve güreşi)*, which takes place over the winter months (mating season) in small towns and villages around the Aegean cost. The biggest festival is held in January between Selçuk and Kuşadası. These one-humped beasts are bad-tempered, and when two moody males confront each other in the ring, a fierce sparring match ensues, in which they use their necks to try to throw each other off balance. The winning beast is the one that stays on its feet, and the match usually ends well before any injuries ensue.

Horse racing may seem rather tame by comparison. Races are held between April and December at the Veliefendi Hippodrome near Bakırköy, 15km (9 miles) west of Istanbul, organised by the Turkish Jockey Club (www.tjk.org). In winter, they move to İzmir.

Sadly Turkey no longer hosts the Formula 1 Grand Prix at Tuzla.

Active Pursuits

There are a couple of long-established golf courses. Klassis (www.klassisgolf.com.tr) is the best known. Alternatively, head for Kermer Golf & Country Club (www.kg-cc.com) situated about 25km (15.5.miles) north-east of the city-centre.

Polluted water around Istanbul means one needs to go to one of the beaches outside the city. The best ones within easy reach are the Black Sea resorts. There are good swimming beaches on the Princes' Islands, too, but extremely crowded at weekends. Kilyos, 35km (22 miles) west of the city, reached via minibus to Sariyer, has clean beaches (charge).

Water sports. The Aegean really comes into its own with water sports, including assorted forms of sailing, windsurfing, kitesurfing, scuba diving, snorkelling, paragliding, waterskiing, canoeing, banana-boat rides, jet skiing and more!

Birdwatching

Istanbul and the Bosphorus are special spots for migrating birds. Raptors are the main attraction, and most European species pass through, although some peak at different times. Keen birdwatchers should look out for honey and common buzzards, the lesser spotted eagle and the Levant sparrowhawk.

Turkish Baths

No trip to Turkey would be complete without a visit to the *hamam*, or Turkish bath. There are three historic baths in Istanbul that cater specifically for tourists, namely the 16th-century Cemberlitas Hamamı (www.cemberlitashamami.com), the 18th-century Çağaloğlu Hamamı (www.cagaloglu-hamami.com.tr) (both in Sultanahmet), and the 16th-century Tarihi Galatasaray Hamamı (www.galatasaray-hamami.com) in Beyoğlu. These places are worth a visit for their interior marble architecture alone, but the opportunity to experience a genuine Turkish bath should not be missed. There are usually separate entrances for men (*erkek*) and women (*kadın*), but if there is only one chamber,

Banana boats at the coast

then different times are set aside for men and women. Most are open from at least 8am to 8pm; longer hours for men.

Leave your valuables in a locker at the desk and get undressed in the changing room. Wearing a towel and bath-clogs, you will be shown to the steamy marble washroom, where buckets of hot water will be poured over you before an attendant sets to work with a coarse glove, removing dirt and dead skin and leaving you pink and glowing. You can also have a massage at this point (for an additional charge). Afterwards you retire to the changing room for tea or a drink, feeling completely relaxed and rejuvenated.

You can also try out mud and spa treatments, and massages, which are considered beneficial for many medical conditions.

Calendar of Events

January/February Camel-wrestling festival near Selçuk.

March Festival of Victory, Çanakkale. Celebrates the Turks' successful defence of the Dardanelles against British warships in World War I. Includes performances by the traditional Ottoman army mehter band.

April Istanbul International Film Festival organised by Istanbul Foundation for Culture and Arts (www.iksv.org), lasting for two weeks, featuring new releases of Turkish and foreign films. Anzac Day, Çanakkale (25 April), commemorates those killed in the Gallipoli campaign. International Istanbul Tulip Festival, best experienced at Emirgan Park with its several tulip gardens.

May Istanbul International Theatre Festival (www.iksv.org), even years only; Festival of Culture and Art at Selçuk and Ephesus, using the Great Theatre at Ephesus as a venue. Fatih Festivities, Istanbul, commemorating the conquest of Byzantium in 1453 by Sultan Fatih Mehmet (29 May).

June Istanbul International Music Festival (www.iksv.org), a world-class event featuring big names in opera and ballet at venues including Hagia Eirene. Associated with it is the Istanbul International Jazz Festival. Istanbul Pride Week culminates in the march for gays, lesbians, bisexuals and transsexuals.

July Istanbul International Jazz Festival (www.iksv.org) takes place at various locations around the city. Rock 'n' Coke, Istanbul (http://rockn coke.com), Turkey's largest open-air rock festival in Hezerfen Airfield. Oil wresting competition Kirkpinar near Edirne.

August Troy Festival, Canakkale. Five-day festival celebrating the discovery of ancient Troy with folk dance and sport competitions, concerts as well as street parades enacting the legend of Paris and Helen.

October–November International Arts Biennale, Istanbul (odd-numbered years), major visual arts event organised around an important political or philosophical theme (www.iksv.org). Marmaris International Yacht Race.

EATING OUT

Turkey has one of the world's richest cuisines, with influences derived from the many cultures of the former Ottoman Empire, and top-quality produce from Anatolia's lush farmland and fertile seas. Many dishes originated in the kitchens of the Ottoman sultans; in the time of Süleyman the Magnificent there were more than 150 recipes for aubergines alone. Many eating places offer standard fare: soups, *meze*, salads, kebabs and seafood, but in Istanbul there's plenty of good international cuisine and top-quality hotel restaurants.

Meal Times

The typical Turkish breakfast, served between 7 and 10am, consists of bread, butter and jam, with olives, cucumber, tomato, white cheese and perhaps a hard-boiled egg, washed down with sweet black tea. *Menemen* is a delicious dish of eggs scrambled with tomatoes, green peppers and sometimes white cheese. People eat out regularly, and there are many restaurants, cafés and food stalls open all day and late into the evening. There are no set times for lunch and dinner, especially in tourist areas, and you can eat at almost any time of day.

Fresh produce from markets

A büfe is a street kiosk selling snacks and soft drinks

A typical Turkish meal begins with a spread of *meze* (starters), washed down with *rakı*, followed by grilled meat, fish or kebabs, and rounded off with fresh fruit or *baklava*, and tiny cups of the famous strong black Turkish coffee. Don't order a main course until you have finished the *meze*; you may be too full to appreciate it. It is perfectly acceptable to have a meal composed entirely of *meze*.

Where to Eat

Many of the eating places in Turkey specialise in serving a certain kind of dish. An average restaurant, offering a variety of typically Turkish food and drink, freshly prepared, is called a *restoran*, and may or may not be licensed. A *lokanta* is a simple canteen-type restaurant, for a quick filling feed rather than gastronomic delight, serving *hazır yemek* (ready food) where you choose from heated trays of pre-cooked food. In the *ocakbaşi* the barbecue grill cooks sizzling meats on skewers, and is a cosy eatery in winter months. A *gazino* is a restaurant serving alcohol, usually with an evening floor show of belly-dancing and folk music.

The range of informal, cheap eateries is vast. A *kebapçı* specialises in grilled meats, notably kebabs served with *pide* and salad, while a *pideci* or *pide salonu* is a Turkish-style pizza parlour, dishing up tasty *pide* (unleavened bread) topped with minced lamb, eggs or cheese. You can enjoy lamb meatballs in a *köfteci*, tripe in an *işkembeci*, soup in a *çorbacı*, and milk puddings in a *muhallebici*. A *büfe* is a street kiosk which sells snacks and soft drinks. (See Recommended Restaurants, page 108)

WHAT TO EAT

Starters (meze)

Meze is the collective name given to a wide selection of appetisers, both hot and cold. They are usually presented on a tray at your table, or in a glass-fronted display case, and you can choose as few or as many dishes as you like. The more popular offerings include *kuru fasulye* (haricot beans in tomato sauce), *patlıcan kızartması* (aubergine fried in olive oil and garlic), *cacık* (yoghurt with cucumber and garlic), *biber dolması* (green peppers stuffed with rice, raisins and pine nuts), *sigara böreği* (cheese-filled pastry rolls) and a range of salads. *Meze* are served with fresh white bread, sometimes hot flat bread, to soak up the oil and juices.

Soups (çorba)

Turkish soups are usually thick and substantial. Try *düğün çorbası* ('wedding' soup, a mutton broth flavoured with lemon juice and cayenne, and thickened with egg), *mercimek çorbası* (red-lentil soup), *tarator* (a cold yoghurt soup with dill, delicious in summer) or *işkembe çorbası* (tripe soup, believed to be a hangover cure).

İşkembecis stay open until the early hours of the morning to serve tripe soup to peckish late-night revellers on their way home.

Main Courses

Ask anyone to name a typically Turkish dish and the likely answer is *kebap* – grilled, broiled or roasted meat. The most common varieties are *şiş kebap* (cubes of lamb threaded on a skewer and grilled over charcoal); *döner kebap* (literally 'revolving' kebab – a stack of marinated, sliced lamb and minced mutton roasted on a vertical spit, with slices cut off as the outer layers cook); *Adana kebap* (spicy minced beef moulded around a skewer and grilled); and *fırın kebap* (oven-roasted fillet of lamb marinated in yoghurt).

The ubiquitous *İskender kebap* is a dish of *döner kebap* served on a bed of diced *pide* bread with tomato sauce and yoghurt, topped with a sizzling splash of browned butter. *Çiftlik kebap* is

Döner kebap

a casserole of lamb, onion and peas. Meatballs of minced lamb, usually served with a tomato sauce, are called *köfte*. Another classic Turkish dish is *mantarlı güveç*, a delicious stew of tender lamb, mushrooms, peppers, tomatoes and garlic, all baked in a clay dish and topped with cheese.

Sweet names

Many confections have names that betray their origins in the harem – *dilber dudağı* (lips of the beloved), *hanım göbeği* (lady's navel) and *bülbül yuvası* (nightingale's nest).

Seafood

The seas around Turkey abound with fish, and waterfront restaurants serve the catch of the day, sold by weight. Fish is usually twice the price of meat, so not a cheap option. Choose yours from the display and find out how much it will cost before having it cooked. The best way is simply grilled over charcoal. Some of the tastiest are *levrek* (sea bass), *barbunya* (red mullet), *palamut* (bonito), *uskumru* (mackerel) and *lüfer* (bluefish). Look for *kılıç şiş*, chunks of swordfish skewered with onion, pepper and tomato, and grilled. *Hamsi* (tiny anchovies), fried whole, are usually the cheapest fish on the menu. Especially good is eating fish along the Bosphorus, whether in a pricey restaurant, or getting a cheap *balık ekmek* (fish sandwich) from a stall.

Other kinds of seafood more commonly appear as *meze* – *kalamar* (squid), *ahtapod* (octopus), *karides* (prawns), *sardalya* (sardines) and *midye* (mussels). The mussels are either coated in flour and fried (*midye tava*), or stuffed with rice, pine nuts, raisins and cinnamon (*midye dolması*).

Desserts

Fresh fruit is often served to round off a meal – succulent *karpuz* (watermelon) and *kavun* (musk melon), *kiraz* (cherries), *kayısı* (apricot), *incir* (figs), *düt* (mulberries) and *erik* (sour plums) but when it comes to prepared desserts, the Turks have a very

Turkish tea

sweet tooth. The best known is *lokum* (Turkish Delight), the most common variety being a soft jelly, flavoured with rose-water and sprinkled with icing sugar. Another classic dessert is *baklava*, made of alternating layers of thin pastry and ground pistachios, almonds or walnuts, saturated with syrup. A traditional Turkish pudding shop *(muhallebici)* serves milk- and rice-based desserts like *fırın sütlaç* (baked rice pudding), *zerde* (a saffron-flavoured rice pudding), and *tavuk göğsü* (a combination of rice, milk, sugar and chicken breast). *Aşure* is sweet porridge made with cereals, nuts and fruit sprinkled with rose water.

WHAT TO DRINK

The Turkish national drink is *çay* (tea), drunk throughout the day, in shops, cafés and offices. Tea is usually served black and strong in small tulip-shaped glasses, with sugar lumps on the dinky saucer. Turkish coffee *(kahve)* is strong, black and served complete with grounds in a small espresso cup, with a glass of water on the side. Sugar is added while brewing, so order *sade* (no sugar), *orta şekerli* or *çok şekerli* (very sweet). Leave it for a moment for the grounds to settle, and don't drain your cup. Most cafés serve cappuccino, latte and the like; for instant coffee, ask for Nescafé.

Avoid drinking tap water, and stick to bottled mineral water, which is easily available everywhere – *maden suyu* is carbonated mineral water; *memba suyu* is still mineral water. A traditional Turkish thirst-quencher is *ayran*, a 50:50 mixture of yoghurt and mineral water, seasoned with a pinch of salt. Refreshing on its own, it's also often drunk with a meal especially in a *lokanta*. Freshly squeezed orange juice *(taze portakal sütu)* is available in season.

It's important to note that although alcohol is widely available, prices are high because of constantly increasing government taxes. The national alcoholic drink is a very potent anise liquor called *rakı*. It is drunk as an aperitif, and throughout a meal. It should be mixed half-and-half with iced water, with a glass of water on the side (when mixed with water it turns a pearly white, hence its nickname, *aslan sütü* – lion's milk). Beware of drinking it without food – it's stronger than you think and the after-effects are powerful.

Turkish wines *(şarap)* have a history going back as far as 7000BC, and some believe that European vine-stocks may have originated here. Despite good quality local wines, Turks are not great wine drinkers although there is a growing appreciation. You can choose from a wide range of reds, whites, rosés and sparkling wines. You will always find Villa Doluca, Çankaya, Kavak and Dikmen; look out also for award-winning labels such as Kavaklidere and Likya.

Turkish kahve

Turkish-made beer is also good. Most popular is Efes Pilsen, which is produced in Istanbul and sold in almost every bar and restaurant in the country. Imported labels are also common.

PLACES TO EAT

We have used the following symbols to give an idea of the price for a three-course meal for two, excluding drinks:

$$$$ over £60 $$ £20–35
$$$ £35–60 $ below £20

ISTANBUL

OLD CITY

Asitane $$$$ *Kariye Hotel, Kariye Camii Sokak 6, Edirnekapı, tel: 0212-635 7997,* www.asitanerestaurant.com. Classic original Ottoman recipes and music in the setting of a peaceful garden neighbouring the Kariye Museum.

Bab-i Hayat $$ *Mısır Çarşısı, Sultan Hamam Girişi, Yeni Cami Caddesi 47, Eminönü, tel: 0212-520 7878.* www.babihayat.com. Above the eastern entrance to the market, this renovated warehouse is a magnificent high-ceilinged space, with good Turkish dishes. Great for a shopping break.

Balıkçi Sabahattin $$$$ *Cankurtaran Caddesi 1, Cankurtaran, tel: 0212-458 1824.* www.balikcisabahattin.com. Top-quality seafood at this family-run restaurant, in a traditional Ottoman house in a quiet backstreet. Lovely terrace in summer.

Dubb Indian Restaurant $$$ *Incili Cavus Sokak 10 (off Divan Yolu), Sultanahmet, tel: 0212-513 7308.* www.dubbindian.com. Pleasant little spot with a roof terrace, serving decent Indian food, including tandoori lamb, chicken and vegetarian curries and hot naan breads. Good-value set meals.

Hamdi Et Lokantasi $$$ *Kalcin Sokak 11, Eminönü, tel: 0212-528 4991,* www.hamdi.com.tr. Overlooking the Golden Horn, this huge, unpretentious venue specialises in grilled-meat dishes; no alcohol. Reservations recommended for the terrace in summer.

Havuzlu $$ *Gani Çelebi Sokak 3, Kapalı Çarşı, tel: 0212-527 3346;* www.havuzlurestaurant.com. Traditional Turkish cuisine in the heart of the Grand Bazaar. Open for lunch only. Closed Sunday.

Mozaik $$–$$$ *Incirli Cavus Sokak 1, off Divan Yoly, Sultanahmet, tel: 0212-512 4177,* www.mozaikrestaurant.com. Cosy, three-floored restaurant in a converted Ottoman house; this is on the tourist trail but a cut above the rest. The menu comprises Turkish dishes, such as *Abant* kebab (lamb with aubergine in terracotta pot), pasta and fillet steak. Good service.

Rami $$$$ *Utangaç Sokak 6, Sultanahmet, tel: 0212-638 5321,* www.ramirestaurant.com. The impressionistic paintings of Turkish artist Rami Uluer are displayed in this romantic restaurant, set in a restored wooden mansion. Serving seafood and traditional Turkish dishes, you can watch the Blue Mosque's sound-and-light show from the terrace.

Seasons $$$$ *Tevkifhane Sokak 1, Sultanhamet, tel: 0212-402 3150,* www.fourseasons.com/istanbul. For a real splash-out meal, head for this rooftop restaurant at the Four Seasons Hotel, with magnificent views and world-class Asian-fusion haute cuisine. Reservations recommended.

NEW CITY

Agatha Restaurant $$$$ *Mesrutiyet Caddesi 52, Tepebasi, tel: 0212-377 4000.* www.jumeirah.com. The fine dining venue in the Pera Palace Hotel Jumeirah is as stylish as you would expect, with top cuisine inspired by venues on the original fabled train route.

Any $$$ *Bebek Caddesi No.71/A, Arnavutköy , tel: 0212-265 0269.* A trendy restobar in a neighbourhood full of fish and seafood restaurants. International cuisine, live DJ shows and a good selection of cocktails make Any a perfect chill-out spot by the Boshporus.

Café du Levant $$$$ *Ramhi M.Koc Museum, Kumbarhane Caddesi 2, Sutluce, tel: 0212-369 6616,* www.divan.com.tr. Gorgeous café in the grounds of Turkey's first industrial museum, serving

French bistro food; wonderful views over the Golden Horn. Closed Monday.

Canim Cigerim $ *Minare Sokak, off Asmalimescit, Beyoğlu, tel: 0212-243 1005.* Serving only skewered liver grilled over charcoal, with piles of salad and warm flatbread, this simple café lacks choice but makes up for in value. Always busy. No alcohol.

Changa $$$$ *Siraselviler Caddesi 47, Taksim, tel: 0212-249 1348.* In a striking Art Nouveau building, the Changa is Istanbul's premier fusion restaurant. Consultant chef, Peter Gordon, creates dishes such as roast salmon with miso-coconut sauce and duck confit with raisin pilau. Reservations strongly recommended.

Hala Manti $–$$ *Cukurlu Cesme Sokak 26, Beyoğlu, tel: 0212-292 7004.* A simple venue for home-cooked specialities, especially *gözleme* (pancakes stuffed with meat, potato or spinach) and *manti* (ravioli) with garlic sauce.

Kafe Ara $$–$$$ *Tosbaga Sokak, off Yenicarsi Caddesi, tel: 0212-245 4105.* High-ceilinged arty café owned by Istanbul's top photographer, Ara Güler, with his works lining the walls. Enjoy an informal meal of ravioli, steak or just have a coffee, inside or on the patio. Great for people watching.

Leb-i-Derya $$$$ *Kumbaraci Yokuşu 57/6, tel: 0212-293 4989.* One of three outlets in a small chain, with a tiny summer terrace, this trendy restaurant is one of *the* places to be seen. The international menu ranges from a full English breakfast to a 40-spiced steak to chocolate fondue – all heavenly.

Mikla $$$$ *The Marmara Pera, Mesrutiyet Caddesi 15, Beyoğlu, tel: 0212-293 5656,* www.miklarestaurant.com. The top-floor restaurant, with a terrace, is one of Istanbul's most stylish, romantic venues, with Turkish-Scandinavian fusion from owner/chef Mehmet Gürs. Dinner only; closed Sunday.

Nevizade Sokak $$$ *Off Istiklal Caddesi, Beyoğlu.* A narrow street filled with noisy *meyhanes* for *meze*, grilled meats and fish. Packed and noisy at weekends, a little quieter in the week, it makes for a fun night out.

Vogue $$$$ *Spor Caddesi, BJK Plaza, A Block, Floor 13, Süleyman Seba Caddesi, Beşiktaş, tel: 0212-227 4404/2345, www.vogue* restaurant.com. Über-chic restaurant with a fabulous range of sushi, plus a vast range of wines. Style is everything here. Gorgeous terrace in summer. Reservations essential.

BOSPHORUS

Banyan $$$ *Muallim Naci Caddesi, Salhane Sokak 3, Ortaköy, tel: 0212-259 9060,* www.banyanrestaurant.com. Authentic southeast Asian cuisine at this sunny seafront restaurant, with tasty satays, Thai green curries, and crunchy Vietnamese salads.

Çiya $$–$$$ *Güneslibahçe Sokak 43, 44 and 48, Kadiköy, tel: 0216-336 3013.* www.ciya.com.tr. Three separate sites for this amazingly popular, good-value kebab restaurant with imaginative dishes from all over Turkey; vegetarians also catered for. Try for an outdoor table on the street. No alcohol.

Kanaat Lokantasi $$ *Selmanipak cd. No:9 Üsküdar, tel: 0216-333 3791,* www.kanaatlokantasi.com.tr. An institution and much admired, Kanaat was established in 1933 and is a family concern serving time-honoured recipes. It's a step away from the Üsküdar ferry terminal. No alcohol or credit cards.

Lacivert $$$ *Körfez Caddesi 57A, Kanlıca, tel: 0216-413 4224;* www.lacivertrestaurant.com. On the Asian side of the Bosphorus, near Sultan Mehmet Bridge, but with boat service from the European side, Lacivert is famed for its Sunday brunch. DJs provide music.

Lucca $$$ *Cevdetpasa Caddesi 51, Bebek, tel: 0212-257 1255,* www. luccastyle.com. A self-styled 'Bistronomique' lounge and bar, this chic arty venue is very popular with trendy local people. Come here for Med-American cuisine, tapas and lemon sea bass. House DJs play after-dinner sounds.

THE AEGEAN

BODRUM

Kortan 365 $$ *Cumhuriyet St 38, tel: 0252-316 1300*, www.kortan 365.com. Seaside fish restaurant with outdoor terrace. Simple menu, delicious food. Great views of sea and castle.

The Marmara Tuti $$$$ *Marmara Bodrum, Suluhasan Caddesi 18, tel: 0252-313 8130*, www.themarmarahotels.com. Top-class dining on the rooftop of this luxury boutique hotel, with stunning sea views. Varied menu includes jumbo shrimps stuffed with ginger, and linguine with bacon.

CANAKKALE

Yalova $$$ *Gümrük Sokak 7, Liman Caddesi, tel: 0286-217 1045*, www.yalovarestaurant.com. The best of a number of fish restaurants lining the seafront in Çanakkale. Good views, a rooftop terrace and convenient location near the ferry port. Open all year.

IZMIR

Deniz $$$ *Atatürk Caddesi 188/B, Alsancak, tel: 0232-464 4499*, www.denizrestaurant.com.tr. Commonly regarded as the best fish restaurant in town, with tables spilling onto the seafront pavement in summer. Open all year

KUŞADASI

Tarihi Cinar Balik $$$ *Next to Kismet Otel, Akyar, tel: 0256-618 1847*. This gorgeous fish restaurant seems far away from the buzz of the resort, and serves fresh fish in a simple setting.

SELÇUK

Okumus Mercan Restaurant $$ *PTT Karsisi Hal Bina 43 (opp PTT), tel: 0232-892 6196*. In the town centre; fresh fish and plenty of vegetarian dishes are served in this pretty leafy courtyard.

A–Z TRAVEL TIPS

A Summary of Practical Information

A

ACCOMMODATION (see also the list of Recommended Hotels starting on page 132)

Hotels in Turkey are classified from one to five stars and there is accommodation to suit everyone. If you want a lively place in Istanbul, go to Taksim-Beyoğlu where many international hotels are located as well as some good inexpensive options, luxury boutique hotel and apart-hotels. Peace and quiet is available in the Old City. Sultanahmet has plenty of reasonable establishments including restored Ottoman houses, while Laleli and Aksaray lack style but usually have lower prices. While Istanbul once had some of the cheapest accommodation in Europe, it's now among the most expensive.

Many mid-range hotels are very pleasant, the rooms equipped with TV, mini-bars, etc. One-star hotels are basic but comfortable. There are also *pansiyons*, often family-run and comfortable.

The Aegean resorts have large numbers of hotels, self-catering villas and apartments, many of which are used by tour operators.

There are also the historic 'special' hotels, usually in old houses or *caravanserais*; they usually offer 3 to 5 star amenities, but often can't have lifts because of the age of the building.

It's important to book ahead in Istanbul, especially in July and August, when many Turkish tourists visit the city, and over the religious holidays of Şeker Bayram and Kurban Bayram. Low season is October–March (except Christmas and New Year), when most places lower their rates. It's worth checking online on discount hotel booking sites.

I'd like a single/double room. **Tek/çift yataklı bir oda istiyorum.**
What's the rate per night? **Bir gecelik oda ücreti ne kadar?**

AIRPORT

The main airport is **Atatürk International Airport** (*Atatürk Hava-limanı*, tel: 0212-463-3000, www.ataturkairport.com) near Yesilköy, 24km (15 miles) southwest of the city centre. A free shuttle bus links the international (*dışhatları*) and domestic (*içhatları*) terminals.

The municipality-owned coach service, Havataş (http://havatas.com) runs between the airport and the city centre, half-hourly between 4am and 1am, journey time around 40 minutes, but much longer during rush hour, and costs 11 TL. Buses depart from outside both international and domestic terminals to Taksim Square, in front of the Point Hotel. Taxis are a little faster and more convenient, 20–30 minutes to the city centre; around 40 TL. The cheapest, but slower option is the Metro to Askaray, then connect to the Tramway (short walk) which is handy for the old city.

Low-cost airlines – including Pegasus and regional airlines (Bora and Anadolu Jet) – use **Sabiha Gökçen International Airport**, Pendik, Asian Side (tel: 0216-588-8888, www.sgairport.com), 40km (25 miles) from Kadiköy and 50km (31 miles) from Taksim. It also has the Havataş bus to the city centre (approximately 75 minutes; 14 TL).

Airports for the Aegean are at **Izmir** (Adnan Menderes Airport; www.adnanmenderesairport.com) and **Bodrum** (Milas-Bodrum Airport; www.bodrum-airport.com) with charter international flights and domestic flights. Some Aegean resorts are reached from **Dalaman** (www.dalaman.dhmi.gov.tr). Transfers to hotels and resorts are available from these airports, although most passengers are forced to take fixed-price expensive taxis. Try to team up with others to share, if possible.

B

BUDGETING FOR YOUR TRIP

Accommodation and meals are on a par with Western Europe. Expect to pay from £60 for a double in a *pansiyon*, above £100 for a mid-range or boutique hotel, considerably more in a 5-star deluxe.

Expect to pay at least £15–20 for a three-course meal in a mid-range restaurant, considerably more with alcohol. A bottle of wine in a restaurant starts at around 50 TL; in a bar a glass of wine at least 8 TL, with a small Efes beer from 5 TL.

The cost of public transport is minimal for buses, tram and ferries (around 4 TL basic rate and 2.15 TL with the Istanbulkart), and taxis are also inexpensive, at about 21–28 TL from Sultanhamet to Taksim although do ensure they use the meter and take the shortest route.

Most sites cost around 10 TL for entry, with the most expensive Hagia Sophia and Tokapı Palace at 30 TL each. Mosques do not charge admission but tips are appreciated. Consider buying a Istanbul Museum Pass (http://museumpassistanbuldistributor.com; 85 TL for three days and 115 TL for five days) to cut costs.

C

CAR HIRE (see also Driving)

A car is a liability in traffic-packed Istanbul, but if you plan to travel further afield, renting a car is sensible, as the rail system is not extensive. Car-hire rates vary – local companies charge less than international chains, and it's possible to pay as little as £25 per day. You can get good rates by booking and paying before you leave home, through the UK office of an international company. Check that the rate includes Collision Damage Waiver, unlimited mileage and VAT (KDV in Turkey). Hire-car insurance never covers you for broken windscreens and burst tyres. Unless you hire a four-wheel-drive, you will not be insured for driving on unsurfaced roads. You must be over 21 and you will need your passport, a valid driver's licence (EU model, with a photo) held for at least 12 months, and a major credit card.

CLIMATE

Istanbul has a typical Mediterranean, temperate climate with warm, dry summers and cool, wet winters. July and August are the hottest months. The best time to visit is April–June when the days are warm, and the shores of the Bosphorus are bright with spring flowers. Winter is generally cold, wet and uncomfortable. Snow is not uncommon in the north but rarely settles for more than a few days. The southern Aegean can have clear, sunny days, even in January. Average daily maximum and minimum temperatures for Istanbul:

		J	F	M	A	M	J	J	A	S	O	N	D
°C	max	8	10	12	17	22	26	28	28	25	20	15	11
°C	min	3	4	5	8	12	16	18	18	15	12	8	5
°F	max	46	50	53	62	71	79	82	82	77	68	59	51
°F	min	37	39	41	46	53	60	65	65	59	53	46	41

CLOTHING

When it's hot, lightweight cotton clothes are the most comfortable, but evenings may turn cool, so take a jacket. In summer, a sunhat is handy to protect against midday sun. In winter, take warm clothes and an umbrella. Respectable clothing should be worn when visiting mosques and other Islamic monuments. For men, no shorts above the knee or sleeveless T-shirts; for women a skirt or trousers or shorts that cover the knee, a shirt that covers shoulders and elbows and a headscarf. Women should avoid wearing tight or revealing clothing, which might draw unwanted attention, although in Beyoğlu anything goes.

CRIME AND SAFETY (See also Emergencies and Police)

You are far less likely to be a victim of crime in Turkey than you are in Western Europe or North America. Nevertheless, take the usual precautions against theft, keeping valuables tucked away out of sight, and be aware of pickpockets in crowded areas and on public transport. In poorer areas, such as Balat, avoid walking down unlit streets alone at night, and be careful when returning from late-night bars around Beyoğlu. Report any theft or loss to the police. If your passport is lost or stolen, inform your consulate. It's obligatory to carry your passport at all times, so keep a photocopy of relevant pages at your hotel in case of theft. Drug use or trafficking is punished severely; avoid it at all costs. Bomb attacks in Istanbul and resorts on the Aegean coast are of concern, but the chances of being involved are tiny. Lately, it's advisable to stay at least 10km (6.25 miles) away from the border with Syria.

D

DRIVING (See also Car Hire and Emergencies)

The standard of driving can be erratic so it's not advisable to drive in Istanbul. If you bring your own vehicle, you need a full driver's licence, an International Motor Insurance Certificate and 'Green Card' (make sure it's valid for the Asian sector if you plan to cross the Dardanelles or Bosphorus), and a Vehicle Registration Document. An official nationality plate must be displayed near the rear number plate, and headlamp beams must be adjusted for driving on the right. Check the website of Turkish Touring and Automobile Club (www.turing.org.tr) for information on driving licences and permits.

Seat belts must be worn in both front and back seats; on-the-spot fines can be issued for non-compliance. A red warning triangle and fire extinguisher must be carried. Motorcycle riders and passengers must wear crash helmets. The minimum legal age for driving is 18, and laws prohibiting drinking and driving are strictly enforced.

(international) driving permit **(uluslararası) ehliyet**
car registration papers **araba ruhsatı**
Green Card **yeşil kartı**
Can I park here? **Buraya park edebilir miyim?**
Are we on the right road for…? **…için doğru yolda mıyız?**
Full tank, please. **Doldurun, lütfen.**
I've broken down. **Arabam arızalandı.**

Rules of the road. Drive on the right, and overtake on the left. Speed limits are 120km/h (75mph) on motorways, 90km/h (55mph) on highways and 40 or 50km/h (25 or 30mph) in towns. Traffic joining from the right has priority, unless signs or markings indicate otherwise. There are fast, empty toll motorways between Istanbul, Edirne and Ankara and around İzmir

Fuel. In western Turkey there are plenty of petrol (gas) stations, and many are open 24 hours, but there are very few service stations on the toll motorways. Petrol is very expensive.

Parking. Look for signs saying *park yapilmaz* or *park yasaktır* (no parking) – police enforce regulations rigidly; they tow away illegally parked vehicles within a very short time and drivers have to pay a fine to retrieve them. Look for an official car park *(otopark)*.

Traffic police. You can recognise the Turkish *Trafik Polisi* by their black-and-white baseball-style caps and two-tone Renault patrol cars. They patrol city streets and highways, and have the power to issue on-the-spot fines for traffic offences. Call 154 for help.

Breakdown. Most towns have a mechanic. Larger towns and cities have full repair shops and towing services. For rental cars there will be a 24-hour emergency telephone number, and the company will arrange repairs or a replacement. For tyre repairs, look for a sign saying *lastikçi*, usually painted on an old tyre at the roadside.

Road signs. Main roads are well signposted; sights of interest to tourists are marked by special yellow signs with black lettering. Below are some common Turkish signs:

Çikis exit
Dıkkat caution
Dinlenme Alani rest area
Dur stop
Gırılmez no entry
Park yapilmaz no parking

Sehir merkezı city centre
Tekyön one way
Yavas slow
Yolver give way
Yol yapimi roadworks
24 Saat Açik open 24 hrs

E

ELECTRICITY

220-volt, 50-cycle current. An adaptor is needed for Continental-style two-pin sockets; American 110-volt appliances require a transformer.

EMBASSIES AND CONSULATES

Embassies are in the capital city of Ankara, but most countries maintain consulates in Istanbul:

Canada: 15/F Tekfen Tower, 209 Buyukdere Caddesi, Levent 4; tel: 0212-385 9700.

UK: Meşrutiyet Caddesi 34, Tepebaşı, Beyoğlu; tel: 0212-334-6400.

US: İstinye Mahallesi, Üç Şehitler Sok. 2, İstinye, tel: 0212-335 9000.

EMERGENCIES

Tourist police **0212 527 4503**   Ambulance **112**
Police **155**   Fire **110**

G

GAY AND LESBIAN TRAVELLERS

Although homosexuality is illegal in Turkey there are plenty of gay bars and clubs in Istanbul, with homophobic trouble practically unheard of. Look out magazines such as *Time Out Istanbul* for good up-to-date listings. Bear in mind that 'rent boys' are relatively common and may target unknowing foreigners. Transsexuality is also fairly common in gay clubs. Avoid going with a new 'friend' to a bar or club of their choice – prices could be significantly inflated and you are forced to pay. The Sugar & Spice Café (Sakasalim Sokak 3A, tel: 0212-245 0096) is a reliable starting point to find out about other gay and gay-friendly venues. The annual Gay Pride march takes place in June, organised by Lamda (www.lambdaistanbul.org/s/).

GETTING THERE

Scheduled flights from the UK. The national airline, THY (*Türk Hava Yolları* – Turkish Airlines; UK reservations tel: 0844-800 6666, www.thy.com), flies to Istanbul four times daily from London Heathrow, four times weekly or even daily in high season from Manchester and twice weekly from Birmingham. There are daily direct flights by British Airways (tel: 0844-493 0787; www.ba.com). EasyJet flies to Bodrum and Izmir from Gatwick (www.easyjet.com) as does Pegasus Airlines (www.flypgs.com), which also has domestic flights around the country.

Scheduled flights from the US and Canada. Turkish Airlines has regular non-stop flights from New York, Los Angeles and Chicago to Istanbul. For details tel: 1-800 874-8875 (24hrs).

Charter flights and package tours from the UK and Ireland. Available from a number of British cities to Izmir, Bodrum and Dalaman (on the south coast near Marmaris) in summer, available as flight only or as part of a hotel or self-catering package holiday.

By road. From the UK the main overland route passes through Germany, Austria, Hungary, Romania and Bulgaria. The distance from London to Istanbul is approximately 3,000km (1,870 miles), which takes at least four days of steady driving.

By rail. Allow approximately three days from London to Istanbul. The InterRail Global pass allows various periods of unlimited travel in 30 European countries, including Turkey (for details see www.raileurope.co.uk). The best single website for planning is www.seat61.com.

GUIDES AND TOURS

Official English-speaking guides can be hired through the local tourist office and through travel agencies and the better hotels. They are usually friendly and knowledgeable, and can prove invaluable if your time is limited. Freelance guides also hang around at the entrance to Topkapı Palace (make sure you agree on a price and ensure they are official, and that their English is good enough). There are increasing numbers of special interest tours: eg archaeology, Byzantine art and tours of historic Jewish sites. Les Arts Turcs (Incili çavus Sokak 19, Sultanahmet; tel: 0212-527 6859, www.lesartsturcs.com) is a fantastic little place with friendly staff, organising specialist tours and events.

You can also combine a city break in Istanbul with a resort holiday in the Aegean, or 14 days of cruising on a *gullet* (sailing boat).

H

HEALTH AND MEDICAL CARE

There is no free health care for visitors to Turkey so take out adequate insurance. However, Turkish hospitals are not prohibitively expensive, and they offer excellent treatment. Note that an EHIC card is only valid for EU countries, so can't be used in Turkey.

The main health hazards are the sun and the risk of diarrhoea, so use sunblock and a shady hat and be careful with food and drinks. Stick to bottled drinking water; ice will be fine in a reputable venue otherwise avoid it. Top restaurants may serve filtered water at the table, which is fine. Take a pack of wet wipes for washing hands. For minor ailments, seek advice from a pharmacy *(eczane)*, usually open during shopping hours. After hours, at least one is open all night, called the *nöbet* or *nöbetci*, its location is posted in the window of all other pharmacies.

Vaccinations. There are no compulsory requirements, but vaccinations for tetanus, polio, typhoid and hepatitis A are recommended.

Where's the nearest pharmacy? **En yakın eczane
nerededir?**
Where can I find a doctor/ a dentist? **Nereden bir doktor/
bir dişci bulabilirim?**
an ambulance/hospital **bir ambülans/hastane**
sunburn **güneş yanığı**
a fever/an upset stomach **ateş/mide bozulması**

L

LANGUAGE

Very few Istanbullus speak English, except for those working in
tourist-related areas, and along the Aegean coast. Local people
will naturally welcome any attempt you make to speak their language. The *Berlitz Turkish Phrase Book & Dictionary* covers most
situations you may encounter. Below is the pronunciation of
some Turkish letters:

c like **j** in jam
ç like **ch** in **ch**ip
ğ almost silent; lengthens the preceding vowel
h always clearly pronounced
ı like **i** in s**i**r
j like **s** in pleasure
ö approx. like **ur** in f**ur** (like German *ö*)
ş like **sh** in **sh**ell
ü approx. like **ew** in f**ew** (like German *ü*)

We'd like an English-speaking guide **İngilizce bilen bir
rehber istiyoruz.**
I need an English interpreter. **İngilizce bilen bir çevirmene
ihtiyacım var.**

M

MAPS

Pick up a free map of Istanbul at tourist offices or your hotel. For something more detailed, check the bookshops, especially Istanbul Kitapcisi (379 Istiklal Caddesi, Beyoğlu; www.istanbulkitapcisi.com).

MEDIA

Newspapers. The English-language *Hürriyet Daily News* (www.hurriyetdailynews.com) and *Today's Zaman* (www.todayszaman.com) newspapers contain national and international news and features. Foreign newspapers are available at several newsstands in Istanbul (in Sultanahmet, Laleli and Taksim) and in the main tourist resorts, usually a day late, and expensive. The monthly *Time Out* has decent listings and a few features. Good news website in English include: www.turkishweekly.net and www.aa.com.tr.

Television. The state-owned TRT (*Türkiye Radyo ve Televizyon*; www.trt.net.tr) broadcasts a number of nationwide TV channels. Most larger hotels have free-to-air satellite tv with a huge range of viewing – BBC World, CNN, Sky amongst others.

Radio. English BBC World Service and Voice of America are available on shortwave radio. Turkish stations for 24-hour music include Number 1 FM and Capital Radio.

MONEY

Currency. The Turk Lira (TL). Coins (*kuruş*) are in 1, 5, 10, 25 and 1 TL denominations. Notes are in 1, 5, 10, 20, 50, 100 and 200 TL units.

Banks and currency exchange (*banka; kambiyo; döviz*). Banks generally open 8.30am–noon, 1.30–5pm Mon–Fri (many stay open at lunch time). Rates of exchange and commission vary slightly, but in general bureaux de change have better rates than banks. The rate in Turkey is always better than in the UK. You can also change cash and traveller's cheques at the PTT office.

ATMs. The fastest and easiest way to get cash with a credit card.

Traveller's cheques *(travelers çek)*. Generally accepted by the banks mentioned above; some charge a high fee per check. The smaller branches may refuse to cash them.

Credit cards *(kredi kartı)*. Major credit and debit cards are increasingly accepted in hotels, restaurants, tourist shops and car-hire companies. Some shops may ask you to pay a premium. Most outlets require you to input your PIN at point of sale.

I want to change some pounds/dollars. **Sterlin/dolar bozdurmak istiyorum.**

Do you accept traveller's cheques? **Seyahat çeki kabul eder misiniz?**

Can I pay with this credit card? **Bu kredi kartımla ödeyebilir miyim?**

O

OPENING TIMES

Banks: Mon–Fri 8.30am–noon, 1.30–5pm (some daily).

Currency exchange offices *(döviz):* daily 8am–8pm.

Museums and major attractions: generally Tue–Sun 9.30am–5pm (some may close later in summer).

Post offices (PTT): main offices Mon–Sat 9am–5pm.

Shops: Mon–Sat 9.30am–7pm. Many stay open later and on Sunday, especially around Istiklal Caddesi. Grand Bazaar: Mon–Sat 8am–7pm.

P

POLICE (see also Emergencies)

The Turkish police's reputation for corruption is gradually improving. Officers wear dark-blue trousers with pale-blue shirts. Motorbike police wear black with red edging. Tourist Police (Yerebatan Caddesi, Sultanahmet, tel: 0212-528 5369) have a 'Tourism Police' logo on their backs. To call the police in an emergency dial **155**.

POST OFFICES

For mail, parcels and phone calls, and often currency exchange as well; look for the sign 'PTT' (www.ptt.gov.tr). The counter marked *'pul'* sells stamps. Mon–Sat 9am–5pm for postal services, until midnight for phone calls.

The main post office is Büyük Postane Caddesi (5 minutes' walk from Sirkeci tram stop); other branches are in the Grand Bazaar and Galatasaray Square. Stamps can be bought at shops selling postcards. Postboxes are scarce – post mail at your hotel desk, or a PTT office. There are usually three slots – *şehiriçi* for local addresses, *yurtiçi* for destinations within Turkey, *yurtdışı* for international mail.

A stamp for this letter/postcard, please. **Bu mektup/kart için bir pul, lütfen.**
express (special delivery) **ekspres**
airmail/ **uçak ile**
registered **taahütlü**

PUBLIC HOLIDAYS

Secular holidays occur on the same date each year, religious holidays are calculated by the Islamic authorities according to the lunar calendar, and thus occur about 11 days earlier each year. Banks, post offices, government offices and many other businesses will be closed on the following secular holidays:

1 January *Yılbaşı*: New Year's Day
23 April *Ulusal Egemenlik ve Çocuk Bayramı*: National Sovereignty and Children's Day.
19 May *Gençlik ve Spor Günü*: Youth and Sports Day (Atatürk's Birthday)

30 August *Zafer Bayramı*: Victory Day.)
29 October *Cumhuriyet Bayramı*: Republic Day.
10 November Anniversary of Atatürk's death

There are two national religious holidays (*Şeker Bayramı* and *Kurban Bayramı*), marked by three and four days off respectively. Most museums and attractions will be closed for the first two days, and shops for one or two, depending on its location. Inter-city transport (planes, coaches and buses) will be booked solid then and hotels will be busy.

R

RELIGION

The national religion is Islam. Istanbul also has Christian and Jewish minorities, and there are a number of churches and synagogues. Details of religious services can be obtained from the tourist office.

T

TELEPHONES

Turkey is on the GSM mobile network (US visitors need a tri-band phone). You can make domestic and international calls from public phones in PTT offices, or phone boxes on the street. They accept credit cards or telephone cards (*telekart*), which can be bought at the ptt and some newsstands and kiosks. For cheaper international calls, buy a calling card from newsstands, which can also be used from your hotel room. There are also kiosks in post offices and private phone offices (*telefon ofisi*), the latter are more expensive.

For intercity calls (including to Üsküdar across the Bosphorus), dial 0, then the area code (212 in European Istanbul; 216 on the Asian side), then the number. For international calls, dial 00, then the country code and the full number including area code. Turkey's country code is 90. Making and receiving mobile phone calls is expensive, but you can buy a SIM card (try Turkcell or Vodafone), valid for up to 7 days – providing it is the first time you've brought your phone into the country. If your stay is for longer, you will have to register your phone, which may take some time to be validated.

TIME ZONES

GMT plus 2 hours in winter, gmt plus 3 hours in summer, making it 2 hours ahead of the UK all year. Clocks go forward on the last Sunday in March, and back on the last Sunday in October.

TIPPING

In a restaurant tip 10–15 percent, even if the bill says service is included *(servis dahildir)*. Often waiters rely solely on their tips as income. Hotel porters should get around 1–2 TL; 10–15 percent is the norm in barber shops and Turkish baths, and a few coins, worth around 10p, should be left in public toilets, although many have a set fee of decidedly more. Taxi drivers don't expect a tip, but it is usual to round up the fare. *Dolmuş* drivers never expect a tip.

TOILETS

Public toilets are usually found in museums and tourist attractions and near mosques. They are occasionally of the hole-in-the-floor variety, and may lack toilet paper, so carry a packet of tissues. Paper should be put in the bin provided, not in the toilet. *Kadınlar* or *Bayanlar* (Ladies) and *Erkekler* or *Baylar* (Gentlemen).

Where are the toilets? **Tuvaletler nerede?**

TOURIST INFORMATION

The main Ministry of Tourism offices in Istanbul are:
Sultanahmet Meydani (by the tram stop), tel: 0212-518 1802/8754; Sirkeci station, tel: 0212-511 5888; opposite Hilton Hotel, Elmadag, tel: 0212-233 0592; Merkez Caddesi 6, opposite Atatürk Kültür

Merkezi, Taksim Square, tel: 0212-2465 313; Atatürk Airport arrivals.
Turkish Tourist Offices abroad:

UK: 3rd Floor, Craven House 121 Kingsway, London WC2B 6PA,
tel: 020-7839 7802

US: 825 3rd Avenue Floor 5, New York, NY 10022, tel: 212-687-2194,
5055 Wilshire Blvd. Suite 850, Los Angeles, CA, 90036, tel: 323-937 8066.

TRANSPORT

Istanbul's public transport system is run by IETT (www.iett.gov.tr),
which integrates buses, metro, tramway and light rail. Most services
run from 6am to after midnight.

Fares. The single fare for bus, metro, tram, funicular, Tünel, ferry
is 4 TL, but it is cheaper to buy an **Istanbulkart** or **Akbil** transit
pass (a stainless steel button with an electronic chip). Single fare
tokens *(jeton)*, Akbil transit Pass and Istanbulkart are sold at the
vending machines at the major bus stops, metro and tram stations,
ferry docks or at the newspapers stands in Eminönü, Taksim Square,
Beyazit and other transport hubs.

Buses. City buses are cheap and frequent, but can be crowded. They
are useful for a some major sights and longer trips in and out of the
city. There are also private lines on the more popular routes where you
can pay in cash.

Trams. The sleek service tram, the T1 Bağcılar-Kabataş, runs every
10 minutes along European shore. Useful stops include Sultanahmet (for Blue Mosque, Hagia Sophia and Topkapı Palace), Beyazit
(Grand Bazaar) and Fındıklı (Istanbul Modern). At the Kabataş Pier
there is a funicular that runs uphill to Taksim Square and catamaran
ferry dock. A restored 19th-century tram runs along Istiklal Caddesi
from Tünel to Taksim Square. Another runs from Usküdar down to
Kadiköy on the Asian side.

Metro. There are several metro lines but the most useful to visitors is
M1 from Aksaray Square through the mammoth Otogar (inter-city
bus station) to Atatürk Airport.

Funiculars. Istanbul's tiny underground train, the Tünel, climbs the steep hill from Karaköy on the north side of the Galata Bridge to Pera. Trains leave every few minutes and take only 90 seconds to reach the top. A second funicular links Kabataş ferry port on the Bosphorus with Taksim Square.

Trains. The suburban rail service is currently suspended due to the opening of a new Marmaray system scheduled for 2015. The only line in operation before then connects stations at Yenikapı and Sirkeci in Old Istanbul in Europe with the Üsküdar and Ayrılık Çeşmesi in Asia via a rail tunnel beneath the Bosphorus.

Ferries. The traditional big ferryboats operated by Istanbul Şehir Hatları (www.sehirhatlari.com.tr) depart from Eminönü for the Bosphorus and Golden Horn cruises, and to Üsküdar and Kadıköy (the Asian side), and Princes' Islands. There is also a private co-operative, Tur Yol (www.turyol.com), from the west of Galata Bridge, which offers an array Bosphorus trips. There are also ferries from Beşiktaş and Kabataş.

Sea bus catamaran. Sleek catamarans (*deniz otobüsü*) zoom across the waterways, and out to Princes' Islands several times daily. There are also Sea of Marmara routes to Yalova and Bandirma on the southern shore.

Dolmuş. A large yellow minibus that shuttles along a set route for a fixed fare. The destination is shown on the windscreen. The driver leaves the starting point when all seats are taken, then drops passengers off along the way (*dolmuş* stops are marked by a sign with a 'D'). Call out '*inecek var!*' when you want to get off.

Taxis. Taxis are yellow, and mostly powered by clean-burning natural gas. They can be hailed in the street, picked up at a rank or ordered by phone. It's better to hail one that is already on the move, rather than those loitering outside tourist sites. Taxis have meters and are required by law to use them. Most drivers are honest, but a few may try to rip you off by 'adjusting' the meter or doing tricks with your money. Night and day rates are the same. If you take a taxi across the Bosphorus Bridge, you also have to pay the bridge toll. Few drivers speak English, so it's worth writing your destination on a piece of paper.

TRAVELLERS WITH DISABILITIES

Few major sights have elevators or ramps, and wheelchairs are not permitted inside mosques, but the new green buses have wheelchair facilities, as do most tram stations. Disabled public toilets are harder to come by. There's a support association called the Bedensel Engellilerle Dayanışma Denerği (www.bedd.org.tr).

V

VISAS AND ENTRY REQUIREMENTS

Visas. All travellers need a passport valid for at least six months. Visas for 90 days are no longer granted on entry; you will need to apply via the Electronic Visa Application System (www.evisa.gov.tr) and pay with a credit or debit card. There are interactive kiosks at Turkish airports when you can get your visa in 3 minutes, but it's recommended to buy it in advance. Fees are £20/$US30.

W

WEBSITES AND INTERNET ACCESS

www.gototurkey.co.uk: The UK's official Turkish tourism site.
www.iksv.org: Organisers of most arts and culture festivals.
www.biletix.com: The official ticketing agents for events.
www.turkeytravelplanner.com: American-targeted site with practical tips and links to vetted service providers.
www.mymerhaba.com: A useful what's on guide, plus features.
www.theguideistanbul.com: The website of Istanbul magazine with listings, news about shopping, lifestyle and arts.
www.muze.gov.tr: Information about all the museums and sites in Turkey

In addition to sleek cafés with free Wi-Fi, tiny internet cafés are scattered around the city centre, especially in the Beyoğlu area. Charges are around 2 TL per hour.

Recommended Hotels

Finding accommodation in Istanbul is rarely a problem as the city has seen a boom in the hotel business, but if you want a room in a particular hotel it is best to book, especially during July and August and religious holidays when many Turkish tourists visit the city. The main hotel areas are Sultanahmet, Sirkeci and Aksaray in the Old City, and Beyoğlu (from Taksim Square to Tepebas) in the New City. It is possible to bargain, especially if you plan to stay for more than two nights. Many offer discounts for internet bookings through their own website or a booking service; some offer discounts for cash. Stay in the Old City if you want to be near the sites (bring earplugs to avoid being woken by the muezzin at dawn), and New City for the restaurants, bars and live music.

As a basic guide we have used the symbols below to indicate prices for an en suite double room, including breakfast. These are not the rack rates, but the more realistic rates available during high season:

$$$$$	over £300
$$$$	£180–300
$$$	£100–180
$$	£60–100
$	below £60

ISTANBUL

OLD CITY

Alzer $$$ *At Meydanı 20, Sultanahmet, tel: 0212-516 6262, www. alzerhotel.com.* A comfortable boutique hotel just across from the Blue Mosque. Rooms range from simple economy ones to the Pasha Suite. Noise from muezzin at dawn in front rooms. 22 rooms.

Ambassador Hotel $$$ *Divanyolu Ticarethane Sokak 19, Sultanahmet, tel: 0212-512 0002, www.istanbulambassadorhotel.com.* In the centre of Sultanahmet, with views over the sea of Marmara, in a restored 19th-century town house. Turkish bath and spa with sauna; breakfast on the top-floor terrace; 22 rooms and two suites.

Apricot Hotel $ *Amiral Tafdil Sokak 18, Sultanahmet, tel: 0212-638 1658*, www.apricothotel.com. This is an inexpensive hotel with a family atmosphere. Six simple rooms of varying sizes; some can squeeze in four people, some have a small balcony, one suite has a sea view.

Armada Hotel $$$$ *Ahırkapı Sokak 24, Sultanahmet, tel: 0212-455 4455*, www.armadahotel.com.tr. Views of Hagia Sophia and the Blue Mosque are a feature of this hotel, in a reconstructed 16th-century Ottoman town house. Many rooms recently renovated but retain traditional decor. Gorgeous breakfast on the terrace; 108 rooms.

Ayasofya Konaklari $$$–$$$$ *Soğukçeşme Sokak, Sultanahmet, tel: 0212-513 3660*, www.ayasofyakonaklari.com. Peaceful, pedestrianised street with nine beautifully restored wooden Ottoman houses, with 4–10 rooms in each, with period furniture and Turkish carpets; breakfast on the terrace; 64 rooms including seven suites.

Dersaadet Hotel $$$ *Kapiagasi sokak 5, off Küçük Ayasofya Caddesi, Sultanahmet, tel: 0212-458 0760*, www.dersaadethotel.com. In a peaceful Sultanahmet neighbourhood, this restored Ottoman house offers the luxury of en-suite hamams in some double rooms. Service in this family-run guesthouse is impeccable; breakfast served on the terrace; 17 rooms including three suites.

Empress Zoe $$$–$$$$ *Akbiyik Caddesi, Adliye Sokak 10, Sultanhamet, tel: 0212-518 2504/4360*, www.emzoe.com. A small, intimate hotel, each room individually decorated and furnished, with antique beds, dark wood-panelled floors and Turkish carpets. No lift and narrow steep steps; secluded garden terrace; 25 rooms including three suites one of which is a duplex two-bedroom.

Four Seasons Hotel $$$$$ *Tevkifhane Sokak 1, Sultanhamet, tel: 0212-518 3000*, www.fourseasons.com/istanbul. Luxury hotel occupying a former prison, just steps from the major sights. Large, antiques and kilim filled rooms cluster around an open courtyard. Fine restaurant with a glass-roofed courtyard; 65 rooms.

Hotel Ilkay $ *Hudavendigar Sokak 44–46, Sirkeci, tel: 0212-511 2270*, www.ilkayhotel.com. It's hard to find such inexpensive accommodation offering cleanliness and friendly service, with simple rooms and a central location. It's a short walk to Sultanahmet and Eminönü, and the tram stop is outside; 60 rooms.

Hotel Niles $$–$$$ *Dibekli Cami Sokak 19, off Ordu Caddesi, Beyazit, tel: 0212-516 0732*, www.hotelniles.com. Friendly little hotel tucked away near the Grand Bazaar, with simple rooms, all with Marmara marble bathrooms. The newest wing has suites and a hamam. Buffet breakfast served on the roof terrace. A real gem and great value; 39 rooms including eight suites, two maisonettes.

Mavi Ev (Blue House) $$$ *Dalbasti Sok 14, Sultanahmet, tel: 0212-638 9010*, www.bluehouse.com.tr. A friendly historic guesthouse within touching distance of the Blue Mosque. Rooms are simply but attractively furnished, with restaurants on the roof terrace and the garden; 27 rooms including one suite.

Sarniç Hotel $$$ *Kucuk Ayasofya Caddesi 26, Sultanahmet, tel: 0212-518 2323*, www.sarnichotel.com. In a restored town house with a rooftop terrace; simple, attractive decor, and a good restaurant. Built over a 5th-century Byzantine cistern, which guests can visit. Ask about their Turkish cooking classes; 21 rooms.

Sirkeci Mansion $$$ *Taya Hatun Sokak 5, Sirkeci, tel: 0212-528 4344*, www.sirkecimansion.com. Outstanding service is the main quality here, together with classically designed rooms, a small pool and hamam. There is a restaurant serving regional specialities as well as a rooftop bar with staggering views. Highly recommended; 32 rooms including one family room.

Yesil Ev $$$ *Kabasakal Caddesi 5, Sultanahmet, tel: 0212-517 6785*, www.yesilev.com.tr. One of Istanbul's most famous hotels, in a restored, four-storey wooden mansion behind the Blue Mosque, that was once the home of an Ottoman Pasha. Rooms have Ottoman brass beds and period furniture. Beautiful garden restaurant and bar; 19 rooms.

NEW CITY AND BOSPHORUS

Anemon Galata $$$ *Büyükhendek Caddesi, Kuledibi Beyoğlu, tel: 0212-293 2343*, www.anemonhotels.com. One of a handful of 'special' hotels outside the Old City, this lavish boutique hotel beside the Galata Tower has it all: plush rooms, superb tower or Golden Horn views from the rooftop bar/restaurant, and close proximity to restaurants and nightlife; 30 rooms including seven suites.

Ansen 130 $$$ *Mesrutiyet Caddesi 70, Tepebasi, tel: 0212-245 8808*, www.ansensuites.com. Tremendous value. Vast, light-filled suites, each individually designed, all with small kitchen areas and large work desks, pale wood floors and large sofas. Breakfast is served in the trattoria downstairs. Close to Beyoğlu's best nightlife; 10 suites.

Çirağan Palace Kempinski $$$$$ *Çırağan Caddesi 84, Beşiktaş, tel: 0212 326 4646*, www.kempinski.com. Prestigious, hotel in restored 19th-century Ottoman palace on the shores of the Bosphorus. Four gourmet restaurants, health club, sauna and heated outdoor infinity pool; 324 rooms including 112 opulent suites.

Galata Residence $$ *Felek Sokak 2, off Bakalar Caddesi, Galata, tel: 0212-292 4841*, www.galataresidence.com. In the former home of a prominent banking dynasty, this apart-hotel offers various sized apartments with basic kitchenettes, 10 minutes' walk from Galata Tower in a quiet neighbourhood. Good for families; excellent value.

Grand Hotel de Londres $$–$$$ *Meşrutiyet Caddesi 117, Tepebaşı, tel: 0212-245 0670*, www.londrahotel.net. A fine old building close to the Pera Palas Hotel, and reasonably priced. Built in 'Orient Express' style, it mirrors the glamour of the age and much of the furniture dates from that era. Wonderful terrace bar; 54 rooms.

InterContinental Istanbul $$$$$ *Asker Ocagi Caddesi 1, Taksim, tel: 0212-368 4444*, http://istanbul.intercontinental.com.tr. By Taksim Park, with superb views over the Bosphorus and city. Luxury facilities include outdoor pool, spa, gym, business centre, and restaurants serving Turkish and international food; 390 rooms including 53 suites.

Mövenpick $$$$ *Buyukdere Caddesi, 4th Levent, tel: 0212-319 2929,* www.moevenpick-hotels.com. Swiss efficiency in the finance district makes this a good choice for business travellers. Large workspace in guest rooms, plus conference rooms. Close to metro for a fast journey to Taksim; 249 rooms including 21 Junior, Executive and skyline suites.

Pera Palas Hotel Jumeirah $$$$–$$$$$ *Meşrutiyet Caddesi 98–100, Tepebaşı, tel: 0212-377 4000,* www.jumeirah.com. Built in 1892 for Orient-Express passengers, and still inhabited by the shades of Agatha Christie (who wrote part of the novel here) and Mata Hari. It is classed as a 'museum hotel' – room 101 is the Atatürk Museum Room. Luxury spa in basement; 115 rooms.

Ritz Carlton Istanbul $$$$$ *Suzer Plaza, Askerocagi Caddesi 15, Elmadag/Şişli, tel: 0212-334 4444,* www.ritzcarlton.com. The hotel towers above the Bosphorus, with tastefully furnished guest rooms, a *hamam* and massage rooms for couples. Divine afternoon tea with live piano music; 244 rooms including 23 suites.

Sumahan on the Water $$$$–$$$$$ *Kuleli Cad 43, Çengelköy, tel: 0216-422 8000,* www.sumahan.com. Hailed as one of the world's finest hotels, this converted *raki* factory on the Asian shores of the Bosphorus is a romantic gem, with chic decor using neutral tones of wood, marble and fabric; 24 rooms including suites.

W Hotel $$$$$ *Suleyman Seba Caddesi 22, Akaretler, Beşiktaş, tel: 0212-381 2121,* www.wistanbul.com.tr. Pure rock-star glam. Deep purple neon in the lobby, huge luxurious beds and Marmara marble bathrooms, some rooms have cabanas onto a peaceful terrace. Istanbul's beautiful creatures flock to the bar at weekends; 134 rooms and suites.

Witt Istanbul Suites $$$$ *Defterdar Yokusu 26, Cihangir, tel: 0212-293 1500,* www.wittistanbul.com. More like spacious loft apartments than hotel rooms, these chic contemporary suites have all the mod cons but don't lose sight of tasteful, minimalist design. All rooms have a kitchenette with a coffee machine; some have large balconies. Good service; 18 suites.

Vardar Palace Hotel $$$ *Siraselviler Caddesi 54, Taksim, tel: 0212-252 2888*, www.vardarhotel.com. A central location, good for business, shopping and entertainment. This well-restored hotel, built in 1911, is a fine example of Levantine-Selçuk architecture; 40 rooms.

PRINCES' ISLANDS

Hotel Merit Halki Palace $$$ *Refah Sehitleri Caddesi 88, Heybeliada, tel: 0216-351 0025*, www.merithotels.com. A reconstructed 1850s Ottoman villa, with terraces and large gardens. Only one hour from the city centre by boat, so a lovely summer option. Swimming pool; jacuzzis in the suites. Cheaper and quieter on weekdays; 45 rooms including nine suites.

Splendid Palace $$$$ *23 Nusan Cadesi 71, Büyükada, tel: 0216-382 6950*, www.splendidhotel.net. Founded in 1909, this Art Nouveau gem has been beautifully restored to offer guests a special retreat on the largest of the Princes' Islands. Beautiful, antiques-filled rooms; swimming pools and gardens; 74 rooms including four suites.

THE AEGEAN

Aegean tour operators have many hotels and apartments available; Kuşadası alone has more than 300 hotels. Here are a few suggestions for the main centres:

BODRUM

Antique Theatre Hotel $$$ *Kibris Sehitleri Caddesi 169, tel: 0252-316 6053*, www.antiquetheatrehotel.com. A smart hotel and elegant, simple rooms and large outdoor swimming pool; 18 rooms, including two suites, all connected to a shared or private garden.

El Vino $$$$ *Pamili Sok. Omurça Mah., Bodrum 48000, tel: 0252-313 8770* www.elvinobodrum.com. Overlooking Bodrum Castle, El Vino offers rooms and suites with all modern amenities in a lush garden setting. From the rooftop restaurant you can enjoy sunsets over the city. The breakfasts are extraordinary.

Hotel Marina Vista $$$ *Neyzen Tevfik Caddesi 168, tel: 0252-313 0356*, www.hotelmarinavista.com. A pleasant low-rise hotel, which is well situated at the quiet end of town near the marina. Rooms are smallish but comfortable, opening out onto a courtyard with a pool; fitness centre, spa and sauna also available; 87 rooms.

Taskule Hotel $$$ *Plaj Caddesi 10, Yalıkavak, tel: 0252-385 4935*, www.taskule.com.tr. On the water's edge, near shops, bars, restaurants and the harbour. Each room is individually designed, with a sofa, fresh flowers and swanky bathroom, and there is a pool and bar; 17 rooms including two suites.

ÇESME

Sheraton Çesme $$$$ *Sifne Caddesi 35, Ilıca, tel: 0232-750 0000*, www.sheratoncesme.com. Luxurious, huge 5-star resort situated within easy reach of all the local attractions. Private beach, plus a world-class Botanical Thermal spa, five pools and entertainment such as a private bowling alley; 398 rooms.

IZMIR

Antik Han Hotel $ *Anafartalar Caddesi 600, Mezarlikbası, tel: 0232-489 2750*, www.otelantikhan.com. A historic 'special' hotel in the market area with simple rooms, bar, restaurant and a pretty little courtyard garden; 30 rooms including five suites.

Hilton Izmir $$$ *Gazi Osmanpasa Bulvari 7, Izmir, tel: 0232-497 6060*, www3.hilton.com. With views of Izmir Bay or the city, one of the tallest hotels in the region has business facilities such as a conference centre and 16 meeting rooms, and spacious light-filled guest rooms. The restaurant on the 31st floor has magnificent sea views. 380 rooms.

Vatan Otel $ *Anafartalar Caddesi 626, Çankaya, Izmir*, tel: 0232-483 0637, www.vatanotel.com. A simple little hotel in a restored building that has been a hotel since the 16th century.

KUŞADASI

Llayda Avantgarde Otel $$ *Atatürk Bulvari 42, tel: 0256-614 7608*, www.ilaydaavantgarde.com. A stylish, recently renovated friendly hotel on the seafront in the town centre, with a coffee shop, a roof-top restaurant and a pool; 75 rooms including five suites.

Grand Blue Sky $$$ *Kadinlar Denizi, tel: 0256-612 7750*, www.grandbluesky.com. A hotel facing the sea, offering a full range of water sports, including diving, and its own stretch of private beach. All rooms have a balcony and a sea view. Prices are on an all-inclusive basis. Open April–November; 325 rooms and suites.

Kismet $$$ *Gazi Begendi Bulvari 1, tel: 0256-618 1290*, www.kismet. com.tr. One of Turkey's most enjoyable and famous hotels is stun-ningly situated on a seaside peninsula at the edge of various interna-tional heads of state. The large rooms all have terraces and face either the harbour or the open sea. Private beach plus gorgeous outdoor pool; 100 rooms.

Mr Happy's Liman Hotel $–$$ *Kibris Caddesi Buyral Sokak 4, tel: 0256-614 7770*, www.limanhotel.com. A small hotel located in a beautiful garden. The service is great and the owners are always ready to help. The rooftop restaurant has harbour views and serves traditional Turkish cuisine. Open all year; 17 rooms with compli-mentary breakfast.

SELÇUK

Kirkinca Konaklari $–$$ *Sirince, tel: 0232-898 3133*, www.kirkinca. com. A charming hotel with rooms and cottages decorated with an-tiques, about 9km (5 miles) from Selçuk in a pretty village. Makes a good base for exploring Selçuk, Ephesus and other sights. Open all year, with central heating in winter; 11 rooms plus four cottages.

INDEX

Berlitz® pocket guide

Istanbul & the Aegean Coast

Fifth Edition 2015

Written by Neil Wilson, Beryl Dhanjal
Updated by Maciej Zglinicki
Edited by Carine Tracanelli
Cartography updated by Carte
Update Production: AM Services
Picture Editor: Tom Smyth
Production: Rebeka Davies and Aga Bylica

Photography credits: akg images 19, 20;
Dreamstime 3TC, 44, 97; Frank Noon/Apa
Publications 3T, 4TL, 7MC, 7MC, 7TC, 76, 79,
81, 82, 99, 101, 104, 106; Getty Images 2ML,
58; Ggia 2TC, 48; iStock 1, 2TL, 3M, 3M, 5MC,
15, 17, 24, 35, 47, 61, 66, 73, 75, 84, 87; Rebecca
Erol/Apa Publications 2MC, 3M, 3M, 4ML, 4ML,
4MR, 4TL, 4/5M, 5T, 5TC, 6TL, 6ML, 6ML, 8, 11,
12, 13, 18, 29, 30/31, 32, 36, 39, 41, 43, 45, 50,
52, 53, 54, 57, 59, 62, 64, 68, 70, 88, 90, 91, 93,
95, 102, 107; SuperStock 26; Turkish Tourism 22

Cover picture: AWL Images

Every effort has been made to provide
accurate information in this publication,
but changes are inevitable. The publisher
cannot be responsible for any resulting
loss, inconvenience or injury.

Contact us

At Berlitz we strive to keep our guides as
accurate and up to date as possible, but if you
find anything that has changed, or if you have
any suggestions on ways to improve this guide,
then we would be delighted to hear from you.

Berlitz Publishing, PO Box 7910,
London SE1 1WE, England.
email: berlitz@apaguide.co.uk
www.insightguides.com/berlitz

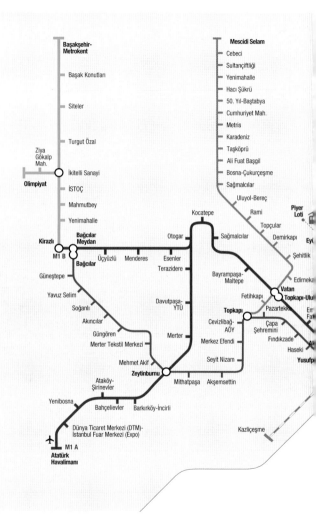

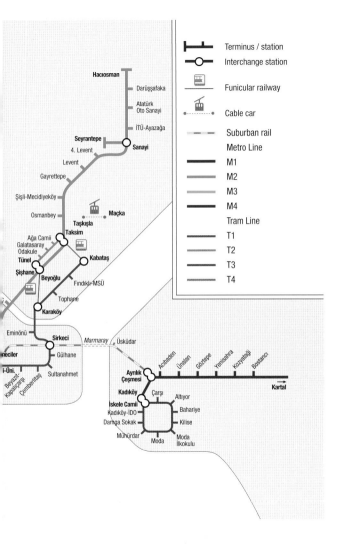

speaking your language

phrase book & dictionary
phrase book & CD

Available in: Arabic, Brazilian Portuguese*, Burmese*, Cantonese
Chinese, Croatian, Czech*, Danish*, Dutch, English, Filipino, Finnish*, French,
German, Greek, Hebrew*, Hindi*, Hungarian*, Indonesian, Italian, Japanese,
Korean, Latin American Spanish, Malay, Mandarin Chinese, Mexican Spanish,
Norwegian, Polish, Portuguese, Romanian*, Russian, Spanish, Swedish, Thai,
Turkish, Vietnamese
*Book only

www.berlitzpublishing.com